# *PHLESH BROTHERS*

## A Science Fiction Novel
## by
## I.E. Kolenda



'Giertz felt uncomfortable about Kadski's statement as Giertz thought about the facial expressions he'd just seen on the surviving Combat Youths, *They all appeared to have the same weird, carnivorous smile as The Festival of Greed posters.* Giertz still resisted believing it however, at this stage. Instead, he tried to reassure himself, *At least we've probably struck a fatal blow to the reality I loathe so much. Surely The Globecon can't survive now?*

He was in for an unpleasant surprise though.'

R

For Joyce Isabel

This novel is purely a work of fiction. Names, characters, places, and incidents are either the products of the author's imagination or are used fictitiously. Any resemblance to any actual persons living or dead, events, or locales is entirely coincidental and not intended by the author.

**About The Author**
IE Kolenda was born in England in 1959, to a Polish WWII veteran father and an English mother. In 1992 he traveled for three years in Southern Africa where he studied traditional rock painting. From 1997 he lived and traveled in Asia.

For more information please go to:

AMAZON: https://www.amazon.com/stores/I.-E.-Kolenda/author/B00EKN6LYM?ref=ap_rdr&shoppingPortalEnabled=true

WEB:   http://www.utopiomatic2000.wordpress.com   / https://utopiomatic2000.wordpress.com/

BLOG: https://alternativedystopias.blogspot.com/

FACEBOOK: UtopiOmatic2000

The publisher is not responsible for websites (or their content) that are not owned by the publisher.

Also by IE Kolenda from UtopiOmatic2000 Productions and available through Kindle:

**Science Fiction:**
Phlesh Brothers – A Science Fiction Novel - ISBN: 978-0-9572080-1-8
Amazon Search: ASIN: B00JAHLUS0
(Print Version: ISBN-10 : 0957208006
ISBN-13 : 978-0957208001)

The Death Wish Man- An Outer Space Novel - ISBN: 978-0-9572080-6-3
Amazon Search: ASIN: B09LJS38H1

Dead Futures - Science Fiction Stories - Volume One - ISBN: 978-0-9572080-0-1
Amazon Search: ASIN: B01BLL9MPA

Dead Futures - Science Fiction Stories - Volume Two - ISBN: 978-0-9572080-3-2
Amazon Search: ASIN: B07BH3PCVD

**Fiction:**
The Naked Art Game - ISBN: 978-0-9572080-4-9
Amazon Search: ASIN: B07MW93GYT

**Faction:**
I, Oswald – The Fictionalized Autobiography of JFK's Alleged Assassin – ISBN: 978-0-9572080-5-6
Amazon Search: ASIN: B08HVL91YR

# PART 1

**PROLOGUE Naked Victim**

As the flint knife rose over the naked victim, his eyes already glaring with terror, he felt a sudden, growing hopelessness. Tied spread-eagled on the cold, stone table, he noted the particularly cruel-looking curve to the serrated, stone blade, while the pulsing drums echoed and re-echoed around the cave chamber, lit by a circle of hand-molded, smoking oil lamps.

The priests chanted and swayed, their shadows jittering over the granite walls decorated with hieroglyphic finger paintings in human blood. Men were shown mutating into half-man, half-beast creatures and devouring each other, as they sank into the spiritual underworld. A crudely carved idol with twisted, misshapen anatomy stood over the table, staring out indifferently as the knife fell.

As the victim's screams faded, a kind of primitive surgery took place. On a granite throne beneath the idol, the ancient Seer surfaced from his trance, his atrophied eyelids lifting for a moment. Leaning forwards, he gradually focused through cataracts, but only half-interested.

Slowly he began to recognize images in the random destruction of life before him. They foretold the future, a strange story of twisted sex, of lies perverted into truth, of out-of-control technology - it was the story of The End.

Now focused beyond the present, his eyes rolled back in his head. With a croaking monotone, in some long-dead language, The Seer began to whisper between the flecks of foam at the corners of his mouth: 'Their world shall end,
They shall be destroyed,
Their great engine shall rot,
It is foretold!
'Metal shall melt,
Stone shall crumble,

Their wombs shall bear monsters,
It is foretold!
'A young, insane warrior,
Shall smite the swollen-headed monster
In his tower,
It is foretold!
'There shall be death,
And death within death,
There shall be no mercy.
It is foretold!
It is foretold!
It is foretold!'

Straining not to miss a single syllable, using the victim's blood, the priests began transcribing, adding the prophecy to the hieroglyphs on the walls. Meanwhile, The Seer caught something, a dim glimmer of red light, somewhere in the far, far future. He blinked, closing his eyes...

## Chapter 1 Hot Rubber

Somewhere in the near future, the weather above the road was bright, the sun glaring off a fake Lamborghini's burnished red enamel, as Dr. James Giertz toyed again with the possibility of killing himself. The tires were on the verge of melting as he tried to gain barely measurable fractions of a second accelerating on straight roads, and feeling for the tread's 'maximum limit of adhesion' on every corner. Even so, because he was insane, he was thinking about world history right now, and how he could end it. In fact, the major question in his permanently deformed mind today, or any day, was, *How can I destroy reality?* In fact, it wasn't just a question, but an overwhelming, visceral need for him, I must to be the one to do it!

As the four exhaust pipes spat a faint blue-green flame, the idea preoccupied him as it had from birth, and perhaps even before that, as far as he knew. He'd even meditated on it more so recently, but so far had found no answer. Meanwhile, he attempted to coax the smallest amount of extra power out of the engine, without over-revving it. He was forever searching for the impossible, perfect point between the speed of the machine and his reactions, by always exceeding both. The car's synthetic leather passenger compartment was laced with the smell of oil, exhaust, burning brakes, clutch, and hot rubber. The chrome-plated, retro gear lever clicked smoothly around its chrome-plated, retro gate. Today, he knew he had to do something. He had to do anything.

In fact, it was also becoming an obsession with him, to find out how far his reflexes could go. *That is the one good thing about me,* he often reflected, in the forever, on-going conversation in his head, *perhaps the only thing: my reflexes. I'm not big or strong, so they are the only real weapon I have for ending reality.* He still wondered though, *Just why are they so fast?* He didn't know why he never seemed to lose on the hologramatic games (or holygames) he played on the Synth-O-Gas station forecourts, in between screaming around 'Consumer Zone D' (what had once been called England) in his red, fake Lamborghini. Why he'd survived it all - up until now.

He was so confident at first; he allowed his mind to wander slightly. *Yes, Synth-O-Gas and Cyclone-Injectors changed the whole game!* The discovery of cheap, synthetic gasoline had dispensed with all the boring hybrids and electric cars; even wind farms had been torn down as uneconomical, 'Too expensive to maintain,' and solar was just allowed to crumble. Giertz roared past a condemned windmill now, the rusty propellers stationary despite a good breeze, and other mills had collapsed altogether, while some just hung at odd angles, blades missing.

Cyclone Injectors also had raised the internal combustion engine's efficiency from about eighteen to eighty-nine percent, giving a 'whole new future' to the old technology, above any of the eco-friendly alternatives. Or so The Consumers were told, by the makers of Synth-O-Gas. Giertz didn't fully understand all the physics, something to do with putting fuel into the cylinders in an already burning state, but every day he offered a prayer of thanks to whichever god had given mankind Cyclone Injectors and Synth-O-Gas. The only unfortunate side effect was that it did all turn the upper atmosphere a noticeable shade of green, which Giertz had to admit concerned him from time to time, despite the corporations' reassurances.

Anyway, to get the full benefit of taking his life into his own hands, he'd torn nearly all the sound insulation out of the car, and every silencing restriction out of the exhaust system. Now, as the sound-box would on a musical instrument, it actually amplified even the minutest sound the enormous W-sixteen motor could make, as he tested just how far his reflexes could go. At full power, it reached a pitch that vibrated his teeth against one another. At the end of each journey, his ears would be whistling and his head throbbing. However, always in conflict with himself, the question was permanently there, *Are my extraordinary reflexes a symptom, or part of the cause of my mental illness?* Yet the following thought was also always lurking, every time he drove like this, *But in the end - does it matter?*

Although the cockpit of the flamboyant car was relatively small, his insignificant body, still in its early twenties, had no problem fitting into it. In fact, his shoulders were not much further apart than his ears. Despite the air conditioning, he ran his hand over his deeply pock-marked face (mostly down one side) to redistribute the sweat. He shook his shoulder-length black hair, on the verge of thinning, trying to get it out of his eyes, which were too close together.

Soon the retro, analogue speedometer needle became pressed so hard against the retro stop-pin at the end of its scale that it bent slightly. He noticed the next bend flashing towards him, and also how strangely calm he felt about it. Nonetheless, a new, clammy sweat appeared on his palms and forehead. *My body seems to want to tell me something...*

Gradually, as if by the sheer power of his will, the time between him and the corner almost seemed to slow down. *Maybe by some effort, I could even stop it there, in defiance of fate itself, and live a little longer just by trying?* Suddenly though, he knew it was too late. He was there, trapped inside *that* moment, in *that* situation. A terrible, sick, moment-before-you-slip-on-ice feeling spread from his legs, telling him the rear tires had finally lost their grip.

There was a fraction of a second of nausea. Then with the tips of his fingers he sensed something through the steering. He went after it. There was an empty moment of limbo, and then the sickness disappeared, as if washed out by a sweet electricity.

Soon he was back on another straight stretch, and in the distance he could see another corner, but he knew, *I probably won't be so lucky on that one...*


**Chapter 2 Mental Hygiene**

*Nothing.* Giertz randomly thought one day, in the Happylands Institute of Mental Hygiene. *Everything is dead here. Bacteria are dead, thoughts are dead - both suffocated by the sterility.* Outside, above the monumental walls, the sky was as gray as death, raining on the lifeless concrete. Since being abandoned here, Giertz often asked himself out loud, with genuine curiosity, 'What did I do to end up in this place?' No matter how he tried, he couldn't remember his misdeed.

The last thing he could recall was resolving to do something unspecified. He knew these lapses of memory always came after his having done something too terrible to remember, and were another symptom of his unique disease. *So perhaps it's just as well I can't recall it.* Yet he knew the more pertinent question was, *So how the Hell do I get out of here?*

Even at this early stage though, Giertz could well understand the inevitable disaster that would eventually take place in this asylum. *It seems the most logical thing in the world, as if I arrived to be the last digit in some equation. It will also be typical of the kind of catastrophe I always leave in my wake.*

In the time he'd been here however, he'd forgotten a lot about the outside world. Sometimes he'd wander out into the exercise yard and stare up at the square patch of sky, framed by the towering walls. As the clouds drifted across it, he wondered, *What exactly are those?* At night he would contemplate the even more puzzling moon and stars.

Confused, he would retreat to the monstrous, Gothic edifice of this 'mental hospital.' Purpose-built hundreds of years earlier, it now seemed more a moss and ivy-covered castle worthy of Count Dracula. This was confirmed for Giertz by the weird, atonal, echoing, organ-like music of the demented howls of the waking nightmares taking place inside, reminding him, *This place is my universe now - almost.*

Over the months he would explore the three-dimensional maze of the asylum, the corridors within corridors of padded cells, and endless specialized wards for ever more obscure mental diseases. Somehow though, no matter where he roamed, he always arrived back at his uncomfortable bed, with its thin mattress and chipped, enamelled-metal tubing. There he spent all his time staring out through the rusty-iron-barred window at his red, fake Lamborghini. The only intrusion of color, it sat in what had been the visitors' car park, with various rusting hulks.

His eyes hungrily studied the long, low, streamlined, wedge. Ducts and scoops for the enormous, complicated engine took up the rear two-thirds of it, which flourished in a massive air foil wing. He'd never been able to work out, *Is it there to hold the car down, or help it take off?* Only the front third of the car made up the driver's cockpit. *That ludicrously-powerful car is somehow connected with my incarceration here. It will also be instrumental in my escape!*

The car gave him no clues to the events that had led to his incarceration however, apart from a few deep, silver scratches in the aluminum skin along one side, but he was no longer that curious anyway, *Perhaps they just put the car there to tempt me in some way, for a test as part of my therapy?*

He could well remember, during an early consultation, facing his First Doctor in the car park, and his treating the car between them as evidence, as he asked Giertz, 'Would you do it again?' Giertz had almost liked his First Doctor, a sensitive, inwardly troubled man, who'd taken a significant interest in Giertz's unique condition. This presented symptoms related to several known mental diseases, but still didn't fit any of the 'standard diagnoses,' while also displaying a few symptoms unique to itself.

Giertz couldn't remember his answer however. All he could recall was narcissistically finding the reflection of the breeze blowing his long hair about in the doctor's dark glasses (which all the psychiatrists wore all the time, even indoors, as was the fashion) more fascinating. *I probably just don't want to remember,* Giertz had concluded, but whatever he'd said must have been the wrong thing. Immediately he was transferred to a doctor he didn't like, on a much tougher wing of the asylum, still with no cure in sight – and so the process continued.

Meanwhile his first doctor, from his initial diagnosis of Giertz's condition, had developed 'A Special Theory of Mutant Mental Illness.' From this, in turn, he'd also developed 'A Special Theory of Contagious Mental Illness,' but by then, of course, he'd already lost all objectivity. Becoming too embroiled in his patient's condition, the doctor himself was now a patient in the asylum. He was still allowed to dress and act like a doctor, but everyone knew he wasn't one anymore. Nevertheless, Giertz would still see him from time to time and pretended to be his client, for old time's sake.

Giertz felt some inverse satisfaction from his being continually transferred however, *By determined effort, I have worked my way down to this: the most intensive wing of the highest security mental hospital in the world!*

**Chapter 3 Strange Disease**

Another day, Giertz's mind drifted to his permanent suspicion something wasn't altogether 'right' in the hospital, *Since I came here, this Asylum has been gradually sealed off from reality. The process began with the solar panels and windmill generators.* He remembered the total indifference of the patients to 'the modifications,' as the 'hospital,' formerly a place of ornamental gardens and gentle therapies, was transformed into a prison around them, and a particularly repressive one. *These inmates will never see any pattern, too preoccupied with their introverted dilemmas - until it's too late.*

*The next stage was the state-of-the-art solar-powered recycling plants.* Once thought to be chemically impossible, much of the food and water supplies were now 'amazingly' regenerated out of waste (but still tasted like it), only a little supplementary nutrition being provided by a few vegetables from the hospital's 'gardens,' and Giertz now understood, *The four surrounding walls were just the final touch.*

Seamless concrete, they were angled inwards to render them impossible to climb, even by the most agile of optimists. In the relative darkness within them, the ornate, eccentric edifice, decorated with carved, snarling gargoyles, was thus self-sufficient, and self-contained. It was illuminated only by the square patch of daylight migrating across it every day. *Someone, somewhere wants to quarantine all the strange ideas here indefinitely,* Giertz mused to himself from time to time, laughing slightly.

There was a huge door in the walls, but it was solid steel, as thick as a man, and welded shut. *To anyone outside, this place must look like some mysterious, truncated pyramid, covered in solar panels, standing on a hill,* Giertz guessed correctly. *What would they think if they knew what was inside? Even then, would they believe this is just a boiler without a safety valve?*

In fact, Giertz felt he could almost see the insanity condensing in the air here, to become an explosive gas. It was the first thing he'd noticed when, strapped half-conscious to a gurney, they had initially wheeled him through the elaborate, stone entrance. He was silently shocked as the clammy dew of this atmosphere settled on him, sticking to everything. *Everyone here just wanders about, as insanity slowly soaks through their skins by osmosis!*

To Giertz, *Every day here is the mental equivalent of trying to climb an ice cliff.* He'd always regarded the idea of an abstract 'sanity' as indefinable, thinking it was irrelevant to anyone, especially himself, but now even he hoped it existed somewhere. *There's no parameter here you can call 'sanity' on which to get a grip! All the patients do is put their energy into manufacturing senseless variations on pointless behavior patterns. My neuroses are mirrored, and multiplied, in the faces of everyone I look at!*

What was even comical to Giertz however, was the idea that, *Whoever created The Happylands Institute of Mental Hygiene actually thought it could work - somehow!* He smiled now, at their naive hope that the patients would gradually form some sort of social unit, and adapt to the place, and eventually society. *Instead, everyone hates themselves, each other, this asylum - and society.*

There was however a form of hierarchy operating, *Even in this ward, the Schizophrenics look down on the Depressives, who look down on the Paranoids, who look down on the Schizophrenics, etc., but all of them look down on me!*

At first Giertz had attempted to socialize with one neurosis category or another, but when he tried to explain his 'condition,' no matter in what way he presented it, they knew it wasn't appropriate to their needs. The patients would only turn their backs on him, going back to their sullen mutterings. Feeling rejected, he realized, *My particular disease is just too weird, even for them! Yet the most these patients ever do though anyway is sit in their symptom-cliques, having blank-faced, cyclical conversations.*

As they smoked the non-cancer-free cigarettes (an unlimited supply of which had somehow been deemed a necessity), these discussions usually began with their bitter memories. These were always of 'World Mental Hygiene Week:' in cities across the globe anyone with 'weird ideas' was rounded up by growling men in white coats and dark glasses. Armed with nets and electric cattle prods, they were titled 'Deputy Psychiatrists'. It had been a last, all-out attempt by the World Government to purge 'insanity' from the collective human psyche altogether. It only ended when they realized that, of course, they were trying to corral the majority of the human race.

Whatever the subject of the patients' conversations, they always concluded with the resolution that one day soon; the walls would be corroded to thin plaster by the concentrated lunacy they contained. Then on 'The Glorious Day,' they would break through them to swarm out and infect the world with their cumulatively-mutated, bizarre concepts. Yet even while their frustration mounted, somehow the possibility seemed to recede still further.

**Chapter 4 Mutated Concepts**

What Giertz ultimately found most curious was the discovery that, *Everyone in here seems to be waiting for something*. It was never openly discussed, but they all watched the only clock intently. (None of the staff or patients was allowed to wear watches.) Giertz observed, *Time moves so slowly here that each second seems almost infinite.* These days the hands on the face hardly seemed to move at all, as if the mechanism contained some slow-drying glue.

Every day, in a pompous ceremony, The Head of the Asylum would theatrically hand, as if it were some sacred object, a small silver key to a burly male nurse. He then used it to wind the clock, which apparently was a task requiring enormous strength, as if he were some mythological figure winding up time itself. Recently Giertz's heart would almost stop between each tick, fearing time may have ceased altogether:

'Tick....................................................................Tock.'

'That clock is really the timer on a giant H Bomb of lunacy!' Giertz heard himself think out loud, somewhere at a distance.

He expected an alarm to ring from it at any moment, and some great spark to leap out to ignite the volatile air. The spark didn't come however, so the air steadily became thicker, and heavier. Giertz concluded, *Anyone who can't take it anymore, becoming violent and throwing a fit, is merely looked down on by the others: 'Here is just another who can't withstand "The Great Waiting."'* In some ways, they even pity the staff, and the whole outside world, because it's felt that, while they are also involved in The Great Waiting, they just have more distractions from it. As to what they were all waiting for, Giertz guessed, *It must be either universal entropy, or just someone to tell them what they're waiting for.*

As usual, Giertz sat on his bed staring at everyone blankly, major explosions fizzing in his brain as, now more desperately than ever, he clashed again and again with that question: *So how do I destroy reality?* At the same time though he despised the patients apathy, especially the feeble geriatrics, *These sacks of potatoes are now paying for their sins, yet doing the bare minimum to stay alive!*

Hunched in their frayed deck chairs, under the sun lamps and dusty, artificial palm trees, they clung to an ever-diminishing hope. Through loose false teeth, saliva creeping down their chins, they incessantly talked streams of pejorative rubbish about their wasted lives, and the world in general. *The worst thing is there are more of them all the time!*

Giertz also hated the middle-aged veterans of World Wars Five, Six and Seven. Forming ranks, they would march heartily up and down the ward in their horizontally-striped pajamas, decorated with tarnished medals, while displaying horrible radiation burns and chemical scars on their hands and faces. *Even with pieces of their limbs and heads missing, they still lustily sing the patriotic songs of their youth.*

He *really* hated the young, fashionable eccentrics as they stood about mutilating their own bodies in the ceramic tiled corridors, lined with porcelain blood-gutters. Singing in meaningless languages of their own creation, their egos were bloated with their self-appointed martyrdom. *Even I'm closer to being a martyr than any of them!* Giertz would observe, angrily.

He particularly hated one case: The Smiling Man. No matter how bad things got, he always beamed at everyone, but even his smile had now begun to degenerate into just an inane grin, with both ends threatening to collapse altogether.

'I HATE YOU ALL!' - Giertz would shout at them at random intervals, but no one ever took any notice. They understood perfectly what the world thought of them, and that Giertz was just stating the obvious.

Above all however, Giertz hated the medical staff, *While appearing to give the truth, they keep something stonily to themselves.* There was no point in telling them about his feelings toward them though, because they took their patients' hatred for granted. Not enough however, as it would prove.

Nearly all the patients were now happy anyway, to have their heads shaved, and wear identical horizontally-striped pajamas with their individual bar codes stenciled across their backs. Even their insane faces all looked exactly the same to Giertz. *It's as if the only thing distinguishing them is the variety of the symptoms of their diseases.* However, he was grudgingly allowed to keep his hair unfashionably long, right down his back, and wear his cheap black jeans and vest, no matter how faded and frayed they were becoming.

The only person in the asylum who Giertz respected was also an exception: the one they called 'Zytopharbb.' *Although Zytopharbb is entirely emaciated, they are too afraid to make him dress in anything but his full-length motorcycle leathers!* It was rumored Zytopharbb was a prophet of sorts, but Giertz believed he was more. *Zytopharbb's mind is beyond The Great Waiting. His eyes look as if they've seen what lies beyond it, and then returned!*

**Chapter 5 Ultimate Asylum**

As it became increasingly apparent The Ultimate Asylum Project just wasn't working, the more oblivious the uniformed staff became, blinded by their privileges. Called 'keepers' by the inmates, (as in 'keepers' of a zoo) the inmates then logically branded themselves 'keepees,' but Giertz noted even the 'keepers' were beginning to show 'signs.' *They are somehow stolidly, dogmatically, and monotonously sane, every logical decision laboriously traceable to a tangible stimulus. 'Sane' to the point where it no longer makes sense.*

*At first, before the walls went up, there was at least some pretense of a 'cure' being available here, but these days, when any 'treatment' occurs at all, everyone just goes through the motions as quickly as possible to get it over with.* Thus, both sides were now heaving in an all-out, barefaced, teeth-gritted confrontation at the theoretical question of 'sanity' itself, and it was clear the 'keepers' weren't winning. *It's all degenerated into a major 'tug-of-war: an all-but-admitted sham!* Therefore Giertz could see the ingredients for the coming, final, cataclysm wherever he looked.

Giertz's first doctor had quietly confessed to him once, 'They send society's rejects here and tell me they're mad. The world is on the outside, the inmates, I mean patients on the inside, and I'm in the middle. I feel I'm busier reassuring the ones on the outside, "Yes, don't worry! You are The Sane."' He seemed to be pleading for Giertz to understand something, but what Giertz did understand was, *I'm dealing with a man in the process of a breakdown here!*

Of course, temporary sterilization was compulsory for all patients and staff. In fact, the situation puzzled Giertz a lot, *Strange how The Keepers don't seem to mind their containment as much as the patients do theirs, and odd The Keepers seem ready to make any sacrifice for the grail of 'sanity.'* Somehow though, Giertz couldn't admire their idealism.

**Chapter 6 Inner Conflicts**

Unlike his first doctor, Giertz's thirteenth and final 'therapist,' who also happened to be the head of the asylum, had no inner conflicts. In fact quite the opposite. Dr. Kortex had also developed a new theory of Giertz's disease, and had explained it to him one day.

'Now you see,' the doctor had clarified to his captive audience of one, 'the basis of my theory is these mental diseases are due to *changes* in the space-time coordinating ability of the victim's mind. Therefore, when mathematical models are constructed of these "disturbances," they sometimes resemble the models Dr. Akthlinger (who is also a patient here) has used to predict intersection points between alternative dimensions and our own.'

Giertz didn't take in much of what Dr. Kortex was saying so excitedly. He never spoke directly to his audience anyway, totally avoiding eye contact, his detached tone that of someone speaking through an invisible interpreter. Instead, Giertz just stared at the psychiatrist: an over-weight, balding man, his remaining hair greased back, but he wore a white coat, *Probably clean enough to be antiseptic!*

Sweating heavily, The-Head-Of-The-Asylum was shuffling small, three-dimensional representations of 'the problem,' composed of geometric solids and sticks. He had the hypnotic dexterity of a master of some outwardly simple, yet infinitely complex, gambling game in a far-eastern marketplace. Giertz watched the twin reflections of the models gyrating through various axes in the doctor's dark glasses. Giertz also studied intensely the small silver clock-winding key that hung around the psychiatrist's fat neck, as would a priest's crucifix. Giertz instinctively knew, *That is the key to my escape!*

Also, because of Giertz's heightened reflexes, he'd often, briefly, caught sight of a number tattooed on the Doctor's palm. Dr. Kortex would quickly clench it, and look carefully at Giertz. This though had been enough to confirm for Giertz exactly what the number was for, which was why, smiling to quietly pretend he knew nothing, he eventually memorized it.

Giertz's disease, as far as he knew, was unique to himself. It had some physical symptoms, but most were psychological. Well before this stage in his treatment, several eminent experts had studied his case, at first taking an academic interest. Gradually though, they had become terrified, as they discovered its true dimensions. Finding it wouldn't fit any standard diagnosis, they drew the most reassuring conclusion: that there was no disease, except in Giertz's imagination. Only Giertz himself knew the opposite was true, still just sane enough to realize he was suspended in a continual nightmare.

The hallucinations he suffered were only one of the more spectacular in a list of symptoms which kept mutating all the time. The worst thing about the hallucinations was that they often blended into reality so well, it was impossible for Giertz to tell the difference. 'Reality' itself was just another hallucination as far as he was concerned. Consequently, his behavior was highly unpredictable.

Usually in these 'therapy sessions,' the psychiatrist always said the same things, and Giertz disregarded them in the same way. Today though, Dr. Kortex said something which caught Giertz's attention, 'You see, this is the reason for your super-human reflex actions.'

## Chapter 7 Mental Confusion

The doctor held up the model and propounded, 'Imagine if you will that this is the universe. Now all of us, who are the human race that is, are inside it, looking out. We try to imagine the future. But your brain,' he went on, 'is about here.' He indicated a point well away from the model, 'Outside looking in. This would account for your exaggerated reflexes, because your perception of time is beyond ours, by maybe as much as *two or three light seconds.*' The psychiatrist smiled briefly, silently congratulating himself.

*Well, that makes sense,* Giertz thought reluctantly, nodding. *My mind was born in another dimension, so I'm outside looking in on this whole universe.* Giertz had always felt he had a sharper focus on what would happen next, and he was invariably right about it, *That would account for the feeling of detachment I have when I hallucinate: I'm simultaneously seeing two or more different universes, and if there's a disparity of about three seconds it explains my unbeatable scores on the holygames. It would also answer the question, I suppose, of whether the heightened reflexes are just another symptom - they very much are.* It didn't make him happy though, to think the one asset he had was only another manifestation of his disease.

'Quite remarkable,' Kortex added. 'You may even represent a new stage in human evolution, a mind able to perceive reality in five or even more dimensions! If you were to breed, propagating your mutant gene, it could transform human society.' They he added more quietly, in a fatherly tone, 'So, of course, that's why you must stay in here forever...'

Generally, Giertz had somehow always known he was insane, but that he could do nothing about it. He could only stand back and watch his actions in this dimension, and their consequences, as would some detached third party. Sometimes he was laughing, sometimes horrified, but never once did he feel responsible for them, except for a kind of distant guilt that, *Perhaps I should?*

The psychiatrist's remarks definitely struck a shrill chord with Giertz today though. Mistakenly encouraged by Giertz's brief show of attention, Kortex, in full flow now, rattled off with the rhythm of a keyboard, explaining, 'In some way as yet not understood, I believe this case is able to perceive the points at which these alternative space-dimensions intersect, thus causing his mental confusion.'

'Therefore,' he expounded further, 'We not only have the opportunity to resolve as yet undiagnosed cases of mental aberration,' and at this point, his voice rose, 'but the possibility of unlimited mental navigation in time, space, and between dimensions!' He held his head erect and pointed at the ceiling, 'Gentlemen!' he said to no one in the room but Giertz. 'It is my contention that this disease originates in inter-galactic Sector-X: an alternative dimension! Therefore it is my intention to lead an expedition to this location in space, in order to prove my hypothesis!'

The psychiatrist returned to his model, sweat drops now gathering at the end of his nose. The planes of the object shifted faster and faster until some came loose and fell onto the carpet, as the doctor's fascination grew exponentially. Giertz now clearly understood, *This man's impending doom in this asylum is permanently built into his mental makeup, and perhaps he already knows it?*

As the model crumbled in the Doctor's perspiring fingers, Giertz gently stood up and left.

**Chapter 8 Pre-Freudian**

When events finally did come to a violent head though, no one was surprised, least of all Giertz. *They just slide into place as if in some well-oiled mechanism.* It was already clear things in the asylum were getting desperate.

The hospital did have a radio station, but it played only old, worn recordings from years before the walls had gone up. Even the soothing tones of Johnny Mathis continually singing 'When a Child Is Born,' couldn't drown out the mounting shrieking and howling. This cacophony echoed down the corridors decorated with browning, flaking murals of Van Goghesque cornfields, embellished with weird graffiti.

Gradually the dwindling arsenal of recyclable tranquilizers had failed to be enough against this collective lunacy, and the non-recyclable ones soon ran out. Placebos were never enough. Therefore bizarre medieval contraptions of thick oak planks, leather straps and wrought iron (the relics of pre-Freudian days) were dragged out of the Victorian basement, and dusted off.

Sometimes, purely to break the monotony, Giertz would hit a male nurse or doctor just to be punished. Perversely, he was even beginning to enjoy being beaten in the freezing exercise yard. When he became particularly unruly, they would strap him to a simple, oak table where he would scream away the sheer pressure of insanity inside himself, until he felt a little better, but he finally decided, *This is all a waste of time.*

He knew he had to do something. He had to do anything.

However, when the day finally did come, at first it seemed so average it could have been remarkable for that fact. Giertz recognized the truth when, as usual, a male nurse in a frayed white coat sauntered up the tiled corridor carrying a syringe, a cup of water, and a single yellow pill. *I must be some kind of 'special case' now. That pill is probably the last of the non-recyclables, there's nothing stronger. The 'tranquilizer' contained in that syringe is really Preparation X315/J and used only as a last resort.*

This over-the-counter drug wasn't only highly fashionable, but highly addictive. The most unfortunate side effect of even short-term usage was that it eventually destroyed the addict's entire nervous system, including, lastly, the higher brain. Paralysis combined with horrible, unnatural convulsions and spasms, frothing at the mouth, and hideous hallucinations being the terminal symptoms of addiction.

Therefore Giertz knew that if even those drugs failed, as they no doubt would, *It can be only a short time before one night the staff will silently take me down to the secret operating theater. There my brain's lobes will be quietly separated from one another, and I will be permanently imprisoned somewhere inside my mind, even more than I am already.* Fear of this fate now took an icy grip on his entrails.

The male nurse stopped at the bottom of the bed. As usual, Giertz twisted his head to look up at him as if he were some kind of deity. As always the nurse didn't try to conceal his smile. He placed the pill in Giertz's mouth and began to tip the water in after it, but this time Giertz spat it back in his face.

He crushed the nurse's testicles with his boot. He smashed the nurse's larynx with his fist. He stuck the syringe in the nurse's eye. The next thing he remembered was racing down the corridor setting off fire alarm buttons, the metallic noise of the sharp steel studs in his boots echoing off the ceramic tiled walls.

As if the alarm was a hunting horn, in the hall-like 'day room,' the patients became agitated as would a pack of hounds. They even looked around from the clock, sniffing the air thick with cheap, non-cancer-free cigarette smoke. The sprinkler system, soaking their dressing gowns, heated them up even more. In fact, the message spread so fast, that even before Giertz reached the end of the corridor, he could feel the building vibrating in the prelude to an earthquake. He nearly began to wonder at what he'd started, almost fearing his own creation, but knew, *There's no going back now!*

A heavily-built, female nurse stepped between Giertz and the door to the 'Staff Only' emergency exit. Her muscular arms folded around her heavy bosom, she drawled in an Irish accent, 'Now just what do you think you're doin' Jimmy Gier...' Immediately, both the door and the nurse were reduced to a mass of blood and splinters of wood.

Giertz swung down the rusted, ornate-iron fire escape, but two figures barred his way. One was a cackling madwoman, with permed, purple hair, fresh from beauty therapy, (which unfortunately failed to cover the many surgical scars all over her forehead). The other was a frail old man with half his head shaved, copper wires sticking out of small blood-clots on the bare scalp. Although they both tried to bite Giertz to death with badly-fitted dentures, he picked up a wheelchair and managed to beat a path between them.

Realizing he would never reach the ground floor by the escape, Giertz reluctantly entered an emergency door marked by a happily grinning skull and crossbones, labeled:

'LOBOTOMY WARD - DO NOT ENTER!'

## Chapter 9 Lobotomy Ward

Giertz soon discovered the warning was good advice. The Lobotomy Ward smelled of sour milk and was full of stainless-steel surgical appliances, while disinterestedly staring eyes observed Giertz's entrance. Even in this hell though, some of the inmates were doing the best they could, clattering the metal utensils, and bleating with optimism.

Then he made a detour through the Terminal Geriatric Ward, where he was even forced to reassess 'the sacks of potatoes.' Running past rows of smiling, perfect teeth, in faces that had done nothing to deserve them, he noted they were at least muttering encouragement. Meanwhile the building was now shaking visibly from what was taking place in the other wards. Large pieces of the ceiling rained onto the patients, but no one here even blinked as Giertz smashed a window. Kicking the rusty iron bars out of the rotten frame, he swung onto a drain pipe outside.

He emerged again, but into a hail of pieces of masonry, doctors, nurses, and other patients, all of which were pouring from the windows above. Although Giertz had never been able to work out fully the three-dimensional maze of the asylum, he knew at least one part well enough. He looked across, and as he expected, a rope ladder hung from The Head Psychiatrist's office window.

Giertz then scanned across the exercise yard to the patients who, long strings of saliva trailing from their mouths, were swarming around randomly. The terrified staff was hopelessly trying to maintain order, but only one member was running with a purpose, and with surprising speed. Giertz knew that psychiatrist and what his destination was, *Dr. Kortex!* His head had already sustained some serious injury, but he was still protectively carrying some of his sweaty, theoretical models, dropping a trail of pieces of alternate dimensions.

It was well-known, especially to Giertz, that any contact with the outside world was impossible, *All radio and telephone links to this asylum are cut or electronically jammed, to avoid even a whisper of the strangeness in here getting out.* Still, one question always remained in every patient's mind (still capable of thinking at all), *Why is there a panel in the steel door, held on by explosive bolts, just large enough for a single car to pass through?*

There was also one, locked, manhole cover near the walls. On his sojourns into the exercise yard, among the dead flowerbeds, Giertz had examined it in detail, and developed a theory, *In a system such as this, in the event of something uncontainable developing inside here, they must have made some provision for one person to get out with a head start, and warn the rest of humanity.*

Now Giertz hit the ground and sprinted to catch the squat, ponderous form in a white lab coat. This wasn't easy, as Kortex was just as motivated by fear of what was behind him as the salvation in front. Angry patients were now oozing out of every fissure of the asylum. Doorways and walls were collapsing. Gradually the rotten institution was beginning to disintegrate, falling in on itself. Even Johnny Mathis now blasting from the PA system, the massive speakers distorting with volume, couldn't drown out the accumulated, inhuman roar.

Above Giertz, panicking psychiatrists were manning heavy, liquid-cooled machine-gun nests on the remaining roof. Still clinging to their Hippocratic Oaths, at first they fired ahead of the masses, but when that didn't delay the stampede, they fired directly into it. However, this only had the effect of a fly swatter on an enraged beehive. The 'Keepees' overcame the guns one by one by sheer weight of numbers, and turned them on the staff or other, out-of-favor symptom-cliques.

By the time Giertz reached Dr. Kortex, he'd already fumbled the small silver key into the manhole lock, heaving with all his insignificant strength at the heavy cover. Giertz began to help him, and the doctor unconsciously thanked him politely, until he recognized who it was. Giertz pushed him back towards the rapidly approaching squad of patients brandishing surgical instruments. Inside the manhole was a key pad, and Giertz pressed the numbers he'd memorized from the Doctor's tattoo. Giertz just had time to see an illuminated digit counter marked:

'EXPLOSIVE BOLT DETONATION TIME.'

It was already beginning to run down the seconds.

Knowing there was no time even to breathe, he dashed for his red car. As he reached it, he was surprised to see the nitrogen-filled tires weren't as deflated as he'd expected. *Perhaps I haven't been in the Asylum for as long as it seemed?* He pressed his thumb to the fingerprint detector on its door, then bump-started the car down the hill leading to the metal doorway. The huge motor coughed into life unwillingly, but he managed to keep it running. The almost-dead battery began charging.

As Giertz pressed the accelerator, the enormous, solid sheet of rusted metal that was the main door of the Asylum grew before him, with no sign of moving. He saw that some patients had already reached it, so he tried to avoid looking at their red, abstracted faces, while pressing down harder on the pedal, *At least I'll die trying!*

Then suddenly the panel in the riveted steel exploded outwards, and Giertz emerged into the light outside the walls from a cloud of smoke and rusty door fragments. Straight away the warming engine howled as if to celebrate its own liberation.

*I'm 'at large' again!* Giertz triumphed.

In the car's rear view screen he saw the rest of the enormous, steel, main door already heaving, cracking and then finally splitting with the sheer weight of lunacy behind it. It spewed out hordes of rabid withdrawal-zombies across the landscape, their terrible, crazed, collective message blazing from their bulging eyes and shrieking mouths.

Feeling satisfied, Giertz wondered what he should do now. He gunned the engine, which after grunting and crackling from its stagnation, was beginning to settle into an even hum. The dull-greenish sky was overcast, but he took his eyes off the road for a long time, fumbling urgently for his astronaut-model Ray Bans in the glove compartment, before flicking them onto his head. He eased his foot down on the throttle, and the world outside the windows became distorted.

'So much for that "reality"!' He laughed.

## Chapter 10 Wild Speeds

He put these thoughts out of his mind however. *In the end, what does it matter?* Now he felt he was safely back where he'd been before his capture, in the weeks spent in this fake Lamborghini, hypnotized by the gray road unraveling in front of it, to the abrasive howl of the engine behind. So his thinking switched once more to its default thought, *So now, how do I destroy reality?*

He'd also picked up his career from exactly where he'd left it, but he wasn't certain what his job was. Not because he couldn't remember, but because he'd never known. It was one of those not-very-clearly-defined job descriptions. All he knew was that it had a uniform and a name. He was a 'Greedeluxe Corporate Youth.' In spite of the title you didn't have to be particularly young, or particularly anything, but none of them knew exactly what they were supposed to be doing.

Nevertheless they usually wore bright-red, Synth-O-Leather jackets, with their names printed across the back in large white capitals, and the Greedeluxe Corporate Logo over their hearts. His was on the seat beside him, just where he'd left it after his capture, to conceal a rather large machine gun.

As the car hurtled along, with only one hand on the steering wheel he pulled the jacket on, while musing on his small glimmer of faith that, *Surely I must be doing something useful? They are paying me for it, after all.* Like almost everyone, the Greedeluxe Youth were paid in World Bank Tokens: the international currency. These were a kind of tin disk that could be bent between the thumb and forefinger. Some weren't even made of tin, just cardboard, or the cheapest plastic. So The Consumers, the majority of whom did no work at all, could buy products, the 'money' was simply paid out to them by the corporations themselves. Therefore, as their name inferred – the Consumers merely consumed. Giertz had a paper bag of such tokens in the glove compartment.

This fiat currency was all 'controlled' by the World Bank. *Almost the only thing the corporations and the World Government can agree on, to any extent.* Within all this also, somewhere, operated the enigmatic 'Council of Ninety' (or CON), which not many people were aware of, or cared about, but Giertz did - a lot. For one thing he knew, *It may well have a lot more than ninety members.*

Everyone also believed the World Bank was safe in The Security Zone, *But nobody seems to know exactly where that zone of 'security' is. Somehow anyway, the 'system' clanks along.* The average Consumer only received so many tokens every week, and Giertz spent most of his on fake Lamborghinis, and the Synth-O-Gas necessary to cruise at wild speeds. Sometimes he even went without food to do this.

As he drove his car today, Giertz reflected, *Strange to think anyone can buy a fake Lamborghini now, or fake anything else. Despite the prevailing economic diarrhea, here in the epicenter of The Consumer Zone, genuine Lamborghinis are now further out of reach than they ever were, as is genuine anything else.* He was well aware however, that those who could afford 'real things' would probably buy a private space shuttle, or at least a Vertical Take Off and Landing (VTOL) jet.

Giertz also knew this cheap, knock-off replica of the original car's design was mass-produced quite legally, just like every fake thing was now: hand-built by clone-slaves in The Pan-Asian Free Trade Zone. There, environmental, labor protection, and any other laws just didn't exist. (Not that they existed anywhere else either.) *Despite that my car's performance and handling are probably almost as good as most genuine cars. There's definitely no other fake car to match this one anyway,* he reassured himself complacently. Even the poorest Consumers now dressed in what looked like designer brand names indistinguishable from the real thing, while the rich Producers were easy to spot, being less 'overt' for one thing, even camouflaging themselves in rags.

Then, in spite of his contemplations, Giertz registered the old Synth-O-Gas station as it shot past.

**Chapter 11 Synthetic Reality**

Even at this velocity, he could see the station was broken down and decrepit. *Or perhaps they just deliberately made it that way, weathering it to make it look more retro? Almost everything is 'retro' now after all, as there's no vision of a future anymore.* Although the tank in the car was nearly empty, it wasn't the nostalgic, non-automated, self-service pumps on the forecourt that interested him. What did was the old machine sitting behind them.

Immediately he span the retro steering wheel, and his car shrieked back out of the distance, skidding sideways into the crumbling station. In one movement Giertz raised the door and stepped out, flicking his long hair dramatically from his face, even though there was no one else in the fully-automated station to witness his practiced entrance. Brimming with nostalgia, after lovingly filling the tank and tires, he turned his attention to his main interest.

The forecourt game machine was even older than he'd first thought, its hopelessly retro casing more reminiscent of an antique jukebox. He approached it feeling somewhat sad for the artifact, *Nobody wants to play this game now. It's so obsolete, it probably can't even remember the last time it was used!* He ran his fingers over the flaking, fluorescent paint on its sides depicting lurid, mad motor races on unlimited highways, as the breeze tugged at bits of loose chrome trim hanging off its chipboard edges. *Maybe it even dates from the Twentieth Century?* However, it was a game he knew well.

His train of thought continued, *The Consumers don't even play the holygames anymore, anyway. All they want to do now is take Preparation X315/J pills, not daring to leave their synthetic reality modules.* These were a kind of sarcophagus that artificially stimulated every sense in the body. Just thinking of that lifestyle, accepted as 'normal' by most of humanity, turned his stomach upside down. He knew he would never willingly climb into one.

'Good morning Dr. Giertz,' said the game.

'Good morning,' Giertz mumbled, as he fitted his head into the dusty viewer, his eyes to the cracked rubber cups, his hands into the frayed control-gloves, his feet to the creaking, rusty pedals. At first, he was surprised it remembered his name, but then he reminded himself, *I've played every game in every station on this road at some time in the past.*

Initially, he looked at the last highest score. It was his own, from all that time ago. It wasn't unusual for him to find this on most machines. He'd never met his competitors, and none of them had ever beaten him, at least not recently, so he was reassured to find his record still standing.

Knowing there were no other real contenders however, caused him to consider, *If what Dr. Kortex said about my reflexes is accurate, and about my mind being in another dimension, perhaps my advantage is unfair?* Giertz knew he'd already honed his reactions as far as they could go on these games anyway, *But there's still one person I can compete fairly against,* he reminded himself. *Now all I have to do is beat that previous record...*

Instantly he was projected down a virtual road faster than any real car could have carried him, digits running up on the score counter, the initial units a blur, as the recorded engine blasted into his ears. As a Greedeluxe Youth, he'd always spent the cold summer days this way, *Nothing else to do besides play these endless games, tearing up and down these limitless, simulated highways, ...*

He was constantly crashing himself in driving simulators like this one, or piloting digital helicopters, jets, and spacecraft, as he zapped unspeakable-looking space aliens. Today however, he suddenly felt very alone in the digital no-man's land of this synthetic highway system, *Nobody here to witness my triumphs.*

Soon though, he would find out he was very wrong.


**Chapter 12 Terminally Apathetic**
Despite being happily absorbed in his game, the artificial road rushing before him, for Giertz the excitement of

regaining his freedom gradually began to wear off. He started to realize he was back facing his old dilemma again.

Before his incarceration, the more he'd asked the Greedeluxe Corp. Youth, 'What am I supposed to be doing?' The vaguer the answers from his superiors had become. He was even beginning to suspect, *Perhaps there's no real job at all? So many Greedeluxe Youths have been unable to come to terms with this aspect of their careers. Becoming terminally apathetic, they just end up staring at infinity, across the existentialist bars of the world!* The idea of that being his fate was something he just couldn't face.

Therefore he found himself doing the job, whatever it was, twenty-four hours a day. He drove with manic intensity, played the forecourt games in a whirlwind, even read the old books, made of real paper, until his eyes stung. In the end, like a priest or doctor, for Giertz there was no point at which 'the job' stopped, and his own life began. *This occupation has just turned into a constant search for its true definition!* However, even his belief in it all was starting to wear thin.

Then he began to notice there was something strange about this particular game, *I can't tell it from reality!* Usually, on games this old there was at least enough difference in the definition to know. It was disconcerting, somehow. He reassured himself, *Maybe they've upgraded it in some way?* It didn't seem likely though, on a machine so archaic.

Then Giertz began to feel his eyes being sucked into the rubber cups, his hands disappearing into the gloves, his legs merging with the pedals. This game was now absorbing him - literally. He screamed, but even his scream disappeared into the noise of the engine.

Behind the scream, he was thinking, *Oh no! I'm hallucinating again, and I've never hallucinated in a holygame before!* He wasn't sure what would happen, but had a strong feeling his life was about to take a turn for the much worse - and he was right.

**Chapter 13 New Realities**

Abruptly, everywhere Giertz looked seemed just the same as what he'd been doing for real a few minutes before. He was back in the cockpit of his car, the sandy, brown of the eroded English countryside swiping past the windows, but somehow he knew it wasn't real, *I'm lost in one of my holygames!* He couldn't see the counter now, but was sure it was still running up his score - somewhere.

He raised his eyes to the artificial sky, which looked exactly like the real sky. *Perhaps even more real? Too real! It's all too sharp and definite!* Everything was attacking his senses. Then the slice of reality before him dissolved, like a bad video signal, and reality began cracking, blurring and breaking down around him, as if it could no longer support itself.

It was soon reduced to its component colors, atoms, and, he believed, other as yet undiscovered particles, but unlike a video signal, it was everywhere. He couldn't look away. The disintegration was so total it seemed to spread to the very cells of his brain. Reluctantly, he had to acknowledge, *I don't know where I am or what's happening to me anymore!*

All the sensual ingredients swirled together before him into a kind of soupy-plasma. Then gradually, as if recognizing pictures in ink blots all around him, sharper, more tangible, new realities began to surface. This particular vision today was a 'blockbuster' as well, slightly worse than any he'd ever had so far. *It's like a hideous, fast-growing cancer on space-time!*

It was also unusual in that they hadn't always been so clear, but this time it formed a definite face. What's more, a face he recognized. It was the standard, dehydrated face of an aging man, but the sphere of the cranium containing the brain was swollen to twice-normal size. Huge veins stood out amongst the remaining silver hair. He wore dark glasses so that you couldn't see his eyes. It was a face anyone could see today, staring down from the hypnotic advertising hoardings, out of holyvision screens, and up from newscomix in gutters - a face that you saw in your worst dreams. It was the face of Dr. Zed, the chief executive officer of Consumeordie Corporation, one of the two, giant hypermultinationals that now supplied all the world's goods and services between them.

Giertz recalled, unwillingly, *Both of those giant corporations are at present wrestling with no-holds-prohibited, to acquire each other in vicious takeover bids! In the early stages they have already used tactical nuclear weapons against each other's robotized manufacturing centers, so one day the victorious corporation will eventually turn the globe into just a single, titanic monopoly.*

The expression on the face before Giertz was growing harder, until it finally became porcelain brittle. It shattered, the pieces falling away to reveal an indistinct broiling mass. This hardened into a new, even more, horrible face, which in turn cracked, the process continuing, with each face growing worse than the last.

Giertz skidded the car sideways to a halt and jumped out unsteadily, hauling the machine gun with him, swinging the heavy, brass ammunition belt over his shoulder. He ran up the road towards the vision (which was just a patch of cloudy, turquoise sky to any outside observer) but the final face he couldn't confront. Giertz screamed, clamping his eyes shut. At the same time he discharged the gun at the empty clouds, in a great whiplash of red tracer bullets, before retreating to the car. Accelerating raggedly back the way he'd come in a haze of blue tire smoke, he pulled his door down as he moved, tears flowing down his face.

The view in front of him was a fluid blur. Pain and terror contorted his body. The car came to the top of a small hump in the road, took off, and flew for a distance. Its tires yelped when they made contact with the tarmac once more, as would those of a landing aircraft. He ran his tongue over his dry lips and changed up into eighth gear. Then the terrible physical convulsions that often followed these attacks began to rack him. He could usually manage to drive through them, but today he was having difficulty.

Eventually, despite the pain, he saw something else before him. It was the face again. He'd felt as if his hallucination was finally beginning to subside, but didn't understand why this particular vision persisted. He wondered if it had some symbolic significance. In spite of everything he tried to interpret what it was, but then found he was heading towards one of the gigantic, hypnotic advertising hoardings. It was strategically placed on the next bend to distract drivers.

These were quite scary in themselves to Giertz, because usually there were several bedraggled, emaciated Consumers standing, entranced by them for days on end, and often even a few scattered, dead bodies. No more than flies caught in the commercial's persuasive, kaleidoscopic web, their minds were permanently cocooned by the infinitely beautiful promises, until they dehydrated and starved to death. So far Giertz had always managed to avert his eyes, usually just in time, but he knew extremely well, *If I were to blink too late, I will perhaps never know.*

He knew though he could never be persuaded by this image, no matter what it promised. The flashing picture of the CEOs malformed head kept alternating with a chunk of freshly killed raw meat, still dripping blood. The legend beneath it read,

'Dr. ZED SAYS, "EAT MORE PHLESH!<br>
OR ELSE...!"<br>
CONSUMEORDIE Corp. '

Successfully distracted by the repulsive image, too late Giertz stamped optimistically on the brakes, but even the fake Lamborghini's twelve-cylinder, power-assisted calipers weren't enough. There was a sickening, crunching bang, as the hurtling steel, aluminum, rubber, and Synth-O-Leather projectile slued violently off the road, spinning eccentrically. It slammed through the board to a sound of tearing metal.

Upside-down, in a moment of zero gravity, almost irrelevantly Giertz reflected, *So perhaps I've finally found the limit to my reflexes, after all?*

**Chapter 14 Horror Creature**

Giertz was forced back into his seat by the impact-suppressing foam gushing from the dash panel, and into his large nose. After what felt like an hour, but was really only moments, he felt the machine shake with a second impact, green water bubbling up past the windshield.

The shock of the collision had the effect of flushing out the last tremors of the hallucination. With his mind fairly clear, Giertz pushed the door up once more, and swam shakily out of the sinking car. As his head broke the surface, hungry for air, he saw a group of people surrounding him on the grass bank.

They were fancy-dressed in elaborate costumes from somewhere in the early twentieth century, the mythologized, hedonistic period around the end of the First World War, and preceding the first Great

Depression. *Or their idea of it,* Giertz observed, taking in the men's tuxedos and the women's bust-less, 'flapper' dresses, their 'bobbed' hair supporting headbands of endangered birds' feathers. Most of the spectators were saturated, despite the day being dry. Then Giertz could see, *The splash as the car hit the water must have soaked them.* Immediately it came to him who, or what, they were. 'Producers!' he hissed, quietly. His tone couldn't have been any more pessimistic if they had been starving lions.

They were applauding him stiffly and laughing politely, but the unhappy expressions on their faces didn't match their gestures. He stood up in the shallows, water running from his long hair and clothes, tangled with slime and pond weed. Even at that early stage though, he was certain they didn't want him there. In fact, he sensed they hated him on sight. Now, resembling some B-movie horror-creature, he waded towards them.

The rear of the car with its airfoil wing was projecting out of the water, the nose stuck in the mud. Surrounded by the baroque house and ornamental gardens, to Giertz it now seemed to be some time machine, as if it had magically transported him to an earlier century. As he neared the bank, peacocks strutted haughtily across the grass, dragging their exquisite tails, which they would fan out in climaxes of vanity.

In the middle of the pool, behind the car, was an eroded marble fountain. Standing in the center of that was the statue of a naked male child, its face and body pock-marked, the nose eaten away by acid rain. It was holding an amphora from which water was supposed to be spouting, but wasn't. Giertz noticed the head was at a rather odd angle and seemed to be moving, before it rolled off and splashed into the dark green water. This drew a further round of applause, but Giertz didn't feel worthy, *The car must have just clipped it on the way over, but they think I did that deliberately!*

One man was, unlike the others, old, short, and fragile. He looked like any tramp in his patched and dirty evening suit, but was applauding and laughing more enthusiastically. He indicated that Giertz should be helped out of the water. Unwillingly, two of the few less saturated men stepped forward and did so, but they smiled rigidly the whole time, showing all their expensive, perfect teeth. Giertz quickly understood, *These phonies will do anything this man says!*

One of the two was dressed as a veteran of World War One, complete with fake, bloody wound-dressings. He placed his relatively dry, khaki greatcoat over Giertz's soaking, scuffed, bright red, Synth-O-Leather jacket. The expression on the man's face though, and on most of the others, instantly neutralized Giertz's gratitude. He also noticed the fake veteran looking furtively at the old man, trying to gauge whether this had extracted any approval from him. The others seemed very interested as well.

Everyone had stopped applauding now, but the old man was still doing so, even more vigorously. In the end, he fell sideways, still clapping and laughing, but it was more a sort of rhythmic retching noise. *Clearly, he's having some sort of fit!* Two of the wet women stepped forward to assist him, and Giertz noted, *It's as if they are familiar with the routine, but are as reluctant as the men who helped me.* Giertz examined the disgust on their faces as they crouched beside the old man with difficulty, in their tight, couture dresses, *Going through the motions of caring.*

'Glaga glaga glaga...' He was saying, staring glassily in front of himself, as they restrained his arms, and the clapping eventually stopped. As the near corpse lay on the ground, Giertz decided, *There is something familiar about this figure.* He stepped forward and inspected the man's face closely. Then Giertz realized he was looking at one of the two richest and most powerful men in the world, in the phlesh. He was also Giertz's boss.

Everyone in the world knew him as just plain 'Uncle Joe,' who ran Greedeluxe Corp. (corporate motto: 'We Love You!') the other of the two corporations that now controlled the entire global economy, or 'Globecon.' Uncle Joe wasn't a public figure though in the way Dr. Zed was. Instead, Uncle Joe had delegated this responsibility to Greedeluxe's board of directors, encouraging it to present the corporation's apparently more democratic front to the world. The full membership list was classified, but Giertz assumed, *That must be this lot standing around me.*

Giertz was confused for a moment. All the pictures he'd seen of Uncle Joe showed someone at least a quarter of a century younger, retaining the cock-confident smile of a thrusting, young entrepreneur. *Those photographs must have been constantly retouched, then reissued, by The Council of Ninety, to hide the horrible truth from the Consumers, and shareholders!*

**Chapter 15 Uncle Joe**
Giertz also understood by now, *Everyone here is under the misapprehension Uncle Joe had prearranged my 'stunt.' The car sailing over the top of the trees was a welcome distraction for Uncle Joe, and a disturbing one for them.* Giertz decided not to counter their illusion, and he was soon to learn Uncle Joe didn't want it disturbed either. Giertz would also learn a lot more besides about Uncle Joe.

Giertz now understood nothing had changed in the 'real' outside world during his Happylands incarceration. *The globecon is still divided into The Producers, who have real money, wealth, power, and information, and The Consumers, who don't, with the Council of Ninety in-between.* Like most

Consumers, Giertz had never met a real Producer before, so he decided to observe assiduously.

In tune with the fancy dress party's general theme, a band of tubercular-looking musicians played tinny New Orleans jazz, as the lead singer crooned authentically through a metal loud-hailer. One thing that wasn't authentic though, was for Giertz to see people here openly injecting themselves with 'Preparation X315/J', but Giertz understood, *Being seen to be going to the most exclusive rehab and detox programs must be a significant status symbol in itself. Something the addicts who are just Consumers can't afford.*

Someone pushed a well-aged alcoholic drink into Giertz's hand, which he never even tasted, as usual. The man who'd given his coat to Giertz reluctantly guided him to an open-air banqueting table. It looked as if it was almost about to collapse under the mountain of food. Giertz was shocked to see the delicacies weren't synthetic, either. *It's all come from a real farm somewhere, that The World Food Corporation's programs didn't destroy!* Wondering what it would taste like, he picked at the dishes experimentally.

He was surprised however, *Without all the additives it doesn't taste as good as the synthetic stuff I was weaned on, even though this must be better for me.* He picked up a whole, roasted, free-range chicken and bit a mouthful out of it, carrying it around with the untouched drink.

Giertz's guide had modern, but thick, grafted contact lenses that shrank his pupils to pinpoints. Giertz could just see the designer serial number around the edge of the irises. Wanting to make the best of the situation, Giertz tried hard to put his prejudice against Producers aside. Trying to think of something to say, he thanked this one for the loan of his genuine World War One coat, with genuine bullet holes, but the man said nothing. He just looked slightly embarrassed, and Giertz noticed he actually seemed about to vomit at the sight of Giertz's eating habits. He found this strange because every Consumer he knew ate with their fingers these days.

Giertz wondered what was wrong. He offered the man his coat back, but could see from this Producer's sneer of disgust he wasn't being generous; he just didn't want it back because Giertz had worn it. In the end, the Producer didn't seem to be able to handle the responsibility given to him. When Giertz offered him a piece of the chicken, it was all too much. He shook his head, plainly nauseated at the idea, and marched away as quickly as he could. Afterward, Giertz only saw him from a distance.

Feeling alone, Giertz wandered aimlessly, attempting to mingle with the party crowd, but they all reacted the same way, many less politely. They talked over his head, or even through it. The women's attitude to him was even worse than the men's. They had a particularly aggressive, spiteful way of ignoring him, and he realized, *I might as well be speaking some dead language, while I can understand them only too plainly.*

He found they only had one, main topic of conversation anyway, a nebulous 'something.' *Nobody refers to it outright, as if it's too vulgar, but in the end it's all they think about.* Giertz didn't fully understand what it was, except to know it wasn't only money, but he couldn't manufacture the necessary curiosity to find out more. There was also a sub-topic they wouldn't talk about at all within his hearing either, but he often accidentally overheard them discussing it excitedly, as if they couldn't wait.

Sometimes The Producers even went quiet, staring at him, when they thought he could eves-drop, but he knew anyway exactly what this issue had to be, *'The Sanitization.'* As most of the Consumers were, Giertz was already primed for the not-so-secret scheme, *The rumor of*

*The Producers' plan to exterminate us Consumers.* Unlike the general population though, he wasn't resigned to it.

Giertz had often debated it with himself, *If questioned openly, The Producers would say the Consumers are indispensable to The Globecon because, after all, where would The Producers be if no one consumed what they were producing? This was certainly true during the construction of The Globecon, but now even the mammoth, new robot-factories in the Pan-Asian Free Trade Zone only need The Producers to buy their output. 'Life' as a Consumer today has only become a matter of which corporate, 'imitation goods' lifestyle one chooses to consume anyway.'* Giertz felt even more depressed at this thought, *And behind it all is each individual Consumer's hope that their chosen corporation will achieve world monopoly, with the nightmare that it won't.*

Although Giertz had chosen the Greedeluxe lifestyle, unlike most Consumers, he was smart enough to know, *It won't make a lot of difference to the overall situation in the end.* So hiding beneath his personal, corporate loyalty was the additional hope that, *The whole system will just end altogether, and this 'reality,' which people take for granted, whichever of the two management philosophies is running it, will just disappear entirely!* Of course, he rarely mentioned this to anyone, because he knew then they would know he wasn't only crazy - but dangerous.

Where 'reality' was concerned anyway, there had been enough rumors and counter-rumors of the planned 'Sanitization' for long enough for him to know it had to be true. The mass extermination of an entire social stratum: *The Consumers!* Giertz thought, with a degree of awe. *It's certainly technologically possible, a few neutron bombs or a virus, or some combination of the two.*

To him however, the impending Sanitization was just another evil aspect of the reality he wanted to destroy so much, only giving his mission a greater sense of urgency.

*Yes, it will be coming soon, so there isn't much time, I have to hurry...* Generally though, he quickly became bored with inadvertently overhearing what the guests were saying. *It's just not as interesting as they think, because their thinking is so predictable anyway.*

What did interest Giertz, as he drifted around, was gradually discovering that while Uncle Joe lived in what looked like a typical English stately home, it was crumbling at its foundations, *Mother nature is rapidly reclaiming the rest of the house also, with ivy and cobwebs.* One antique wing had already collapsed, and the rubble still lay with weeds growing through it.

Nonetheless, Uncle Joe encouraged his party guests to dress in the flowing clothes of periods appropriate to the house. They parked their helicopters and private VTOL jets behind the trees, out of sight. Anyone looking at the scene as Giertz had, for the first time, would have felt they were looking through some time-window into an earlier century.

However, closer inspection revealed the mildewed costumes, crumbling masonry, overgrown ornamental gardens, and vinegary wine. The guests danced with cold, blank faces, as the musicians' renderings of Bix Beiderbecke's greatest hits echoed emptily through the atmosphere. The event gave Giertz an eerie feeling, *Perhaps Uncle Joe is trying to illustrate some point to all of them? They all seem to be ignorant of it though.* As Giertz looked around at the guests' frozen faces, he perceived, *There's something else going on here that I don't understand.*

Trying to analyze it, he began to expand on his first observation of the crowd. *These people do not seem happy. In fact, there's a miasma hanging over this estate, and I'm beginning to feel it too.* The media had always assured Giertz that if he had bigger money, he would have a more enjoyable life, but he felt, *There's a prevailing inertia with these people, a suffocating lack of any real challenges, and a preoccupation with trivia. It's not so different to the Happylands asylum, in that sense, and in some ways it's even worse!*

He also had a suspicion that he would soon find just how bad it really was.

**Chapter 16 Food Chain**

Giertz began to recognize some of the other faces at the party from the holyvision, and saw everyone who was 'anyone' came to 'mingle,' but he felt disappointed. *Holyvision stars, generals, dictators. So this is 'The Overclass,' and this is all they get up to?* It was something of a shock, after being told all his life he should aspire to be one of them. Their desperate quest for pleasure as an end in itself seemed ironically degrading to Giertz, somehow. After witnessing the second or third orgy writhing in the eroded marble fountain, Giertz began to feel, *I'm only seeing an exercise in mass boredom, and felt wiser.*

At that moment too, Giertz also felt he knew Uncle Joe more closely than anyone else there. Despite their opposite positions on the food chain, Giertz felt he could see the deeper significance of the old man's condition. *Even with his health problem, he's just too sane for all this.*

Because of his initial naiveté though, Giertz still accidentally dropped his guard from time to time, when he met young Producers his age at some of the food tables. He found himself naturally trying to strike up a conversation, but the only reply was to see the corners of their mouths curling down slightly. *It's not that they are ignoring me, it's more as if I don't exist for them. Their minds are so focused on the 'something' here; I am no more than a marginally annoying insect distracting them from it.* Some even bumped into him as they rushed to meet the arriving VIPs, as if Giertz was invisible.

He wondered at first if it could have been his spectacular gate-crashing that had alienated him, but soon found, *It's more as if they recognize something about me, identifying me as just not one of them.* Therefore, Giertz eventually realized that his earlier social prejudices had been correct.

He also understood that since his 'stunt,' he'd instantly been cast in the role of court jester for Uncle Joe, but Giertz didn't care, at first. He was glad in fact, because he mistakenly believed, *I can play along with this show for the time being, until something more interesting comes up, and the more they ignore me,* Giertz vowed, *the more I will become a splinter under their skin!* Now Giertz even felt incredibly lucky. *After all, if I am going to destroy reality, these stuffed shirts must be the first to go, because they are the ones with the most control over it.* Therefore he could now see his unique status gave him an ideal vantage point from which to experiment on them, *I will use my unfavorable position here to learn their weaknesses!*

Despite his youth, Giertz wasn't fooled by this 'civilization,' which he'd always been informed was 'reality.' He knew, *What everyone calls 'reality' is just something manufactured by civilization. So reality and civilization cannot exist without each other.* Despite The Globecon spanning across the world, he knew, It's getting near the end for it anyway. *'Reality,' or at least the enormous, over-complicated machine defining it, is already unable to support itself.* He also had an inkling however that, *Destroying these Producers' 'reality' probably isn't going to be as easy as it was that of the Happylands Institute.*

Giertz's private theory was, *It isn't one big cataclysm that destroys a civilization, but an infestation of smaller problems.* In his brief life so far, he'd seen them every day: major disagreements over easily-resolved issues, jobs not finished properly, the wrong people appointed to the wrong positions, and on and on. *These are tiny, festering microbes, which have undermined some once-dignified animal, now terminally sick and crawling on its belly.*

Just looking around at the 'civilized' gathering here made him feel ill, until he just couldn't stand the sight anymore. *I, Dr. James Giertz, just want to be the one to euthanize this sick animal, to simply put a bullet through its head, relieving it of its misery forever. Civilization is so weak, it would only take one small catastrophe, and somehow I must initiate it, then 'reality' will finally be dead, or at least well on its way.* He still didn't specifically know the reason why he wanted to do this; he only knew that he had to do it, somehow understanding, *It is my destiny!*

What he still didn't know however, was that one way or another, nobody ever completely left Uncle Joe's party, or that for himself, Giertz, this particular stage of his life would come to a violent and bloody end.

**Chapter 17 Unsettling Intrusion**

As the months of partying passed, Giertz's dark hair and beard grew even longer, well beyond his shoulders, giving him the appearance of a young, demented Jesus. Wandering alone around the limits of the rolling estate, Giertz felt like some Victorian explorer, wading through the bracken and weeds, making expeditions into the jungle-like corners of the once-ornamental gardens. As if discovering some lost civilization, he uncovered ruined gazebos and toppled marble nudes swathed in ivy, *Relics of a more optimistic age.*

He also found out that when Uncle Joe wasn't attending his never-ending party, he only lived in relative poverty in one small room of his stately home. He normally subsisted on meager meals he cooked for himself over a small camping stove. Giertz was surprised, but not disappointed. *Uncle Joe seems to be the only one here with any real personality.* Therefore, overall, at first Giertz began to feel there was no fundamental difference between The Producers and 'other people,' despite what The Producers and 'other people' thought.

To his joy, Giertz also discovered a lot of machinery in one of the archaic garages, converted from stables. There were decrepit cars and motorcycles from the Twentieth Century. Giertz ran a hand over a dusty, genuine Bugatti T35 which sat corroding on flat tires. He worked the stiff controls on a hydraulic inspection lift and played with a workbench of carefully organized, but rusty tools. *Uncle Joe must have had a passion for this kind of equipment at one time.* It was all covered by several decades of dust. Giertz started to wonder about what could have gone wrong, but then preferred not to.

Giertz soon found though, that he'd just escaped from one prison into another. *I am a captive on this estate, despite knowing no one will prevent me from leaving. In fact, they would willingly do the opposite.* The temptation to stay here was an invisible straight jacket, and he'd nowhere to go anyway. *I am trapped in my role here; they won't let me be anything else.* He understood again, just like in the asylum, *My car is my only hope of escape.*

That night, Giertz adopted the air of a grave robber. He went to the moonlit pool where the winged tail of the car still projected out of the water, but instead of carrying a spade, he tied some ropes, chains, and pulleys that he'd also found, to a nearby oak tree. With intense, physical effort, Giertz began to drag the machine out of the mud and onto the bank, a few centimeters at a time. No one showed much interest in this part of the estate these days. The party was now focused on the tennis courts on the other side of the house, where the duels took place. *There seem to have been a lot more duels recently,* Giertz thought idly, as his thin arms heaved at the ropes.

Finally, the dirty, dented, maritime wreck of the red vehicle emerged from the pond, water running out of the door seams. As he pushed it towards the garage, he was relieved to see the damage hadn't been substantial. The mud must have cushioned the impact! *Miraculously no water got into the engine or major components either.*

Over many more nights, he began cleaning, straightening and rebuilding with the old spanners and sockets. Giertz would use the antique, Bakelite phone in the hall occasionally, and small packages of parts would arrive in plain wrappers, unnoticed amongst the endless stream of food, wine, and Preparation X315/J.

As he worked on the car, he considered his situation, *Time seems to be running backward on this estate.* The guests were now dressing like early Victorians: the women in long crinoline dresses with their hair in ringlets, while the men wore brightly colored military uniforms carrying ceremonial swords, which made him wonder, *Why are rich people always so obsessed with the past?* Displaying his cheap, black jeans and running-vest amongst them, Giertz was some unsettling intrusion from the millennium seething outside the estate, but he knew well by now, *This isn't the real reason for them not liking me.* Giertz also suspected that, *Under the affable senility, Uncle Joe has some purpose for me,* but Giertz never bothered to ask what it was.

During the balmy autumn days, Uncle Joe would just encourage Giertz to arrange more 'surprises' for the guests, similar to the one he'd provided when he arrived. Strangely this didn't seem to make anyone want to leave, and everything Giertz did was tolerated by them, although bitterly. It didn't appear to stop more of them arriving either, and at least two of them were bad news for Giertz.

# Chapter 18 Systematically Taunting

Often these days, despite them being declared enemies, Dr. Zed himself would visit Uncle Joe's party. Giertz was extremely disturbed by the presence of this tall, ageing man in a sharp suit with his beach-ball sized cranium, as if he had physically stepped out Giertz's last major, nightmare hallucination, but he tried hard not to show it.

Throughout the tarnished banquets, everyone would sit around the table politely avoiding any mention of the size of Dr. Zed's head, except for Giertz, of course. He would be entirely outspoken, mentioning it at every opportunity, 'What a fat nonce!' He exclaimed at his first real sight of it, genuinely surprised at just how big it was.

Giertz also made a point of eating with his fingers, while spilling food and water down himself. In a quiet moment, he would sneeze across the table. The guests, laughing politely through clenched teeth, pretended to be amused, but Giertz was only beginning to comprehend just how much they fundamentally hated him.

Conversely, if Giertz had hated them in the early days, he positively loathed them now, and wanted to destroy their reality even more. *I despise their patronizing laughter and applause.* In fact it had turned into a pure battle of wills, as he probed and feinted to find some way to provoke them into openly acknowledging their real attitude to him. The more they disguised it, the harder he tried, systematically taunting them at every opportunity, and so the vicious circle span ever faster.

Therefore, always trying to top his first stunt, and entrance, he regularly performed his favorite trapeze acts from the dusty chandeliers above the guests. Swinging by his heels, his long hair dragged across the table as he head-butted dishes to the right and left. The diners would sit quietly as lobster and foie gras flopped into their laps. They didn't mention this either, pretending to be entertained, despite it now being unusual for anyone to get as much as a mouthful from a plate.

Meanwhile, Uncle Joe wasn't in the least embarrassed. On the contrary, he would drink toasts to Giertz, banging on the table with a pewter tankard, laughing heartily with his mouth full, shouting, 'BRAVO! BRAVO!' - encouraging Giertz further, to even more spectacularly embarrassing feats. Uncle Joe would even display him with pride, as if Giertz was the son he'd never had, much to the confused disgust of the guests.

Once they'd all been ready to tuck into a sumptuous recreation of a 'Dickensian' feast, whispering expressions of relief, because 'that dreadful Jimmy Giertz' was notable by his absence. They chose to ignore the sound of a revving motorcycle engine, and didn't see a shadow growing darker on one of the stained glass windows.

Suddenly there was a thunderous crash, showering them with particles of colored crystal, when Giertz leaped onto the dining table on a large, chrome-plated BSA motorcycle. He'd found the relic in the stables and repaired it, as a side project to his car.

He rode the weighty, growling antique around the vast table several times, chewing up the starched tablecloths, kicking hors d'oeuvres into their aghast faces. He even made a victory lap, and laughed snarlingly down at them, before launching himself back out of the shattered window.

Uncle Joe was so catatonic with laughter he had to lie on the floor again. Many who ran to his assistance went through the motions of fearing for the worst, as his head turned almost purple, and his trousers stained with urine once more. He was even slightly paralyzed down one side for some time afterward, but he promised Giertz he could have *anything*. Anything it was within his power to give. 'Anything! Anything! Anything! Ah-ha-ha-ha!' He laughed, with his open mouth still half-full of food. Behind their icy smiles, the guests, from looking disgusted with Giertz, now seemed afraid of him.

They needn't have been though, because while Giertz tried hard, he just couldn't think of anything he wanted that Uncle Joe had got. Somehow Giertz felt that in spite of all Uncle Joe's wealth, he didn't want to be anything like Uncle Joe. In fact, Giertz ultimately wanted to destroy everything that man had, and represented.

However, the guests didn't know that.

**Chapter 19 Serious Mistake**

One day at the party, Giertz recognized even more celebrity faces from the holyvision screen than usual: there was the hollow countenance of Leonard Kornn, a career 'artist.' Nibbling on a rich tea biscuit and sipping at a priceless wine with an amusing bouquet, as he nervously ascertained that he was seen to be rubbing with the 'correct' shoulders. However, Giertz couldn't remember when Kornn had last created any 'art.' *Nobody else seems to be able to either, or when he first created any for that matter.* Kornn's critics termed his' work' 'Post-Neo-Obscurist,' which mostly seemed to consist of being invited to parties like this one, and the invitations kept flowing.

There was the predatory smile of Reinholt Schnartz III, 'The World's Most Self-Created Man.' He looked relatively normal, except his smile ran almost unnaturally up one side of his face, even exposing his molars. An 'ornament of polite society,' he was the master of magically wafting entire fortunes out of thin air, without actually producing any goods or services benefiting anyone. With a single phone call, he could liquefy whole industries or even economies, piping the results directly into his anonymous accounts in the Security Zone. Part of his 'charm' was the way he generously gave a small percentage to causes he vehemently believed in, such as making Preparation X315/J more freely available to children. His flock of disciples would follow him everywhere, even into the bathroom, hoping some of his 'Midas touch' would rub off on them.

Today though, Giertz headed straight for The Evil Poet. A fat, brawny man in a velvet cloak with a fur collar, his thin hair was drawn dramatically back to his neck, a thick, gold chain around his substantial belly. Giertz liked to listen to him as he talked, *I hate his pomposity so much, I derive a perverse pleasure from hearing his pronouncements.* Looking over people's heads into the distance, it was as if he were on some pedestal, deigning to hand down information gathered from the clouds. Giertz quietly joined the small circle of white-haired men absorbing his every word, and nodding sagely.

'...I do not find the human animal enigmatic,' The Evil Poet was saying today. 'Its actions are entirely predictable. It has but five fundamental motivations: the urge to eat, respire, move, grow and reproduce its kind. Its every act, no matter how complex, can be explained in terms of these, just like the lowest microbe.'

Giertz reflected on the rumor that the Evil Poet was presently engaged in reaping 'priceless scientific information,' on his private island. This was at terrible, inhumane costs to his research assistants and human guinea pigs, but this didn't seem to bother the Evil Poet unduly. 'I do not feel human beings have any significance in the universe,' he continued, 'they could not be and *are not* "loved" by its creator, because they are *forgotten*. After all, the only thing separating Man from the other beasts is that it has the ability to kill all the rest.'

It had taken some time for Gietz to ascertain that, *These, and others present, are members of The Council of Ninety!*

Mainly he could tell from the way some guests drew more attention than others, and it wasn't just about money. *Just why are they here, though?* Giertz wondered, unaware that he would soon find out.

As he contemplated this, Giertz was annoyed however, as his attention was disturbed by a minor commotion coming his way. A rather silly teenage girl and her silly teenage friends danced up to him. She was wearing an extremely low-cut dress, loosely patterned on the eighteenth-century fashions all the guests were now wearing. Giertz guessed, *I suppose part of the effect is the possibility that it might slip away from her artificially developed bust altogether, at any moment.*

'Hello, Jimmy!' Giertz just smiled back cautiously. She informed him happily today's party was 'special,' as Dr. Zed's infamous sidekick, known as The Bad Actor, was present, and she wanted Giertz to fight a duel with him.

Becoming more persuasive, she told Giertz her name, which he instantly forgot, but she also told him to come to one of her parties sometime, and passed him an embroidered table napkin with the geo-coordinates and security code written on it. As she skipped away again, Giertz was shocked, realizing someone at the party had finally spoken to him. He would eventually be even more surprised at how significant this encounter would be in his bizarre future.

It was doubly a strange experience for him because most women never usually paid him any attention. He guessed, *She must be too young, and even more naive than she looks, to understand the 'something' that's in the air here.* Despite this, he wasn't really in the mood for another stunt, but realizing it would be unexpected of him to accept, he accepted.

## Chapter 20 Bare Knuckle

Giertz had fought duels with some of the guests before, but they'd never been as challenging as the ones in his holygames. To Giertz this one was just another stunt, at first. His only real combat training had come from the happy days when, like most children, he'd learned bare-knuckle boxing in the World War Two bomb craters, overgrown with weeds, still peppered around his parents' home.

From the expressions on the guests' faces though, Giertz began to realize that from 'court jester' he'd been promoted to the role of 'single-combat warrior.' He was now Uncle Joe's champion, but for exactly what cause he still wasn't sure. *I only know that I hate The Bad Actor*, he decided, *and that's mostly because I hate Dr. Zed.*

Dr. Zed and The Bad Actor were a team. The Bad Actor was everything Dr. Zed wasn't: young, leisured, and normal-looking. He had a spoiled, sharp-featured face, with ears which stuck out, making him somehow look a bit monkey-like. He was prematurely gray, and when smiling, he showed all his gums. He regularly wore next month's style of light-gray suit, with a large blood-red carnation in the lapel.

He'd started off as a television news-comedian, good at putting a saccharine coating on the increasingly hard-to-swallow 'latest developments,' but had grown to become Dr. Zed's champion in the arena of the mass media. He was always endorsing Consumeordie Corp. products (corporate motto: 'You will love us!'), arguing Consumeordie's 'case,' and seen living the Consumeordie lifestyle, in both 'soap operas' and real-life situations. In fact, there was no line between the fiction and the reality of his life. People either loved him or hated him. Most hated him, but envied him so badly it was painful. Some only hated what he represented, while Giertz just hated him.

*Will this particular episode be broadcast for mass-consumption, like all The Bad Actor's other exploits?* Giertz wondered, vaguely hoping it would be, because he mistakenly thought it would feel good to be on holyvision, but he would eventually learn that lesson the hard way.

## Chapter 21 Casual Facade

By now Giertz's hair, almost reaching down his back, no longer seemed so out of place among the retro styles the guests were wearing. Giertz assumed, *Soon they will be dressing as medieval barons and maidens, heartily drinking mead over roasting boars.* He wondered where it would end, *Perhaps Uncle Joe will have them in animal skins, tearing at raw meat with their bare teeth, living as hunter-gatherers in the thickets of the jungle-gardens?*

It had taken time, but in an isolated way, Giertz almost managed to enjoy himself at these parties. He also liked the general feeling of privilege at being able to witness the two greatest forces in the world come together. He did still wonder from time to time however, about the 'something,' *Exactly what's going on here?* Meanwhile, his general, youthful delirium prevented him from fully realizing these people weren't just the cardboard mannequins they appeared to be. Yet he was developing a vague notion, *There may be terrific tensions heaving beneath their happy facade?*

An involuntary tremor would often pass across Dr. Zed's otherwise stony countenance, or Uncle Joe's distorted joviality would fracture into a look of stung soul-searching. The guests were continually swanning between the two, as iron filings would the poles of a magnet. Giertz had observed by now, *Under their glassy looks of respect, they're only trying to see which one has more to offer.*

Therefore Giertz had guessed, *Maybe there's just no dividing line between pleasure and business here?* What he didn't know however was that pleasure was business, that the party games weren't just 'games.' To people for whom almost any amount of wealth was trivial, money couldn't be used to measure the real prize, or penalty, in any contest. Therefore, everyone at these parties, except Giertz, knew they were really complex competitions. Whole careers or even empires could be made or ruined by a word or gesture in the right or wrong place. All the weapons of the two great corporations were so well counterbalanced, any chink in the opponent's defense was now a legitimate tactic.

The embroidered, sparkling crowd followed Giertz and The Bad Actor to the old tennis courts, with their sagging, rotten nets. The ingrained, dried bloodstains on the dead grass testified that the area was now solely reserved for dueling, and the two duelists selected their rapiers. Giertz had never been able to take the duels he'd witnessed here seriously, even when they were to the death, and even when he was fighting them. As he looked at The Bad Actor however, Giertz noticed him taking this one very seriously indeed. In fact, there was a particular brand of nervousness Giertz had never noticed in him before. Giertz became slightly curious. *Exactly what's at stake here?* Even if he'd known what it was though, it couldn't have prepared him for the outcome.

The Bad Actor tested several swords, slashing at the air with them, before finally appearing to select one from the rack. Giertz just grabbed the first one, more interested in chewing on the veal sandwich in his other hand.

As The Bad Actor quibbled, Giertz looked around at the crowd. He found it unsettling the way all the over-fed, pampered faces had an identical expression on them, a kind of nervous anticipation. In fact, their eyes were almost bulging, making Giertz feel he was in some pornographic spectacle. It was also given a weird cast by the way some were biting into capsules of Preparation X315/J to enhance the experience, the unnatural high glowing in their dilated pupils.

However, especially after Giertz's last hallucination, one, very large, face disconcerted him the most, because it had no expression at all. Although he'd often observed Dr. Zed from a distance, Giertz had never been so close to him before, and somehow this felt even stranger. Then just before it started, Giertz already knew the fight was on.

**Chapter 22 Genuine Terror**

As Giertz launched himself at The Bad Actor, he saw him as embodying everything Giertz hated about the world and universe in general, *He's the personification of the reality I want so much to destroy.* The Bad Actor even seemed confused at first, as he tried to assume some level of defensive stance against this fevered onslaught.

Most of the duels were usually over in five minutes, but this one was running well beyond the normal time span, the two were slashing at each other for a full twenty minutes. Giertz's reflexes, and hate, were prolonging it against The Bad Actor's advanced skill. From nervousness, Giertz now saw genuine terror in The Bad Actor. It was obvious the undiluted, insane loathing in Giertz, coupled with his speed of reactions, was something The Bad Actor had never encountered before. Giertz was even still taking bites out of his sandwich at least five minutes into the battle.

In fact, Giertz now felt he had a chance at something he'd been waiting for since before his birth. Therefore something inside him was taking over, guiding every movement. The air in front of him appeared to turn red, then black.

Despite Giertz's lack of training or experience, it wasn't a fair fight, and now everyone was beginning to see it. The Bad Actor's ability, science, and years of practice were no foil for Giertz's secret aptitude to divine what would happen in three seconds time, and the way he'd sharpened this talent with practice. Even Giertz was almost puzzled, *Just like in one of my holygames! It's easy!* He also had time to notice the audience hastily reversing many bets.

Eventually, the padding in The Bad Actor's shoulders was sticking out like wads of quick-growing fungus, and Giertz's arms and black vest were covered in minor cuts and blood. He now knew, *So that's why he earned the name Bad Actor! It's because while his eyes are wide with terror, he somehow manages to disguise it as a kind of forced enthusiasm.* Giertz also now understood, *Someone must have trained him very rigorously for these kinds of situations.* Additionally, Giertz suspected, *The Bad Actor probably doesn't enjoy his job quite as much as is widely assumed.*

Finally, Giertz drove him into a corner of the tennis court's rusted wire mesh fence, but when their backs were to the crowd, Giertz heard something unusual. There was a metallic click from The Bad Actor's sword. Only Giertz and The Bad Actor saw a small, curved, second blade flick out of his sword's handle.

Even with his advanced reflexes, Giertz still took too long to register what was happening. As the prong closed on his sword, which snapped with no more resistance than paper cut by scissors, Giertz found all his loathing hadn't prepared him for the possibility that The Bad Actor could actually cheat. Again also, Giertz was reminded, *My reflexes really do have their limitations!* Meanwhile, the tool in his opponent's weapon discreetly clicked back again into the handle.

The next thing Giertz knew was The Bad Actor had him by his scrawny neck, the chipped edge of his sword creasing the skin over Giertz's carotid artery. Giertz still clung to his useless, ornate handle disbelievingly. Both panting heavily and soaked with perspiration, they looked to Dr. Zed, who did nothing for a moment. He just stared impassively down on the scene, and Giertz felt his complicated life dangling in an unpleasant state of suspension.

**Chapter 23 Broken Sword**

In the end, Dr. Zed shook his enormous head slightly, granting Giertz an extension of his life, but he would soon almost wish Dr. Zed hadn't, as The Bad Actor theatrically threw Giertz to the ground, to the usual mannered clatter of applause from the guests. This always followed a duel, but Giertz noted it was the same in tone as the one heralding his spectacular arrival in the pool several months back. Behind the light laughter today though, Giertz detected something else - the confirmation that this had never really been just about sport.

As the guests drifted away from the tennis courts, Giertz also noticed an atmosphere of relief amongst them. *It's as if some point has been proven, at last.* Everyone knew the party was finally over. The air was soon full of the departing fanfare of private VTOL jets, blasting into the sky from behind the trees, a louder echo of the guests' laughter - in Giertz's bitter silence.

Soon there was no one left on the tennis courts besides Giertz and Uncle Joe, standing either side of the broken sword. Under the autumn, dusk sky, Giertz was still on his knees, exhausted, angry, and bewildered. He didn't want to even look at Uncle Joe's gray, washed-out face, comparable to that of a man who'd just been shot. He couldn't even see Giertz, but just stared at some invisible, unreachable horizon. *It seems some last, temporary buttress supporting his life has finally shattered.*

Uncle Joe's jaw hung sideways slackly, as if he was contemplating a life of struggles which had all come to this. Strangely, although like Dr. Zed this man also represented everything Giertz despised about reality, he now felt a paradoxical sympathy, partly due to their shared animosity towards the other Producers. So Giertz gently carried him back to the mansion, and up the sweeping, broken staircase, his head lolling over Giertz's supportive inner elbow. The near-corpse was much heavier than he looked, especially now. Saliva dribbled down his chin from the collapsed hole of his mouth, which hung open showing the empty gums.

Giertz laid him carefully on the insignificant camp bed in the small cross between a kitchen, bathroom and bedroom, then hunted for any medicine, but couldn't find any. After checking Uncle Joe was comfortable, in the bathroom area, with its dull brass taps and fittings, Giertz then sprayed anti-scarring foam and applied rapid-healing dressings to the minor cuts on his own body and face. Actually, The Bad Actor's assault had made little difference, especially to Giertz's face, which was already heavily pitted by adolescence.

Considering the situation, Giertz actually resented the way he'd been manipulated by the old man, but also wondered why it had happened, *What point was he trying to prove? What was the real prize I lost up there on the tennis courts?* Giertz wasn't even fully sure about what he'd been opposing during the duel, apart from Consume or Die Corporation's leaders in some vague way, and what he didn't like about them. Meanwhile, Uncle Joe lay in bed for days losing weight, as he refused the food and water Giertz desperately tried to share with him.

Then Uncle Joe died.

## Chapter 24 Spiritually Wounded

Sadly, Giertz contemplated Uncle Joe's shriveled form on the cheap, single bed, not sure what to do. Emotionally wounded as he was, Giertz didn't believe it had been suicide, *It's more as if he finally lost control of his sense of purposelessness.*

Although he wasn't really interested, at this stage, Giertz watched share prices visibly plummeting on the old, neglected, secure-information-terminal next to the bed. The thick dust on its control testified to Uncle Joe's disinterest in Greedeluxe - his brainchild. Giertz continued to wonder, almost obsessively, *What's my true degree of responsibility for the problem? 'The Council of Ninety' will now completely take over the running of Uncle Joe's corporation,* but this wasn't what worried Giertz.

He wandered around the deserted estate, the sharp metal studs in the soles of his boots crunching over a carpet of party hats, tinsel, torn underwear, broken bottles, cancer-free cigarette butts, hypodermics, and empty blister-packs of Preparation X315/J ampules. Surveying the uncut lawns, he tried to make sense of it all. On one level, something kept reminding Giertz the whole situation was ridiculous, *Dr. Zed and Uncle Joe are mature men, with wealth and power, but with ironically childish rivalries.* Gradually, Giertz almost managed to convince himself whatever had really happened wasn't his fault - but not completely.

Eventually a couple of board members turned up to arrange a funeral. Giertz recognized them from the fancy-dress parties, but now they wore just normal business suits and Homburg hats, as was the fashion. Uncle Joe was buried on some forgotten part of his estate, in a small, cheap wooden coffin, with only a few, paid mourners in attendance, A pauper's funeral, Giertz observed, surprised and confused. There was no priest, and no words were said, only a plywood marker that was already splitting. Standing beside the open grave Giertz shed no tears, but did somehow miss the old man, despite the brevity of their encounter. Eventually though Giertz would change his mind.

Finally, he went to his car, which was now in running condition again, with only a few remaining dents and needing a coat of paint. As he dropped into the dried-out, but now water-stained Synth-O-Leather seat, a different feeling began to develop deep inside him. It wasn't a new emotion, but it had never been as strong as it was now. Although he didn't know how or what, he knew he had to do something. He had to do anything.

As he twisted the retro ignition key, he could think of only one place to go, 'Asclepius Institute for Biotechnological Research,' he muttered out loud, as the mighty engine burbled again, coughed, and then screamed.


**Chapter 25 Motorcycle Youth**

A few weeks later, there was a small surgical mark on Giertz's forehead. This was the only indication of the complicated, advanced medical techniques which had been used by the Asclepius Clinic over the past weeks, in an all-out, vain attempt to repair Giertz's deformed mind.

Originally, sometime even further back, it was also they who'd given Giertz his synthetic Ph. D. It was a direct download into his memory of all the learning from the brain of a top prize-winning student called Snodgrass. Therefore Giertz could remember the graduate's entire academic life of study, more study, and further study. The institute's scientists had told Giertz this implant was just a minor experiment, to see what effect it might have on his disease, but overall it had only confused him even more.

One of the 'benefits' of being a Greedeluxe Youth was that one could volunteer for the scientific experiments of the Asclepius Institute, a Greedeluxe enterprise. This paid no money; it was entirely voluntary, and for the good of Greedeluxe Corp. Knowing that the experiments didn't always work, and sometimes even caused terrible physiological problems, hadn't deterred anyone, including Giertz. In fact, the scientists there had always taken a 'special' interest in his case.

Sometimes Giertz was curious, *So why was The Asclepius Institute so desperate to work on my case?* He could no longer even remember when he'd first contacted them, or even if they'd contacted him. This time though, after he'd volunteered yet again, they'd finally admitted defeat. Mainly he'd just wanted refuge anyway, after his escapes from the Happylands Institute, and Uncle Joe's seemingly endless party. By the end of the summer however, Giertz would not only know the answer, but be extremely surprised by it - if not shocked.

It was also significant to Giertz that it was Professor Asclepius, (affectionately better known as 'Professor Skull-face,') himself who'd suggested Giertz should transfer to the Greedeluxe Combat Youth division. He'd thought it might help Giertz work out his problem for himself, so the idea had taken root in his aberrated mind - and wouldn't let go.

Therefore Giertz stepped out into the winter-morning heat from his battered car in the parking space beside the armored, post-neo-obscurist office-tower of Greedeluxe Youth headquarters. It stood by some disused, dirty-brick Victorian warehouses next to the stagnant, soupy river. Not put off by the setting, Giertz considered, *Maybe being part of a collective point of view rather than trying to destroy reality single-handedly might make a difference?* Really though, as it was with most of his decisions, Giertz didn't even really understand why he was here.

He only knew he had to do something. He had to do anything.

So he turned and looked across yesterday's newscomix blowing around the empty road, in front of the scarred concrete and bulletproof glass front of the skyscraper. Erected near the disused docks, it was a monument to Uncle Joe's flirtation with philanthropy. The dead neon sign up the side had letters missing though, so that it proclaimed the enigmatic equation:

'GREED X YOU H'

Giertz also noticed preparations everywhere for the annual Festival of Greed: Day-Glo flags, banners, and strings of colored lights were already going up amongst the general grayness, despite it still being almost a year away, and the last Festival still not even completely finished.

This was a celebration favored by Consumeordie Corp. Basically, the Consumers were supposed to consume as much as was physically possible, for as many days of the year as the economy would allow. The symbol was a big, red-lipped, self-satisfied smile. It had a sense of familiarity to Giertz, that he somehow didn't want to recognize. Around it was printed,

'Dr. ZED SAYS: EAT MORE PHLESH!'

People were encouraged to label anyone who didn't, or refused to, participate in The Festival as an 'ascetic.' This was not a compliment, in fact as a pejorative comment it was often followed by 'liability.' The later expletive was also a terrible epithet now. It was even worse than accusing someone of being mentally sub-normal, or of unspecified parentage, or of copulating at random, or even with their mother. Therefore, everyone used this single 'L' word sparingly, because it could bring instant, terrible retribution.

Interestingly though, Giertz noted, *None of the Consumeordie Festival flags or banners are anywhere within a good-sized radius of the Greedeluxe Youth headquarters.*

Although Giertz had entered the building once or twice before, he'd never seen it at this time of the morning, the hot winter sunrise turning its damaged front into a sheet of blinding orange light. He didn't fully understand why this should instill an element of fear in him, as if he was walking into a furnace, but he acknowledged, *It's probably at least partly due to the prospect of my interview today for the Greedeluxe 'Combat Youth.'*

Each Youth sub-division occupied a floor of the lofty building, and he knew Dr. Asclepius had been right of course; it had to be *The Combat Youth.* Not The Fundamentalist Youth, who shaved their heads and violently evangelized their religious-extremist, 'Xeracist' dogma, nor The Motorcycle Youth, who dressed in black leather and fought each other all the time, nor the Intellectual Youth, who all had hollow-looking eyes from spending their time in endless libraries, searching for 'The Answer,' nor any of the other specialized, fanatical, corporate-youth sub-divisions sponsored by Greedeluxe Corporation. *No,* Giertz decided, *it has to be the Combat Youth.* He found it strange the way Asclepius seemed to know Giertz's need so well, but later he wouldn't find it strange at all.

As he crossed the road, he analyzed the fear inside him. *I'm not afraid of the interview itself, because they seldom turn anyone away, after all. It just matters to me more than anything else at the moment. Somehow I can't face the possibility, however slight, of my application being rejected - but why? Perhaps it's because they offer me at least some kind of high ground, from which to attack reality?* Giertz felt overwhelmed by the task however, *Surely I can't do it by myself, after all - can I? But I don't even know what I've got to offer them.* He wasn't even slightly aware though this was going to be his second serious mistake.

Just as he was half-way across the road however, his contemplations were disturbed by the approaching sound of a cyclone-injected motorcycle engine, as a Greedeluxe Corp. Motorcycle Youth attempted to run him over.

**Chapter 26 Bullet-Resistant**

Without even thinking Giertz somersaulted, and at the other side he dusted his red, Synth-O-Leather jacket's upper-arms off. Further up the road, the Motorcycle Youth nearly wobbled off his mount, confused at how someone could have avoided death with such ease. Meanwhile, looking around for more threats, Giertz reminded himself, *Well, the Combat Youth might be interested in my reflexes, I suppose. They're something no one else seems to have, after all.*

He also had to admit he admired the Motorcycle Youth, despite their myopic focus on their internal leadership struggles. *They're certainly the least tame of the Greedeluxe Youth factions, and constantly bucking for more and more recognition. Perhaps I should join them instead?* Again though, something told him his path had already chosen him. He also reminded himself, *The Motorcycle Youth are famous for being so unruly, they are more of a danger to themselves than Consumeordie Corp. In fact, they are more hostile to the other Greedeluxe Youth gangs than any outsiders.*

As Giertz approached the heavy, bullet-proof, glass doors, he encountered two tall Motorcycle Youths lounging either side, in rugged, black, Synth-O-Leather jackets, pants and boots, with their blond hair artificially greased intricately over their heads. They appeared to decide between them, on some unspoken level, that Giertz was beneath their attention. They wouldn't beat him up today, or even grace him with as much as a sneer. Nevertheless, as they eyed him with undisguised contempt, he cautiously observed their positions from the corners of his vision. Passing quietly between them, and through the reception lobby filled with trash, he made his way to the dented elevator, embellished with graffiti.

After the riveted, bomb-proof office door on the appropriate floor slid back, Giertz's first real view of the Combat Youth's 'leader' Ceebix, (pronounced See-bicks), was of a man in a wheelchair. His over-developed shoulders seemed to make his legs appear even more atrophied, but this still didn't give him any second thoughts about wearing their uniform: a bright yellow Synth-O-Leather jacket, augmented by chunks of black, bullet-resistant padding. At the sight of Giertz, he pressed an intercom button on his desk, despite having no secretary, and mumbled some words into it. Giertz wondered who was on the other end.

He noticed a small slip of hard copy in Ceebix's hands. He'd been studying it intently, just before Giertz entered, but let it fall to the desk. He didn't seem to want Giertz to notice it, affecting an air of exaggerated disinterest. *Like a guilty self-abuser,* was Giertz's immediate analogy. Nevertheless, he tried in vain to see what was on it, without appearing too curious.

At this point, Giertz couldn't have guessed the part this man would play in his quest to destroy reality. The only clue was his office was almost completely bare, except for a few utilities. The bulletproof steel shutters over the only window kept the room very dark. Giertz's observation was, *For someone to work in a room like this by choice, it must take some extraordinary discipline, or another mental capacity.*

Consequently, he felt an instant affinity with the hunched silhouette, as Ceebix flicked at the wheels of the chair with the tips of his fingers, to glide across the room.

Then, Giertz was overcome by a strange feeling, *I want to be liked by this man!* This was doubly unusual, as he'd never wanted to be liked by anyone before. As Ceebix drew closer though, Giertz could see immediately, *Ceebix definitely doesn't like me.*

Giertz found particularly intimidating the way the frozen-blue eyes were fixed on him from beneath the broad, pale forehead. Above it, sparse hair was between blond and going white with age. The thin lips were permanently drawn tight, as if they were always about to utter something derogatory. Despite his preserved appearance however, aside from his obvious disability, Ceebix looked generally unhealthy, *As if he's trying to hide the beginnings of tuberculosis.*

Giertz recognized him now as someone he'd only noticed from a distance at Uncle Joe's party, but Ceebix had always just sat in his wheelchair, seemingly never doing or saying much, just intimidating everyone with his very presence. Giertz hadn't known who he was, and just wondered, *Why has he never had his spinal injury repaired, now there are nerve-grafting cures available in the Asclepius Rapid Healing Clinic?*

Standing awkwardly in the office, not quite knowing what to do, Giertz offered his hand. Ceebix's mouth smiled up at him, showing small, whitened, saw teeth, but the rest of his face remained immobile. He didn't take Giertz's hand, and so, feeling stupid, Giertz let it drop to his side once more.

## Chapter 27 Private Joke

Ceebix reached up with his thumb and forefinger to feel Giertz's stringy biceps and then, unimpressed, returned to his desk and clicked a steel pen against his teeth, as if on the verge of making a decision. He scrutinized the scrawled, smudged, crumpled, application form Giertz had hesitantly offered him. Giertz knew the clicking was meant to disconcert him, but pretended he didn't.

'So,' Ceebix began after some time, 'you're a Greedeluxe Youth, but now you want to specialize, and transfer to the Greedeluxe *Combat Youth?*' He looked up directly into Giertz's face. 'Why?' Giertz only shrugged and mumbled, 'It's an alternative to suicide.' Ceebix laughed a little at this, the small joke everyone in Greedeluxe Corp. told about the Combat Youth, despite probably having heard it until he'd stopped hearing it. It had virtually become their motto, but it was more as if Giertz had reminded Ceebix of some private joke, than made him laugh directly. Then Ceebix was momentarily distracted by a commotion coming from somewhere on the road by the waterfront, far below.

He leaned over and prized apart two of the bulletproof metal slats to peer out impassively. Giertz guessed accurately from the dissonance, that the two motorcycle youths he'd seen on the way in had found no-one worthy to challenge, *Therefore they are now beating each other insensible with chains, while wearing exactly the same black Synth-O-Leather uniform as each other.*

'The Youth are restless,' Ceebix commented as a general observation, still without emotion. Then unwillingly focusing on Giertz again, Ceebix wheeled himself around from behind the desk once more. The heavily-used wheelchair creaked as he raised himself to look more closely into Giertz's eyes. There was the usual moment of communication between two lunatics, they both understood the same thing, but Giertz perceived a kind of somber surprise on Ceebix's part. *It's as if I'm someone he was anticipating, but doesn't think I'll live up to expectations.*

Unenthusiastically Ceebix quickly scribbled a signature onto a form, photocopied and re-photocopied so many times it was almost illegible, mumbling, 'This consigns your uniform, weapons and new car,' handing it to Giertz, but seemingly more interested in the form itself than its significance to Giertz. As he was about to snatch it hungrily from Ceebix, it was withdrawn quickly, as Ceebix added, '...On completion of 'basic training,' before letting Giertz's fingers savor it.

Giertz noted the serial number stamped on the top of the form: 'CY 827.' *So I'm the eight hundred and twenty-seventh Combat Youth. There are only about fifty left now, and very few ever leave, and so all the rest must be dead.* The thought sobered him, but only slightly.

Next Ceebix tried hard to be friendly, which only unsettled Giertz even more. Ceebix even managed to beam broadly and say, 'The standard Greedeluxe Youth are certainly losing their operatives recently!' Giertz just mumbled a slightly less well-known cliché, but one precipitated from the every-day conversations of The Consumers. At the same time he made a non-committal gesture, as if anything would have done, 'It's too late for the truth.' Even Ceebix didn't laugh at this, because no one did - these days.


**Chapter 28 Smiling Coldly**

He asked Giertz if he wanted to see the indoctrinatory holyvid, despite knowing he must have seen it, along with all the other official 'holys,' several times, as all the Greedeluxe youths had. Giertz still said, 'Yes!' Ceebix warned him the sound wasn't working on the terminal's holy screen, but Giertz persisted.

'Have a seat,' Ceebix said resentfully. With no effort at all, he swung a heavy steel chair across the floor. Ceebix clicked the near-antique screen on with the broken manual control, held together with dirty adhesive tape. Giertz noted passingly that it was the same old-fashioned design of secure holy-terminal as Uncle Joe's. Ceebix also warned that he would have to do the commentary himself, but Giertz already knew it off by heart as the title jumped onto the screen,

'GREEDELUXE YOUTH INDOCTRINATORY
PROGRAM 63-A. COMBAT YOUTH: 01'

Giertz knew it would be sub-hypnotic, but didn't care. A slow-motion, two-dee monochrome shot of Adolph Hitler preaching flickered onto the screen, as Ceebix recited rapidly and mechanically, 'In the mid-20th century, fear of thermonuclear war and an increasingly faltering civilization manifested itself in violence among the young.' There was some old, scratched, black-and-white film of two opposing fronts of adolescents violently chanting at one another. One side was dressed in black leather, the other in green army-surplus. There was a shot of an overturned, burning car, then a close-up of a girl with dyed blonde hair and large earrings. She wore a black nylon raincoat and was screaming with hate until it hurt.

Scenes followed of adolescents beating each other up in clouds of dust at various sporting events and rock concerts, frightened policemen gradually losing control of the seething masses. Water cannons and tear-gas were being overcome and turned on the police themselves. The dazed and bleeding victims were carried away on stretchers. 'Attempts were made to redirect these energies, Ceebix continued, 'but the end result was always the same. These street battles, or "situations," as the media termed them, only grew in size and intensity.'

Grainy color scenes of two gangs of motorcyclists followed, stabbing and shooting each other. Some even had rocket launchers. This time there were no visible differences, they were all wearing the same uniform. 'With the advent of World Wars Four and Five, it became apparent a new morality and culture were emerging.' There was crude, early, low-definition three-dee footage of rioters tearing each other to pieces in the streets, with the bodies of Consumers hanging in two's and threes from every lamp post. Giertz could see clothes and tattoos carrying various advertising sponsors' logos aimed at 'the youth market,' but observed many of the opposing sides were bearing exactly the same corporate tattoos. *The advertisers had already moved in by then.* It was getting closer to the 'Situations' as Giertz understood them, but there were no genetic mutations in evidence yet.

There was also another pattern the holy-vid didn't mention, but Giertz often nonchalantly considered it, *Even then, wars were getting more decentralized, long-term, and closer to the civilians. This society has become so fragmented; war has now almost gone back to being a tribal thing. The terminology has been getting vaguer as well; wars were already being renamed 'conflicts' or even 'disagreements.' Now fought on an ever-smaller scale, they take place right in the cities themselves, and are just called 'situations.' There are no battlefield 'theaters' anymore, war is in nearly all urban, in the streets now, and mostly a civilian affair. Where's it going to end?*

'With these and other social problems,' Ceebix droned indifferently. 'Great faith was placed in the "League of Geniuses." On the one hand...' There were shots of genetically modified, middle-aged men, each with a deformed, swollen, forehead, protruding over deep-looking eyes. They were walking through wooden-panel doors, nodding and smiling coldly, in a salvo of camera flashes. '...and the Reverend Norman Brown with his concept of "The Antisatan" on the other.' There was a sequence of a fat, belligerent man in a cassock, one hand clutching at the sky, as he bellowed to an audience stretching to the horizon in all directions. Giertz could lipread his famous, old war-cry, 'I feel God in my phlesh!' As Ceebix commented, 'But with his self-immolation and World Wars Four and Five, this faith gradually ebbed.' Giertz felt dissatisfied with this explanation though. He thought silently, *That's not all of it. World wars and all the rest are only symptoms of this civilization's basic morbidity.*

In fact he realized now this was the crux of what he didn't understand. Mentally he extrapolated from the holy', *Most of the great dreams of the Twentieth Century have been fulfilled: a world where no one has to work hard, or in most cases at all, where Consumer goods and even luxuries, although fake, are practically free. Where there's no more war as such, and permanent peace of a kind. (Well at least since World War Seven.) The police and armies are all being disbanded as obsolete. Personal security and freedom are all now managed by corporate insurance. At least technically there's no more prejudice, poverty, oppression, or illness for anyone - technically, yet somehow it still isn't enough.*

Many 'great' minds had tried to explain what was wrong. Why, after all the art, science, and culture, people now only wanted to destroy each other. Neither Giertz nor anyone else could articulate what the cause was, but the masses all knew exactly what evaded the 'experts.' *Its symptoms have been suppressed one after the other over the decades. No one likes to talk about it because there's no name for it, in any existing language. So the only way left to express it is through violence.*

**Chapter 29 Antitrust Wars**

There had been terrible wars in the past, but Giertz recognized that those had been more idealistic times. He could remember with a shudder the later World Wars, better known as The Antitrust Wars, when the World Government had literally fought against the giant monopolies, forever merging and re-merging into one, omnipotent economic monster, with no competition. *Someone had to do it!*

Giertz still felt an uncomfortable coldness though, as he remembered the awful 'Protein Riots' caused by The World Food Corporation, after World War Six. *That monopoly almost succeeded in turning the Earth into an enormous dust bowl, with their genetically 'improved' yields.* Then there was the shortages caused by The World Transport Corporation, the chaos generated by The World Communication Corporation, and the blackouts caused by The World Energy Corporation. Meanwhile every day the ground would vibrate as another major manufacturing center vaporized in a nuclear blast.

In the end, when they'd all merged anyway, the compromise had just been for the last shreds of The World Government to cleave them into two competing, yet ungainly, private companies: Greedeluxe and Consumeordie. This 'victory' by the World Government however, left Giertz uninspired.

'As the two hypermultinationals crystallized,' Ceebix droned further, 'it was ascertained young peoples' energies could be channeled towards corporate ends. Firstly as a direct force for undermining the other company's marketing strategies, and secondly as a safety-valve to prevent them growing to dangerous proportions.' *I suppose it's a natural step, as they sell us our 'lifestyles,' what we wear, eat, and even what we think. So they might as well sell us what we do, as well.*

Giertz had always been surprised the two corporations could be so open about this policy, but to him, *The strategy is pretty obvious. The Producers keep us obsessed with trivial arguments to play us off against each other, making us hate and fight one another, in case we start to think about them, and what they are doing over our heads.*

Giertz tried, but failed, to visualize the Corporate Youth on both sides uniting and using all their frittered, virile power to change things radically, and he felt gloomy, *The most they'll ever do is battle for the marketing policy of the corporation they support. They'll merely make their little contributions to its struggle for world domination, and the return to a single monopoly on every commodity.* He didn't even bother to think about why he was now volunteering to do the same.

Even while Giertz favored Greedeluxe, realistically he knew the truth, *Ultimately, it will make little difference which corporation rules, as the whole system itself is failing.* He saw only the dimmest ray of hope, *If I can just use this opportunity to make even a dent in this 'reality,' wouldn't that at least be something?*

Meanwhile on the screen, the first Non-men were shown marching in ranks down an empty street. These were widely believed to be Dr. Zed's prototype for his 'New Adam,' a milestone in his biological quest to create the perfect future Consumers. They wore plain black coats down to their ankles and wide-brimmed black hats, to hide their 'faces,' which were really plain, featureless expanses of skin, with no visible orifices for breathing, eating, or sensing. How they actually 'lived,' and what on, was a secret. Perhaps solar power...? Giertz theorized. There was no reliable proof this project existed, *But even if it didn't, Dr. Zed would have to create it.*

Some of the early Combat Youth were shown wearing the first crude version of their yellow and black Synth-O-

Leather uniform. *Minus the bullet-resistant padding!* They were standing proudly beside a light tank, as children would with a new toy. Ceebix commented, 'Issuing the youth with tanks was tried, but the cars have proved more effective so far. They are more maneuverable and cheaper to replace.' Then Ceebix added disinterestedly, 'We're already experimenting with helicopters now...' Giertz looked at the youthful, derangedly smiling faces to see if there were any he recognized, but there weren't. There followed more scenes of riots stretching to the horizon. Columns of black smoke rose from cities, and Giertz lost track of Ceebix's commentary.

Bored, Ceebix sang. 'The Greedeluxe Corp. "Council of Ninety" founded by Uncle Joe, in turn, created the Greedeluxe Youth Movement, Including the Combat Youth - the first attempt to coordinate the energies of gangs with similar ideologies. Dr. Zed's equivalent Consumeordie Youth divided the rival gangs into two definite factions.' Then Ceebix ad-libbed, instead of finishing the commentary, 'And the rest,' as I think you know, is history...' He switched the terminal off.

'Thank you!' Said Giertz, meaning it. He felt strangely flat though, despite knowing he'd passed the interview.

He'd admitted to himself he wanted Ceebix to like him, but it was clear by now Ceebix liked him even less. Giertz sat in the chair, outstaying his welcome in the dark office. Ceebix, noticing he was still there, misinterpreted the moping expression on Giertz's face. So Ceebix reassured him, 'Don't worry! You will enjoy The Game! For as long as it lasts for you - that is.' With the word 'enjoy' however, a strange smile flashed across his pursed lips, casting Ceebix and the Combat Youth in a completely different hue for Giertz.

He pictured what Ceebix would be doing if he wasn't with the Combat Youth, immediately visualizing, *The most illicit kind of drug pusher, handing addictive 'candy' over to children, his predatory smile masquerading as benevolence.* At the same time Giertz developed a sudden, urgent curiosity, *Just what will the experience of being a Combat Youth be like?*

Although it would soon be satisfied, the answer would only leave him even more confused.

## Chapter 30 Safe Distance

Giertz had just stepped out of Ceebix's office feeling somehow transformed, but at the same time sensing a strange dissatisfaction, when Giertz abruptly came the closest he'd ever been to some Combat Youths. He was walking down the dimly lit, scrubbed concrete corridor, wondering why all the light bulbs were inside wire cages, when the youths stood up from the walls they'd been lounging against. A pack of stray, hungry dogs sniffing fresh steak, they surrounded him.

He'd only encountered Combat youths before from a safe distance, but this close he noticed that, *While Ceebix is a shattered, emaciated, Greek god, the rest of them just look unhealthily thin and wiry.* They had hot, shifty eyes which avoided contact any way they could - or just stared straight through you.

Before then, Giertz's only real thought about the Combat Youth had been, *Why do they all wear the same nihilistic smile?* They always smiled a lot, as if everything was really all right, but at the mildest cue the Youths instantly became withdrawn, and unpredictably violent.

Now Giertz tried to decipher their faces, but they were completely expressionless, apart from the hint of disapproval at the corner of each mouth. Their totally emotionless eyes studied him carefully. Knowing this to be some kind of unofficial initiation, Giertz smiled in an attempt at friendly, introduction. 'Hi! My name's Jimmy Gier...' He then took the worst beating he'd ever had.

All the time Giertz knew that with some effort, and his reflexes, he could probably have taken, and thus permanently distanced, all of them, but he also knew, *These kinds of unofficial initiations are important.* However, even while wanting so much to belong, his resulting physical state made him question his emotional sacrifice in - somehow - managing to hold down his urge to retaliate.

The attack ended with a leather-gloved fist, and Giertz saw a white flash as it knocked a cuspid out, crashing his head back into the wall. He was only stunned, but slumped to the floor. After a few final kicks, they walked off, quietly muttering derogatory comments about him to one another, but it wasn't completely over. Giertz didn't know yet this was just the first ritual of a process that would fundamentally change him forever, and not necessarily for the better.

**Chapter 31 Self-Torture**

Giertz wasted several days recovering at home, staring at the many cracks in the ceiling of his room through a mask of bruises. He carefully reconsidered his decision, not just because of the pain, but because he already, correctly, suspected each stage of his 'basic training' would take away more than it gave. 'Stage One' of the process began in the 'Self-Torture Chamber.' At first, he thought this was just some sort of joke name for a gym, so he was almost horrified when he found it was something of an understatement.

When he first entered the large hall, which was almost an entire floor of the building, he saw naked male bodies on its bare concrete walls, floor, and ceiling. They were stretched above and below him over sadistic mechanical devices, lattices of iron bars, chains, and cogs. *In fact, this whole room is just some enormous engine for manufacturing agony!* The nude men were screaming and howling from horrible, distorted grimaces. There was a digital counter on each machine, indicating exactly the level of pain each was inflicting on himself.

For a terrible moment, it also reminded Giertz of the 'therapy' scenes he'd personally witnessed in the final days of the Happylands Institute. Even more horrifying was observing how, *These men are their own torturers!* The devices were designed so they could simply have released themselves and walked away, but this only appeared to make them more inhumane to their own bodies.

Giertz saw one, nude figure spread-eagled on a metal rack, seemingly near death. Purple veins bulged around his neck and forehead. Giertz felt almost nauseated as he recognized the wolf-like face, disguised by its mask of pain. This was someone he knew, and knew fairly well. Then, as if opening his eyes from the bottom of some deep pit of agony, the man recognized Giertz also.

Nailbrand was the leader of the Motorcycle Youth, or at least came as close to 'leading' them as anyone could. Usually, he lived in their headquarters on the upper floors of the building, kept well away from the other gangs for their own safety. Giertz therefore assumed correctly, *Nailbrand is training with the Combat Youth in the hope of healing the Motorcycle Youth's ever-growing, general rift with Greedeluxe Corp., and to prove some obscure personal point.* He admired this. In fact, he admired everything Nailbrand did, no matter how extreme. Apart from Zytopharbb, Nailbrand was probably the only person in the world whom Giertz had ever admired, up to now.

Their paths had first intersected at some early point in Giertz's psychiatric treatment, before he'd been transferred to Happylands, and Giertz recalled Nailbrand as a particularly schizoid biker, *But now he seems to have found his true direction at last!* While Giertz had gone as far as 'introducing' him to his girlfriend, he and Nailbrand had never really talked much, but Giertz had always lived with the hope they would.

Giertz also found it strange seeing the closest he had to a friend in this state. *I could never have done much worse to this person than he's already doing to himself!* Seemingly in too much pain even to acknowledge Giertz, Nailbrand nodded him towards the metal handle which would advance the machine by another cog-tooth. Confused for a moment, Giertz finally shrugged and did as requested. Wondering if it had been the right thing to do, he tried smiling sympathetically at Nailbrand, but Giertz was only more confused when Nailbrand shrieked with the additional agony. It was almost as if he immediately regretted the decision, but he still didn't let go of the machine's handles.

Giertz saw some Combat Youths training in pairs, coaching each other to ever-greater bone-bending, ligament-twisting agony, as they fired curses and blasphemies at each other. When Giertz dropped his clothes and straddled one of the appliances to try it for himself however, he found more pain than he'd ever anticipated was bearable. *The trick is just to administer as much of it as possible, without causing any permanent damage,* he reassured himself. The problems only came afterward.

Giertz had already started to understand that 'Basic Training' was a stage-by-stage psychological process that would grind any remaining humanity out of him, but he assumed the final result would be worth it. When he finally stood up though, he found he could hardly walk. He only managed to stagger as far as the large zinc bucket in the corner reserved for vomiting. Secretly though, deep inside, he felt he'd now found the arena he wanted. In it, he believed he could finally earn the emotional refund he'd felt such a great need for in Ceebix's office.

Greater than the physical pain however, was Giertz's discovery that he gained no respect for his efforts. In fact, his status among the other Youths only fell the more he tried. He was generally ignored and literally spat on as he attempted to survive the 'training' sessions. When they did notice him at all, he received the occasional blow or kick for no reason. When they lost their tempers altogether with him, over what he'd no idea, he was beaten with some cheap wooden staves hanging - always ready - on the wall. He was even concussed once when a stave broke, but eventually they showed signs of becoming bored with baiting him.

Still hoping to blend in eventually, Giertz somehow clamped down on his urge to kill all of them, by presciently reassuring himself that, *One day I probably will.*

He also began to notice how closely their attitudes towards him reflected Ceebix's. *It's as if each of them is just an extension of Ceebix's will, no more than a finger on his hand.* Now Giertz felt that hand was pressing down upon him, but he still didn't dare hope that soon he too would be a digit on it, just like the rest of them - almost.

**Chapter 32 The Strength**

Giertz was well aware by now he was saying goodbye to a part of his human self at every stage of the Combat Youth's Basic Training. He was therefore intrigued when he found, once they were immune to pain, the second stage consisted of exercises based on Yoga, and a quiet, gentle kind of solitary, slow dance. He was disappointed however that there were no martial arts as such. Taking it for granted that they would initiate him into some elaborate discipline, Giertz speculated at first, *Perhaps I'm being cheated here?*

He also discovered though that the Combat Youth believed in one perfect moment of anger. During this, the subject lost all conscious control of his body, and certain unconscious mechanisms took over. At this instant, he was at his 'Optimum Destructive State,' or ODS. The unofficial name for this phenomenon was 'The Strength.'

It was the time when an otherwise puny man would bend iron bars trying to escape a fire, or a woman would break her own back lifting a car off her mangled child. There was very little build-up to it, but early signs were excessively shallow breathing, dilation of the pupils, sudden paleness of the skin, and so forth.

Giertz could now see the objective of 'basic training' was, *To produce this moment almost at will, by isolating it, purifying it, and even improving on it - ultimately building one's entire life around it.* Giertz had once seen the canteen at the headquarters after it had been entirely taken apart by a single Combat Youth, who'd gone into this state prematurely. Plywood tables were just shattered wafers, and there was blood everywhere. They sometimes seriously injured or killed themselves during the process. At the very least they were in a condition of exhaustion and shock. If two went into it together, they'd been known literally to tear each other apart.

Even before this stage of Giertz's training was over, after discovering this condition existed he was no longer disappointed, already hoping to experience those few seconds of devastation. He was never sure however, *Do I control it, or does it control me?* The answer, however, would eventually shock him.

From there it was a minor step to the third stage: 'The Simulators.' These were giant, metal robot-arms that would slash at the trainees with machetes, or fire live ammunition at them. Some trainees were seriously injured or even killed during this exercise. The first thing Giertz noticed in 'The Simulation Room' was the old, brown bloodstains spattered across the concrete walls.

Suddenly he was distracted from his contemplation, as he watched one unhappy victim catch the sleeve of his real leather jacket in a robot's mechanical finger. Giertz was doubly shocked to see it was Nailbrand once more. This fact was still just registering with Giertz, as the indifferent contraption lifted Nailbrand effortlessly, and dashed him at the ceiling, as a child would some toy.

Giertz jumped forward to help, but Nailbrand was already being hustled away by other Combat Youths to the building's Rapid-Healing Clinic, an annex of the Asclepius Institute. They aggressively told Giertz to mind his own business. *I suppose they are concerned about the effect this news will have on the Motorcycle Youth, if it ever leaks out.*

Seeing his best acquaintance injured in this way also gave Giertz a strange feeling, as he looked more closely at the machines. He noticed that, like the self-torture devices, these simulators also ran up each trainees' scores on digit counters, to be totaled up on the old terminal in Ceebix's office. After Giertz's initial sessions, he was interested to learn from the thin, paper printout tacked to the notice board, his scores were well above average. *Just like in one of my holygames! It's easy!* He rejoiced.

He noticed some of the other Combat Youths were noticing his scores also, but he saw it only appeared to add another dimension to their contempt for him, in spite of his out-doing them at all stages. *Or maybe because of it?* Therefore he began to understand they were focusing their dislike for him on something more fundamental. This also may have accounted for his other suspicion, *Perhaps Ceebix is being particularly hard on me?*

One day, Giertz even saw Ceebix laughing to himself, behind the bulletproof glass partition to the control room, as he turned the dial on Giertz's simulator up into the red-danger mark. Even with his reflexes, he at least twice only-just sidestepped death, as the monstrous riveted, hydraulic appendage lunged at him.

This final insult was almost more than Giertz could tolerate. Also, he felt, *At last I've found a temporary target for my mounting hate for Ceebix and his private army!* A small crowd of surprised faces gathered in The Simulation Room as Giertz's machete rung and flashed against that held by the double-jointed machine, as he fought back against it.

Actually, it wasn't as difficult for Giertz as fighting The Bad Actor had been, *This machine is more predictable, and incapable of cheating.* So, in the end, Giertz was able to work his way close enough to attack the machine's more exposed parts. Its tubes sprayed hydraulic fluid, lunging wildly as its programming switched from aggression to self-protection, but Giertz continued hacking.

Finally, the machine lay limp, occasionally twitching, bleeding the last of its oil. No one said anything as Giertz leaned almost his whole weight on the handle of his spring-loaded machete to retract the blade, and walked out of the room feeling smug. Behind the safety of his bulletproof glass, even Ceebix looked surprised, but this only reinforced Giertz's suspicion that Ceebix hated him even more by now.

Eventually, Giertz would find this to be true.


**Chapter 33 The Crucible**

In spite of Giertz's accumulated triumphs during his 'basic training,' his scores now the highest in all categories, he felt ambivalent about progressing any further. He even questioned the whole process more than ever, to the point where felt like giving up, but it wasn't because of the physical agony. In fact, he wanted to give up on the whole idea of the Combat Youth. The horrors of Basic Training had only made him wonder, *Can the end result be worth it?*

Initially, he'd thought it was a worthwhile trade to surrender what remained of the human being in him, for his membership of something - or anything. However, as the 'The Fourth Stage' approached, the prospect of another test, whatever it was, and of losing even more of himself, only left him feeling less motivated. He and the other novices feared it so much it even had a special name, referred to in whispers as 'The Crucible.'

The lack of any real information only made it all the more mysterious, and ominous, yet Giertz wondered how it could be worse than any other stage. *I've already dragged myself beyond the limits of endurance and pain.* When it finally came though, Giertz discovered that more than anything else, his growing fear of giving away another irreplaceable piece of his soul, far outweighed his curiosity.

Giertz was getting ready to make the decision to quit, but found something stopping him. He wasn't even sure what it was, but only knew, *There's no going back to the life I had before, because I know now it was no life. I can only go forward.* He also saw it was the same for the other trainees also. Plus, he knew his own unique problem – his quest to destroy reality - wouldn't let him go, no matter how bad the tests became. *It will eventually either force me to be victorious - or die trying.*

In the end, there was just no way out of it for him.


**Chapter 34 Nihilistic Expression**

On the day of 'The Crucible,' Giertz found he was involuntarily shaking as Ceebix handed him a plain blue vest, which he was told to put on over his gray vest, and not to cover in any way. He was searched for weapons and asked to hand over his watch, but he explained that he never wore one. He was led to a doorway that Ceebix unlocked and then, preempting any hesitation, he roughly pushed Giertz through it.

Giertz found himself in a very cramped room, not much larger than an old telephone booth, with half of the other trainees: a handful of sullen males in their late teens or early twenties, like himself. Some now had fresh, bizarre Greedeluxe corporate tattoos on their necks and shaven heads. Giertz also noticed most of them were beginning to develop the ugly, nihilistic expression that was an unofficial part of the Combat Youth uniform: their eyes already completely devoid of emotion. *Just as mine are now*, Giertz lamented.

They also wore blue vests identical to Giertz's. He was reassured to note that they seemed to be as scared as he was. Apart from this, Giertz felt no common bond with them, and they appeared to actively dislike being in such close proximity to Giertz. Meanwhile, no one said anything, not knowing if that was part of the test.

With nothing else to do, looking for clues, Giertz examined the room, which continued the theme of the entire building by having no decoration at all. He squinted against the neon strip lights in wire cages, which gave out a harsh glow, but barely illuminated the raw concrete walls. He played his boot against one feature: a small drain in the center, and saw the floor was canted towards it. Giertz was disturbed that the room was like a shower, but there were no shower fittings. *Just like the blood-gutters in the corridors of the Happylands Institute.* He also noticed the other trainees were equally disturbed by it. He found it strange as well that one wall of the room, opposite the door, was made entirely of rusted metal, and another unusual feature was a letterbox slot in one wall, covered with a small metal gate on the other side.

Nothing happened for a long time.

Giertz felt the heat in the small room increasing from the closely confined bodies, making it seem more stifling. He began to feel an intense claustrophobia as well from the smell of the others, and the air was becoming staler as the oxygen disappeared. After a while, Giertz was sure he could tell what the body closest to him had consumed for breakfast.

Giertz wondered, knowing the others were thinking it also, *Perhaps this is the test? Just to see how long we can go without killing each other?* Soon, Giertz could hear his own heart jumping rapidly in his chest, and knew, *It can't be long now, surely?*

Yet it could.

**Chapter 35 The Enemy**

After a few minutes, which seemed like hours, Ceebix's voice crackled from a small, tinny loudspeaker in the ceiling. It felt almost reassuring to Giertz to hear the familiar monotone, in spite of what it had to say, and the speaker being so cheap they could hardly make it out anyway, 'YOU ARE THE BLUE TEAM.'
'What did he say?' asked one of the youths.
'We're the blue team!' another participant barked at him, but apparently not understanding the significance of their categorization either.

They began to relax a little though, as this information had given them an orientation as to what was going on, and also some kind of bond, but still not with Giertz. Then after a while, when nothing happened, Giertz knew all of them had begun to think the same thing, *So what color, or colors, is or are the other team, or teams, and who and where are they?*

Another half an hour passed, seeming more like a day, before they heard Ceebix's voice again, 'IN A MOMENT YOU WILL MEET "THE ENEMY." YOU MUST KILL

"THE ENEMY" IN ORDER TO PROGRESS TO THE NEXT STAGE OF YOUR TRAINING. OTHERWISE "THE ENEMY" WILL KILL YOU.' 'What did he say?' demanded the same Combat Youth again. The other was beginning to answer him once more, when just then the metal wall slid up, as a guillotine blade would.

They immediately saw the five other trainees standing in an identical, tiny room, all of them physically larger, and wearing red vests. Even as the wall was sliding up however, Giertz had ducked under it three seconds early and gone straight for the largest youth on the other side. Giertz knew, *What I lack in physical size can only be made up for by surprise.* Therefore he had the fat neck locked under his elbow, his entire weight braced against the vertebra, even before the others had followed his lead - with a strange, collective animal bellow.

What happened after that Giertz had no memory of, and tried never to recall. The only thing he did remember was seeing the letter-box slot in the wall open and briefly staring through it, into Ceebix's icy, disinterested eyes.

After some time a cannon of near-freezing water jetted through the slot, ending the slaughter. Soaking, but not feeling the cold, Giertz lay panting, his hands still clamped to the dead throat. The water in his ears stopped him from hearing Ceebix's exact words from the speaker, but he knew what they would be saying, 'CONGRATULATIONS, BLUE TEAM,' but with no real feeling.

Giertz only felt a sense of self-revulsion however.

**Chapter 36 Self-Indoctrination**
As Giertz had expected by now, the fifth stage of a Combat Youth's training took place in their purpose-built shooting gallery. It seemed more like a reward for surviving the earlier stages. Giertz spent many happy

days in there, blasting at an endless supply of cardboard targets, each in the shape of Dr. Zed's misshapen head, with explosive micro-bullets. Yet, as Giertz watched them fly apart, he still couldn't have dreamed that one day he would do this for real.

The final stage was a surprise, as it just consisted of self-indoctrination. For this Giertz stood in an empty room, in front of a large, old, full-length mirror, diagonally cut in two by a crack running through it. He touched his face with the tips of his fingers, saying out loud, 'No one will love this face.' He touched each arm, 'No one will love these arms.' He touched his chest, and so on. Finally, a weird, fundamentally blank feeling absorbed him, as he stared at the bisected form in the broken glass - a total stranger.

*Who am I now? More to the point, what am I? What has this training process done to me?* Also, his disease had always been out of his control, but it worried him greatly that it was now probably in someone else's.

Giertz also found that, while further training wasn't compulsory, the Combat Youth put themselves through it to extremes, especially in the Self-Torture Chamber, and he saw at least one benefit to it all, *Although absolutely anyone can apply to join them, no one ever does with any ulterior motive.*

At the end of his Basic Training though, the dissatisfaction he'd felt on leaving Ceebix's office was now gnawing at the interior of Giertz's stomach. In spite of his excessive scores, he hadn't gained the thing he'd most wanted from Ceebix. *In fact, I seem to be getting the opposite.*

This was the point at which Giertz began to fundamentally hate the Combat Youth.

**Chapter 37 Death Bed**

There was an unexpected side-effect to Giertz's training. While he'd been away, the entire Greedeluxe Youth Movement had become more deeply absorbed by the theological studies of The Fundamentalist Youth. Known as 'Xeracism,' it was a cult that Giertz had previously only vaguely comprehended.

He found that the mythological 'Judazz' had initiated it, when not yet 16. Conceived in a test tube, brought up and educated by old holygames, Judazz's highest ambition had been to become a statistic. Then one day he'd had a vision. This idea appealed greatly to Giertz. *Yes! What would happen if someone really thought? If one just sat in a room, with no distractions at all, and really concentrated. What concepts, what ideas would come?*

According to the official legend, whatever enlightenment had come to Judazz had caused him to leap off his deathbed, and tattoo that vision all over his body. Running naked from city to city, he'd left a trail of destruction in his wake. He'd last been seen heading out across the world, divisions of tanks unable to stop him - or so it was told.

Giertz's hazy understanding of 'Xerak' was a concept somewhat more powerful than any mere god. *Judazz was his human embodiment, Ziachrad his main prophet and Zytopharbb his disciple, who had set down The Idea, and conveyed it to the Greedeluxe Youth!* Giertz was pleasantly surprised when this last name, Zytopharbb, was mentioned, because of their encounter in the Happylands asylum, *Now I'm beginning to see what kept him sane in there!* Although Giertz wisely decided it was best to keep quiet about their meeting.

He also discovered that besides The Fundamentalist Youth, no other faction was more fanatical about this religion than the Combat Youth. Giertz couldn't fully understand all the tenets as he struggled with the complicated, ancient, hieroglyphic language of the sacred texts as much as he could, but in the meantime he just had to make do with the official translation: 'Capital requires sacrifice. Xerak has said future, possibly uncertain, consumption (to consume itself wholly) is the difference between ecstasy and rapture! Zyt' 23-15.'

The basic point Giertz did understand was that Xerak didn't love his creation, but he hated it, which was why it was in a constant state of destruction. This made perfect sense to Giertz, based on the evidence he saw all around him. *I see! Creation is only there to feed destruction! As long as you are enjoying yourself destroying, then Xerak is on your side!*

One day, as he closed the small, tatty paperback with a crude, garish and irrelevant front cover of a bug-eyed, mutant creature clawing the clothing off a terrified young woman:

'THE THOUGHTS OF ZYTOPHARBB ON THE IDEA'

Giertz felt enlightened at last, *Yes, the means justifies the end,* he summarized. Really though, Giertz was willing to believe any garbage, in order to fill the dark, empty void deep inside himself, slowly corroding what little of his soul he'd ever possessed, and that 'Basic Training' had left him.

As he'd trained with the Combat Youth, in spite of his differences with them, Giertz also began to see the reason why the old hated the young so much these days, loathing their very existence. *'Old' people are afraid of a pure truth and energy that Young people have. Old people have lied to themselves that they never had that energy, because they couldn't bear it anymore. For them, it's like being forced to* stare into a bright light. Therefore their unbearable jealousy is like acid in their hardening arteries.

Giertz now understood the bitterness he perceived ingrained in every wrinkle, every broken vein, the narrowed eyes accompanying every derogatory remark, every put-down from their papery mouths. It's just the demeanor of someone bedazzled. In spite of his dislike for The Combat Youth, Giertz at least believed, They will stare into that light until it blinds them! Or so he thought, at first.

Conversely, everyone told Giertz he was 'young,' but he didn't feel so young. He felt old already, unable to imagine how it was possible to feel any 'older' than this. He saw every day as just a matter of pulling himself out of bed, to wander around long enough to climb back in, sixteen hours later, and it was getting harder all the time.

Over-all, Giertz always felt he was on a personal, rapid, downward spiral. When aging drunks or Preparation X315/J addicts in the street patted him on the back and told him he had 'it' all in front of him, 'Son,' with a faraway look in their eyes, he felt they were lying to themselves at his expense.

He also began to see now, Perhaps the Combat Youth have the potential to resolve this dilemma for me, somehow? Even while he already hated them so much, they were still the only hope he had. Yet he'd never considered that they could eventually make him feel much worse.


**Chapter 38 Terrible Retribution**
A few weeks later, Giertz, still wearing his old, red-with-white-stripes-down-the-sleeves Synth-O-Leather jacket for the last time, was waiting for his new uniform, but had his hair cut shorter. It only flowed to his shoulders now instead of down his back, as he slammed down the deeply-scratched door of his battered, red car, and walked out of the late spring snow, into his insipid girlfriend's

post-neo-obscurist apartment building. Instead of taking the elevator, for the sake of it, he bounded up the many flights of stairs. Despite not having seen her for a very long time, he knew she would still be waiting for him. He wasn't sure why he was here, except for a gut feeling that, *Somehow she is a necessary component in my self-prophesied destiny.*

She opened the door wearing a scarf knotted around plastic curlers on her head, and a pair of spectacles with perfectly circular lenses. The mousy roots of her blonde hair were showing, and her makeup was smudged. Actually, her hair was naturally blonde, and the roots were dyed. (She often just deliberately dyed all of it to look mousy.) Giertz noticed her hands hanging onto the door frame, as if for moral support. She also wore false fingernails which were artificially cracked, bitten, chipped, and covered with flakes of two different colors of nail varnish, over her perfect, healthy natural ones, as was the fashion.

She yawned, but when her brain registered who this was, she exclaimed partly with joy, partly with terror, 'Ahhhh! Jimmy!' As usual, the two emotions canceled each other out. She was pining to invite him in, but at the same time felt compelled to slam the door in his face. Therefore, Giertz waited as the two expressions battled for supremacy on her face, while the couple just stared at each other across the threshold.

Finally, half of her politely invited him in. He immediately stumbled over the jumble of half-read glossy fashion magazines, non-cancer-free cigarette ends and putrefying cups of coffee, scattered across every horizontal surface. The hooded eyes of pin-up boys roughly two-thirds her age, ripped from the magazines, met his gaze. Their torn edges adorned every vertical surface. Giertz picked up and examined some items of grimy underwear hanging over the backs of chairs, and from it all, he caught a sense of her claustrophobic bachelorette existence, concluding, *Like her, this room is a contrived mess. It is only the carefully arranged chaos of someone trying to convince themselves their life is more hectic, and exciting, than it really is.* Therefore he understood what was missing in her life, and what his dual role would be, *I am her savior. I am her destroyer.*

As she observed him with her arms folded, she also conceded to the other side of her nature, by giving him the lowest insult anyone could deliver in these times, 'You *liability*!' She spat out venomously, 'You should know you couldn't get away with things like that!' Giertz was taken-aback, as he rarely saw this vindictive 'other' side of her, but he'd always known it was there. He still couldn't remember what they'd locked-him-up-and-melted-down-the-key for in The Happylands Institute either, or what the significance of the deep scratches down the side of his car was, and didn't want her to remind him. So he managed to rapidly change the subject, 'I escaped weeks ago!' He said it with a degree of pride, to open his end of the conversation.

'Um?' she responded, beginning to psyche herself up to humor him again. She'd learned the hard way this was the best strategy through all his more unpredictable behavior patterns.

'Literally!' He emphasized, gesturing wildly with one hand.

'My backside you have,' she muttered, with exaggerated loss of interest, returning to her kitchen. She called from over her shoulder, 'One way or another, you'll never 'escape'!'

Giertz instinctively knew however, he appealed to the suppressed part of her divided personality that mirrored what he was entirely. 'Since I last saw you,' he continued, ignoring her disbelief, 'I went to Asclepius Clinic, and they used me as a guinea pig again. He's developed even more new, rapid-healing surgical techniques. He also gave me a treatment called Age-Lock, which makes me virtually immortal! Did I ever tell you as well, some time back, about his experimental education process that gave me a Ph.D in one hour! So I've been *Doctor* Jimmy Giertz for a while now.'

'He implanted you with *someone else's* Ph. D, you mean,' she jibed, but he added cryptically,

'Asclepius gave me a few other things besides!' Giertz fingered a cylindrical, brass locket on a stainless steel chain around his neck.

Even as he ranted however, he was surprised to see her emotions make a quicker switch than usual. She became slightly humbled as she returned from the kitchen drying a plate that was already dry, and said, 'Yes, I heard about his recent experiments on the holyvision, I suppose. They said he was looking for volunteers.' Then she forced herself to ask the embarrassing, all-important question, 'But did he say he could *cure* you?' Giertz just looked at her, puzzled. The question had hardly even occurred to him.

'I've transferred to the Combat Youth,' he answered instead, again evading the topic.

Then he continued to elucidate what he was going to do with his extended future, 'I've already been training with them. It was prophesied a young, insane warrior will single-handedly kill The Bad Actor and defeat Dr. Zed! I intend to be that warrior! The will of Xerak flows through me!' He was also surprised though, to see her reaction shift to slight concern at this.

In the end, she just shook her head. 'You're mad Jimmy!' she concluded as she retreated to the kitchen again, still polishing the plate, but he still knew, *I can feel my emotions beginning to manipulate hers again.* He also reflected on how truly sad this was, and it also made him feel guilty, even more so because he knew what he would be dragging her into this time, *But she doesn't - yet.* Then, for some reason, he recalled the image of Ceebix's enigmatic smile, hanging over her now, yet it was an inevitable process. Both she and Giertz knew neither of them could stop it, even if they wanted to, or, in retrospect, the eventual cataclysm it would spawn.

This was Giertz's third serious mistake.

**Chapter 39 Voyeuristic Window**

Still uncomfortable in each other's presence, Giertz took a cold shower to calm down. As he sat back on the couch, she stood in front of him wearing her apron and said suddenly, 'Do you want to see my new dance routine?' This was nothing new to him as he'd often seen her dance, *It's obvious she just copies them from whatever is the trend on holyvision this week,* he assumed silently. This idea was reinforced by her putting one of as singer called Pandora's latest frothy dance-ballads onto the player, too loud. He liked to see his girlfriend dance though, there was something innocent about it, which was part of what little charm she had for him.

This time she incorporated more whirling, high kicks into her movements, swinging her hips almost violently. Giertz was slightly impressed this time, *She has been practicing!* When she finished however, sweating slightly, he gave her the same, small round of applause he always did. Panting, she bowed theatrically, happily high on endorphins, and that she had got this positive reaction out of him.

Then she sat down next to him in front of her brand new, but retro, holyvision screen. More than just three-dimensional, its solid, life-like images spilled out into the living room, enveloping their entire senses. In fact it seemed more like a voyeuristic window on a world even more three-dimensional, and real, than the one from which they were viewing.

He still wondered why she didn't have a synthetic reality module like most people did these days, but he reflected, *It's was probably just as well. Those who climb into one very often never want to climb out again, and in many cases, never do.*

Giertz called out channels at random to the holyscreen, and it switched through the thousands of generic shows. Most of it was just commercials, the advertising breaks lasting twenty minutes or more, when the actual programs were about five minutes long, if that. His girlfriend commented, bored already, 'Even all the Snuff Channels are mostly repeats.'

He became desperate for something worth watching; *I'm always looking to this box for some kind of answer!* Eventually, he felt almost sick, because the following thought was, *Is this how desperate I've become?* He experienced this kind of frustration every time he watched HV. More viewing only exacerbated it, but he'd no inkling that today he would finally get the answer he'd been watching it so long for.

Eventually, the screen automatically switched by default to the worst peak-viewing time garbage. To his joy and dismay, he was just in time for the Consumeordie Corp. sponsored, eight-hour daily extravaganza known as 'Real Life.' It had all evolved from the first attempts to 'lighten-up' the old news programs, as the facts they presented became less and less palatable.

Immediately after the murder-rate forecast, The News Dummy popped onto the screen as always. His hinged wooden mouth clicked up and down in its permanently cheerful, papier-mâché face. 'Hiya folks...' The young, nervous operator sat stonily behind it, still with a kind of rigid smile. His lips occasionally quivered as they struggled silently with a multi-syllable word, but he needn't have worried, because the canned laughter flowed out of the audience with everything The News Dummy said, 'Well there's been another nuclear meltdown in The Free Trade Zone, millions contaminated. Another big earthquake in Lower Tokyo, millions more families buried alive. Genetic terrorism threat in...' Meanwhile Giertz wondered, *Who's really doing the talking? Whose hand is inside the operator's back, and whose is in his? Whose is the arm at the end of the chain? Perhaps though, The News Dummy actually does do all the talking, after all? Who is operating who? Perhaps The Operator is really the fake? Therefore, when my time comes to destroy reality, The News Dummy must be the first to die!*

The News Dummy was just the hors d'ouvres however. The canned laughter cut off abruptly, and then Pandora swanned onto the World's stage. She compered the show wearing a different, white, couture dress, seemingly every half an hour. While it happened almost every day, at first no one applauded - they were too stunned. 'Good afternoon, fellow citizens!' She purred, looking down her nose into the camera, her face as blank and cold as a fashion hypermodel's.

'That's so shrewd!' Giertz commented aloud, bitterly, 'Her reminding people of the days when they were citizens and not just Consumers.' His girlfriend said nothing, which was her usual response to Giertz's outpourings. He'd always assumed she just had nothing to say, but today he noticed the beginnings of a strange, knowing smile on her face, which seemed to portend something he didn't like.

Reflecting the times, Pandora was a humorless, unsmiling, optimally proportioned woman. She'd been mass market-researched to perfection, made-to-order for the human race, especially the males. Her height, hair color, and length, bust size and choice of narcotics, were all better than perfect. She was so clean; she appeared to have the air of a surgeon about to perform some intricate operation, rather than that of somebody comparing an HV show. *She embodies 'the spirit of the age' all right*, Giertz believed, *because she has no spirit*.

Trying not to let his girlfriend see, Giertz ground his teeth, formed fists around his sweating palms, digging the fingernails in deep. This was the thing he hated Consumeordie Corp., The Bad Actor, Dr. Zed, (and ironically) Pandora herself, the most for. *She gives Dr. Zed an unfair advantage over my emotions!* Above all, he hated himself, because he wasn't as different to the masses as he liked to think he was. Just like everyone else in the world, he secretly loved Pandora. Therefore, watching her only made him feel more lonely and inadequate.

She was everything he could have dreamed of, what everyone with a Y-chromosome could have dared imagine. With the rest of them he shared the sad, collective, male day-dream of that chance encounter, when unexpectedly, they would all realize the woman they were sitting next to was Pandora. Men were free to switch her off at any moment, but they never did. Giertz was even tempted to smash the screen just to stop the pain, but he couldn't. He didn't want to miss one second of her. It was his weakness, and everybody else's. The worst thing was she seemed to know it. Giertz could never forgive her for her all-encompassing indifference to her worshipers though: the unreplied-to messages of adoration. *I could probably forgive her for anything else, but not her unawareness of just how necessary she is to us all.*

Consequently, Giertz couldn't stop himself from examining his girlfriend out of the corners of his eyes, hoping she didn't notice him doing it. As was also normal, Giertz wished she could be more Pandora-like, even though he knew well, *Like every woman, she also yearns to be Pandora, and is only too aware of it.* Of course, he'd resolved to hide this, knowing that if his girlfriend found out, it might be the end of whatever their relationship was. *Even worse, it might cause her to take some form of irritatingly pathetic, emotional retaliation, such as starving herself to death.*

In fact, adolescent and menopausal women were always trying to eat, starve, and vomit themselves into Pandora's exact shape. Her wardrobe was continually mass-marketed, but by the time these women had arranged enough credit to pay for it, she would be wearing something else anyway. It never looked so good on her audience either, somehow only exaggerating their imperfections.

This didn't make any real difference to Giertz, because by now he felt almost indifferent to women in general. The few beautiful ones only gave him a feeling of emptiness. In its presence for too long, he just felt his intestines tying themselves in knots anyway. Mumbling some excuse, he would squirm out of their unimpressed gaze.

Strangely though, his girlfriend did have something for Giertz that no other woman had. Beneath the rough complexion (from wearing too much makeup for too long), the ultimate in dyed, dull hair, no discernible bust or hips, he felt he filled some gap, however small, in her confined existence.

In the end, he just desperately needed her limited gratitude.


**Chapter 40 The Undercaste**
The basic idea behind the Real Life show was that roving cameras mounted on helicopters would flutter around

looking for any kind of crime or disaster. These would be transmitted `live' into the studio, and the contestants would be made to answer relevant questions. If they got the questions right, they won prizes such as private planes, but with two-week airworthiness guarantees, etc.

Dr. Zed's `Wheel of Destiny,' a sparkling mill wheel, encrusted with semi-precious jewels and flashing neon question marks, decided who caught 'it' and became a news item next. Many people totally believed it could foretell the future, and even if they didn't, they still watched Pandora always spinning, spinning, spinning it - as disaster struck with terrifying arbitrariness.

Today a brave young family of Consumers had dared to adventure out of their 'point-of-consumption.', (What had once, technically, been called a 'home.') Giertz winced as they accidentally took a wrong turn in their caterpillar-tracked, armored camper. *They must have sacrificed everything to pay for that status symbol. They seem doomed, somehow. Some people just do.* Suddenly it was rammed out of the way by a driverless cargo truck that just carried on along its programed schedule, not even noticing them.

The occupants weren't too badly injured - at first. The protective crash foam automatically spewing out of dash saved them, but soon they would wish the truck had killed them outright. Giertz's anxiety rose as a gang of heavily-tattooed, mutant members of the undercaste surrounded the wreckage. *They probably patrol that sector, scavenging from wrecks to earn extra tokens from the scrap.*

Everyone knew this was the penalty for almost any kind of mechanical breakdown these days. There was a close-up of the thugs' dirty, deformed faces, overlaid with a kind of inhuman bitterness. One had an extra eye blinking on the side of his head. There was an even closer-up view of the ringleader, a spider's web branded over the left side of his face. He ran his tongue over his stubble-curtained lips at the sight of the wife's pink thighs thrashing through the shattered passenger window, and the dazed children in the back seat. Even the armor plating on the Greedeluxe Corp. manufactured vehicle wasn't going to protect them, only prolonging their agony.

The camera switched to a view of the audience. They were doing the same with their tongues, eyes bulging slightly with anticipation, many of them chewing on gummies of Preparation X315/J to enhance the experience. This was all just the first course though. They knew there would be more, the main course, to come...

At that moment, there was a strategically-timed, hypnotic commercial break, and the audience moaned. They would have to wait for twenty minutes, slavering with curiosity for the outcome, despite already pretty much knowing what it would be. Like most people, Giertz had trained himself to blink in time to avoid being hypnotized by commercials. Or so he hoped, but he was never completely sure. *Perhaps the laser hidden behind the screen might just be able to creep under my eyelid, and still program the commercial's message through my retina? Maybe that's why I, and everybody, seem to feel permanently dissatisfied these days?*

Of course, The Wheel of Destiny was never wrong, or that would be the end of the ratings, and the show. Therefore the helicopters, with their prying zoom lenses, were always magically arriving just in time to witness the latest carnage, to frame the dying facial expressions of terror and injustice from dramatic angles. Consumeordie Producers vehemently claimed the Real Life 'situations' were 'live.' That was the whole point of a news-game show after all, but even the least cynical viewer couldn't help noticing it wasn't all so random. 'No one wants to admit, or even believe, they record the 'news' items well before the wheel spins,' Giertz said out loud, not necessarily to his girlfriend, but to the indifferent world in general.

'Oh I don't know...' she began, but this was more than Giertz could take,

'Oh, come on! Sometimes events aren't even coherent! Bullet holes appear in bystanders and then disappear. Cars explode, and buildings collapse, only to reappear in different scenes! The wheel never predicts anything unpleasant happening either, to anyone driving a Consumeordie Corp. manufactured car, or living in a Consumeordie Corp. apartment. They never threaten anyone rich enough to purchase a revenge clause in their insurance policy that could pay for a hit on Dr. Zed, or even The Bad Actor. No Producer is ever touched by The Wheel of Destiny. It's only The Consumers that get it!'

Giertz was getting ready to also point out that in every show at least one incident would involve The Bad Actor himself. He always managed to look suitably surprised however, before dealing with the situation. There was never even a single gray hair out of place during the choreographed fight scenes, and other elaborate stunts, but all this contrivance didn't shake the audience's faith. It was even obvious they were actively being encouraged to laugh at the victims, which the spectators did quite willingly.

So Giertz gave up on trying to destabilize his girlfriend's belief in The Wheel of Destiny today, or any day, as she said reasonably, 'It could be argued the "crimes" and "disasters" are real enough in themselves.' Giertz had a strange feeling though that, by pointing at the screen, she was trying to convince herself more than him, so he only threw in a final comment,

'Surely everyone must realize they are just set up by Consumeordie Corp. hit squads?' No one appeared to however.

'It's arguable though the wheel is not rigged, as fate itself is pulling the strings of whoever is rigging it,' his girlfriend expanded.

To Giertz this just sounded as if she was still trying to reassure herself, but he hadn't thought of it that way, so he didn't answer at all this time. He was also surprised again she was actually arguing with him these days, wondering what had happened to her while he'd been away. *Has she been seeing someone else?*

Either way, none of the people on the panel of contestants seemed to care about the matter, as they were now expected to answer multiple-choice questions about what the 'unfortunate victims' should have done to avoid their fate. *Whatever answers they give, everyone knows the only way to 'beat the wheel' is to consume as much as possible for as long as they still can, living not just for the minute, but for the millisecond. After all, it could be their turn next.*

However, even with all Giertz's nihilism, he could never have imagined that one day soon, the contestants would be answering questions about, and the audience laughing at, himself.

**Chapter 41 Violent Reactions**

The questions in Real Life were relatively simple, but there was nothing easy about the way they were fired incredibly quickly. Then the contestants had to sprint over a skidpan to stand under the right multiple-choice answers, printed on neon signs thirty paces across the studio. If they stood under the wrong sign, it would change to describe a person who was of less-than no value whatsoever,

'LOSER!'

Giertz watched amused, as a middle-aged Consumer slipped and crash into the wrong sign. The whole piece of gold-painted scenery shook, and his spectacles flew off in a comical manner. The neon sign flashed `LOSER' as the audience shrieked with shrill laughter that had an unsettling, discordant note of Preparation X315/J in it.

The camera zoomed in on those audience members giving the most violent reactions to his predicament. Some were waving their fists, threatening to kill him, as the contestant struggled to salvage what dignity he could, attempting to stand up on the skidpan. One man even climbed onto the stage, and the security guards allowed him to viciously kick the contestant twice before the assailant was manhandled off, making threats.

Then the guards with their electric cattle-prods restored order to the crowd as The Bad Actor sang a song about how his passion raged for some 'lucky' girl. It was about how he would take her and possess her and just how grateful she would be to him, 'Baby, I don't care about your age, I just want you in a cage!'

He shook his hips with the agility of a teenage dancer, while Giertz thought bitterly of his own face-to-face encounter, *Rumors will circulate that in reality he's just a twenty-year-old, with his hair dyed gray, and middle-aged Producer-executives will try desperately to contact his masseur.* Giertz's eyes narrowed to incision-like apertures, *But I know you now!*


**Chapter 42 Personal Secret**

The Bad Actor was the main compere to the `Real Life' show, while they kept Pandora in the background, dimly lit amongst abstract scenery - something ephemeral and mysterious,. The Bad Actor was usually vaguely 'saucy' and sneering when he referred to her. It appeared he wanted the public to believe the two of them had some kind of more-than-just-a-working 'relationship,' and there were always plenty of guesses as to what it was.

Teenage boys fervently bought gray hair dye and line-deepening agents for their faces. They would inflect certain words to copy The Bad Actor's mid-Pacific accent. They dreamed of owning a wardrobe full of gray suits, each with only extremely subtle variations, each of which they would wear no more than once.

As he watched The Bad Actor, Giertz summarized for his girlfriend a cherished belief he held, 'The Bad Actor is really three people. There are rumors that they are clones, but I don't believe they are. For one thing,' Giertz went on, 'it doesn't explain his enormous diversity of talents, including skier, racing driver, dancer, and acrobat, etc. Secondly, they are not good enough replicas to be clones. What's more likely is they are three similar men, carefully selected and then given plastic surgery to make their resemblances almost total. Not to each other, but to a set of rules. So there never really was a Bad Actor as such.'

However, Giertz didn't want to mention his own, embarrassing first encounter with The Bad Actor to his girlfriend, *Which she probably wouldn't believe anyway.* It also occurred to him, *This would also explain his mildly different personality traits every time I saw him, such as accent, education, tastes in color and so on. However much I dislike Dr. Zed, I have to admit it would take at least three men to replace him anyway. Therefore, The Bad Actor would be his most logical successor when Dr. Zed's time comes.* 'No he's not!' Giertz's girlfriend exclaimed, interrupting his thinking.

He was surprised by the strange tone of self-assurance in her voice, as much as her directly contradicting him. *What made her say that?* He looked at her for a moment, and she swallowed hard what she was about to say next, but again Giertz said nothing. He'd no idea it was the first clue to what would be the biggest surprise of his life, and whether Giertz's theory was correct or not, it explained how he would eventually kill The Bad Actor several times over.

**Chapter 43 Hellish Vision**

During the gaps between calamities, 'Real Life' was sweetened with various distractions: acrobats, clowns and troupes of young, enthusiastic, naked dancers. There were other games as well.

For instance, in The Elimination Stage, there was the 'Physical Test.' For this, the contestants, linked to a 'truth detector', first had to answer questions about their 'personal lives.' At the same time, appropriate averages for the world population were projected onto a board behind them for comparison. Next, they had to strip shamelessly in front of the audience. Giggling golden-girls then took vital measurements with golden tape measures. All these statistics would contribute to the 'successful' contestants' final scores. Then they attached Electrodes to the competitors' genitals.

After that they were made to jump into a swimming pool full of offal. The green animal intestines floating on the surface were swelling and steaming in the heat of the studio lights. As if it were some strange baptism, the contestants were immersed up to their necks in the filth, and some of them over their necks. Scattered on the bottom of the swimming pool were a few hundred identical-looking Consumeordie tokens, but only one of these was the prize-winning token. The others were wired to give a near-fatal electric shock.

Giertz watched impassively as these shocks convulsed the contestants, causing great sprays of slime to fly off their bodies as they groped at the bottom of the pool, fighting each other for the winning token. He wasn't surprised that sometimes people were even killed at this and other stages in the contest, *No one has died of pure embarrassment yet, but several seem to come close.*

This all went on to the same, thumping, John Philip Sousa march music that was the theme of the whole program. Today as it thundered, one nervous, teenage male Consumer was having second thoughts about descending into the Hellish, Darwinian vision. The Bad Actor just called him a 'liability' and casually gave him a contemptuous shove. The young contestant fell face-first into the viscera to get an immediate electric shock, while the audience guffawed.

After this, The Bad Actor showed the losers the prizes, emphasizing, 'This is what you could have won!' Then he gave them consolation 'rewards' specifically matched to their failings: exercise machines, memory improvement courses, or deodorant, and in some cases all three. The show made a shimmering ceremony of the presentations, 'Everyone's a winner!' The Bad Actor would smirk, as the athletic dancers wobbled and gyrated around the naked, shivering, slimy losers.

Then silence and calm would descend as the apparition that was Pandora would materialize from the wings to sing. Today it was a sad song, about a young Producer waiting at a spaceport for her to turn up for a date, looking hopefully at his Consumeordie Corp. manufactured iridium wristwatch. (Accurate to a microsecond a millennium!)

Finally, she arrives late, and he apologizes for not waiting patiently enough for her, but whisks her away for a relatively distracting evening over well-aged champagne. Then, unfortunately, he makes a mistake! Attempting to assure himself she is real, he tries to touch her. As he does so, she notices that although his watch is a genuine Consumeordie brand, it's not *this* month's style of watch. Therefore she says, 'No,' and he's forced to agree.

She sang the last lines of the song in barely a whisper, 'And he said, "I can never touch you,

   I can never touch you."'

## Chapter 44 Endlessly Flogged

Giertz reflected however that, *Over the years they've optimized the entertainment value of 'Real Life,' but the mixture has gradually changed. First, they added more hypnotic commercials, then various pieces of Consumeordie Corp. propaganda - including full speeches from Dr. Zed!* In fact, recently, as part of the lengthy build-up to The Festival of Greed, Dr. Zed had spent almost more time than Pandora on his holyvision channels, and sometimes all the Consumeordie channels at once.

Today Giertz forced himself to watch Dr. Zed raving through one of his speeches about his 'New Age of Optimism.' In spite of himself, Giertz always marveled at Dr. Zed's ability to overcome the enormous gaps in the logic of Consumeordie Corp.'s policies, with more declarations, more condemnations, more promises of retribution, and more plain, meaningless nonsense. Giertz noted loudly however, 'He always seems mainly under the misapprehension all anyone has against him is Consumeordie Corp.'s marketing strategy on fresh meat: that if we consume more phlesh it will solve everything!'

Everyone, especially the shareholders, knew Consumeordie Corp. had almost overstretched itself developing a new method of preserving and packaging raw meat, that didn't involve refrigeration. Instead, kept in a kind of mild suspended animation, it could reach the table in exactly the same state as the moment of slaughter, still warm and steaming, even pulsing, months later. Most of the advertising played on this fact, encouraging the Consumers to eat it raw. The slogan was, 'Now you can have your pound of Phlesh...'

Giertz listened unwillingly as Dr. Zed argued, even while there was no one present for him to debate, 'The phlesh price theory is flawless when the mean market price has no competition!' He gesticulated with weird, abstract motions. 'The market cost is therefore given and adapts to it as a reason other than the form of reality!' And so it went on for some time.

It was only interrupted by another hypnotic commercial, showing a family of Consumers kneeling on their deep-pile carpet, tearing at an animal's whole, severed foreleg, and growling. Two children were fighting over the bone. The housewife, in her freshly permed hair, belched. The husband, his spectacles tilted at a strange angle, closed his eyes, looked up to the ceiling, and barked. Then he cheerfully wiped his bloody hands on his clean tie and white shirt.

Strangely, although there was no profit to be made from this at all, it was more than just a pet project of Dr. Zed's. To him, it wasn't only 'The pinnacle of Consumeordie Corp.'s ambition.' but, 'The zenith of civilized man's achievement!' Consequently, Consumeordie was already reeling beneath the financial strain, but the marketing divisions were being endlessly flogged to create a campaign that would practically force the Consumers to acquire a taste for it. Giertz concluded, 'It's just Dr. Zed's way of expanding the gap between himself and the Consumers. He's only trying to put them in a position where they've no choice but to acknowledge his definition of them as 'sub-human.'

In fact, recently Dr. Zed had taken to openly laughing down at the Consumers from their holyvision screens. This underlined the 'uncomfortable problem,' which still no one openly discussed, and despite being depressed about it, even Giertz couldn't say it out loud, *It's true; the Consumers do serve no real purpose, at all. 'The Sanitization,' it's got to come - and time is running out for us Consumers.* He tried to be fatalistic but just couldn't manage it, instead wondering, *Can I destroy reality before it starts?*

There was by now a whirlwind of 'leaked' rumors about The Producers' master plan for exterminating the 'non-productive' members of the human race. The media's silence just made them louder, but quite often these days, top Producers, mostly in Consumeordie Corp., would hint they viewed the Consumers as more of a hindrance than anything else, but Giertz didn't understand, *A hindrance to what, exactly?* Meanwhile, the Consumers had no choice but to passively nod and agree to their lack of value, because there was no evidence to the contrary, after all. Giertz was only surprised the neutron bombs hadn't started to fall already, *Or whatever, other fate they've arranged.*

Of course, The Producers met any questions about all this with the hottest of denials from reassuring smiles, but the way they showed all their gleaming teeth didn't reassure Giertz.

**Chapter 45 White Phlesh**

Far from being entertained, Giertz just continued reflecting sadly, *The 'Real Life' show is a great worry to Greedeluxe Corp., because they haven't managed to come up with any HV show to rival it, or Pandora, in the ratings. People just aren't interested in being educated by nature documentaries, classic art cinema, intellectual debates, or opera.* Even sadder to him was that, when it came to HV, he wasn't either.

Most people wouldn't admit it, but they watched Real Life all the time. *It always seems safer than going outside their homes to experience real real life after all.* Even Giertz, after having his senses battered by the show for just these few minutes, wondered, *Maybe it's true? Perhaps Dr. Zed does create reality. After all, if it's on HV all the time, what's the difference?* It was a frightening thought somehow, but then an idea entered Giertz's warped mind, *Perhaps I should just kill Dr. Zed first? Never mind the News Dummy.*

Then Giertz's noticed that, by now, his girlfriend had stopped disagreeing with anything he said, *But she still seems to be holding something back, and probably more than ever.* Taking Giertz's silence as a kind of cue, she got up and returned to her kitchen to make a cup of tea. When she was gone, he noticed her hand-written diary on the coffee table. He furtively picked up the tacky, Consumeordie Corp. plastic bound book, with a picture of a side of beef on the cover, and began flicking through it.

This was typical of what he didn't understand, *Her job, whatever it is, pays her enough extra tokens to be able to afford higher-quality products manufactured by Greedeluxe. While her apartment itself is well designed enough, everything in it is cheap, tasteless, and made by Consumeordie Corp.* He weighed the inexpensive book in his hand. *As well as that, nobody hand-writes anything anymore, as there are the more convenient pocket thought-dictators now.*

Amongst the advertisements for various cuts of raw meat, or 'Phlesh,' he read about the time they'd first met, '...I have nothing except for Jimmy, and it's so strange the way he seems to know what I'm going to say at least three seconds before I've said it. Until we met, I would sit just staring at the wall for hours, or listen to a few pop songs. I know I am going to die with Jimmy eventually, but I don't care. I told myself he was just confused when I met him, but then he started bringing around that man with a face like a wolf called Nailbrand. I always gave them what they wanted, even when it wasn't always necessarily what I wanted...'

He flipped to the time just before he'd been admitted to the Happylands Institute, '...now Jimmy just smiles when I say anything to him, and sits all day in front of the holyvision cleaning his machine-gun, but I know I must go with him. My only life is with Jimmy. If I suffer because of it, that will just be the price I have to pay.'

Curious, he turned a few pages further on, 'My fears about Nailbrand are materializing. Today he said to me with that dog-like grin I've never seen on anyone else but him, "You think you're so safe inside that soft, white phlesh don't you!" I must be getting terribly desperate if I think Jimmy will protect me from him if he comes back. Most of the time he seemed to be more interested in Nailbrand than in me.'

Giertz made an effort for a moment to try to feel jealous, *So Nailbrand continued to come here while I was away.* However Giertz had to admit he didn't, and so he let it go, turning to the most recent entry, 'The job is getting more unbearable. Sometimes I feel so much like "the product" I literally find it difficult to move. I so hate the whole lie! Every time I complain they just offer me a bit more money, which just makes it harder to decide. I even think about asking for enough to buy myself out of the contract.' Giertz realized now that he'd never asked her what her job was. Sometimes he was mildly curious about why she got paid so much for only working only one day a week, but he soon forgot again, as he wasn't that interested anyway.

**Chapter 46 Superhuman Effort**

Finally, he lost interest altogether and tossing the book back onto the table started watching Real Life again, but unlike most people wasn't captivated by Dr. Zed's diatribes either. Giertz knew how the show would always end anyway: *Dressed in sparkling gold costumes, the 'winners' will mount The Stepped Pyramid, which will be surrounded by dry-ice fog, as if it's some shrine. As they ascend, its summit will be veiled by a gilded curtain, with The Bad Actor and Pandora looking coldly down on them. What will the 'winners' find there?*

*As soon as they are halfway up, The Bad Actor and Pandora will whip the curtain aside. There will be The Prize, brand new and shining! The cymbals will clash, and the audience will always gasp, even when they know this model will be rusted out in six months, has the least economical motor, will be uninsurable, and nobody would ever buy it from them second hand. It's just a 'white elephant' for a young Consumer couple already burdened with credit, yet they will always falter slightly with awe. They swallow the lumps in their throats as they kiss each other. They've won! There will even be a passionless kiss for the husband from Pandora. He'll roll his eyes and stagger slightly, the camera framing the look of jealousy on the wife's face. Then they will both admire the prize again, and turn back for more congratulations, but find themselves alone.*

*As the credits roll, the teenage fans with dyed-gray hair and artificial lines on their faces will be shown throwing their jackets over puddles, and pleading with Pandora for her attention. They will clutch at her skirts, but she will act as if they aren't there, literally stepping on their faces into the VTOL executive jet. The boys' unashamed tears will spiral upwards into the sky after her, sucked along by the turbulence, as she just leaves them to be brutalized by her eunuch Sumo bodyguards, sporting dark glasses and real silk suits.*

Changing channels became quite a dilemma for Giertz though, even as Dr. Zed continued to drone on and on. Giertz was becoming bored enough to scream, but he still didn't want to risk missing a moment of Pandora. The prospect of being sick of The Bad Actor's sneering, patronizing face wasn't enough of a deterrent either. As well as that, although Giertz was now more than bitterly frustrated at not being able to find his 'answer' somewhere in all the color and noise of the HV, it still took some time, and a superhuman effort, for him to eventually switch channels.

**Chapter 47 Revenge Clauses**

Immediately, he found himself watching the Greedeluxe Corp. slant on the news. A relatively sane man in a suit was reading it with no gimmicks, but this 'news' was no surprise to anyone. In a minor item, amongst the big stories about The Festival of Greed and Pandora's new hairstyle, it was announced that the World Government had disbanded itself. The last motion had been that since World War Seven, the whole concept of 'government' was now obsolete. The surprising thing to Giertz was that the tired-looking former World President, whose name Giertz couldn't even remember, still sounded bitter as he proclaimed, 'We have to accept that no system of government has any relevance in the world we have today. This entire planet is out of control.'

Giertz was surprised because, *Surely he's aware that as far back as living memory can go, the cry has been for small government, smaller government, no government! When all the governments of the various surviving countries from World War Seven banded together to form The World Government, it was only for self-preservation. Everyone these days knows insurance policies, especially those with 'revenge clauses,' and private security schemes, have replaced any laws for a long time. The elimination of anti-gun laws has shifted crime prevention to personal responsibility. Even five-year-olds carry concealed weapons these days. It was obvious the World Government had become just a puppet of the two hypermultinationals, and now they no longer have any use for it. No one ever wanted to pay them taxes anyway. "No countries, only corporations! No democracy, only consumption! No citizens, only Consumers!" That was the battle cry, even as far back as World War Four. So we don't need any 'balance.'*

Giertz missed his old illusions of citizenship though, somehow. He was not fully able to account for the sad kind of stateless limbo he now existed in. *It's still strange to think The World Government initially carved out the two hypermultinationals, but everyone knows The World Government lost their power base long ago, when America and Russia accidentally blew each other up in World War Five, and are now radioactive shadows of their former selves.*

Nobody knew what had happened, just when the two, main superpowers were in the final stages of dismantling all the dangerous old defenses, and ideas. Giertz still shuddered at the sight of American Consumers with terminal radiation sickness, their skeletons sticking through their designer clothes, rubbing their hollow stomachs, begging the camera lens for food. Only the strange little strip of countries that lay between the two continents had somehow been left relatively untouched. Therefore Dr. Zed and Uncle Joe had moved in quickly, and bought up everything that was going cheaply - which was all of it.

### Chapter 48 Unintelligibly Screeching

Giertz didn't like the former World President telling him what he already knew, so he didn't wait for the end of the sound-byte. Switching channels again, he was overjoyed though to see old footage of Shrieking Joe Megastar (also known as 'SJM') the front-man of Giertz's favorite band 'Psycho Kiss,' bounding onto the World's stage again.

Cavorting, posturing, and postulating in the most effeminate manner, SJM's long, greased hair slithered down his back, decadence dripping from his every gesture. With his twisted emotions hidden behind large, dark glasses, and the microphone halfway down his throat, he wasn't so much singing, as unintelligibly screeching and ranting over a backing of out-of-control guitar solos. The band was just attacking the audience with noise. Therefore, Giertz couldn't make out any lyrics, or tune for that matter, which was just how he liked it.

This pop group were always hopelessly behind the trends, but Giertz didn't care. He still loved them, maybe even because of their paunches, obvious toupees, and noses eroded by decades of cocaine abuse. In fact, by now Giertz simply couldn't live without their solid wall of ear-hemorrhaging distortion.

It caused Giertz to dwell for a while on the history of the band, *SJM's real name is Trevor Wilcox, and his manager taught the band one or two chords, yet everyone could hear Wilcox had a less-than mediocre voice, but was a fairly good-looking boy, so a label got behind him and his band. They were all good-looking boys as well, but couldn't play at all. They were happy enough though, miming with their guitars, doing bubblegum rock at trendy teen clubs. Even with all the vocoders and pitch correction everyone could still hear Wilcox couldn't sing, but he was coasting along OK, raking in the bucks and the chicks. Teenage girls would pin his sunshine-smiling picture to their bed posts, at first.*

*However, he probably became more famous for being hideously disfigured in a motorcycle crash, and then refusing to have the damage cosmetically reconstructed. In fact it's now more like a Picasso interpretation, repelling his female fans especially. So all the pin-up pictures came down, and there are even rumors that the crash also damaged his brain. That was when he really became Shrieking Joe Megastar: Trevor's invented stage persona, which attracted a new following of rather demented people. The band's music has also became more disjointed and chaotic, seemingly reflecting SJM's physical appearance. They still can't play of course, they never could, but to the new audience his propulsive, half-chord rock represents freedom.*

*Shrieking Joe Megastar was just a character Trevor gave birth to, but it started to take him over. At first, as part of his stage act he'd do things like smear peanut butter all over his naked body, then jump into the audience and get them to lick it off. Consequently, afterward the fans would smash up the theaters and run out to overturn cars etc., but not knowing it was all set up by the World Government, who wanted The Youth to think their anarchic behavior actually achieved something. Really though, the World Government just wanted to channel their youthful energy and dissatisfactions into trivial, destructive behavior, so it could justify yet more repressive laws.*

*Meanwhile, the band still can't play, so they've computerized everything. They just stand behind their instruments, which play themselves, and now the members have created holograms of themselves, so they won't even have to turn up to the gigs. By now though, their audience have grown up and moved on to 'mature' bands like Death Slot and Kill Switch.* Yet Giertz still loved Psycho Kiss loyally.

Additionally today, the noise and the vision in general all seemed to be saying something specific, just to Giertz. He still couldn't make out the lyrics, except for something about a 'system,' but something *beneath* the cheap, trashy pop-song was talking directly to him, encouraging him in his quest to destroy reality, *And seeming to portend something cataclysmic!*

He noticed his girlfriend's sour expression and thought about explaining it all to her, but knew, *She wouldn't be interested as she only likes Abba.*


**Chapter 49 Psychological Advantage**
Once the song was over, Giertz quickly lost interest in whatever came next. He called out more random channels to the holyscreen, but without much optimism of finding something to watch. However, he was surprised to notice,

amongst all the hypnotic commercials and usual garbage: Ceebix.

Giertz was shocked now to see him clean-shaven and wearing a gray business suit, *Like any other Producer!* He sat calmly in his wheelchair as he was introduced by the interviewer, whose fluorescent green hair was permed into small question marks standing out all over his scalp, 'Ladies and Gentlemen, for your approval, Professor Anthon Ceebix, it says here, "researcher into Asymmetrical Warfare for Greedeluxe Corp. Military Division." Wow!' This just got a small laugh.

Still disbelieving, Giertz had to study Ceebix hard, to make sure this was definitely the same man who'd interviewed him weeks ago. What finally identified him was, while he was another tired-looking man in his late thirties, he still fizzed with the dissatisfactions of adolescence.

In an ironic tone, he explained a new weapon they were developing, 'We call it 'The Idea Bomb,' he said quietly, with the same enigmatic smile Giertz had seen at the interview. Some of the audience members were already yawning, unimpressed. Even in his short association with Ceebix, Giertz knew by now, *They could never know Ceebix's personal discipline that keeps him in his wheelchair in a dark office all day, allowing him to observe life with heightened clarity, probably even more than he would wish. Of course, if the audience did know, they would be paying rather more attention!*

What Ceebix said this time certainly captured Giertz's attention however, 'It's a weapon,' he explained, 'based on the theory that the introduction of certain factors, in the right time and place, can upset the balance of any society, even causing an entire civilization to topple.' Ceebix went on to propose that an army's main weapon was its *psychological* advantage over the civilization it was attacking. He cited examples from history, such as the relative ease with which Alexander had conquered half the world with such a small force, or the Spartans' stand at Thermopylae.

Giertz also noted one of the information boxes in the corner of the holyscreen with interest. 'Consumeordie Military Academy had expelled Professor Ceebix because it summarily rejected his final thesis. This called for a small, highly mobile, urban army that created most of its own orders by using its imagination, instead of stifling it with a hierarchy of orders.' *Consequently Uncle Joe's arms had welcomed Ceebix into Greedeluxe's academy.*

Then Giertz bit his lip as he began to notice something. The Interviewer's job was complicated, as he had to serve Ceebix and his ideas up to the audience as entertainment. They were clearly not very entertained though, he wasn't talking about sex, money, sport or Pandora, after all. Therefore, the interviewer had to desperately play him for laughs, 'So even one man, acting alone, could change the course of history, you say?'

'Or end it altogether!' Ceebix confirmed quietly.

'Even one man in a wheelchair!?' The interviewer jibed. The audience laughed openly, but Ceebix wasn't offended. His smile just broadened - but so did the enigma.

As they wheeled Ceebix away, the interviewer and the audience had no problems with the next item. This was something really interesting: leaked information about what would be the color of the shoes Pandora might be wearing tomorrow, 'And the word, folks, is - Pink!'

The crowd went wild.

**Chapter 50 New Dogma**

Not sharing the crowd's enthusiasm for the last announcement, Giertz had been greatly disturbed by their reaction to what he'd just seen and heard from Ceebix. Additionally, Giertz had been listening between Ceebix's lines to the extent that it was as if Ceebix had been enunciating a coded subtext only he, Giertz, could understand. In fact, the screen itself seemed to turn into the mouth of some idol, the blurred, shifting colors almost became talking hieroglyphs, speaking directly into his mind's ear. Abruptly, everything in the room was assaulting Giertz's senses, all-too sharp and definite. Then, as usual, reality began cracking, melting, and breaking down around him. He was almost physically thrown back from the screen by the lingering memory-image of Ceebix's smile, knowing it was the prelude to another hallucination.

The room was now changing shape, the walls becoming shifting parallelograms, and Giertz perceived it was all just part of a much larger chain of geometric formations, stretching in all directions. *A grid of terrible illogic, infesting the whole universe, just like Dr. Kortex's model of my disease!* Therefore Giertz saw himself as only the size of the smallest microbe, curled in its corner.

He only vaguely recalled his girlfriend's cooling hand stroking his forehead, trying to calm him down. This was followed by the usual feverish lust-making, which he soon forgot, while knowing, *That could all just be a hallucination as well?!* He also saw that this one was different, as it appeared to never end. That was because in the following weeks, through the filter of his disease, the world twisted itself to resemble his waking nightmares.

At first, like most Consumers, he didn't think much about the dissolution of the World Government. Soon however, in all the nations that had survived World War Seven, poets, führers, messiahs, and plain lunatics were battling to fill the power vacuum, by emerging from the rotting woodwork to make war for airtime. There were endless close-ups of their bloodshot eyes and foaming mouths, attempting to surpass the fanaticism of each other's declarations. Seemingly, every few minutes a new dogma, an even more 'final solution' was born.

Entire societies were soon toppling over one another as would a house of cards in an earthquake. Every night Giertz gleefully observed his holyscreen overflowing with scenes of populations who mostly just fought each other, *The 'situations' are growing out of control!* In fact The Consumers never seemed to stop fighting themselves, even to sleep or eat, in streets soon carpeted with the dead, while their 'leaders' swept their arms above them in cosmos-encompassing gestures. Eventually, even entire populations were being marched, with much happy chanting and cheering, on lemming-pilgrimages into the nearest sea.

As time went by though, Giertz viewed this general, cumulative chaos in terms of Ceebix's prophecy of an Idea Bomb, seeing clearly now, *The end of The World Government was only a symptom, rather than the cause, of this ongoing disaster - an extension of a long process of evolving chaos that started decades back. Ceebix's Idea Bomb, whatever it is, and however he will deploy it, will only be the final exclamation mark in what began with the end of World War One, or perhaps earlier. Yes, Ceebix knows the truth!* Or so Giertz thought.

As the hurricane of violence raged though, its 'eye' around Giertz was relatively calm: in Consumer Zone D 'life' went on as best it could.  Although the rest of the world was gradually crumbling, it wasn't happening fast enough here for Giertz, and he was most disappointed his surroundings weren't disintegrating as fast as the rest.

One theory Giertz had about his area's survival was, *I suppose the weapons systems, and counter weapons systems, and counter-counter weapons systems, are so evenly balanced they eliminate each other very efficiently. So maybe they are preserving this target I'm standing on? Perhaps old-fashioned, large-scale war, even nuclear, has almost become a half-hearted affair? So the infrastructure is just about holding up through it all, probably because it's so decentralized these days. The flow of food and Consumer goods from the robot factories won't stop, so I can even still get unlimited Synth-O-Gas. Therefore, in spite of the odd famine or plague, communications continue, and there aren't the expected levels of starvation. The Globecon has probably been hardened by so many wars anyway, that now it just acts as a permanent wet nurse for this world slowly destroying itself.*

Pleased as he was to see it, Giertz could now understand, *The resulting global disaster is only smoldering rather than exploding.* Yet he consoled himself, *Soon, just like in the Happylands asylum, only one small spark, in the right time and place, could finally detonate it all! For good! Therefore he knew, The end result will probably be even more cataclysmic!* Also, from time to time, happily recalling what Ceebix had said about his Idea Bomb, Giertz hardly dared to hope, *Perhaps the final destruction of reality is coming at last! And I will at least be playing some part in it.*

Suddenly, Giertz knew he'd finally got his answer from the holyvision. The message engraved on his mind by Ceebix's smile had told Giertz everything. Therefore he felt he had to do something. He had to do anything.


**Chapter 51 Unclean Gods**
Even as what remained of the world teetered, Giertz's first day as a Greedeluxe Corp. Combat Youth seemed just like any other to him. Like yesterday and tomorrow would be. Well before the retro, clockwork alarm clock started its metallic ringing, its phosphorescent numbers swam into view when he awoke as he always did - to The Screamers.

Having completed their hours-long climb to the top of their enormous columns, they'd begun calling to the disenchanted. Placed at strategic points around the city, no one knew who'd built those pillars, or recruited The Screamers. They just appeared one day, as if they'd always belonged there.

Most of what they were shouting was just indiscernible howling, as if they were only out to damage their lungs. It was possible to make out some proclamations, but these usually followed the same pattern, 'SLAUGHTER! SLAUGHTER! VILE ATROCITIES VISITED UPON THEIR BODIES! FORCED TO ACKNOWLEDGE UNCLEAN GODS!' (This last item always sickened Giertz more than anything, as he visualized faces contorted with revulsion, being bent to kiss the gnarled foot of some hideous idol.) Then The Screamers would then spend further hours descending the ladders from their columns. After collecting news of the latest atrocities, they would spend all night ascending the ladders once more. They never slept.

Giertz had awoken from the same dream he had almost every night: he was standing in a landscape that had once been a city, but was now just smoldering rubble. Usually, his only sensation was feeling extraordinarily happy, but this morning he felt a particular kind of nausea on waking. Reluctantly, he forced himself to recall that the dream last night had a nightmarish variation. He'd been in the same landscape, but holding his own skull in his hands, somehow staring deep into the vacant eye sockets.

Next, as he lay in bed for a while, feeling how stiff and tired his body was, he listened to the great towers of machinery that ran the city. They made deep, empty, bellowing sounds as they pulsed enormous clouds of greenish-black filth into the dawn sky. He always visualized the Consumers oozing out into the streets, blinking in the daylight, to march in forward-staring ranks to the rhythm, as the city ground into gear for another day.

Shortly after that, a slice of cold, early-summer sunlight cut through the gap in the curtains, and played over the texture of the flower-patterned wallpaper next to his bed. He always ran his fingers over its surface, somehow expecting to feel the light. He felt slightly foolish when he realized what he was doing, but still, irrationally, wished he'd been able to touch it.

Then he would then just lie, not wanting to get up, hoping he could force himself back to sleep and stay there, probably until he died. He would also dwell on the feeling he'd always had, stronger now than ever, that he was somehow stunted. *Perhaps I'm a deficient, not-quite-human being, with a mere talent for passing as living?* Sometimes he could even believe his unremarkable body was merely a thin shell, and 'he' was only some shriveled, stillborn fetus, somewhere inside it.

Finally, knowing he couldn't delay any longer, he rolled heavily off the old mattress as if it had become a bed of nails, his thoughts stabbing deeply into him. Standing naked in the damp darkness, looking around, he shook his head and then felt his way along a wall covered in tattered posters of Zytopharbb, the disciple of Ziachrad. Taken from a low angle, making Zytopharbb appear enormously tall, the black and white portrait was lit from behind, so seeming to give the prophet an ambient, holy glow. The unkempt, bearded man's wild eyes were staring, half in awe, half insane, at something, somewhere, far off in the sky.

Finally as Giertz opened the tattered curtains, the chilling sunlight blasted in, but he still acted as if he was in total darkness.

## Chapter 52 Eroded Gargoyles

Giertz 'lived' in one room of his parents' grotesque, little terraced house, still soot-stained from The First Industrial Revolution. There were eroded gargoyles carved into the red brick around the front door. It was one of the few in the area that didn't have its windows boarded up. Instead, there was just rusting, bullet-retardant mesh over the cracked glass, which nobody had cleaned in decades.

His parents had long ago moved 'up-market' to a cramped apartment in the Lo-Rent Zone. These were seemingly endless ranks of identical, gray concrete blocks scraping the sky, each with a number stenciled on the side - the World Housing Corporation's idea of the ideal Consumer home. His parents had won their tiny apartment in an episode of Real Life, but the adolescent Giertz had chosen to stay in this house. This was despite having to regularly battle the growing population of local mutants.

He waded towards the bathroom sink, through and over drifts of well-fermented rubbish piled up against the walls, which gave off an organic, composty smell. He often got severe retching coughs from this, and was also continually at war with a tribe of mutant rats that shared the house. Occasionally he would shoot a two-headed one as it scuttled across the floor. At night he could hear them under the skirting boards whispering to each other about him, in the primitive spoken language they'd evolved. The thought of clearing the garbage away only dimly occurred to Giertz though. He just put more poison down, shot the rats when he saw them, and sprayed it all with air freshener now and again.

Finally, after reaching the sink, he never dared to look at his youthful, but ravaged face in the spotted mirror. At first, he would just spray experimentally under his arms with an aerosol of deodorant. Then he would have a better idea and spray himself all over. As he did this, he would always notice the small serial number that was branded, probably with a laser, under his left armpit. When he'd first discovered it as a teenager, he'd wondered what it meant, and who'd put it there, but now he hardly thought about it at all.

Next, he would stretch into a freezing, clammy vest, still soaked with the previous day's sweat. It was light-gray Synth-O-Cotton that had been black once, years ago, and he would also pull on a pair of no-name jeans in the same condition. Lastly, he pushed his ugly feet into his scuffed, brown Synth-O-Leather boots, testing the sharpness of the silver, shark's-teeth, metal studs covering the soles, as was the fashion.

Today was different however, because for the first time he also pulled on his Combat Youth uniform: the yellow-and-black Synth-O-Leather jacket. It had chunks of bullet-resistant padding down the sleeves, and at various strategic points around the torso, with holes left at other points for cooling. *It's more a complex web of straps than a jacket, like some item of perverse underwear!* He observed. The whole effect made the wearer appear to be some insect, to be avoided by the rest of nature at any cost. Giertz's surname was stenciled across the back in large capitals, so he could be easily identified in the situations.

The next unusual thing was that he knelt and performed the simple ceremony of absolute subservience to his creator, and eventual destroyer: the omnipotent Xerak. It still felt strange, acknowledging this new deity who hated him, and all mankind, who would kill him on a whim one day. 'Hail Omnipotent Xerak, slaughterer of innocent and guilty alike!' Giertz mumbled, regardless.

Then Giertz stood up straight and tried to forget everything for a moment, except for himself as a Combat Youth, but the thought disturbed him. He wondered, Did it happen? *Did I actually become a Combat Youth? Or was it just something between a dream and a nightmare?* The minor religious ritual this morning had only made him wonder .further whether he'd done the right thing in joining. He even considered going back to being just a plain Greedeluxe Youth again, as pointless as it would be. He didn't want to admit to himself that since deciding to make the change, he'd gained a sour feeling in his stomach. He suspected it was giving him ulcers, while still wanting to know why all this was so important to him.

Eventually however, he would find out it was even more important than he'd anticipated.

## Chapter 53 Grimacing Unhealthily

Giertz's ancient, suffering, grandmother's room was next to his. She lay in her bed all day, every day, in a senile world of her own. She was incredibly old, and had been dying ever since he could remember. In fact, he could recall her dying and himself attending her cheap funeral, somewhere in his early teens. Therefore he thought she might be another of his hallucinations, but he carefully looked after her anyway: every morning and night sympathetically spoon-feeding her, and gently bathing her horrific bedsores.

In return she would relive her childhood for him, telling partly-true stories of her life before World War III. She often asked him about the world outside, and if the long-forgotten trams were running on time. At night he could hear her talking to the dog that used to lie by her bed, but had expired years ago, to be buried in the backyard. On her room's mantle-piece was a very faded photograph of Giertz as an apple-cheeked child, which he knew was more real to her than he was. Sometimes, looking at it, he could feel the same way. He could only dimly remember his grandfather, a vulgar, laughing, old man, with lapels covered in snuff.

In the kitchen Giertz took two slices of a papery white substance, 'I've Failed To Comprehend It Isn't Bread', and spread it with some 'product' to make it worth eating. In fact, this Consumeordie product was quite literally branded as just 'Product.' Also, all the large, colorful, elaborate cardboard and plastic packaging was less than a quarter full when he tore it open. Nobody noticed this anymore, except for Giertz, but he tried to resign himself, *I suppose in this sort of area, there just isn't the market for the better quality stuff from the Greedeluxe Corp.'s Synth-O-Food outlets.* He also attempted to reassure himself by reading the obvious lies on the packet about the contents' nutritional value, but among the smaller print were long lists of chemical additives. Cursing Dr. Zed and Consumeordie Corp., Giertz forced himself to swallow a mouthful, wondering by how much it was really shortening his life.

As he chewed, his eyes drifted with sad longing over one of the kitchen shelves at the titles of some of the books he'd used to read: 'The Third Wave' by Alvin Toffler, 'The Interpretation of Dreams' by Sigmund Freud, 'Seven Pillars of Wisdom' by T.E. Lawrence, 'The Decline of the West' by Oswald Spengler. When he analyzed the feeling of longing, he understood, *It isn't because I want to start reading again, so much as I miss the state of mind that made me think it was worthwhile.*

In fact, Giertz's secret, and the ambition that had kept him going, was that he wanted to be not just a poet, but a successful poet. He'd never understood why he wanted this, and reasoned it could only be for some kind of ego satisfaction: a vague notion of it perhaps floating him above the sedimentary level of human existence. His ambition was made even more ridiculous by knowing so many people were illiterate these days. Since education had been handed over entirely to the holygaming industry schools were a thing of the past, and poetry was the least read thing anyway. It made him feel bitter, *Everyone prefers to live in their synthetic reality module, too apathetic even to play holygames anymore, getting their 'edutainment' from the HV, when they venture out of their sarcophagus at all. Over-all, nobody believes in words anymore, because there are too many about anyway: every argument is immediately neutralized by some counter-argument.*

There was one book on the shelf with nothing in it but blank paper. Giertz had bought it long ago at a vital stage in his poetic ambition. He sat and contemplated its title-less, Synth-O-Leather bound cover, embossed with fake gold leaf. Finally, he put his sandwich down and took it off the shelf. He opened it on the first page and found his laser pen.

Despite his ambition, he'd never actually written anything creative before. He tried hard now for a moment, but as usual was overcome by a terrible realization that even though he could write anything he liked, it would be an entirely inconsequential act, never to be read. Somehow, he just couldn't put the dead words onto the dead paper. His whole body felt a sense of revulsion at the very idea of writing - or even thinking. *I'm now at the limits of language. Words have run out. Action! Action is what's demanded!*

Even so, something made him force a few words onto the empty page. Straining to recall the holygame that had taught him to write, he scrawled the only thing he knew for sure, 'There's something wrong with my mind.' He thought for a few moments more, then wrote something else in large, childlike capitals, 'I HAVE TO ACT.'

He sat and contemplated the words standing worthlessly on the page for a while. Knowing the world is entirely indifferent to this message of mine makes it feel even more worthless. He threw the book onto the kitchen rubbish pile.

He thought now about Leonard Kornn and his Post-Neo-Obscurist 'art'. Giertz despised Kornn, but in a moment of clarity Giertz believed he could see what he meant, *I'll give the liabilities a poem!* Giertz thought, grimacing unhealthily. *My actions shall be my poem. My switchblade machete shall be my pen, and I will write it in their blood! I swear by omnipotent Xerak I'm going to use this opportunity to destroy this civilization, and their so-called 'reality,' forever!*

## Chapter 54 Distilled Hatred

He turned to look out of the muddy filter of the kitchen window. Under the greeny-gray sky were the backs of the opposite row of houses, also stained by ancient coal soot. The occasional broken roof or bomb crater from World War II left gaps in their regular, paper-chain pattern.

His curious gaze traced the strings of colored lights festooning the neighborhood, embellished with summer icicles. As the breeze nudged at the bulbs, he could see they had the same layer of muddy dust that coated everything around here. They'd been put up in preparation for another Festival of Greed long ago, and for some reason never taken down, or switched on again.

Generally, he believed, *This place doesn't like me.* Everywhere he looked, whichever way he looked at it, reality gave him hints that it would rather he didn't exist: the filthy brick walls, weeds clinging to life in corners, the expressions on people's faces. He was a relatively short man, and the crumbling buildings always seemed to tower over him monstrously. This wasn't the main cause for why he wanted to destroy it all, because really he didn't specifically know the reason, *But it certainly gives me a good enough excuse.*

In addition to this, ever since he was a child, he'd always had a mild belief that everything was hollow, giving him a cold, empty feeling, *These buildings, people and so on, appear to be made of some tissue-thin substance, of various colors and textures: so they are merely filed with air, or even vacuum.* They certainly looked that way.

Socially, although by the standards of the time this was an average neighborhood, Giertz was too wise by now to use the front door and risk making himself an easy target. Instead, he exited through the kitchen window as usual, still eating his breakfast, and waded through the thick weeds of the alley. He had to step cautiously around some children playing intently with a human skull.

As well as the stream of cars, robot trucks and armored taxis ripping down the cobbled street at racetrack speeds, Giertz dodged around the usual sidewalk circus, *Recently it all seems more frantic as well.* He carefully avoided toothless madwomen, shrieking at him from the gutter, while Preparation X315/J addicts, in the terminal stages of their vice, danced and jittered aggressively past him, as he noted, *They all have the same bizarre, abstract expression on their sickly faces.* At the same time, walking scrap-yards of obsolete industrial robots politely tried to interest him in their case to be accepted as 'human.'

Religion appeared to play a big part in it as well: bizarrely-dressed, Xeracist-fundamentalist fanatics tried to convert him on the spot, while crazed prophets attempted to out-rave each other in declarations of divine retribution and doom. Street corner zealots would admonish, and kill, anyone they saw as violators of 'The Five Temptations of Judazz' (or just they didn't like).

As if in answer to it all, starving, naked geniuses strode the freezing sidewalks, their chemically enhanced brains denouncing the leaders, the gods, Dr. Zed, The Council of Ninety, and other geniuses. On the other hand, Torchbearers from 'The League of Geniuses' (who were nothing to do with the individual geniuses), ran around bearing their symbolic torch-flames. Lustily, in the face of all the evidence to the contrary, they would cry their motto, 'There is still hope for man!' They also reminded The Consumers, 'The League of Geniuses' genetically boosted brains are working as a team, day and night, with everyone's best interests at heart! They are bound to come up with The Answer soon!' Giertz was still waiting.

Amidst it all, as always, wandered Old Dog, the local pariah, his sorry, aged, decrepit, self-starved body swathed only in a ragged loin-cloth, barely able to stagger bare-foot along the streets. Matted strings straggled from his balding skull as hermaphrodite breasts swung among his gray chest hair. His eyes were permanently rolled back in his head, revealing the yellowed, bloodshot 'whites' while, as if chanting a mantra, he prophesied, 'Their world shall end,
They shall be destroyed,
Their great engine shall rot,
It is foretold!
'Metal shall melt,
Stone shall crumble,
Their wombs shall bear monsters,
It is foretold!'

'A young, insane warrior,
Shall smite the swollen-headed monster
In his tower,
It is foretold!'

'There shall be death,
And death within death,
There shall be no mercy.
It is foretold!
It is foretold!
It is foretold!' He waved his gnarled, wooden staff at the Consumers who laughed at him, and even spat directly into his face, but Giertz couldn't even manage a smile.

Somehow though, the most disturbing sight of all for Giertz every morning was The Organ Grinder. In his dirty olive-drab raincoat, standing before the backdrop of dingy, soot-stained red-brick walls. It's as if I've stumbled into some horrible Victorian time warp! As he looked up at Giertz from under his flat cap, The Grinder's eyes burned with a distilled hatred. On top of the flaking old barrel-organ was a small monkey in a tight, yellow, bellboy's uniform. Its fur was too pale, as if it had never seen daylight, and it skittered about angrily, holding an aluminum mug, rattling a few tokens. The instrument must have had some notes missing, because it was always plinking out no tune Giertz recognized, or that could even be regarded as a tuneful. Giertz had to admit it added a weird, discordant, background music to the whole street scene, *The perfect accompaniment to the wails and gnashing of teeth of the faithless.*

Therefore it was almost reassuring to see a Human Fly jump in front of him, reminding Giertz of where and when he was.

## Chapter 55 Genetic Warfare
Literally a cross between the genes of a human and a fly, The Human Fly was just one of the genetically engineered mutations now infesting this class of neighborhood. This one made a big mistake however, pausing too long to aggressively hiss its long, black proboscis at Giertz.

Instantly he saw it was an opportunity to try out his new gun, which The Greedeluxe Weapons Division had specially designed for the Combat Youth. With his heightened reflexes, Giertz whipped it from the quick-release holster.

Casually taking aim, Giertz hugged its strangely-shaped, ergonomic stock, squinted into its complicated, heat-seeking, telescopic sight, caressed the nickel plating that made it shine as would some holy object. Activated by nerve impulses from the hand, it reacted more quickly than a standard gun, firing the latest, high explosive, super-high-velocity micro-bullets. Its small digit counter ran up a score of kills. Giertz wasn't used to how light it was however, compared to his machine gun. The tiny bullet took a large chunk out of a metal lamp post, as the human fly ducked.

Then, trying to escape, it then leapt with super-human agility across the street, over the suicidal traffic, but uselessly fluttering the small, atrophied wings on its back. Zigzagging the lines of rusting, abandoned cars, then swinging deftly from lamp post to lamp post, it used all the usual tricks Giertz was used to by the time he'd killed his tenth one, *These are relatively easy prey, compared to a spider-woman or human-crab.* For a moment though Giertz could even, perversely, admire it.

Despite being faster than any other mutation on the planet, Giertz was still able to keep the sight on it. Also, feeling a faint, irrational pang of conscience, Giertz reminded himself, *It's generally accepted they, and all the other weird miscreations, are probably some kind of genetic warfare experiment that went wrong. I suppose I've just got to put an end to its misery by swatting it quickly.* The Fly was halfway up a wall when it loosed some misshapen appendage, ready to fire a disgusting ball of chromosomes at Giertz. This was the human fly's way of defending itself, and also recruiting more to its miserable line.

Giertz had witnessed this spectacle before: on contact the ball would spin a sticky, black cocoon around the victim, injecting them with the necessary DNA polluting substances. Giertz could always hear the 'fresh' Human Flies screaming in the night with the pain of rapidly combining, barely-compatible genes, and Giertz always answered the same question every time, *Nobody knows who created any of these mutants, whose numbers grow faster than us remaining humans can exterminate them.* If the shock didn't kill them, after a few days a new human fly would stand up and clean itself off. *Soon there will probably be more of them than us!*

Still finishing his ersatz breakfast, Giertz fired twice. The first shot just blew two bricks out of the wall beside the mutant, but the second took away one of the red, compound-lensed eyes which accounted for half its head. It dropped with a high-pitched yelp, and Giertz rejoiced, *With this new gun it's easy!* The following thought disturbed him though, *Just like in one of my holygames?*

As the insectoid lay in the weeds, giving the odd, spasmodic death-tremor, Giertz went matter-of-factly to inspect what he'd done. Luckily there was a public crossing nearby. He put a few tokens in the meter, and as the lights turned red two powerful industrial lasers on either side projected a path for him, giving him just enough microseconds to sprint across the road. He skipped the flattened bodies of 'road-kill' Consumers, usually the elderly or infirm, as the snarling, growling traffic jam started to build up on either side, its horns giving Giertz a kind of random fanfare. As the cars' thousand horse-power front ends bounced up and down with torque, the drivers got ready to 'pop' their clutches the moment the lights changed, and the lasers no longer threatened to singe their front bumpers. Then hopefully they would have an excuse to run this annoying, paranoid pedestrian over, but he just made it - this time.

The kill-counter on the gun now read 'zero, zero, zero, one,' but as he approached the twitching corpse, like most hunters, Giertz still felt some guilt. Despite the unnaturalness of it all, he couldn't help feeling there was something beautiful about the blue-black exoskeleton of a human fly, *They seem less alien in this environment, and in these times, than I feel, somehow.* Therefore this small victory felt hollow. *I've destroyed something superior to myself, in some ways, but I still hope someone will do me the same favor if I'm contaminated.*

He didn't do anything with the cadaver, because sooner or later the whole area would be washed by migrations of large, mutated, orange, phlesh-eating spiders, as big as dogs, consuming everything too slow to get out of their path. Over-all though, Giertz didn't notice these scenes anymore, unable to imagine life any other way, but looking around today he decided, *I prefer this place at night, when the street is relatively deserted, with just dust and paper blowing under the orange sodium lights.*

As Giertz looked up, he had a real surprise today however, as he recognized Mrs. Soroko, one of his few non-mutant neighbors. He had a blurred, childhood memory of her as a fresh-looking, neatly-permed newlywed, but now she was staring wildly in front of herself. Her gray hair was streaming down her back, and she had no shoes on her feet as she stood on the frosty cobbles, her nightgown billowing around her. Giertz called, 'Good morning Mrs. Soroko!' She didn't reply however.

**Chapter 56 Obsession Level**

After his synthetic 'breakfast' his mouth had a horrible burnt feeling, which lasted the whole morning, as if from consuming too much sugar. In retrospect to Giertz, this seemed like an ominous foretaste of what was to come. Despite this, as always Giertz began to run the distance to the garage where he kept his car. It would have been easier for him to jog directly to the Greedeluxe Youth headquarters, but he wanted to drive his red car one last time.

As he ran, apart from the mutations and lunatics, what were known as 'muscle-men' bestrode the streets in ranks of classical-god physiques. Most Consumer men now indulged in steroid bodybuilding to some extent. They wore tight, tank-top vests, and sometimes only G-strings, even in this icy summer weather. Strutting with inflated dignity, intricate corporate tattoos flexing on their arms and faces, they acknowledged each other's presence with barely a curt nod, but nobody acknowledged Giertz of course. By their standards he was physically insignificant, mainly as a result of his parents' over-protection. His body had never really developed in any particular way, but Giertz wasn't bothered much by this anymore, secretly knowing, *My reflexes can compensate for a lot!*

However, since he'd started training to be a Greedeluxe Combat Youth he'd been running, carrying the gun and other equipment on his shoulders. The overall shape of his stringy frame couldn't be improved much, but his general fitness had been. In fact, this workout had gone beyond obsession level, *It's strange, the more I do, the more I feel I'm not doing enough!* So he'd also been preparing himself in the Combat Youth's computerized gym in his own time.

Giertz arrived at the garage with steam swirling off his skin. It was in an area of deserted houses and boarded-up shops full of mutants, who shared it with Preparation

X315/J users, at various stages of addiction, and other miscellaneous degenerates. It had all been wrecked one especially bad night during the first of The Protein Riots, and then abandoned. Because there was so much apathy here now, his car was relatively safe. Nevertheless, he used the heat-seeking sight on his new gun to scan for any mutants who might be hiding inside.

He disarmed the hidden security system and heaved open the metal door. It was covered in strange, intricate graffiti, which on closer inspection he'd found was, in fact, complicated algebraic formulae. Knowing that 'Math-heads' had produced it saddened Giertz, *Addicted to intelligence drugs, they are forever trying to find an outlet for their tragic, synthetic genius, before their over-clocked minds burn out, reducing them to vegetables.* They appeared to think it was worth it though. Giertz had once, briefly, tried analyzing some of the equations, but even through the filter of his surrogate Ph.D., he only achieved the beginnings of a headache.

Inside the garage was a kind of Aladdin's Cave of fake Lamborghini parts. There was a small workbench, welding gear, and three fake Lamborghinis. Two were twisted irreparably. The third was now still only slightly dented from Giertz's entrance to Uncle Joe's party. The garage floor was littered with tools and more parts, each with 'Made in the Free Trade Zone' stamped on it. Before he joined the Combat Youth, he'd spent much of his time here, repairing the cars and making them go even faster.

Today he left in a cloud of rubber smoke, not even giving the cherished engine time to warm up, or bothering to close the garage doors.

**Chapter 57 Nauseous Nostalgia**
Eventually, he arrived at the Greedeluxe Youth headquarters, and again saw the frigid, summer sun

reflecting off the damaged building. Filtered through a near insomniac's morning stupor, the sight gave him a kind of nauseous nostalgia for the first time he'd seen it this way, at his interview only a few weeks before. Already he believed, *That was a 'time of innocence,' of a kind.*

Knowing he was late for his first patrol made him unhappy, not because there was any punishment involved, but because he very badly didn't want to miss even a second of it. He left his old car outside with its door open, and ran down to the underground car park from where a new patrol was launched every eight hours. He came charging out of the fire exit, carrying his weapons into the circle of yellow and black fake Lamborghinis.

These differed from the standard, fake Lamborghini. The Combat Youth modified them by, amongst other things, bulletproofing the tires and other vulnerable mechanical parts, fitting ejector seats and bigger Cyclone Injectors, which boosted the already enormous horsepower. Their yellow finish was augmented with a black, dashed-stripe down each side, matching the one down the arms of the uniform jacket. The driver's name was stenciled beneath the side window. The Combat Youth wrote off at least five or six cars a week.

Ceebix, looking neutral as always, but slightly more dazed than usual, had positioned his wheelchair in the center of the circle of cars, under the gaping, dusty, mouths of the ventilation system. On seeing Giertz he said nothing, only lifting a hand to run it across his unkempt, thinning, blond hair, barely bestowing him a glance. Giertz watched carefully, *It's as if his dazed state has been building up for some time. Something's really preoccupying him!* Giertz could never have imagined however, that it was himself.

As Giertz pulled up the door of his car, Ceebix continued with the sermon he gave before every patrol. It was common knowledge Ceebix heard 'voices' from inside his skull, telling him, and subsequently The Combat Youth, what to do. Usually, when they spoke via him it just sounded like streams of apparently meaningless nonsense, but today the message sparkled with clarity, infusing the Combat Youth with enough of The Idea to get them through the next eight hours, '...And I say unto you,
In the beginning was the Idea,
And the idea was Xerak,
And there was only ever one Idea,
And there has only ever been one Idea,
And there shall ever only be one Idea,
And it is unquestionable,
And the very foundations of the universe shall tremble,
Its mention shall level the mountains,
It shall cast aside the clouds and split the sky,
It is absolute and all-encompassing,
It is totality,
And all other ideas shall be smitten from its path,
And those uncircumcised fornicators,
Unable to embrace it in the depths of their souls,
They shall be made not alive,
They shall be OBLITERIZED!'
As Giertz hurriedly loaded his gun and other equipment into the car, and climbed into the ejector seat, a black leather-gloved hand reached out to help. Giertz knew by now it belonged to a Combat Youth called Kadski. All novice Combat Youths were initially partnered with an experienced operative, but at first Giertz didn't have much faith in Ceebix's decision. Giertz ran his tongue over the still-tender gum in his mouth, where the new tooth had been implanted by the Asclepius

Institute dentist, remembering Kadski was the one who'd landed that final punch several weeks earlier.

In the intimacy of the car's Synth-O-Leather cockpit, Giertz observed that Kadski's eyes bulged slightly under his greasy black hair, to which he added yet more grease, framing an even more deeply pockmarked face than Giertz's, mostly down one side, *As if it's been chewed up and spat out!* His mouth was also somewhat malformed, curled in a permanent sneer, from which he spoke with an affected, private school accent, intoning each word precisely in perfect, received-pronounced diction. Shortly, Giertz would also learn Kadski had an unnerving habit of telling you exactly what he thought of you. Giertz would similarly be surprised to discover that, eventually, he would regard this young man enough to die for him – or worse.

**Chapter 58 Shock Troops**
In a star formation on their turntables, the cars faced the appropriate exits for the part of the city they were to patrol. Stenciled over the one before Giertz was:


'SECTOR H.'


Ceebix's voice became muffled as Giertz pulled down the door, but somehow the words still carried,
'Omnipotent Xerak,
Slaughtering innocent and guilty without discrimination,
Laughing as he nudges his pawns!
Merciless Xerak!
As the stars coalesce,
We, your shock-troops against inferior Gods,
Take our cue!
Man was made to crawl on his belly,
There is no good or evil, only survival!'

As Ceebix proselytized, Giertz noted the empty parking spaces of the standard Greedeluxe Youths that he was no longer one of, but there were still a few red, fake Lamborghinis, although mostly abandoned on flat tires. Giertz reflected that eventually the handful of remaining, generic Greedeluxe Youths in their red jackets would sadly wheel his own red car down from the street to join these. Most of the standard Greedeluxe Youths seem to have drifted away now, including me.

Watching the foam forming around Ceebix's mouth in the rear-view mirror, Giertz tightened his safety harness. He also noticed the corners of Ceebix's eyes were bloodshot as he slashed the air unconsciously with his machete, to emphasize each point, as he spoke the last words, 'Their world shall end,
They shall be destroyed,
Their great engine shall rot,
It is foretold!'

'Metal shall melt,
Stone shall crumble,
Their wombs shall bear monsters,
It is foretold!'

'A young, insane warrior,
Shall smite the swollen-headed monster,
In his tower,
It is foretold!
'There shall be death,
And death within death,
There shall be no mercy.
It is foretold!
It is foretold!
It is foretold!'

The very last words though were lost in the sound of the ten W-sixteen engines barking into life, and then disappearing up their respective ramps, in clouds of ultra-high-octane, green Synth-O-Gas smoke, 'IT IS FORETOLD!'

# PART 2

## Chapter 59 Uncircumcised Fornicators

There was a brief, discordant scream of metal and sparks as Giertz grazed the back of the car slightly on the wall of the sloping tunnel that led out of the garage. He was shocked, *For all its realism during my training, the driving simulator hasn't prepared me for how even more potent than my old fake Lamborghini this one is!*

In fact, the engine shrieked as would some animal straining to break out of captivity, when the car leapt out into the daylight. He had to fight with the steering to avoid hitting the wall of one of the disused warehouses opposite, watching the old, red bricks slide past the windshield.

He projected his imagination to view the scene from above, guessing correctly that the buzzing yellow and black cars emerging from the concrete hive of the skyscraper looked like some strange swarm of flightless insects. It headed down the broad alleyway leading to the main mega-highway, not racing each other to get there so much as attempting to reach the road quickly, at any cost. Therefore they disregarded each other's safety - and their own.

Trying to overtake Giertz, one car hit a pile of garbage and overturned. It skated along on its roof in a spray of sparks, as aluminum grated against asphalt. Giertz watched its wheels spinning in the air in the crosshairs of his rearview camera. Despite the safety foam ballooning out of the shattered windows, no one got out.

As they reached the sweeping, cracked concrete maze of the mega-junction, they split up to follow their separate patrol routes. Kadski silently indicated the direction for Giertz to take. Kadski hadn't spoken to him since they'd met, but he decided to ignore Kadski. Giertz rapidly took the car up through all eight gears because all the cars on the mega-highway were traveling at near their maximum speed anyway. As usual, the minimum-speed signs were urgently flashing three-figure numbers, and on bad, 'high digit' days like today, many drivers couldn't keep up. Every few minutes Giertz would see the green explosion somewhere of another collision.

Predatory, prehistoric monsters of salvage helicopters with huge electromagnets or cruel-looking metal grabs swinging below them patrolled the road, but the burnt out, contorted wrecks of the uninsured lined the roadsides. Occasionally it occurred to Giertz, *Why does everyone have to drive so fast?* This question felt pointless though, like asking, 'Why is the sky always green?'

In fact, rusting scrap stretched to the horizon in all directions, turning the entire landscape into one enormous landfill. Corroded skeletons of Consumer products such as not only holyvisions and cars were flashing past, but helicopters, even planes. Much of it had been tossed out because it just wasn't this month's style, never to be recycled. Giertz didn't think of it as waste however, or even think of it as anything. It was just 'economic reality,' as Dr. Zed referred to it. Even Giertz couldn't argue with that.

Still strangers, the two Combat Youths had only been on the mega-highway for a few minutes before Kadski spoke his first words to Giertz. They were in the same kind of patronizing tone someone might use to point out an obvious obstruction in the path of a person who insisted on wearing a blindfold, 'They're following us!'

Giertz checked the crosshairs of the rear monitor again. Indeed he saw three of the large, dark blue-black limousines, (actually replicas of nineteen fifty-nine Cadillacs) used by the Consumeordie Corp. Non-men. The cars' enormous tail fins flashed as they knifed in a wedge formation between other less powerful cars of The Consumers, which were skidding, or being shunted, out of the way. 'By Xerak! Don't let the uncircumcised fornicators overtake us!' Cried Kadski.

Changing down to sixth gear, already weaving between cars going at half his car's velocity, Giertz pushed the accelerator all the way. Exactly as he'd learned in the simulator, the boosted engine's extra cyclone-injectors cut in automatically, and its horsepower grew cumulatively. All four of the car's tires screeched in a short burst of smoke. Kadski, despite his outburst, appeared unsettled by the way Giertz was paying more attention to the vehicles receding in his rearview, than to what was in front of him. He only just missed several cars, but his main thought was, *Just like in one of my holygames! It's easy!*

Giertz even took out his astronaut Ray-Bans and was trying to attach them to his head with one hand, when he dropped them. He began groping on the floor between his knees. Occasionally he actually took his eyes off the road altogether. He was aware of being observed carefully from the edge of Kadski's vision, but Giertz didn't care, *Because confrontations of this kind now plague the roads, they retain only a fraction of their popularity as a mode of transport. Most people either spend everything on buying a helicopter or stay in the relative safety of their 'point of consumption,' viewing the world through the holyvision, or synthetic reality module.* So it wasn't long before Giertz came to the empty stretch of highway he'd been gambling on.

**Chapter 60 Dark Glasses**
Finally, his fingers caught the sunglasses, but they'd become wedged under the seat. As he tried to pull them free, he slowed the car spectacularly to a virtual stop, applying the hand-brake and then full lock on the steering, so the car span on its axis to face in the opposite direction. Then he accelerated once more, the headlight pods rising out of the nose.

Eventually, he freed the dark glasses and began trying again to attach them to his head, the frames occasionally interrupting his vision. The few cars now cautiously hugging the 'slow' lane careered out of his way, but the further he went against the stream of traffic, the more he had to swing the steering wheel. He slalomed between an increasing number of cars going the opposite way, their relative speed added to his own.

At one point he swerved into the verge at the edge of the road, the dead soil sending up a column of dust from each wheel. Taking a full moment to glance across at Kadski, Giertz saw his fingernails digging into the Synth-O-Leather of his seat. Then Giertz looked directly ahead, and through the crosshairs etched onto the windshield saw his targets.

At last, he hooked the sunglasses around his ears and grabbed the steering firmly again with both hands. The three Consumeordie limousines, still in formation, almost blocked the whole road, but now they saw Giertz's headlights coming towards them. Eventually, becoming confused metal hippopotamuses, they began shunting against each other in a disorganized attempt to split up.

Finally, they managed to separate enough to allow Giertz to shoot harmlessly between them, but the speed was too much for their ponderous handling. Giertz studied them in the rearview screen, now no more than skittles bouncing end over end. One huge car pirouetted on its chrome nose before its windows burst, green Synth-O-Gas flames billowing out of them.

Still traveling in the wrong direction, Giertz now started looking for one of the frequent damaged sections in the central crash barrier, which the insurance companies didn't bother to repair these days. Loudly praising Xerak, and the insurance corporations, he quickly found it. Braking heavily, he slid the car sideways through the gap in the barrier, taking a certain amount of previously undamaged barrier with him. In the opposite lane, going in the right direction again, he gradually slowed to the same speed as the other traffic - nearly.

Giertz hadn't been particularly surprised by his enormous scores during training, but he'd become aware that a lot of the Combat Youth were. Some had gawped open-mouthed at the cheap, printed lists of each operative's name and number, pinned daily to the notice board. The same look was trying to appear on Kadski's face now. With some effort, he turned to Giertz and said straightforwardly, 'You did relatively well.' Giertz also thought he noticed a mild tone of apology. Ignoring the patronizing attitude behind Kadski's compliment, but otherwise not sure how to respond, Giertz just nodded, feeling slightly smug behind his dark glasses, *At last Kadski seems prepared to acknowledge my existence in some way!*

**Chapter 61 Physical Contortions**

While waiting for the call to Giertz's first 'situation,' he drove unspectacularly for some time, placated by the screeching noise from the radio. He insisted to Kadski it was music, even if it was of the retro-generic, corporate genre. Generally Giertz preferred the radio to holyvision because it seemed every minute another legend was born: 'Marilyn on the Slab', 'The Church of God the Criminally Insane', 'Johnny Newblood and the Transfusions', even if each new band to come along was screaming exactly the same message, just more pessimistically than the last. They all offered only one solution anyway, demanding the leaders should 'Kill! Kill! Kill!' as many as it takes, and more besides.

However, as Giertz drove further into the city, he watched the empty faces of young Consumers drift past the car's windows, *Despite all this music, the youth today are relatively apathetic. The ones who don't join the corporate youth gangs, and `end it all' in The Situations, just hang about on street corners in long black coats. Desperate for any clichés to hold onto, they chant these pop-songs while staring blankly into space. They change their haircuts every other day with the trends, but once their favorite bands have sold a billion and immediately escape to The Security Zone, their fans will only hear the record now and again on the nostalgia shows, bringing back distant, faded, teenage memories.*

Giertz was almost entirely neutral about this station's DJ though: Ekkodd Gleego. He orbited the earth in a satellite, relatively safe from any music sub-corporation who violently objected to a play-list based purely on his personal whims. What Giertz liked about him was that he played more of `Psycho Kiss.' When that band's grating metallic cacophony announced itself, Giertz's always reminded himself, *They're still producing 'music,' but they always seem a doomed sort of band.*

Shrieking Joe Megastar's voice was that of a man trying to shout his way out of a soundproof cell. Giertz could easily recall all SJM's HV performances, *The audience, almost out of revenge, wildly encourage him in the dangerous physical stunts and contortions which dramatically illustrate his vocal style!*

Giertz was personally fascinated by SJM, often musing about his idol, *At the beginning of his career he was just another wholesome, apple-faced boy with a tooth-capped smile, but as his career progressed he metamorphosed into a decadent, fey character with flashy clothes and a bad complexion over sunken cheeks. Even without the disfigurement from the motorcycle accident, trying to compensate for his reversed 'Dorian Gray' decline, with layers of plastic surgery has somehow only made it all worse. Most people are only really interested in his weird sexual appetite anyway, and what directions this could indicate for them in the future.*

Giertz had always assumed Psycho Kiss's noise had some degree of popular following, but so far had never found anyone else who could bear to listen to a single note of it. Their recordings were always overtaken in the pop-charts by Pandora singing something soporifically middle-of-the-road, like, 'I'm in Love with a Total Stranger,' but this didn't diminish Giertz's faith. It was just another reason for his adoration.

Another thing Giertz liked about the DJ Gleego was, *He appears to have a physical need to broadcast. Indeed, he does so almost twenty-four hours a day, seven days a week, often high on Preparation X315/J to keep him going. Perhaps he never does sleep at all? Gleego gave Giertz the feeling that, All over the world, teenage rebels are jumping into thousand horsepower hot-rods, and driving straight into walls of solid concrete!* Which was mostly true, it was quite a final fashion statement at the moment.

What ultimately neutralized any admiration Giertz had for Gleego though, was that in between the songs, he was always ranting about 'The Power of Love.' He would go on for hours, talking at almost super-human speed, without playing any records, 'And that one - "Exterminate All Uncircumcised Fornicators" - by Psycho Kiss - is dedicated to - and brought to you by, The Power Of Love!'

Ultimately Giertz accepted the situation, *Even a DJ has to believe in something I suppose, but nobody else believes in 'The Power of Love' anymore, least of all me, but Gleego does have a point. Like him, I have to believe in something. Otherwise, I will end up like all the other hopeless liabilities, wandering the freezing streets alone with my collar turned up, and last week's newscomix blowing around my ankles.*

Then, when Giertz and Kadski had just managed to calm down, Ceebix's monotone crackled out of the radio.

A 'Situation' was now in progress. Reminding himself his first time had to come, Giertz tried to swallow the hard lump of fear and expectation in his throat.

## Chapter 62 Protein Riots

Giertz had never been involved in The Situations before, only watching them on HV, so had no real idea of the terrible experience awaiting him today. He could well remember when the term 'Situation' was first used by the media, *When the early `Protein Riots' grew into something less comprehensible.* While he'd initially been excited by the idea of the riots, Giertz had steadily become disillusioned, *They've just degenerated from ideological free-for-alls into dismal, pitched battles between two entrenched, corporate, points of view.*

As he drove urgently to this one though, trying to be optimistic, he thought, *Perhaps being a Combat Youth might give the `Situations' an extra dimension for me?* He would shortly find it would indeed do this for him, but in more ways than he'd anticipated, or would have wanted to.

Soon he was nearly convulsed with fear, trying to stop his hands from shaking on the steering wheel. At the same time, he felt a sense of expectation that was almost painful. The geo-coordinates Ceebix had given guided Giertz to the blackened, flaming ruin of a disused rubber sex-aids factory. *Somehow, it makes a perfect setting.* It also left a strange, acrid smell of burning rubber hanging over everything.

As they approached the gray, boarded-up buildings surrounding the flaming ruin, Giertz read some of the fresh graffiti embroidering them,

'LIABILITIES GO BACK TO HELL,'

announced itself in fluorescent orange paint, and over it in black, someone had superimposed,

'TEENAGE JUDAS.'

Wandering among it all were some stragglers from the Situation, still screaming their frustrated points of view. Blood ran over their faces, contorted into living masks of pure loathing. Their torn clothes hung in drapes around their well-defined torsos, somehow casting them to Giertz as classically tragic figures.

On Kadski's urging, Giertz slowed the car to allow a Human Bullet to attach his magnetic towline to the back. Dressed in one-piece motorcycle leathers, covered in steel studs, zero-friction boots and a crash helmet sporting sharp, metal spikes, human Bullets claimed allegiance to no particular corporation or ideology. Seeing themselves as catalysts more than anything, the impact with whatever target they selected usually killed them. Vehicles from either side would tow them to their self-imposed doom, purely out of good-will.

As Giertz accelerated again, the Human Bullet crouched behind as a water-skier would, but the boots were sending up a wave of orange sparks rather than ocean foam. Giertz lapsed into a mild daydream of becoming a Human Bullet himself, *It might make more sense, after all, to go out in a single blaze of idealism, rather than just prolonging the process with the Combat Youth.* For all his fanaticism and agility though, this particular Human Bullet tripped against a corpse as he released his towline. His helmeted head took a piece out of a wall before he hit the group of rioters he'd been aiming for, impacting them with a relatively harmless cart-wheeling motion, his neck clearly broken. Observing this in the rear view screen, Giertz reflected, *Perhaps it might not be such a good idea after all?*

Then the car shook rhythmically when a line of small hills appeared in the bullet-resistant panel next to Giertz's leg, a stream of machine-gun tracers drumming into it. He almost lost control, but he managed to stop. He and Kadski raised the doors and simultaneously dived out, firing back at the roof the shots came from. Then Giertz had his first shock.

## Chapter 63 Methodically Shredded

Out in the rubbery-smelling air, the first thing Giertz noticed was the noise. He believed the cacophony wouldn't only permanently damage his hearing, but his memory also: bellows of rage and pain; shattering glass; snatches of amplified, fanatic diatribes; threats; accusations; and even music, thundered somehow into a single, terrible wail of desperation, over an uneven rhythm of gunshots and the odd explosion.

The second, but no less terrible, thing was the horrifying spectacle. As Giertz surveyed the scene, his first impression was, *It's much bigger than I expected!* It almost paralleled his last experience in the Happylands Institute. The Situation was illuminated by the giant chemical flames leaping into the air from the old factory, and some cars and other buildings around it were also burning. Giertz wondered at the many bodies already scattered across the street, as he often would from now on, *What's it all over anyway? Clearly, the original argument has been lost.*

Screaming angels of death, jet-pack fliers swooped over the show below; firing shots at random into it. The odd Synth-O-Gas bomb was thrown upwards at them, describing a fiery, green arc across the crowd, but the 'Jet-Packers' were somehow always just out of reach.

Already weak with fear, Giertz also began to feel an even worse poison filtering through his veins, paralyzing him. Soon he thought it would reach his heart. He knew this must be 'The Terror' he'd heard the other Combat Youth mention in quiet voices, but he hadn't thought about what they meant until now. He felt something warm and wet running down the inside of his leg. At the same time he ducked three seconds before a Synth-O-Gas bomb sailed past his head, but he still felt the intense heat as it burned green close behind him.

Canceling out the smothering fear though was his overwhelming loathing for the opposing factions, but when he thought deeply about it, he'd nothing specifically personal against any individual gang. All he cared about was whether or not they supported Consumeordie Corp, *But that's all it takes.*

Hanging from everything were the usual colorful banners and other decorations relating to The Festival of Greed, but Greedeluxe supporters had even methodically shredded these. The self-satisfied smile hung flapping in tatters in some places, now a weird, idiot grimace, which appeared to be appropriate somehow to the battle broiling beneath.

Looking around, Giertz heard the screech of sintered metal brake pads from other Combat Youth's cars that were now skidding to a halt next to his. Then he felt another shock, *The Combat Youth have no real tactics or anything else!* He watched open-mouthed as they just leaped out of their cars and formed a loose phalanx. This was enough to make the crowd, as one huge monster, send a tentacle of extremists charging towards them.

Meanwhile, Giertz stood motionless, wondering what was done now, but nothing happened. He felt his legs beginning to melt under him. He'd never really thought about 'courage' before, since his most fundamental impulses always guided most of his actions. Even now it didn't mean much to him, but soon he began to see, *Courage doesn't even come into this fight!*

One fresh-faced novice Combat Youth, trying to mask the nervousness in his voice, started a chant of 'No compromise! No compromise!' This was the Combat Youths' official motto. It quickly built into an enormous, wordless, gut-battle-cry, before transforming into something else still - a kind of animalistic group-bellow.

Then Giertz found that far from running for safety, unlike any creature with a fraction of reasoning capacity, the Combat Youth spearhead was illogically charging against the entire monster. Not only that, but as a comet would, they were drawing into their tail a mass of otherwise disorganized and disillusioned Greedeluxe stragglers, somehow seeing hope at last. Strangest of all, Giertz was also charging with his own cry drilling into his ears.

Even knowing he was about to have one of the worst experiences of his life didn't matter to him - initially.


## Chapter 64 Riot Chic

As Giertz came closer to the monster, rather than the amorphous rabble he'd expected, he found The Situation was somehow self-organized into concentric rings of rioters, each circle trying to destroy the one inside it, the core consisting of a mounting pile of corpses. As the weeks passed, he would find this always to be the case, getting used to the idea that the deeper he penetrated the monster, the more intense it would be.

The Situations had also become as much fashion shows as they were battlegrounds. Each faction, no matter how splintered, had its characteristic idea of a uniform, but most were just variations of the classic Synth-O-Leather-and-studs vogue. This even momentarily sidetracked Giertz's thinking as he almost felt his yellow and black outfit was rather dowdy in comparison with the general 'riot chic.'

Noticing some heavily armed, but uncertain-looking Producers on the less dangerous fringes, Giertz was also dismayed, *The Situations are now so fashionable almost every level of society takes part to some extent. After all, there's a whole industry now promoting this lifestyle as a kind of therapy for bored executives.* It had become 'the latest thing' amongst the middle-aged to pass one's self off as a member of some teen faction or other, but the menopausal fakes were easy to detect. Their uniforms were always expensive and flashy, giving too much protection. Giertz noticed that most also wore expensive bullet-proof metal masks molded in terrible expressions, to create fear in the opposition, *The question is always there though, what's behind the masks? The Combat Youth don't need any masks because their own faces are their best weapon.*

In a skirmish nearby, Giertz saw a balding Producer, still in his shirt and tie after a day at the office, wearing an expensive muscle-extension suit. Hydraulic servos and pistons all over his body turned his smallest movements into colossal gestures, shattering rotten-apple skulls left and right. *He thinks his suit will protect him,* Giertz smirked.

The high-powered megaphone clamped in front of the Producer's face was blasting out his opinion, but this couldn't disguise the lack of conviction in his voice. Someone skillfully severed his hydraulics from behind with a single cut from a switch-blade machete. There was a look of pained surprise on the Producer's flaccid face, covered in squirting hydraulic fluid, as he drowned under the mass of heaving bodies.

Nevertheless, Giertz found that those Producers even often employed gaily-colored minstrels and tumblers who would go before them, singing and acting out their supposed exploits in small dramas. Giertz also knew that some of the more affluent Producers were not present at The Situations at all, but sent professional champions. The ones who could afford it even sent clones of themselves. *What kind of liabilities could delude themselves with such an act, and how could anyone fall for it?* Whatever the case, it certainly never stopped them from trying.

**Chapter 65 Bazooka Battles**

The third thing Giertz noticed was that, *Strangely, for all the anarchy here, there's a paradoxical code of ethics operating. Generally the rioters show a disdain for the use of arms, I suppose one's point of view is itself the real weapon, the physical tools only there to back it up. The fundamental idea behind The Situations, after all, is not just to kill the opponents, but first try to change their minds, at least.*

However, most participants specialized in the use of some weapon: a simple club or switchblade machete appearing to be the most popular. Wielding these with some degree of skill gained more respect than any sophisticated gun, even if, in the end, the former weren't as effective. Despite this though, many firearms and portable rocket-launchers were unashamedly in evidence.

Not all the rioters were as specialized in their function as the Human Bullets. For example, some had merely tattooed themselves all over with the advertising slogans of the particular corporation they supported, and fought desperately with their bare hands. *These minimalists are the most respected, perhaps because they have the lowest life expectancy.* Some didn't even fight physically at all, but only emphasized their opinions by shouting through powerful amplifiers. Yet at the other extreme, some had fingers, limbs, or other parts of their bodies surgically replaced with steel implements, even cachets of alkali or acid, or explosives detonated by certain sequences of thoughts. Giertz was also baffled though, *There is a notable absence of the martial arts, as such?*

Today, Giertz and Kadski were instantly surrounded by a group of men who were naked, except for full-face crash helmets, carrying sledgehammers. Their agenda, whatever it was, rapidly became irrelevant though, as Kadski instantly disarmed the weakest member. His hammer was then used by Kadski to assail the ringleader, and others, with a ferocity they saw they could never match. Therefore the survivors disappeared as quickly as they'd arrived.

Still, as Giertz had anticipated, the longer a particular situation continued, the more weapons were used. Starting with taunts and then hand-to-hand fighting, towards the end they would often eventually degenerate into pure bazooka battles. Therefore he saw, *This was the main excuse for forming the Combat Youth, in order to have a force available to deal with the worst the other corporation could throw at the Greedeluxe-related gangs.* Again though, as he penetrated still deeper into the monster, he felt the same sense of futility at the sight of so much wasted energy. *Why does it have to be this way? If only I could somehow unite these factions, perhaps then I'd have a chance to destroy reality?*

He didn't know yet he was thinking prophetically.

**Chapter 66 Grotesque Carnival**

Now almost in the bowels of the collective monster, Giertz saw, *A more recent trend in riot chic is for serious participants to have their DNA mingled with some of the most unpleasant members of the animal kingdom.* These rioters had quickly evolved a snake's venomous bite and scales, or a bad-tempered ape's fangs and agility. When a young woman with pancaked make-up confronted him, from the hairy, sectioned appearance of her lower body Giertz deduced, *She appears to be partly mutated with the DNA of some insect, probably a spider. Sometimes there's more animal than human left by the process!*

The spider-woman also appeared to be a veteran of previous situations. Covered in machete scars, one of her six 'arms' missing, she laughed at Giertz, clicking her mandibles at him. Without asking himself if it was the 'done thing' or not, he released the blade on his machete and removed her multi-eyed, over-made up head. His first thought was, *Just like in one of my holygames! It's easy!*

Of course, she was by no means the first mutant Giertz had dispatched, but he noticed it felt uncomfortably strange again, in much the same way killing the human fly had this morning. As he looked around him, overall he felt an unusual mixture of fascination and revulsion, *This is just like watching some grotesque carnival destroy itself!*

**Chapter 67 Sinister Function**

Giertz could see now, *This Situation is going to end up in an episode of Real Life, because The Bad Actor himself is gracing us with his presence.* On a rooftop nearby was, at least superficially, the same tall, gray-haired man who introduced the show with Pandora. Giertz also noted a substantial presence of Non-men at this Situation, a line of them standing close behind The Bad Actor, and lurking in the dimmest alleyways to the left and right, as they always did. Everyone knew they were Dr. Zed's secret police force, barely visible in their long, black coats and wide-brimmed hats, *Yet no one is certain what they specifically do, or how they do it, so even people on their own, corporate side fear them.* No one knew either how The Bad Actor controlled them, and some guessed it might even be some form of telepathy. *Or perhaps they control him...?*

At The Situations, The Bad Actor always bellowed at people through a bull-horn, even if they were standing directly beside him. Today, this particular Bad Actor was also something of an acrobat. He performed his feats on top of telegraph poles above the rioters, as he shouted at them from behind the safety of a transparent, bulletproof screen. This accompanied him everywhere, but was never shown on the holyvision.

He used the megaphone to lead a chant of, 'KILL! KILL! KILL!' Or Consumeordie's motto, taken from Dr. Zed's famous theory, 'EMPIRE AND GENIUS! EMPIRE AND GENIUS! He would punctuate this by laughing contemptuously at the rioters below, on both sides. He would also quote Dr. Zed's latest speeches at them, such as, 'Mankind's only redemption lies in increased production!' Or just, 'Consumeordie sales topped Greedeluxe's by three point two percent this year, Ha Ha HA!'

Meanwhile, the Consumeordie factions were throwing back a chant of tenets from The Idea,
'Their world shall end,
They shall be destroyed,
Their great engine shall rot,
It is foretold!
'Metal shall melt,
Stone will crumble,
Their wombs shall bear monsters,
It is foretold...!'

The sight of The Bad Actor today was more than Giertz could take. His initial fear had by now been converted into fanatical rage. He even felt as if he could take on the entire monster single-handedly, and for a moment he very nearly tried to. Afterward, he had a vague recollection of being entirely engulfed by the monster, but everything else was blank.


**Chapter 68 Splinter Faction**
When Giertz's senses swam back into consciousness, he was lying on the side of the road, surrounded by the dead and concussed. Even some of the merely stunned were

crawling on all fours, still begging for mercy, despite no longer being under attack. It was beginning to rain, which should have cleaned it all, but instead made it dirtier, somehow.

Giertz looked around at the dead, and clouds of flies had already moved in, crawling over their expressionless faces. He guessed, *I must have put them in that state,* but he couldn't locate what specific feeling he'd originally held against them, now experiencing no animosity towards their corpses at all. He also noted many of them were dressed as clowns, their bloody cadavers had painted-on smiles, orange wigs, and bright, baggy clothes, but even in death they still clutched their assault rifles. He guessed, *They must represent some bizarre, ironic splinter-faction or other,* but Giertz didn't bother to try to work out what convoluted, ideological statement they'd been trying to make.

Now Giertz understood why he'd never really been trained in any martial arts by the Combat Youth, *Such disciplines have no bearing in a sub-human, animalistic frenzy such as this. There's no 'art' here, only 'survival of the fittest,' at its most primal level.* Then gradually the realization came to him, *I've gone into my `Optimum Destructive State' the first time out!* Rather than bringing any sense of achievement however, it felt strangely unpleasant. It was as if he'd taken a step away from, rather than toward his ambition to destroy reality.

He finally had to admit though that despite his survival, he felt the opposite of what satisfaction he'd expected. He examined himself methodically to find, apart from superficial injuries, he only had one large gash in his left forearm. *Lucky it didn't hit an artery!* Somehow the thought didn't cheer him though. *Then again, maybe I would be luckier if it had? Oh well, one evening in the Rapid Healing Clinic will fix my physical injuries, at least.*

His revulsion at the whole experience even made him feel ill however, and eventually he vomited into the gutter. The synthetic breakfast left willingly enough, but he couldn't so readily cleanse whatever was paining him deep inside, questioning the whole scenario.

So it stayed within him, and grew.

**Chapter 69 Interesting Case**

Giertz spent the first of many nights in the Rapid Healing annex of the Asclepius Clinic, which occupied two floors of the Greedeluxe Youth skyscraper, 'For physical and mental testing.' In contrast to the rest of the building, the clinic was so decontaminated it resembled one enormous operating theater. It was filled with softly bleeping, state-of-the-art equipment and efficient, blonde nurses with large breasts in crisp white uniforms. They all had identical faces and spoke minimal English with commanding, foreign accents.

As he lay in the sterile bed, he contemplated his situation. He'd learned long ago the clinic was an experimental research center, run by the corporation, *The Greedeluxe Youth provides a steady stream of interesting cases, I suppose.* This was where his suspicions began though, *So I'm still just an 'interesting case,' even here.* Therefore he felt the same isolation he had in Happylands.

As the summer unfurled, there were plenty more Situations, and stays in the clinic, following in very rapid-fire succession. In fact, as his 'career' progressed, in all his time as a Combat Youth he would never be able to shake off the feeling of, I'm just a guinea pig. Not even when once in a situation he'd had his lower leg nearly severed by a machete. Kadski had driven him urgently to the clinic, but by the end of the week there was hardly a scratch to show for it, and Giertz had required minimal rehabilitation. One day an indifferent nurse held a mirror up to Giertz's desolate face. *They've even reduced most of the scarification left by my sword-fight with The Bad Actor!*

Giertz eventually lost count of how many times the yellow and black cars roared out of the skyscraper. The Combat Youths' eyes were always blazing with the blue heat of idealism, but while he was initially optimistic about Ceebix's promise, that Giertz would 'enjoy' the experience, Giertz soon felt locked into a process of disillusionment. Each event that confronted him only seemed to take him successively further away from his most fundamental goal, *The total destruction of reality, but rather than destroying it, I'm just becoming part of it!* Also, even further from himself. Finally, The Situations all blurred together, the whole summer seeming to be one, prolonged battle, the feeling of nausea from his first situation only getting still worse.

Even after the second or third Situation, Giertz couldn't ignore anymore being reviled by the ugliness of what he was seeing and doing. Therefore, despite Ceebix's promise, Giertz found he didn't actually 'enjoy' The Game much, at first. Even when 'righteously' slaughtering the mutants, the same mixed feelings Giertz had when he'd killed the human fly on that first morning persisted, to the point where the merest sight of discolored mutant blood now made Giertz queasy. Something else overrode it all though - knowing it just had to be done. *It's the will of Xerak, after all.*

What made it worse, however, was his knowing, *I've lost count of the number of people, or even mutants, I've killed!* The 'kill counter' on his gun had already gone around the clock. *I don't know how many times I've gone into my ODS either, and somehow it doesn't matter to me at all.* A part of him still felt it should though, and so he began to develop a secret theory, *Perhaps all the rottenness and evil is emanating from somewhere inside my head? Maybe if I were not here, Dr. Zed, The Situations, Non-men and everything else would just disappear?* This idea started to dominate Giertz's thinking.

He believed that, *Somehow, perhaps in some other dimension, I was personally responsible for some great sin humanity committed? Maybe I am carrying it with me now, being made to suffer the results. If I could atone for it, or even just think the right thoughts, it might all go away? This is another reason why I must destroy reality!* He knew really though, this was just an excuse.

Giertz also began to see he wasn't the only one with a negative perception. One day as they were patrolling, Kadski said quietly, yet bitterly, 'By Xerak I hate this city!' To Giertz it was as if Kadski had spoken for both of them. As they surveyed the Hellscape of rusted machinery, Giertz just nodded, which was all he needed to communicate, but he added anyway, 'You always feel the city could run perfectly well, and probably better, without any people in it; especially yourself.' He could even visualize the metropolis one day with nobody in it at all, entirely barren and lifeless. *All The Consumers will be gone forever, nothing moving on the sidewalks except for the wind blowing the dust, but somehow the city itself will still be whirring away efficiently beneath it all, as if nothing has changed.*

Every day Giertz drove under a summer sky the color of sheet metal, pregnant with snow-clouds, through expanses of abandoned industrial capital: bricks and concrete cracked by weeds. *I'm lost inside this city, despite living here since my birth. The deeper I go into it, the more I feel I'm in some maze, with no exit.* As the massive, smoking towers of rusty machinery drifted past, he considered, *Nobody even knows what they're for anymore, only something to do with running the city.* In fact, Giertz wondered, *What exactly is keeping this city going, and why?* The question made him optimistic however, *This city is dying, and always has been, and that's because the entire world is dying, and no-one cares anymore. Perhaps reality in general hasn't got much longer to go after all, and someone has to just to give it one, final nudge?*

The more he drove around though, the more monotonous waiting for The End began to feel. He noticed he was now spending almost every day in the bullet-resistant cockpit full of weapons, equipment, and ejector-seat warning notices, only getting out for the situations. Giertz never got used to Kadski's long bouts of non-conversation either. Consequently, Giertz began to feel the cold, hollow, feeling, as if he contained a vacuum, even more intensely. Ceebix's fanatical droning on the radio, calling them to the next Situation, alternating with the screeching, trash-pop songs, somehow compounded it all.

This miasma however, was only the beginning of Giertz's spiritual transformation.

## Chapter 70 Holy Ravings

Even after some time, Giertz still couldn't see any immediate benefits at all in joining the Combat Youth, but then he began to notice, *It has caused some shift in my general focus on the world.* He felt it most at night, as he drove Kadski through the empty neon streets. Both of them wore dark glasses, mainly for effect, the big engine growling behind them as the hard, commercial, neon colors shone in the car's yellow and black finish. Amongst it all were yet more of the gaudy banners, posters, and flags heartily proclaiming The Festival of Greed.

Unwillingly even Giertz had to admit, *The Festival of Greed is already gathering momentum. This year will probably be bigger than The War Celebrations, National Conformity Week, or even The Summer of Hate; all put together!* The ever-emptier faces of the Consumers also drifted past however, ingrained with greed and hopeless bitterness, overlaid with symptoms of addiction to alcohol, non-cancer-free tobacco, and Preparation X315/J. *It's almost as if The Producers are using the festival to hide something? After all, The Consumers have never looked unhappier.*

Therefore, mainly as an act of revenge, on his few days off Giertz took to striding through the Consumerplexs of multiple superoutlets. The robot security cameras, with their built-in sniper rifles ready to pick off shoplifters, tracked him suspiciously as he loudly derided The Consumers, while they clawed at and trampled each other to death for the discounted merchandise. From his studies of Xeracism, he would quote at the frenzied customer-mob the holy-ravings of Zytopharbb, which he'd memorized, 'You are *excrement*!
Your pathetic philosophies and putrid ambitions will not protect you!
Worshiping your less-than worthless tokens!
Groveling before your idols of paper!
Jumping into holes and scraping dirt over yourselves!
Sniveling back to your mother's breast!
Diving into stagnating filth to drown!
Rather than be purged clean,
In the holy incinerator of The Idea!
For I say unto you,
Man is conceived in lust and dies in agony!
And the very Gods shall tremble as the mountains crack,
As the heavens are rent!
The losers to be turned out to wander the face of the earth,
Alone and naked,
Driven from city walls with stones and derision!
So woe be to them that give suck in these days!'
  Zyt' 15-8.

The bruised and bloodied Consumers, their fashionable garments in tatters from the strife, just looked at him as if he was crazy - which he was, before returning to their violent 'bargain hunting.' From his point of view though, their mindless faces just hung in front of him, no more than a gallery of meaningless expressions. So as a parting shot, Giertz would assure them, 'The will of Xerak flows through my veins!'

Gangs of unemployed policemen hung around on street corners smoking cigarette stubs, still affecting their worn, tatty uniforms, while eying Giertz hungrily. He knew they were just itching to arrest him, in defiance of their own obsolescence, to beat a confession out of him, or anyone, *'Like the old days,' but they have no power anymore, he* reassured himself, *their jobs handed over to the corporate insurance companies.* Strangely though, like most people, Giertz still felt slightly nostalgic for when those uniforms had meant something.

In fact Giertz also began to see the world and other people in general as if the light had finally been switched on, noticing everyone had strangely-shaped faces, *Now there is hardly anybody without any deformity or major imperfection, not-quite concealed with cosmetics. Perhaps it was inbreeding as the wars and disasters depleted the gene pool? Or maybe it was some radioactive contamination that was hushed up? Either way, everyone looks unhealthy, as if there's some layer of gray just beneath their skins. The Combat Youth themselves are no exception, myself included.*

Despite all this though, after a few more Situations, something strange began to happen to him.


**Chapter 71 Self-Destruct**
Over the weeks, in a detached sort of way, Giertz found himself getting used to it all. Then, and there was no mistaking the feeling, he finally saw what Ceebix had

meant by, 'You will enjoy The Game...' Giertz discovered he was enjoying it, *Now I understand why the Combat Youth hardly ever leave, continuing until they are finally killed. It's an experience that just can't be categorized!*

Gradually Giertz came to believe he only felt truly alive when he was fighting back to back with Kadski, surrounded by hordes of the worst mutants. Paradoxically however, Ceebix's fulfilled promise of enjoyment only made Giertz question his predicament more, *But what have The Combat Youth turned me into?* He still suspected he'd only taken another step backward, distracted from his true destiny.

Giertz had always been told he was insane, to the point where he now accepted it without question, but the perception he'd first had of Ceebix's enigmatic smile became stronger still. As the chaotic summer continued, Giertz always saw the grinning image superimposed over it all, to the point where he was finally feeling, *The universe has now almost entirely twisted itself around to comply with my, Jimmy Giertz's, view of it, instead of demanding I do the opposite!* Now, after allowing himself to be reassured by Ceebix's promise, Giertz felt as close to 'at home' as he ever had, but he was still always disturbed by, *How strangely similar Ceebix's smile is to the selfish smirk that symbolizes The Festival of Greed?*

It all reached a climax when approaching a situation one night; an image Giertz had never expected to see flashed in front of him. His entire soul leapt as he saw a red nineteen fifty-nine Cadillac nearing the junction before him. *That color is reserved for only one person in the Consumeordie food chain!* He recognized that, centered in the crosshairs engraved on his car's windshield, was The Bad Actor. Giertz instantly estimated the distance, Two hundred meters.

He didn't need to consult Kadski, as he knew by now the two of them would be thinking the same thing. Giertz jumped on the accelerator and the machine, as if reflecting his joy, sprinted willingly towards its destruction. A second later Kadski suddenly became aware of what was happening.

*One hundred meters.* Giertz fumbled the necessary code onto the keypad of the car's self-destruct. This was wired to a TNT explosive charge buried somewhere in the nose, under the spare wheel. Kadski exclaimed something Giertz didn't hear.

*Fifty meters.* Giertz let go of the steering wheel and reached between his legs for the two orange and black handles under the ejector seat.

*Twenty-five meters.* The explosive bolts in the roof panel detonated. It flew away, filling the narrow cockpit with a seeming hurricane.

*Ten meters.* Giertz just glimpsed The Bad Actor's face through the glass, and for a moment their eyes locked. Giertz saw the same confused expression he'd seen at Uncle Joe's party now turning to terror, but this time The Bad Actor didn't have time to disguise it, or cheat.

*Five meters.* The nitroglycerin charge in the seat kicked the base of Giertz's spine hard, out of the car. For a moment all he experienced was sudden near-silence, except for the wind rushing in his ears, the car's engine growing distant, the pain of exacerbated elevator compression in his spine and stomach, and the horizon slowly spinning in front of him. He was aware of Kadski off to his left, both of them floating somewhere in space. There was a moment of blissful weightlessness, just before the seat began to fall again. For a moment, the freezing summer, the situations, the Combat Youth and everything else, seemed to almost make sense to Giertz. In one way, he almost felt reborn.

Beneath him, Giertz was aware of the yellow and black David impacting the side of the black Goliath, which folded it in two. Locked together they went into a kind of waltz, minor parts flying off them. Giertz knew the impact alone would have been enough to eliminate The Bad Actor, but then Giertz's car's warhead obliterated the scene in a flash of white light, which stung his retinas. Helpless as he hung in the air, he saw chunks of the wrecks come tumbling up towards him, out of the flames.

Then however the rocket motor in the seat took over, throwing him even more painfully higher, and the burning parts fell harmlessly away, just before the seat's explosive parachute opened.

As he and Kadski unstrapped themselves on the ground, twenty meters apart, they said nothing. When Giertz looked over at the two immolated wrecks, he had only one thought, *I've just killed The Bad Actor!* It even took his mind off the bruises on his body, from where it had rolled on the pavement. Giertz also noted however, that within the 'enjoyment' really there was an empty feeling. The 'righteous wrath of Xerak' was not as satisfying as Giertz had been lead to expect, and so was another disappointment.

There was also a strange twist to the expression on Kadski's face, which Giertz only saw for a second. He tried to dismiss it as shock, or Kadski's confusion after the ejection, but Giertz couldn't eliminate the thought, *There's now a trace of jealousy in Kadski's silence!*

The overall experience though helped push it, and the other growing doubts out of Giertz's mind - temporarily. However, Kadski's expression was an omen of worse realizations to come.

## Chapter 72 Frozen Contempt

Trying to fill the persistent hollow feeling, on the few days when Giertz wasn't patrolling, he continued with his 'advanced training.' This was really just more torturing himself to zeniths of agony in the Greedeluxe building, or blasting line after line of targets in the shape of Dr. Zed's head in the shooting gallery, *I am not practicing my aim, so much as expressing it!* He found, as he impassively watched them disintegrate in clouds of cardboard fragments.

His scores on the machines were still improving to the point where the other Combat Youths, and Ceebix, were now very shocked indeed. Also, Giertz often almost reduced his fists to bloody pulps on the punch-bag with the image of The Bad Actor's smiling face printed on it, but still with no sense of catharsis. In fact, Giertz was becoming more disturbed, *This is only symptomatic of the 'something' The Combat Youth awakened in me, which is now definitely out of my control, but was it ever entirely within it?*

He soon also discovered that any attempt to question the Combat Youth's point of view was immediately washed away in a tidal wave of Xeracist econo-theological texts,     'With-the-help-of-Xerak-to-be-able-to-describe-a-return-in-the-realm-of-infinity-of-consciousness-determines-the-aggregates!' They would cry, 'Cartels-determine-the-existence-of-The-Blessed-One!

Zyt' 18-3.

This was all chanted in a kind of four/four rhythm until it became progressively more unintelligible. In the end, it was reduced to the same meaningless, aggressive whine he'd heard in his first situation.

Giertz also found attempts to probe beyond this were highly dangerous, *I can see they are addicted to this brand of fanaticism, like any other drug! Their violent acts are just symptoms of withdrawal, when they feel anyone is challenging their beliefs. So why don't I feel it also?*

In spite of Giertz's relative lack of faith however, he still found the Combat Youth were having a definite effect on his personality. He began to walk through life wearing his own body like a suit of armor, as if he was surrounded by an invisible iron pillbox, staring at the world through its slit-window. People would speak to him occasionally, but he would stare straight through them as they jumped out of his way, to avoid a collision.

The only other people he felt a need to communicate with were the Combat Youths. When conversing with them, his face was almost as completely expressionless as theirs. He even began to develop a seething contempt for anyone who wasn't a Combat Youth, almost as much as he hated the Combat Youth themselves.

In addition, he became used to an almost constant state of 'The Terror.' It gave him a perverse kind of exhilaration to discover, *I'm running on the thin, arbitrary border between life and death!* Somehow he was excited by the feeling that his fate was in the hands of an unseen, third party.

Also, strangest of all, he felt an unexpected respect growing in himself, not just for Kadski, so much as Kadski's point of view.

**Chapter 73 Serious Mistake**

Kadski's philosophy could be summed up in one of the unprompted remarks he would make at arbitrary intervals in the car's cockpit, 'If you love people enough they'll nail you to a cross...'

Giertz was awed, *Unlike most philosophies, which were developed to console suffering, or give life some direction, Kadski's is there solely to justify his impulses, and inspire him to greater fanaticism! He sees human life as entirely valueless, but he has an absolute belief in the Combat Youth. It's like an irony he was born with, beyond any question of mere purpose!*

From time to time, also without warning, Kadski would reveal other facets of his philosophy to Giertz. They were driving as usual past the meaningless, neon-washed, lines of shops, all selling the same things, when Kadski expostulated, 'Human beings think they are the most intelligent animals on the planet, but they are only the most self-deluding. Many species of rodents, insects, and bacteria will be around long after the last human.' Giertz had just nodded again, entirely in agreement.

Another time Kadski said, 'Some people admire insects, Ceebix for example, his "ant-hill society" etc., but I don't. The insects probably *think* they're happy, but only human beings have the capacity to know how bad things really are.'

On yet another occasion Kadski expanded, 'Human beings are only herd animals. They will follow whichever one of them bleats loudest, no matter what he's actually saying.' He waved his arm in a nonchalant gesture. 'Individuality is a myth...'

For the first time, Giertz began to feel admiration for somebody besides Nailbrand and Zytopharbb, and then it became more than that, building into something even greater still - and stranger.

As he drove, Giertz came to understand that, *Kadski sees mankind as existing solely to destroy itself! Therefore, Kadski believes everything he does is just a contribution to the process.* This idea excited Giertz very much, but he still wondered how Kadski lived with his own nihilism. *It's as if the Combat Youth is the only thing keeping him alive!*

Giertz also noted with some surprise, *Women throw themselves at Kadski's feet, despite his face's ravaged appearance.* Giertz accurately visualized Kadski only using them with a kind of frozen contempt, and soon Giertz would have a graphic demonstration of it.

He still didn't fully understand his personal feelings about Kadski when he also began to wonder, *What does Kadski feel about me?* In the early stages, as they charged into The Situations together, Kadski had sometimes endangered his life to shield Giertz's. Once, when the thin, high-carbon steel on Giertz's switch-blade machete had shattered, as they sometimes did, Kadski even threw him his own to use. Giertz had noted, *This is not standard practice for the Combat Youth!* In fact, as a new Combat Youth's life expectancy was measured in minutes, Giertz wondered, *Even with my advanced reflexes, how long would I have lasted without Kadski's help?*

Soon Giertz had also come to understand, *Kadski is just not interested in other people at all.* There was usually an embarrassing moment when Kadski met someone for the first time. He would only stand staring through them, his hands merely hanging at his sides. Therefore the next surprise came when Kadski invited Giertz to meet his friend, who also turned out to be his only friend. Giertz was overjoyed to discover Kadski already knew Nailbrand, the incredibly tall motorcyclist with a face like a wolf.

Nailbrand was slightly older than Giertz, and everything Nailbrand said or didn't say seemed to speak directly to something inside Giertz, who daydreamed, *He always seems so free on his motorcycle.* Giertz had to face it though, *I've never fully communicated with anyone in this world, as if I'm speaking a separate language. So if there's anyone who could understand me at all, surely it has to be Nailbrand?* However, while they had known each other well enough for Giertz to 'introduce' him to his girlfriend some time back, like having a cake but not quite eating it, somehow the interchange Giertz was so desperate for had never happened.

Therefore, when Giertz, Kadski and Nailbrand met in the rapid healing clinic, it was an 'occasion' for Giertz, but there was hardly even time however to hear Nailbrand announce enthusiastically from his bed, 'I've almost recovered, and I'm ready for a Situation!'

As he was being wheeled away by three identical nurses for yet another brain operation, he grinned secretively, showing his backward-curving incisors to Giertz. *The word 'recovered' seems to hold a special meaning for him.* Giertz decided to just not mention the entries in his girlfriend's diary. *They don't seem relevant to anything anyway,* but he could never have believed that he'd just missed his last chance to converse with the closest he'd ever had to a friend.

This mutual acquaintance seemed to finally dissolve all the remaining caution between himself and Kadski however, or at least as much as it ever could be with one so taciturn. Kadski appeared to believe anyone acquainted with someone like Nailbrand couldn't be all bad, even Giertz.

Unfortunately, the resulting false sense of emotional security led Giertz to make the next serious mistake, when he 'introduced' Kadski to his girlfriend.

**Chapter 74 Pessimistic Frown**

Giertz's rendezvous with Kadski was during their 'special day off,' granted in reverence to The Greedeluxe Youth rally, the Corporation's answer to Consumeordie's Festival of Greed. Like everyone else, the two Combat Youths were unable to afford tickets, and so they consoled themselves by arranging to watch it together at Giertz's girlfriend's tasteless apartment. After a cold shower, Giertz frustratedly sat watching Real Life all morning, waiting for the rally to begin, and Kadski to arrive.

Then Giertz noticed his girlfriend's diary once more. To distract himself he turned to the most recent entries, 'Most of the time Jimmy is so apathetic he can't make lust to me. Instead of getting more worked up, he just gets less and less. He usually wanders away and starts listening to his Psycho Kiss recordings, or just drives off. He doesn't get embarrassed about it or blame me, so I suppose that's a good thing. Perhaps you've got to be optimistic to do it, but he hasn't even flagellated me recently. Jimmy seems to drift in and out of my life, sometimes for years at a time...'

Giertz was forced to acknowledge, *Lust-making just doesn't mean much in itself to me, intellectually at least.* He was past being concerned, but he did still wonder, *Why does it mean so much to other people?* All Giertz knew was, *The only idea that positively excites me is destroying reality.* As the diary confirmed, his girlfriend didn't seem to mind his attitude or lack of it, but then she hadn't appeared to mind anything he did or didn't do - until recently.

In fact, she was usually so apathetic Giertz could visualize, *Some thread, barely as strong as a cobweb, is all that is anchoring her to reality. One day it will probably snap, and she will withdraw, entirely lost in a pastel-shaded world of her own creation, to become some form of vegetable.* Partly to break her out of her apathy, he would do terrible things to her, but the most she would ever do was flail hopelessly at his chest. *Even during lust-making, I can tell her mind is elsewhere, if anywhere.*

He often analyzed her angrily, *It's as if she makes only token gestures at everything life demands of her. Sometimes she will even go for days without eating! The only things she ever does with any enthusiasm are to write her diary - mostly about my exploits - or sit staring at the four walls of this apartment, with a pessimistic frown.*

It was even mostly a toss-up for Giertz whether he preferred driving his fake Lamborghini or making his brand of lust to her. Sometimes he even questioned why he stayed around her at all. Whenever he really thought about it, he decided, *It's just something about the way she slouches her head forward, looking at me through that fringe of her artificially mousy hair.* Even then it was mainly because she reminded him vaguely of somebody else, but he couldn't make the connection, as if it was too ridiculous.

In time though, he would be surprised to find it was only too plausible.

## Chapter 75 Emotional Cage

Giertz felt it was fortuitous he'd read her diary today. For a long time, an idea had been growing in the back of his mind, until it had now reached the front: a general feeling of dissatisfaction with their relationship, such as it was. *There must be more there that I just can't reach?* He felt constricted, *It's as if our emotions are in some bottleneck. At least now I know she feels the same way I do, I suppose.* In one sense he knew they'd gone as far as they could, but in another, he couldn't help feeling with some degree of guilt, *Perhaps there is some contribution to the 'relationship' I'm not making?* Yet nobody had ever told him what it should be.

In fact, being honest with himself, he hadn't really thought about their relationship at all; hadn't even viewed of it as 'a relationship.' Mostly he just liked the idea of keeping her in a part of his mind where he didn't have to think about her. He just enjoyed flagellating her, more than anything.

Being even more truthful with himself however, he knew, *I like to think of her as being inside some emotional cage. Making lust is devalued now anyway. Temporary sterilization and immunization against nearly all the major diseases have made it infinitely available, and infinitely worthless.* There was only one doubt about this for Giertz though, *But then there's always the dreaded 265/76G-F Virus.* It was virtually undetectable, incubated for at least twenty years, and there was no cure. The symptoms were the victim's body would almost literally turn itself inside-out in a slow process over several months, before death.

Giertz was reassured however by knowing even this wasn't enough to deter most people, who made lust at random all over the place, in spite of the risks. *Or perhaps because of them?* There were expensive drugs to suppress some of the symptoms, and prolong life for a few more years, so spreading the disease further. *Strange how these appeared on the market shortly before the first cases of the actual contagion?*

However, It doubly reassured him to know, *Generally, nobody knows what they should feel anymore, or even how to feel it - because people's emotions are so stifled by holyvision and reality-in-general. It's all become pointless, but it's true I haven't even flagellated her for weeks.*

When she'd finished whatever it was she was doing and came back into the room to see Giertz reading her diary, she didn't seem bothered. In the end, Giertz didn't care either what she thought. He dropped it back onto the table, as he would any other ornament.

She joined him on the large couch in front of the holyvision as always. Events took the usual course, but for the first time he sensed something was definitely not right, *There's a kind of resistance here! Perhaps it's only because I read her diary that I'm now seeing us in a different light?* It also occurred to him, *Maybe she left it there on purpose?*

Then Giertz found they were being watched.

**Chapter 76 Congenital Sneer**
Leaning in the doorway was the silhouette of Kadski's lank frame. He was dressed entirely in black: a thin

turtleneck sweater and narrow, black, Synth-O-Leather jeans tucked into polished, black jack-boots, surveying the room through dark glasses. In spite of the deep pockmarks and bulging eyes, Kadski's face still looked handsome, in an unconventional way. *Handsome and brutal,* Giertz thought. *Brutally handsome.* Expecting him earlier, Giertz had assumed he wasn't coming, but now he felt slightly disconcerted.

As always with Kadski, there were no greetings. Nothing was said at all, and when he came closer, Giertz noticed his face was almost completely devoid of expression and emotion, as usual. There was only the hint of its permanent, congenital sneer. Even so, Giertz sensed, *Kadski understands everything about the scenario before him, just from what he can now see.* Through his sunglasses he looked down his nose into Giertz's girlfriend's eyes. Despite never having met Kadski before, staring up at him, she gently began undoing his clothes.

Meanwhile on the holyvision, a half-naked youth ran effortlessly into the gigantic stadium, built especially for The Rally. It had stylized nude statues of male and female giants standing at regular intervals around the perimeter, their perfect anatomies contorted into agonizing postures, as if begging the heavens for mercy.

The youth, at least two-and-a-half meters tall with white-blonde hair and eyes glowing blue with fervor, ran to a monotonous rhythm beaten on a single, giant kettledrum. He bore a metal torch as tall as himself, impossibly glowing almost red hot in his hand. He ran a lap of the stadium to an earthquake of shouting and applause.

He eventually ascended the stepped pyramid in the center, but this event was eclipsed by the entry into the arena of forty male-virgin geniuses, bearing the body of The Prophet Zytopharbb, who had slaughtered himself in ritual Xeracist suicide. When Giertz looked closely, he could see the message of his predictions branded in hieroglyphs on the body, but when Giertz remembered the figure he'd encountered in the Happylands asylum, he felt puzzled, *He didn't seem the suicidal type.* While Giertz assumed it must have been some sacrifice for 'The Greater Cause,' he still felt a sense of dismay.

As if to symbolize the positive nature of Zytopharbb's final gesture, flocks of small girls skipped alongside the pallbearers. Dressed in white smocks, with white garlands circling their blonde, braided heads, they sprinkled the corpse with showers of pure, white petals.

At the same time a Xeracist high priest chanted the sacred names of the prophets of Judazz, as more priests were carried in shoulder high on litters in various states of holy, mystic trance. At the same time a youth, (no, a child!) waved a shimmering flag, three times his size, emblazoned with the new logo of Greedeluxe Corporation - two crossed strokes of black lightning.

The crowd's ecstasy then appeared to become howls of mass orgasm as the running youth finally reached the summit of the pyramid, to salute the heavens with the torch. He touched it to a large, shallow bowl, which immediately leaped into a tower of fire. Then the crowd's reaction went beyond whatever it was, as the geniuses also ascended the pyramid, and cast Zytopharbb's carcass into the flames.

This was followed by a display of agonizing calisthenics performed by armies of youths dressed in only white shorts and vests. To Giertz, *This seems more like an exercise in mass self-torture!*

As the festivities accumulated momentum on the screen though, Giertz and Kadski performed their own kind of celebration, exploring almost every possibility with the willing enough girl. Giertz knew it had been an unspoken, 'gentleman's agreement' that this would happen, and it was nothing new for him. *I've already done the same to her with Nailbrand after all, and everybody does this kind of thing all the time now anyway.*

Giertz was even used to this three-way lust-making almost to the point of boredom, but this time he still felt a conflict within himself throughout the whole exercise. Something new in him made him think, *Maybe this really is perverse?*

**Chapter 77 Mutual Intimacy**

Bathed in the radiation of the holyvision, enveloped by the colorful, three-dimensional images washing over them, and overwhelmed by the spectacle on the screen, the naked, sweating trio writhed around somewhere between the floor and the couch. Giertz was by now awe-struck, *What we are doing seems perfectly in tune with what's taking place on the screen!* For him, it was as if the emotions in the rally and their bodies had fused.

With a kind of grunting, teeth-gritted desperation, Kadski grappled the girl's skinny frame over the cheap coffee table. The colored patterns of the holyvision surged over her exposed, insignificant bust as if reflecting the emotions within it. To Giertz it looked more as if, *Kadski is trying to prove something to the world, and himself!* However, Giertz wasn't quite sure what it was.

From Giertz's point of view, the background noise of cheers and insane howls from the crowd almost appeared to be meant for Kadski alone, *As if they are encouraging him in some Herculean feat!* Giertz couldn't have blamed the audience either, even if it had been true. He knew by now he admired Kadski almost more than any person in the universe, on a par even with Nailbrand, and Zytopharbb, *Kadski does it all perfectly. Everything about him is so perfect, he's the Combat Youth's Combat Youth. When he kills in a*

*Situation, it's more like some art-statement. Even his imperfections seem necessary! When he dies, no doubt it will be a beautiful death.*

Giertz marveled further, *Kadski's face stays almost blank behind his dark glasses, most of the time, even during this exercise!* Giertz carefully watched the way the multicolored light played across the pockmarks on it. Scars from the rapid healing clinic never disappeared one hundred percent either. *Almost* invisible, they were there for anyone who knew where, and how, to look. This close, Giertz felt he was being allowed into some of Kadski's secrets, witnessing that his body had so many injuries, *Even one machete wound that runs diagonally right through his face!*

Despite their mutual intimacy with this girl though, Giertz knew, *There's still a barrier between myself and Kadski.* When, while exploring her phlesh, his hand accidentally brushed Kadski's black-gloved one, Giertz's fingers automatically winced, snatching themselves away - but Kadski's didn't.

Through the girl, Giertz started to sense there was something in Kadski that was trying to reach him. *Does Kadski see her as nothing more than an emotional conduit, running between him and myself?* Suddenly Giertz had a giddy sensation, as he felt his feelings somehow over-balancing into some region out of his control, as if the three of them were now blending into some single organism, bonded by one emotion.

His thoughts were broken up though by the holyvision, as the speeches began. Eight muscular, eunuch bearers carried some official shoulder-high up to the rostrum on a gilded litter. The figure was just introduced as a member of 'The Council of Ninety,' which was enough to bring an instant hush to the proceedings.

He didn't stand up, but remained seated. Behind the bank of microphones, he wore the standard gray suit of a Producer, except he also wore a black, real leather cowl zipped around his whole head, with just holes for his eyes and mouth. From the unzipped mouth hole came, 'LET THE WORD GO OUT TO ALL UNCIRCUMCISED FORNICATORS! WE ARE FIGHTING A HOLY WAR!' He then launched into a flood of condemnations, accusations and open threats against Dr. Zed, taunting him personally, and even calling him a 'liability' several times. Giertz thought there might be something familiar about the speaker's voice. He was unable to quite place it, but later he would be astonished to find out who it belonged to.

As the masses surged forward, desperate to kiss the speaker's jackboots, he was quickly surrounded by a contingent of Motorcycle Youths, high on Preparation X315/J. Giertz noted they were armed with the same guns that were supposed to have been issued exclusively to the Combat Youth, and guessed absently, *So we're probably just being used to test prototype weapons?*

There were graphic, slow-motion close-ups of the motorcyclists smashing the ergonomic butts of the guns into the crowd's faces, but this still didn't deter them. Giertz learned later some people were shot as well. Meanwhile, the speaker continued as if this all wasn't happening, just beneath his feet.

## Chapter 78 Leather Cowls

As the various speakers in their identical gray suits and leather cowls came up to the microphones to blast the crowd with statistics and ideology, Giertz gradually realized he'd no precedents for what he was now feeling. *At once I feel degraded and exulted! This is something I've needed all my life, like air, but without knowing of its absence until now!* It was obviously nothing new to Kadski though.

Giertz wondered what emotional territory the three of them now occupied. *It's almost frightening!* He also speculated that Kadski had deliberately manipulated his emotions. *Ever since our first 'meeting', probably.* He also saw Kadski was now doing the same to the girl, despite having just met her. *Kadski has been in complete control the whole time, the same way he is with everything else.* Giertz also wondered how many other Combat Youths feelings Kadski had manipulated in this way.

Before the final speaker came onto the stage however, the camera panned to a figure wearing a suit composed of contrasting, conflicting colors. Bright green, red and purple clashed with each other until the whole effect grated nauseatingly on Giertz's senses. 'Oh No!' He exclaimed as he recognized who it was.

Gritig the clown was the one thing Giertz really didn't like about Greedeluxe Corporation. Originally one of 'The Three Bennys,' when the company first paid him to endorse their products, like most people back then, Giertz had found the rotund 'cheeky-chappie' reasonably amusing. Gradually though, the humor had become more bitter as he grew thin and drawn while gaining more personal jets, and more celebrity golf tournaments in his honor. In the end, there was no humor at all, just a virtual human skeleton squawking acidic comments at various people he didn't like.

Now a long, greasy fringe flopped over his face as he leered knowingly into the camera. Mincing about in front of the rostrum, he struck various theatrical postures to emphasize each statement the speaker was making about Consumeordie Corp., adding, 'We ask them for explanation! But they send us an actor! We ask them for plenty! But they send us only tokens! We ask them for truth! But they send us a fiction...' It was so embarrassing Giertz expected the audience to turn violent and pelt Gritig with fruit and garbage at any moment, but they never did. The polite canned laughter was always on cue, but the audience's collective facial expression showed Giertz they also found Gritig more disconcerting than anything else. *After all, you can never be sure of how much power and influence he now has.*

It was easy to visualize Gritig laughing at them all as their world, and lives slowly disintegrated. They also even had to face the possibility of Gritig being involved in engineering it all. *There are even rumors he's now on The Council of Ninety.*

Finally, despite his passion for the rally, Giertz was forced to admit he couldn't stomach Gritig any longer. Giertz averted his gaze and was somehow reassured to realize he could watch his girlfriend being made lust to by Kadski, and feel no jealousy whatsoever. Or so Giertz thought.

**Chapter 79 Thigh Length**
Giertz now noticed his girlfriend was responding to Kadski in a way she never had to himself, or even Nailbrand. Giertz also wondered further about what his feelings regarding Kadski had become, and what Kadski's were in his own case. He already knew by now, *My own and Kadski's feelings for 'my' girlfriend are just a kind of emotional glue, uniting myself and Kadski for some as-yet-unspecified purpose. Whatever our feelings are though, I know he can only express his through her.* Giertz felt reassured by this thought, but it somehow concerned him also.

Slowly, over the following weeks and situations, Giertz and his girlfriend came to recognize they were now locked together in 'something' with Kadski, and the world was on the outside. His girlfriend even went to some of the situations, substituting Kadski or Giertz when they were spending longer than usual in the Rapid Healing Clinic. It was then Giertz began to see other, previously unknown, sides to her.

Initially, he noticed changes in the way she dressed. First to go were the spectacles with perfectly circular lenses, replaced by bullet-resistant, dark glasses. Next, she began to wear thigh-length Synth-O-Leather boots with steel toe-caps, and a new selection of skin-tight, bullet-retardant, rubber-look dresses. Giertz knew well how she enjoyed dancing around her apartment to her pop-tunes, but it was a shock when he witnessed her whirling high kicks become practical, performing the most gymnastic of attacks on other rioters, with a malevolence which made even Giertz wince.

It was the changes under the surface however which irritated him, seeing something else behind them, *A sort of overall, cold contempt for the Consumers, and the whole human race!* Again this was mainly because it reminded him of somebody else, who he could still not associate with her - yet.

While Kadski showed little or no interest in her as an individual, Giertz came to believe, *Kadski has no real interest in women, so his only true passion must be for the Combat Youth.* Giertz was wrong though about both ideas.

Over-all, Giertz now felt at once free and yet captive inside the whatever-it-was between the three of them, a simultaneous claustrophobia and agoraphobia. *It's as if we have achieved some perfect three-way balance.* He couldn't believe it could be so pure, their sharing this triangle without competition, without jealousy, without hate, to pollute the mixture. *Or can we?*

The thought immediately jolted him, and the uncomfortable inkling persisted of the mistake they'd already made, *Where will this end?* Finally, however, he just shrugged to himself, *I suppose it's like an emotional roller-coaster ride, and we don't care where it's going, or what the consequences will be!* So they continued not to care - until it was too late.

In fact generally, as Giertz's relationship, or non-relationship, with the other Combat Youths developed, he began to realize that at no stage in his 'career' had there ever been a time when he felt confident in his decision to join them. *In spite of my study of Xeracism, and my commitment to my training, I can never quantify the particular decision I made. All I know about myself is still only that my reflexes are faster than other people's. I suppose it was just those and the will of Xerak which somehow led me to this point.*

He was also becoming cumulatively more frustrated, squeezing his hands into white fists, at the sight of all the wasted effort, and life, in the situations. He was beginning to see behind Ceebix's smile when he'd promised, 'You will enjoy the game.' Giertz's knowing, *I could leave it at any time, but am now too absorbed in it,* had only served to underline his general confusion with the life, *Ceebix hadn't lied after all. Yes, I am enjoying it, in the most perverse way. It's even probably the most 'enjoyable' experience I could ever have, but it's hollow. All the conflict is going nowhere. The youth, whether Greedeluxe or Consumeordie, is just killing itself, instead of reality.*

He also perceived something else, *The Situations always take place in some real estate of little value, worth more for its insurance anyway, like the rubber sex-aids factory. They never threaten the areas occupied by The Producers. So does that prove my point?*

This knowledge only added to what had been Giertz's overall doubts about his mission as a Combat Youth, and he wondered if it was beginning to show. Therefore it didn't surprise Giertz when Ceebix ordered him to be killed.

## Chapter 80 Uneasy Relationship

Giertz also began to understand that all the Combat Youths, in turn, had their own uneasy relationship with Ceebix. Although, as Giertz did, they all wanted to be liked by Ceebix, Giertz could see, *They don't like Ceebix, and at best only grudgingly respect him. This is merely because he's been known to shoot them from his wheelchair, for reasons that aren't always clear. After all, no one knows what his long-term plan is for the Combat Youth is, or how each of us fits into it.*

In this context, as Giertz drove out of the skyscraper under another frosty, summer-morning sun, he had a strange feeling some voice, very far away, was calling him. As always he slip-streamed onto the multi-level tangle of the mega-interchange, but didn't follow his assigned patrol route. Instead, he just continued in a straight line. Kadski stared across at him for a moment, but said nothing. He probably knew by now that while no one could persuade Giertz, he usually seemed to know what he was doing, although today he drove even more wildly than usual.

A satellite monitored all the Combat Youth's cars, so it was obvious straight away that Giertz had deserted his assigned route. As usual Ceebix's hypnotic drone was speaking from their radios directly into their collective subconscious, '...Judazz entered the first trance raising structure of capital! He entered the second trance raising simulated profits and reserves! He entered the third trance raising market capitalization...' Then there was an abrupt silence, indicating Ceebix was having one of his periodic 'visions,' when the voice of Xerak communicated to the Combat Youth directly through him.

Sometimes he would even start speaking in tongues, but today the message was only too clear, 'Eliminate operative

Giertz! The will of Xerak has spoken!' Ceebix then droned on for several minutes more, but with no real explanation for his directive, as always.

Giertz looked over at Kadski, but he said nothing. Giertz observed, *He seems to have developed a kind of trust in my judgment.* With surprise, Giertz also saw that, *Despite Kadski's unofficial position as the Combat Youth's combat youth, he probably doesn't care at all what Ceebix says, or thinks.* This was only as far as Giertz could read the expression on Kadski's face. Giertz still had no real idea what Kadski was thinking about most of the time, so silently. This was why Giertz would be shocked when he would eventually find out.

Within an hour, as they sped onto the Channel Bridge, with the gray sea undulating around them, the first attack came. A contingent of Motorcycle Youth on their modified, fake, cyclone-injected Harley Davidsons appeared to relish the 'righteous chance' to destroy a Combat Youth vehicle, and its occupants. At first, they just fell in behind Giertz and Kadski's speeding car, following it at a distance, weighing the possibilities.

Eerily, there was no other traffic on the twenty-lane bridge, or even any abandoned cars. Giertz hadn't ventured far out of the city recently, and was surprised at the still smoldering, gaping shell-holes in the road everywhere, *I knew things were getting bad on the outskirts, but not this bad.* Sometimes the gaps almost spanned the ten-lane carriageway altogether. Yet Giertz didn't even have time to consider that this could be an omen of what was to come on this journey.

In fact, the bridge-road was more like an elongated obstacle course. Giertz slalomed between the missing chunks of concrete and occasional broken slabs at high speed, tearing at the small, Synth-O-Leather steering wheel, licking his dry lips. *This isn't too difficult. It's just like one of my holygames. It's easy!* Meanwhile, Kadski lowered the rear window and casually shot two or three youths off their mounts. Trying to avoid being shot, one rider accidentally disappeared into a hole. As one by one they rolled into the gutters, their chrome-plated machines bouncing and sliding, the attack gradually broke off.

Giertz wasn't particularly interested in them though, or anything Ceebix might send after him. He didn't even consider turning back. He couldn't ignore the soundless voice inside his head now, because it was paradoxically much stronger than Ceebix's outside it. Giertz couldn't understand what this interior voice was saying, but for a long time his doubts about the Combat Youth had gelled into a question burning inside him, to the point where he believed, *This voice probably has the answer.* Therefore it was drawing him like a black-hole's event horizon, to which he had no resistance, and to an equally mysterious conclusion.

**Chapter 81 No Explanation**

Almost across the bridge now, Giertz knew the Motorcycle Youth had failed in their attempt on his life, *So Ceebix will probably send a helicopter, which will be the end.* Giertz knew Kadski knew it also, but just didn't want to show it. He said nothing as always.

The Combat Youth had begun experimenting with light helicopters recently. The previous week Giertz had witnessed the youths whooping as they made their usual ritual dance around three brand new ones. It had been a party, as they happily stripped the cardboard and plastic packing off the glinting Gatling cannons.

Now Giertz watched the machine flutter through the smoke, a distant metal mosquito hanging over the road. Steadily it gained on them in the crosshairs of the rear-view screen. It flew low, releasing a few rounds to gauge range. Giertz flipped between the collapsed pylons of a shattered section of the road bridge, but the helicopter gracefully swung between them also, on an identical path. 'The pilot is good,' Kadski observed fatalistically.

However, occasional fires from cars still burning on both sides of the road distracted the infrared guidance on its Gatling cannon. Meanwhile, Kadski released a few armor-piercing rounds at the helicopter, but both he and Giertz knew it could make no real difference.

Giertz knew far ahead of him was the deserted, concrete tollgate, and he thought he might hide there from the helicopter's infrared sights. He had the car's cyclone injectors turned on full, the throttle pedal against the bulkhead. He could even smell the hot engine's insulation beginning to smolder. Now the helicopter was the size of a large bumblebee and still growing. They could almost see its yellow and black coloring, but before him, Giertz could just make out the details of the bomb-damaged blockhouse, and some of the mathematical graffiti on it.

In the end, the helicopter was the size of an angry, metal moth when the first bullet bit through the car's rear wing. Giertz braced himself. In the rear-view screen, he could now make out the rivets on the helicopter's fuselage. He tried to prepare himself for the strings of depleted uranium bullets to tear the car, himself, and Kadski to shreds. He knew the pain couldn't hurt him much now, after the self-torture chamber, but something else in him couldn't accept the idea.

He'd already risked his life so many times, *But dying this way, and without achieving my destiny, is somehow unfaceable.* Also, the worst thing was the distant, Siren's voice calling him, growing louder as he came closer to it. He couldn't deal either with the disappointment of not hearing whatever answer it had to give only him.

Then he saw before him and entire section of the bridge was missing, between his car and the blockhouse. With his ability to see ahead he knew he had time to brake, but with the helicopter behind them, he also knew he only had one choice.  He kept his foot down, and there was a strange, weightless moment as the cars wheels span in space, and the engine revved freely.

Then the two Combat Youths bounced heavily in their seats and the engine growled as the car landed. Perhaps because of this, Giertz unexpectedly heard Ceebix's voice ordering the attack to cease, again with no explanation. *It's as if he, or more specifically the will of Xerak, has simply changed his mind.* Abruptly the helicopter slued off and disappeared. Nevertheless, as Giertz shrieked the car to a halt under the darkness of the empty toll bridge, he sat shaking in his seat, and Kadski seemed just as puzzled as Giertz that they weren't dead.

Through the cooling breeze of relief wafting over him from the air conditioning, Giertz found himself wondering at the intricacy of the plan hatching in Ceebix's mind. Now more urgently, Giertz tried to guess, *Exactly what is going on in there?* He wouldn't be ready though, for the conclusions he eventually reached.

**Chapter 82 Smoking Rubble**

Giertz finally calmed down enough to drive off the other side of the bridge; the toll-gate barriers bent from being rammed open some time back. It was then he and Kadski saw why the bridge had been so deserted. Open-mouthed, they witnessed the results of the recent power struggles on the other side of it, and Giertz rapidly understood, *These conflicts must have been going on for much longer, and with more ferocity, than The News Dummy's reports have admitted!* Or even Giertz could have imagined.

Consumer Zone D had expanded over the years to now be relatively closer to the continent, but Giertz felt angry he still knew so little about what had been happening here. 'Real Life and Pandora distracted The Consumers from the precise extent of the devastation pretty well!' Giertz observed, bitterly, as he and Kadski sped through a landscape of gutted buildings, smoking nuclear craters, and twisted, rusting machinery. Kadski said nothing, not seeming surprised.

Strangely, standing pointlessly amongst the rubble were brand new hypnotic hoardings. Big cuts of fresh meat were displayed with the usual legend,

'CONSUMEORDIE CORP. - EAT MORE PHLESH!'

*As if it offers some solution?* The bases of the boards were covered with equally fresh graffiti, mostly telling Dr. Zed to eat it himself, and the odd equation.

As Giertz drove further, the panorama then became something worthy of Hieronymus Bosch. Among intermittent, green, Synth-O-Gas witch-burnings at the side of the road, were broken corpses tied to cartwheels, raised on tall poles. To Giertz, *Time appears to be running backward here as well, but more quickly than it did on Uncle Joe's estate. This civilization now seems to be sliding back into the Dark-Ages and beyond, never to return.*

Further on, decomposing Roman-style crucifixions, at almost regular intervals, made Giertz even more curious, *It's as if concentric rings of history are reemerging, but from what center?* Only the distant voice calling in his head seemed to offer any clue.

The sky here was now an unnatural shade of yellow-orange, becoming an indistinct smoky haze in the distance. Under it, ragged masses of Consumers wandered around amongst all the chaos in no particular direction, their eyes staring wildly. Most were clutching their defunct, worthless savings plans to their emaciated chests, and gleefully Giertz saw some hope at last, *It's a landscape from my most optimistic dreams! It seems as if some unknown phenomenon is dissolving whatever glue holds reality together.* It gave him a strange, overall feeling he was somehow driving into his own mind, but he had to be realistic, *Then again, perhaps I'm just hallucinating?* He hoped he wasn't.

Soon there were no buildings or people at all, just nightmare plains of smoking rubble, a rusty metal weed of twisted steel rebar growing from the broken concrete. Even here though, decorating it all in garish colors was more of the strange, formula-graffiti. He guessed, *It must all be part of some single gigantic formula, a collective side effect of the intelligence drugs – but searching for what conclusion?*

Further on he also saw it was all being eroded and buried by a hot wind, sandblasting it from what Giertz speculated must be the rumored, ever-expanding Red Desert. Gradually it was all being smothered with a substantial blanket of crimson dunes, as if finally soothing the sick Hellscape to sleep.

'Perhaps it's all some new climactic change?' Kadski volunteered with a tone of finality. They both knew it had to be something more though. In fact, Giertz felt a strange inkling that the voice in his head, the benevolent sand, and the shrinking timeline, must all be emanating from the same epicenter of destruction. Moreover, it just felt right, to Giertz, *Something long overdue.*

Giertz could see now, *This civilization calling itself 'reality,' is not just ill, it's dying! This desert is where I belong! So maybe my chance to euthanize reality is closer than I thought?* He could hear the wind sometimes echoing the terrible voice inside his mind, which seemed to want to speak to him so badly now. *I know it comes directly from somewhere in here, speaking of The End, spreading its ripples across the world!*

Therefore he continued all night without stopping. This was strange to Giertz as he'd thought it was too early for night. *Maybe it's just part of a hallucination? Or perhaps it has some symbolic significance for me?* Whether it was or not however, the darkness certainly appeared to be in tune with the landscape.

Giertz carefully studied the road rushing ahead in the headlights, but still ran the cyclone injectors on full. Now he just wanted to save the full fuel tanks the car had started out with, even if it meant the engine was nearly red-hot in places.

Gradually however, the car went faster, continuing to accelerate until even Giertz was amazed at the speed, but he looked across at Kadski and saw he was oblivious. In the end, it was so fast Giertz knew he definitely must be hallucinating again. Reality started to fracture once more as the car disintegrated around them. Finally, the entire machine exploded silently and painlessly into a billion, glittering fragments, the steering wheel turning to dust in his hands.

Weightless, Giertz was left hurtling alone, slowly turning end over end in silence through the various dimensions of his illness.


**Chapter 83 The Pianist**

When Giertz recovered it was daylight again, and the car was intact once more, the engine softly whirring, the straight road still unreeling. After congratulating himself for managing to drive through this hallucination, peering out of the now dirty, sand-scuffed windshield, all he and Kadski could see were endless kilometers of lifeless Red Desert, everywhere. Giertz had a vague guess at where they were, but he wasn't sure if it was a hallucination. He first began to hear the piano as a faint noise inside the cockpit, not so much 'over' the symphony of the engine, as *behind* it.

Giertz looked at the radio, but it was off. When Giertz asked Kadski about it, he only said, 'I can't hear anything.' Not interested, he was more intent on returning to sleep. Therefore Giertz began to accelerate nervously, overcome with curiosity as it got louder. Soon it was a clear hi-fi sound in his head, drowning everything else, echoing within his skull even over the distant, siren voice, and Giertz knew he was hallucinating yet again. That's new, he thought, slightly disturbed, *A hallucination within a hallucination?*

Giertz began to follow the music, even distracted from the voice that was calling him, by someone playing elaborate, classical piano. *Maybe Chopin?* It didn't sound quite like anything he'd heard before however, or would hear again. *It's more like Chopin backward.* Irrelevantly he envied the player, wishing he could play some instrument like that, and that well.

Soon he knew that the music was off the road, and so reluctantly he turned the car in a billow of dust at ninety degrees into the desert. The volume was now so loud it was beginning to make his head hurt. Then he saw a tiny, dark speck in the far-distance.

It drew closer, now a grand piano materializing out of undulating heat haze, with someone playing it. Giertz stopped the car, swung the door up, and reluctantly climbed out. The desert was perfectly flat, and everything was still. The pianist had his back turned three-quarters towards Giertz, and he approached him gently.

Now that Giertz was out of the car the volume seemed more reasonable, even slightly tinny. The pianist had long, shaggy black hair, and wore a bow tie with a pressed, black tuxedo. He was pounding delicately at the keyboard, seemingly oblivious to the melting heat. In spite of the dust and harsh conditions, the piano was so clean its French-polished top shone like a mirror.

Almost convulsed with curiosity, Giertz wanted to see the pianist's face, but annoyingly, he could only make out the back of his head. Tentatively he went closer, walking around him. Strangely, it was a face he knew well.

## Chapter 84 Blackened Stubs

The pianist was himself, and the shock of so much hallucination, combined with his overall exhaustion, was enough for Giertz to lose consciousness.

When Giertz awoke, the car was standing still, skewed diagonally across the middle of the empty road, somewhere. Kadski was still asleep at first, but awoke unwillingly after some time. Slowly they both began to see they'd lost all sense of direction and didn't know where they were. Then they both noticed a house some way off the side of the road.

Wearily they swung the doors up and walked up to it. There was nothing spectacular about it. It was just a large, comfortable, post-neo-obscurist residence, with a flat roof and large windows, vaguely reminiscent of Frank Lloyd Wright's inspirations, blending with the desert horizon, amongst the blackened stubs of dead palm trees.

The large front door, carved from a single oak panel, was open, but it had been open for too long. Both Giertz and Kadski barged against the rusted hinges, and eventually it gave enough for them to squeeze through. Kadski released the switchblade on his machete and held it in front of him with both hands, his eyes searching warily, not believing anywhere so quiet could be unthreatening.

Inside, most of the house was a single, large living-room. Giertz recognized shreds of rotten canvas which had once been a painting hanging from a wooden frame on one wall, *Probably once some priceless masterpiece.* Looking carefully at the corner he could still read the signature: 'Leonard Kornn.'

Giertz sat down on one of a tasteful arrangement of original Bauhaus Barcelona chairs, but they were rusted, and the leather on them was dried out and cracked. He ran his fingers over a corner of a large, genuine teak coffee table, eroded to the grain from a hole in the ceiling, but there was no water now. The whole area was very dehydrated. Kadski kicked through a course-grained, red sand drift in one corner of the room, which had blown through the open door.

Giertz tried to thumb through some magazines on the table, but flakes of paper came away in his hand. He couldn't even make out the dates, just a few faded color images of Consumer products, with indistinct shots of Pandora's unsmiling face. Kadski examined a large, empty tropical fish tank, poking with his machete at the skeletons of some exotic species.

At the back of the house, the two pushed their way through dirty rags of curtains, wafting limply through the screen windows, then walked around a massive, ornate marble fountain. It reminded Giertz of the one at Uncle Joe's mansion, but this was empty, just a few dehydrated weeds in the dust at the bottom. Looking out on it was an antique Eames lounger, which Kadski took an interest in, calling to Giertz, 'Hey, look at this?'

Giertz walked up and saw someone had left a coffee cup, a pair of glasses, and an old-fashioned newspaper with a towel beside it. The cup was full of dust also, and there were only a few yellow fragments of the paper left. Kadski commented, 'It looks as if whatever took the owner arrived very quickly. Giertz tried on the glasses. 'Long-sighted,' he commented.

Searching the rest of the house, they found other elegant furniture and appliances, all equally unusable, but what drew Giertz's interest was the car sitting on four flat tires in the basement garage. He carefully brushed the flaking paint off the rear panel, 'Lamborghini 450 GT! Genuine!' For a moment something in him toyed with the idea of bringing it back to life, but that didn't seem appropriate somehow. *Everything about the condition of this place just seems so right. Outside, another huge sand drift was building up against the wall. Soon this will be all buried for good.*

Kadski had dropped his machete-guard sometime back, when the same realization had come over both of them. They didn't need to say anything to know they both felt the same way. There was no one, just a small, translucent yellow scorpion scuttling across the floor, leaving tiny tracks in the dust. Therefore they left.

Once outside again they both noticed the area wasn't entirely flat. The single geological feature on the horizon was a shallow, blue mountain. Kadski said he was going back to the car. He appeared to have lost whatever interest he'd had, but Giertz was immediately convinced that what was calling him, now more loudly than ever, was inside that mountain. He compromised with Kadski, saying, 'I'll go to it on foot to conserve the remaining Synth-O-Gas.'

Kadski promised to wait. Carrying only his gun and the small emergency water ration from the car, Giertz began running across The Red Desert. The mountain didn't look *that* far away, but soon the heat was burning his throat.

**Chapter 85 Irresistible Voice**
After what seemed like hours of running, the mountain didn't appear to be any closer. Giertz's feet quickly

became numb on the cracked, red earth. The stale-tasting water ration was soon gone. He began to sense this particular desert was actively, malevolently trying to kill him, *It's sucking life out of me with every breath!*

Giertz had always assumed that every desert had life hidden away in it somewhere, but after stopping for a moment to survey the barren, sterile, heat-blasted landscape, he knew, *This place is just dead. In fact, it is death, and I'm going to die here!* In a sense he was right, but he'd no real feeling of surprise or regret.

He dropped his gun, knowing it was just useless weight. Then garment by garment he began to discard his uniform and clothing until he was naked. As he did so, along whatever path he was following, sticking out of the dust he occasionally noticed other scattered pieces of uniforms, and weapons. There was a Lee Enfield rifle from the twentieth century, covered in rust, *First World War!* Then after an hour, there was an equally rusted breastplate from a medieval suit of armor. Giertz noted the sword-gashes running across it. *Probably from The Crusades.* Later there was an elaborate bronze helmet. *Roman!* Then intermittently there were more, even older, spears, swords, and armor. *So I'm not the first here!* This knowledge didn't reassure him though, as the red dust wafted among the relics, slowly building into small mounds over thousands of years, to bury them.

Meanwhile, he could see nothing in front of him but the overwhelming heat haze. The malicious, suffocating temperature was now making his mind feel somehow distant from his body. Then, and he wasn't certain, he thought he saw indistinct figures standing in it, somewhere, as if they'd materialized out of the heat itself. *Perhaps they're just hallucinations?* He somehow knew though, whoever they were, what they represented couldn't be good. He also thought for a moment the wordless, soundless, irresistible voice which had drawn him here might be theirs, but he also somehow knew, *There's another stage of this journey to go before I meet the owner.*

As he came closer some details became apparent. They wore simple robes of a crudely woven cloth, tied at the waist, *Like monks of some kind?* They were not young men, even at this distance, they looked ancient and undernourished. Their sunken eyes looked infinitely weary, as if they'd been waiting forever for something, but today those eyes were glowing with a spark of expectation.

By the time Giertz hobbled up to them, he was exhausted, and collapsed panting at their feet, almost too tired to breathe. Nothing was said, and Giertz found that although they were small, they were stronger than they looked, as they picked up Giertz's now relatively large body. Reverentially, they bore him the rest of the way to the mountain.

Before he lost consciousness, Giertz had a sudden, terrible thought as he looked up at the empty sky, 'Oh no! They think I'm Judazz!' He thrashed about gesturing weakly, but he found his throat was too burned to contradict them. So they only heard the word, 'Judazz.'

**Chapter 86 Panic Stricken**

Before he lost consciousness Giertz had a brief memory of being carried through an underground passage with ancient chisel marks on the walls, and broken flints lying around. He was only able to think vaguely, *This was probably some natural cave which has been widened by these people, over eons.* It was the drums that awoke Giertz, with their deep, malevolent throb.

His eyelids felt almost too heavy to open as he looked around the chamber, carved from the rock. It was naturally cool, and Giertz guessed he must be somewhere deep in the mountain. Despite still being naked, he didn't feel cold. *The heat outside must be maintaining some balance, like natural air-conditioning.* Then Giertz discovered he was lying spread-eagled on a rough, stone table, lit by a circle of hand-molded oil lamps, reeking thickly of animal fat.

The priests were ringed around him, chanting and swaying. Jittering shadows cast by the torches played over the granite walls. They were decorated with crude yet intricate paintings in human blood and vegetable dyes, of distorted-looking half-man, half-animal creatures. Giertz noted the table had centuries of old bloodstains soaked into it. He believed he could almost feel the suffering that must have taken place here. *This whole place stinks of The Stone Age.*

Giertz reached out to touch one of three, roughly-carved idols with misshapen, twisted anatomy standing around the table. Eyeless, they nevertheless stared with stony indifference across the scene. From his theological studies, Giertz recognized them straight away, The Three Guardians of Xerak! This only served to reinforce his feeling that the priests were making some terrible mistake. Then it slowly came to him, *I'm actually in the fabled Xeracist Tabernacle, which everyone believes is probably just a myth.*

Giertz himself had always envisioned some shining, marble edifice, worthy of ancient Greece, but by now he just absently wondered what the priests were going to do with him, only half caring about anything. He felt too weak and ill to stop whatever it was.

One of the 'younger' priests nervously put a carved wooden bowl of something that didn't smell too good up to Giertz's mouth, pouring a little of it in. He choked as it went down, feeling most of it running down the sides of his face. At first, he thought it was some natural medicine, but then after a few more gulps tasted it was just water, but not that clean. He began to feel slightly better, but now generally more disorientated by the whole situation.

Giertz could tell straight away the oldest of the priests was the mythical 'Seer.' He sat on a primitive throne scraped out of a large stalagmite, near to Giertz's feet. Towering behind that, in the near-darkness, was a huge, roughly-carved idol. To Giertz it looked as if it had been chiseled long ago by some race even preceding the priests. Giertz recognized the effigy immediately, despite never having seen it at all before, *Omnipotent Xerak!*

The evil-looking, stone countenance with a malformed mouth, full of misshapen teeth, surveyed the proceedings indifferently. There was something familiar about the expression on the distorted lips also, but Giertz couldn't categorize it, at first. He now knew however, that the voice that had called him here had emanated from it.

Before it, The Seer seemed so frail he should have been dead years ago, looking as if he was in some permanent trance. His prolapsed face hung as if it were about to fall off his skull, a few, random wisps of white hair straggling from his scalp. Giertz also noticed the other priests were somehow afraid of this tiny old man, and there was a general atmosphere of heightened expectation in the chamber. *Perhaps they're afraid of what The Seer might see?*

It was still painful for Giertz to focus his eyes, but he looked again at the paintings. He could easily tell they were very antiquated, *Hundreds, perhaps thousands of years!* It was as if the number of eyes staring at them had faded them, which brought many questions for him, *How long have these old priests and their ancient belief been down here, and how much older is their faith? How many other religions did it precede, if not all of them? Perhaps their belief is even older than the human race? Is it something they've been guarding for us?* Looking at the priests carefully also, he couldn't define what race they were.

Short and stocky, unable to stand fully upright, with over-hanging brow ridges, they seemed more like some forerunner of homo-sapiens. *Maybe holding onto something too powerful stopped them from joining human evolution?* He also noticed how pale they were, as if they rarely saw daylight, and he speculated dreamily, *Maybe they're even immortal, always living in this mountain, just becoming progressively more decrepit - without actually dying out?*

Then, looking around again he recognized something familiar about the paintings, *They are close to being Xeracist hieroglyphs, almost some forerunner of the script.* Also, from his theological studies, Giertz had begun to pick up some of the weird, ancient language. More for something to do than anything else, he made a half-hearted attempt to interpret the symbols. Then he felt a moment of shock when he finally understood, *There's nothing difficult about reading them at all, it's only too clear!*

While still feeling too ill to stand, he managed to roll off the table and staggered about the small chamber, the priests breaking their circle and flinching away from him in terror, raw fear in the 'younger' one's faces. *It's as if they are witnessing an earthquake, or some other natural cataclysm!*

Eventually, Giertz managed to get himself upright. Most of the priests stood up also, now panic-stricken, as if Giertz had risen from the dead. The drumming stopped. A relatively young priest draped a blanket of their crude cloth around Giertz's shoulders, but then the priest jumped back, wondering if he'd done the right thing. Only The Seer remained immobile, indifferent in his trance.

Giertz pulled the rag around himself, and grabbed one of the smoking lamps, leaning close to the picture. They told a simple story, *There's no mistaking it.* 'A young, insane warrior...' Giertz didn't want to read anymore. He turned to them, gesturing to himself with his free hand, 'Look, he started to say. 'My name's Jimmy Giertz. I'm not...' But then he checked himself.

From the looks on their time-eaten faces, Giertz quickly began to see, *They've based their whole culture on a simple hope that one day Judazz will come to them. It's as if this is all that's kept them alive! Perhaps this alone is what has maintained them for so long? Their entire existence is about just holding their message here for him, whatever it is.* He therefore wondered, *Have I any right to contradict their faith?* Then he began to think hard, and another thought struck him.

He went back to the inscription, and scrubbing his finger along it, strained his knowledge to decipher the rest. After checking it two or three times there was no mistake, '...shall smite the swollen-headed monster,
In his tower,
It is foretold!' He whispered.


**Chapter 87 Terrible Puzzle**
Now Giertz felt very aware of an overwhelming claustrophobia in the prehistoric tabernacle. Staggering backward away from the paintings, he hit his head on a large stalactite. The priests stood around him, now rigid with fear, still not sure what to do.

Giertz could see through the painfully small entrance that the cave was a network, leading to other chambers, other shrines, a maze within the mountain, and he reminded himself, *I'm here! In The Tabernacle! Where I always secretly wanted to be.* It only felt like being inside some terrible puzzle though. Then he stumbled over some things on the floor, not sure what they were.

Giertz looked down and then realized half a human skull was staring back at him. The floor was almost covered with human bones. Many of them were carbonized, and some had the scratches of teeth marks. Dazed with pain, Giertz tried to reason, *I gave my soul to The Idea willingly enough. I almost believed the Xeracist Tabernacle existed somewhere, and The Idea was enshrined there - here. Now I'm truly confronted by it though; it feels very - different.*

He was well aware of the prophecy, as was every Combat Youth. and like all the others he'd hoped he could be the one to fulfill it, slaying the swollen-headed monster, especially in the context of his personal quest to destroy reality. Yet now he was beginning to see what it all truly meant, *All my life I've been willing to volunteer, but I hadn't known specifically what, or who for.* Those questions seemed irrelevant now, when he felt his destiny wasn't under his control, and never had been. *Being swept up in a tide of events that has been gaining momentum for eons, is a different responsibility altogether.* In the context of these thoughts, trying to deal with it all, Giertz now began to feel as if his mind was spinning in his head. Consequently, his memories of the hideous events which followed were rather vague.

The priests lit a fire in the chamber which cast more, even weirder, distorted shadows on the wall. It filled with an ugly smoke that clutched at Giertz's lungs. The drumming restarted, becoming louder, and faster, *and deeper.* Giertz's head began to throb in time with it, and he vaguely knew he was now hyperventilating. Through the smoke, he could see the indistinct outlines of the priests dancing around him, but there was nothing crude about the dancing itself. In fact, the steps were quite elaborate, in spite of the aged feet carrying them out.

They wore crude animal masks, actually made from human skulls, with added, broken animal bones and fangs jutting out. These looked very old, so much that parts of them were falling away, making them look even stranger.

For Giertz it was as if the mythological creatures had just stepped out of the paintings on the cave walls, in some unusually horrific nightmare, *How many times have they performed this ritual? There's something even older in the rocks down here, older than the priests' themselves, something going back beyond time, something too terrible...*

For Giertz the paintings had now become as clear as a holyvision screen. They showed a landscape stretching around him. He even felt he could walk into it, becoming one of the deformed figures in there. Now he was looking out at himself, his human body, lying back on the sacrificial table. This wasn't one of his hallucinations as such; it was an experience caused directly by the ritual in the chamber.

Then he felt he was growing taller, hundreds of times his usual height, and something inside him, buried for perhaps thousands of years, was coming alive. It was stretching towards something. Or, more accurately, something was drawing him towards it. It was the same call which had brought him here in the first place, except now the voice was so loud it seemed to be melting his ears. The message was old as well, *Maybe older than the universe, older than space, older than time...* Staring up above The Seer into the ugly, badly sculpted face of the large granite statue once more, Giertz felt The Terror as he never had before.

He finally recognized the expression on the terrible, distorted mouth. It was a smile, and a smile Giertz knew well. Now the ugliness was unlimited. What was more he understood where the voice in his head had come from as that stone mouth now opened, eventually becoming the size of the idol's whole head, the entire chamber. It was turning into a sort of tunnel, and he felt himself being sucked into it. From being a distant whisper, the voice now boomed, hammering in his ears, filling the entire universe.

It wasn't that his question was being answered, it was that it was eliminated altogether, as he was flying through other dimensions of space and time again, on the final stage of his journey to receive the message, and there was no avoiding it: he was finally confronting The Idea itself.

**Chapter 88 Tangled Remains**

The only thing Giertz could recall afterward was permanently entering the landscape on the walls of the chamber, and materializing there in the desert, where it was early morning and a lot cooler. Therefore running back to the car, and Kadski, was easier. After some time, following his own footprints in the dust, he came to the last piece of his uniform he'd discarded, pulling it back on again as he ran.

Eventually, fully dressed once more, he even found his gun where he'd dropped it. Then in the distance, he saw the small, yellow sliver of the car, still parked outside the empty house. Giertz could just see Kadski was still there but lying in its shadow, weak with dehydration. *He could have left me here, but he stayed!*

Giertz loaded him into the car and began driving, yet Giertz had no clear memories of the return journey, not sure either if it was just another hallucination rapidly metamorphosing the landscape around him. Eventually, he was back in the now familiar urban Hellscape, soon approaching the tangled remains of the Channel Bridge, and returning to Consumer Zone D once more. He looked carefully at the fuel gauge. *Unless it's faulty, the tank couldn't have carried enough Synth-O-Gas to get us to The Red Desert of Death, even with the cyclone injectors on full. I must have hallucinated most of that, surely?* In fact he hoped he had.

Back at the Greedeluxe Youth headquarters Giertz delivered Kadski to the rapid-healing clinic and found he was indeed suffering from the after-effects of extreme dehydration. *So I couldn't have imagined it.* Even so though, Giertz still wasn't sure.

Ceebix seemed to have entirely forgotten his earlier attack on Giertz as if it had never happened. *So perhaps it didn't? Maybe that was a hallucination as well?* On returning to the basement however, he found the real-enough, silver-lined bullet hole the helicopter had left on the car's rear wing, but he still couldn't even be sure of that either. Yet the bruise on his head from the Tabernacle was real enough. In the end, he just trusted Ceebix even less now, but incredibly, Giertz found he still wanted to be liked by him, and perhaps even more so.

When Kadski recovered, he could remember nothing at all beyond setting out for the patrol. Gradually Giertz also pushed the whole episode to the back of his mind. When he thought about it at all, he concluded, *Perhaps I just imagined it all?* Even if it had all been an illusion, Giertz had taken it his encounter with the voice from The Tabernacle as a kind of warning or prophecy, but deep down, he knew he had the answer he'd gone there for, no longer feeling any doubt about the nature his mission, in fact it was the opposite, *Some part of me did die there - I'm not the same confused person anymore.* He knew exactly what he was meant to do, beyond just wanting to destroy reality. *I know whatever Ceebix says, I am truly the vessel for a holy quest – The Idea - given unto me by Xerak!*

Beneath Giertz's bravado though, the 'hallucinatory' experience in the desert had somehow made him less, rather than more, confident in his ability to fulfill his destiny, now that deep down he knew what The Idea truly was. In fact, now his question had been answered, and he knew what he was really serving, he secretly doubted he could fulfill the mission at all. However, the prophecy would come truer than he could have imagined - or would have wanted it to.

**Chapter 89 Suicide Squad**

The news of the formation of a new division within the Combat Youth also compounded the negative feeling. It was on a single sheet of lined paper torn from a cheap notebook, covered in Ceebix's spidery, scratchy handwriting. It was pinned with a single tack to the otherwise bare notice board, outside the self-torture chamber, next to the Cancer-Free cigarette dispenser. It announced the formation of `The Sacred Oath of Judazz Suicide Squad.'

It gained little overt reaction from the Combat Youth however, but one by one they quietly signed up. Their general lack of celebration for this opportunity surprised Giertz, but he concluded, *They probably see themselves as a suicide squad already*. The announcement still had a very unusual effect on Giertz though.

He didn't understand why, but in the context of his recent experience, he just had a feeling the notice had been written specifically for him. He would eventually also be surprised to find it had been. During the recent patrols and since his 'journey,' he'd started to wonder even more about Ceebix, *Sitting there in his wheelchair, his desk always draped in maps, charts, and computer printouts. It's all covered in tiny, colored, plastic counters that he shuffles around as he barks instructions and theology into the microphone on his desk, in between talking about kill ratios. His face is almost permanently red as well, going on purple, as if he's on some medication.* Giertz hadn't thought of it as so unusual before, but now he wondered deeply, *What does it all add up to, if it adds up to anything?*

After a while however, Giertz saw the Combat Youth did find something significant about the Suicide Squad. They suspected Ceebix had a particular mission ready for them, but were only half-curious as to what it was. Giertz was as well, but later he would be a lot more so. However, as the end of the bizarre summer drew near, it was the morning of the day Nailbrand was killed, when Giertz finally understood something fundamental about the whole situation.

**Chapter 90 Phlesh Brothers**

Before the fateful patrol, Giertz and Kadski sat in the empty lunchtime canteen, surrounded by the garish Synth-O-Food dispensers with their flashing neon lights, staring across the unclean table at each other. The walls were just bare concrete, with no decoration of any kind. Giertz looked down at the plastic cup of Synth-O-Juice in his hand, and noticed ripples from his fingers vibrating across its surface. He glanced back up at Kadski and saw he'd noticed it too.

Giertz hadn't known his accumulated doubts were this strong by now, his body telling him something his mind didn't want to admit, but although Kadski had seen the hand shaking, he said nothing. He just continued to stare blankly, as he usually did, at Giertz. So he decided to introduce the topic of his wavering self-confidence, but indirectly,

'Kadski?' Giertz said eventually.

'Hmmmm?'

'Do you think our motives are pure?'

Kadski continued to say nothing for some time, but his eventual answer took Giertz by surprise, 'It doesn't matter.'

'What do you mean?' Giertz asked, now very curious, willing to reach for anything that offered hope. Kadski closed his eyes and sighed, then looked directly at Giertz once more,

'It doesn't matter whether our motives are pure or not. We're like Siamese twins Jimmy,' he continued. 'It's as if we share the same phlesh. We don't need the Greedeluxe Youth, Combat Youth or any other youth, or even Judazz or The Idea if it comes to it.'

Giertz still felt very puzzled, especially at hearing this blasphemy from Kadski, and even with Giertz's heightened foreknowledge of what Kadski was going to say next, Giertz couldn't have imagined it, as Kadski said slowly, 'You've heard of blood brothers? Well, we're phlesh brothers, Jimmy. This on its own justifies anything we do. We don't even need "motives."'

This introduced an entirely new concept to Giertz, and he turned it over in his buckling mind, examining it from various angles, *The means justifying the means?* Despite Kadski's reassurance though, Giertz's doubts became even more complicated when he began to see the rules of 'The Game' were changing, and nothing could have prepared him for the outcome.


**Chapter 91 Strange Conversation**

After the strange conversation, during the patrol, there was a routine situation call, but it was taking place much further out of the city than usual. Four of the Combat Youths' cars formed a convoy, traveling towards the geo-coordinates. Giertz was pleased to hear Nailbrand's car was one of them. Today was notable because it was his first patrol with the Combat Youth. Recently the Combat and Motorcycle Youth had been known to fight pitched battles with each other. So Giertz thought optimistically, *Perhaps there's a chance I can have that conversation with him at last?*

Ceebix had droned during this morning's sermon, 'There is a general hope this kind of co-operation could lead to a cessation of the Motorcycle Youth's gradual break-away from the Greedeluxe Youth.' But this had prompted Giertz to recall his old dilemma, now nagging at him like an incurable headache, *If I could just find some way to unite the youth! Only together can we destroy reality!*

Giertz was also pleased to see one of the other cars was that of the Abominable Bastido Brothers. Identical twins, they only had three eyes between them. Somehow they'd never found the time to visit the Rapid Healing Clinic for a new eye; such was their dedication to the cause. It was easy to tell them apart because one of them wore a pirate-like eye patch, but Giertz never understood, *Why is it always the one with the worst eyesight who does the driving?*

They were also the only Combat Youths besides Kadski who Giertz had come to know to any extent. Most of the others either openly hated Giertz or were killed before he even learned their names. Always a team, the twins seemed indestructible, and despite their reputation, while not openly despising Giertz as the other operatives did, they appeared relatively indifferent to Giertz, which was enough for him to almost love them in return.

Nailbrand's car was the first to arrive and report there was no Situation, only a complex of deserted, half-demolished office blocks, relics of the early Protein Riots. Giertz would realize later they should have known something was very wrong at this point, yet he only had an inkling, *If it's a mistake, it's never been made before.*

The other three cars screeched to a halt in a circle as usual. The Combat Youths got out and stood around, squeezing their sweating fists like addicts facing withdrawal. Nailbrand tried to contact Ceebix through the waves of radio static blanketing the area. At least three seconds before it happened, Giertz was ready to jump, but Kadski was the first to work out it was a trap.

He shouted something unintelligible to the others. They dived back into the bullet resistant, temporary safety of their cockpits, but a sniper caught one Combat Youths in the neck before he could close the door, puncturing his carotid artery. He sat dazed and bleeding to death in the open doorway. The passenger pulled him inside and the door down, as snipers opened up from the roofs at the cars. In the distance, Giertz could see heavy, retro, 1959 Cadillac limousines approaching the entrance.

Every few seconds Giertz's whole car would heave on its suspension as a bullet slammed into it, but along with The Terror, Giertz felt even more puzzled, *They could have shot us all straight away! So why did they wait?*

Above the revving engines and gunfire, Kadski commented, 'They are obviously trying to make us panic! There are easier ways of eliminating us than this!' They all agreed the radio was probably being monitored, and so they decided to remain silent.

The four cars lined up, Giertz igniting all his tires by reversing into the formation. Kadski waved the complex sign language the more experienced Combat Youth used for communication in situations. Giertz hadn't achieved fluency yet, and so Kadski shouted a translation for him over the noise of engines and ricochets. 'The Abominable Bastido Brothers believe it's possible to out-run the Non-men's cars! They say Xerak is with us!' The cars surged towards the entrance in a fog of tire smoke.

As Kadski checked all the guns, he observed, 'The car in front with the injured driver is drawing more concentrated fire!' Just as the car he was talking about swerved fifty paces short of its target, embedding itself uselessly in a brick wall. Most of the rest of the building collapsed on top of it, billowing dust.

Nailbrand took advantage of the snipers' feelings of achievement and opened his door to release a few dozen micro-rounds at the surrounding rooftops. He accompanied his bullet's explosive impacts with a torrent of profanity from his canine mouth. Strings of saliva fell from it, staining his black, real-leather motorcycle jacket. For a moment, to Giertz it seemed more as if Nailbrand's epithets themselves were ricocheting off the concrete. Kadski also expressed admiration as he saw it had the effect of driving back the snipers momentarily. Meanwhile, the Bastido brothers' car flew past the first car's smoking wreck and through the narrow gap.

Nailbrand's and Giertz's cars somehow shot through the opening together. Nailbrand was still pulling his door down, and Giertz buckled one of the car's rear fenders on the metal gatepost. Kadski adjusted the rear view camera from the control on the dashboard, to watch the limousines, a group of Consumeordie Motorcycle Youth, and a Consumeordie helicopter, form into a pack behind them.

**Chapter 92 Heat Seeking**
Since joining the Combat Youth, Giertz had become used to fear, to some extent. By now he almost welcomed The Terror as a kind of partner who would inspire him to further extremes, but he'd never become entirely immune to it, in the way some Combat Youths appeared to be. Also, his strange suspicion that something else was wrong with today continued to grow.

He wondered out loud what the Consumeordie Youth and the Non-men were trying to achieve, 'This whole thing makes no sense!' He raved at Kadski. 'Until now, a Situation, no matter how violent, was always a struggle between two or more opposing points of view. The aim was to convert the opposition to the others opinion, even if the process meant destroying them, not just to destroy them as an end in itself!' Kadski was too busy double-checking the weapons to reply.

The three surviving Combat Youth cars drew alongside each other once more while still moving, and another silent, semaphored conversation took place. Kadski translated again, 'They've decided to split up and rendezvous at the main road junction in ten minutes, to divide and lose the opposition.' Giertz was silently skeptical, *It doesn't sound like much of a strategy, probably exactly what the Non-men want us to do. He knew though, There's no time to disagree.*

He also learned that because his car was the newest, it was the only one still carrying some of its stock of hand grenades. They were not considered to be 'sporting' weapons in a situation, but that didn't stop them from being used. He and Kadski looked down at the last four of them shining dully in their hypermarket blister-packaging.

Giertz knew this area vaguely from his holygame simulations. Just over the brow of a hill it was dominated by the contorted, rusting remains of a nuclear reactor that had melted down some years back. Consequently, it was mostly deserted. He slid the car off the road through a broken gateway marked 'KEEP OUT,' heading it in a trail of dust across a field of weirdly shaped plants. A faded sign announced the land had once belonged to The World Food Corporation, but a newer Consumeordie sign defiantly declared food was still being harvested there.

Kadski was having trouble organizing the grenades with the buffeting from the uneven surface. They spilled out of the brightly-colored packaging and rolled across the floor. He strained against his harness groping for them. Meanwhile, Giertz crashed through a second, rotted gate, onto another side road. However, it was only to see the motorcycles coming towards him, *The agility of the motorcyclists and the probability they are carrying heat-seeking missiles rules out a confrontation at this time.* Kadski recognized the dilemma, 'Can you do it?' he asked Giertz suddenly.

Giertz had never seen him in this state before, the question taking him by surprise, *An unusual question for Kadski.* Giertz understood the feeling however, while considering to himself, *Realistically, no.* The tone of Kadski's question nagged at Giertz though, reflecting his own puzzlement, *This just isn't right!* Until now they'd become used to running towards death, Giertz even driving with a self-destructive urge, but it was an entirely new experience to drive defensively. *We're running for our lives! It's not death we're running from so much though. It's just dying here, like this, in a smashed car, like two hunted animals, two losers, two liabilities, my destiny unfulfilled, and reality still intact...* It was inconceivable, somehow.

Therefore he applied the hand-brake, spinning the car on its axis. It headed the opposite way, towards the main road, but the motorcyclists had no problem with this. He knew his performance in his holygames over the years well enough to recognize his personal limitations, *It's going to take more than my reflexes to get us out of this.* He decided to keep this to himself as well however, *If they can't, soon we'll never know about it anyway.*


**Chapter 93 Chrome Grille**
Not far behind, two of the replica Cadillacs began to snake ahead, through the rapidly gaining motorcycles. Giertz knew, *Those heavy cars couldn't normally keep up with Lamborghinis, even fake ones.* 'Their cyclone-injectors must have been tuned up especially for this, the motors set to burn out,' he guessed out loud. Meanwhile Kadski

carefully lined up the grenades with a launching mechanism in the floor near his feet.

It had been installed by the Greedeluxe Youth specifically for releasing these, but he'd only ever used it in the simulators. Giertz tried to ignore the knowledge that the grenades had been known to catch in the suspension. As Kadski bit the pin out of the first one, Giertz tried to line the screen's crosshairs up with the first car, and shouted, 'Now!'

Although it was more of a guess, the dot bounced in the rear-view. There was an unbearably long silence in which nothing happened. Then there was a muffled flash directly in the middle of the pack of assailants, which illuminated the whole cockpit. A chain of events followed.

A Cadillac was lifted bodily into the air and dashed at the side of the road. One of its wheels came loose and bounced randomly. It landed on the front of another car, which had to stop immediately, smoke pouring out of its chrome grille. The rearmost of the two motorcyclists didn't quite manage to avoid its tail fins. His machine broke into large pieces as he was thrown from it - a torn, rag doll.

This so disconcerted the second motorcyclist that he lost his concentration. His machine glanced off the crash barrier, wobbling as he cartwheeled off it, lying stunned in the path of one of the limousines. The weighty car shunted his machine out of the way and drove over him, as if neither had been there. Therefore, Giertz became more confident as he zigzagged through the thin traffic, *Just like in one of my holygames! It's easy!*

In their own uninspired, methodical way though, the Non-men's limousines further back were keeping pace with him, even gaining. Kadski informed Giertz, 'You've got about sixty seconds left to reach the rendezvous.' Then a third Cadillac started to push its way through the pack, bending its panels and smashing its heavy chrome grille in the process. It was a different color to the others – red.

'The Bad Actor!' Kadski almost spat, but Giertz didn't feel as intimidated by the driver's attitude as he was meant to, *Perhaps my death here might have some significance after all!* He prophesied, *I've killed you once, I'll kill you again!*

The approaching, main mega-highway also reassured him, and another yellow blob of a Combat Youth car became visible, but it was the only one. There was also the Consumeordie Corp. helicopter behind it, maneuvering further down the road. Giertz's car was the first to reach the junction, but only Nailbrand's car pulled alongside this time.

**Chapter 94 Easy Target**

The occupants seemed to have had a much worse time than Giertz. Their car was badly dented, smattered with machine-gun fire, and even burned in places. A third, hasty, sign-language conversation informed that the Abominable Bastido Brothers were no more.

As Giertz's car screamed into one of the road's speed-banked corners, the horizon gently twisting through forty-five degrees, he felt himself being pressed down into the seat by the centrifugal force. In the rear-view screen the remaining limousines, motorcycles, and helicopters were forming a single pack once more, slowly gaining. 'They'll soon be in easy firing-range,' Kadski observed, his voice stilted with nervousness and hate.

Giertz knew, *The obvious thing to do is to use this car's superior acceleration, which would lose the relatively sluggish limousines, if not the motorcycles.* He also had to find somewhere to hide from the helicopter, but there didn't seem to be any bridges or tunnels along this road. He dropped back to allow Nailbrand's car a clear run, but nothing happened.

One disadvantage of Cyclone Injectors was that they projected out of the top of the rear engine cover, making an easy target. Then Giertz noticed a fine jet of Synth-O-Gas was smearing oily-green stains over his windshield. 'Nailbrand is losing speed!' Giertz shouted.

He drew alongside once more, and Kadski urgently signaled that Nailbrand's motor was pumping fuel into the vehicle's slipstream, instead of the engine. 'He'll be lucky if his engine doesn't catch fire!' Kadski commented. Then Giertz felt the first bullets hit the back of his car.

**Chapter 95 Fatal Mistake**

Kadski opened the side window and fired back at the Non-men, ducking back in quickly before the door's mirror was shot away. The Non-men's' empty, non-faces didn't try to duck, or even flinch, as the shots ricocheted around them. The fake Lamborghini's bullet-resistant tires would yelp every few seconds as another round tested them. Giertz dropped further back, trying to shield Nailbrand's car as best he could.

He worked the windshield wiper trying to stop Nailbrand's fuel blurring his vision on the surging road. 'It's clear the armor-plating on the rear of Nailbrand's car can't take much more!' Giertz warned. The cockpit air was near unbreathable with the unhealthy combination of Synth-O-Gas fumes, and the firework odor of spent cartridges.

Then, booming through the turbulence via powerful loudspeakers, in his best private-school tones came the voice of The Bad Actor. It even almost drowned the combined howl of the engines and ricocheting bullets. Every word was so loud, Giertz felt them vibrating his teeth against one another. It was as if they were somehow speaking directly to Giertz's whole body, rather than just his ears.

The diatribe opened with the usual fusillade of statistics and quotations from Dr. Zed, 'This is the age of sales, net assets, etc.! The Phlesh-price theory is perfect when the average market is in monopoly!' Giertz guessed the loudspeaker must have been behind the limousine's grille, because it was as if the enormous, grinning, chrome mouth was doing the speaking. It was now bent at the corner also, giving it a kind of mechanical leer.

The voice went on to emphasize Consumeordie's pricing policy had outstripped Greedeluxe's, and there was no necessity for The Consumers to be taught to count above fifty, and so forth. Kadski switched the radio on to drown it out. It blasted Psycho Kiss at a volume which threatened to shake the doors loose, but The Bad Actor was still as loud as if he was in the cockpit with them. Then the voice revealed the reason for the day's events.

They'd been chosen by Pandora's Real Life randomly spinning 'Wheel of Destiny,' and would be 'guesting' in today's episode. Kadski shouted various suggestions about what The Bad Actor should do with his anatomy, but Kadski's voice was itself drowned out by the combined noise of the radio, engines, and The Bad Actor.

Meanwhile, Giertz examined the helicopter in the rear-view screen, *Now I can see why it's so lightly armored, and hasn't attacked us. It's carrying holyvision cameras! It makes sense, in a way. The recording of whatever happens here will be edited to make it look as if we attacked The Bad Actor, and he successfully fought us off.* This thought made Giertz feel almost physically sick. Therefore, as the limousine was now so close, Giertz retaliated by touching the brake pedal.

The rear of his car collided with its aggressive chrome face, but there was little effect. The added distortion just made the chrome mouth look even more malevolent, and the voice didn't stop either. The collision also broke off the fake Lamborghini's damaged rear fender, which was dragged momentarily in a shower of sparks. It finally tore off like tinfoil, leaving a naked tire bobbing temptingly.

Giertz glanced into his rear-view screen again. Through the Cadillac's tinted, bulletproof windshield, he was staring directly into the disinterested face of The Bad Actor. Giertz could actually see him mouthing his statistics and condemnations, as he cruised languidly with one hand on the wheel. Somehow though, Giertz got the impression that The Bad Actor's heart wasn't in this, *It's probably just in his contract he has to attend these staged events – or maybe it just distracts him from his overall boredom?*

Then, just as Kadski was getting one of the two remaining hand-grenades ready, Nailbrand made his fatal mistake.

## Chapter 96 Flaming Remains

Nailbrand was no longer able to restrain himself. Giertz watched, horrified, as the Motorcycle Youth forced the door of his car open against the wind, to get a better aim at The Bad Actor. Giertz guessed, *Nailbrand is trying to top his earlier shooting feat, as he always does. Away from his motorcycle he probably feels restricted.* Even before Nailbrand leaned out though, a shot caught him in the chest.

He disappeared so quickly it was as if the bullet had turned him to vapor. What happened next also took place almost faster than even Giertz could react. He just had time to think, *Nailbrand's driver is probably stunned!* Giertz could visualize the Combat Youth staring at the empty passenger seat for a fraction of a moment too long. Therefore Giertz watched the car go roaring into an oncoming bend with its door hanging open, much too fast.

Briefly it scraped along the steel barrier, spraying sparks, the driver straining against the steering, but in the end it plunged through. Somersaulting crazily out into space, it trailed smoke and a long, jagged ribbon of crash fencing. The driver's scream was briefly even louder than the roar of the freely-revving engine, as one of the sparks caught the fuel in the damaged injector.

**Chapter 97 Warning Light**

The car exploded. The flaming remains spiraled through the air like a loose, green Catherine wheel, as the camera helicopter fluttered gleefully around it all. Even Giertz had to admit, It makes great holyvision, I suppose.

Until now, Giertz had felt almost no emotions at all when he thought about his own death. It had just seemed an abstract prospect, but as he watched the burning wreck dropping, something in him was changing, *I've so regularly confronted death with the Combat Youth, I thought the very idea itself no longer has any significance for me, but perhaps it still does?* For some reason however, the death of Nailbrand, or more accurately the death of the hope he'd represented to Giertz, wasn't like any other he'd witnessed recently.

In fact, Giertz was so stunned that even with the road now clear in front of him, he felt unable to act. The Synth-O-Leather steering wheel somehow felt lifeless in his hands. There was only one thought in his head, which wouldn't go away, *Now we'll never have that conversation!*

At first, being too busy, Kadski didn't notice Giertz's reaction. With a partially insane grin Kadski fumbled one of the last two grenades into the chute. Again there was a very long wait. Then The Bad Actor's PA system quickly went quiet, and Giertz saw him back off rapidly. It was as if some sixth sense had told The Bad Actor what was happening, but this time there was no explosion. There was nothing at all.

'It was a dud!' Kadski said, disbelievingly. Giertz and Kadski looked at the last grenade, silently asking the same question, but only Kadski was really bothered. Then he switched his stare to Giertz as he began to recognize Giertz's condition. It was obviously something Kadski had seen in other Combat Youths before - and didn't like. Then with no warning, a bullet finally penetrated the car's tiny rear window. Like some terrible insect, it ricochet around the cockpit, into the roof, door sill, Kadski ducking instinctively, before it smashed into Giertz's hand on the steering wheel.

Giertz looked down, and it took a moment before he registered it had almost severed his middle finger. He found it strange, the way his emotional state had even nullified his reflexes. They hadn't saved him this time, but the pain penetrated Giertz's emotional inertia enough to make him use the accelerator pedal. Kadski had to grab the steering, as the tires screamed, complaining about the weight of torque.

Kadski found the tiny first-aid kit as Giertz got used to the sensation in his hand enough to steer. As the car lurched raggedly along the narrow road, Kadski applied a tourniquet to Giertz's injury, then crudely bound and splinted it. Meanwhile, Giertz pressed the retro clutch pedal and told Kadski when to change gear for him.

The car appeared to go on and on accelerating, almost as it had in his 'hallucinatory journey.' In spite of the shock, or maybe because of it, Giertz began to think, *Perhaps Dr. Zed could be right after all? Maybe this literally is Real Life. I want to destroy reality, but what's reality anyway? Dr. Zed thinks his orthodox view of it is the only one worth having, but who's to say he's mistaken?* It reinforced Giertz's now general sense of something really being wrong with today, which would soon be further confirmed.

His contemplation was broken by a warning light winking from the dashboard. Then he saw the oil pressure gauge was falling, *The bullet-resistant material around the engine is no longer resisting!* He guessed correctly the back of the car was now a lace-work of holes. Decisively Kadski grabbed the spare gun from its clips on the cockpit ceiling, and told Giertz to stop the car.

Giertz knew at once what Kadski was going to do, also recognizing the futility behind Kadski's desperation, but felt too disorientated to argue. Even so, Giertz made an effort to disagree, but it was clear Kadski wouldn't listen. Giertz knew by now anyway, *Kadski never could.*


**Chapter 98 Bared Teeth**

Despite the failing engine, they flew over the crest of the next hill. Giertz changed down the gears and applied all his weight on the brake pedal, before realizing it wasn't enough to stop the hurtling machine. He reached down and pulled the red release handle marked, 'EMERGENCY STOP.'

The enormous sail of the parachute billowed out behind them, and the car lurched violently, jerking them both in their seats. Under the car, two shock-absorbing cables with small steel anchors fired into the road surface. Kadski and Giertz were thrown forward against their harnesses. Giertz's chest was compressed as if his ribs would crack.

Despite this, it was still some time before the car sat at a dead stop, and finally, Giertz could pull the second handle to release the parachute and cables. The engine burbled unhealthily and almost stalled. Kadski jumped out, and Giertz, more stable now, tried to make him take his gun as well, but they only stared at each other for a second. Then Kadski slammed the door down once more.

In the rearview screen, Giertz watched Kadski as he dematerialized in the blue haze of tire smoke. He straddled the dividing strip in the middle of the road, a gun on each hip, his head thrown back, his breath steaming in the cold summer air, saliva glistening on his bared teeth. As the remaining Cadillacs and motorcycles howled over the hill, they only noticed Giertz's car accelerating up the opposite slope. Nevertheless, a few shots were already hissing around Kadski, as the Non-men woke up to what was happening.

Kadski waited carefully until the range was perfect before he lifted one gun, dropping over it in his trademark, crab-like stance. He released single-fire rounds, each accompanied by an obscenity, and one car with a shattered engine block catapulted off the road, taking two motorcycles with it. A second turned end over end, pushing a third car off the other side. Only The Bad Actor, who'd cunningly retreated to the back of the pack, and one motorcycle got through. They rapidly surged ahead after Giertz's car.

Kadski gamboled out of the way as The Bad Actor attempted to run him over. Kadski came up on one knee and discharged both guns after the Cadilac as it was already cresting the second hill. As Giertz descended the other side however, he'd already discounted Kadski as dead. Yet the numbness Giertz had felt towards death now metamorphosed into a fundamental, bitter anger that made him just want to make a worthwhile end of it. He also guessed he was about to join Nailbrand, and he supposed, Kadski in their final experience, as the engine began to sound more and more discordant.

The speedometer needle joined the oil gauge in its decline, as more warning lights and buzzers came on.

Thick, gray smoke was beginning to issue from the fake Lamborghini's engine cover, and Giertz caught the smell of burning rubber and magnesium. Eventually, the dashboard began to look like some colorful decoration for The Festival of Greed. Then, inevitably, Giertz was seeing the distorted, grinning front of The Bad Actor's car behind him once more. Giertz desperately wondered what he could do about it, but quickly found there was nothing. So he just tightened his seat harness, hurriedly checking his gun and the last hand grenade, *In case I need them*, but didn't believe it was likely. Then the world appeared to turn inside out.

**Chapter 99 Blood Pressure**
Without even deflecting from its path, The Bad Actor's car expertly clipped Giertz's, spinning it around. It flipped over the crash barrier and rolled sideways down the embankment. The Bad Actor just drove on as if it all hadn't happened.

Giertz hung from the floor of the car, with the blood pressure whistling in his ears. He tore at the harness buckle and dropped onto the ceiling. He couldn't see anything as the cockpit was filling with oily smoke. The hand grenade was still where he'd thought it would be, but he had to search for his gun.

Kicking out what remained of a bullet-resistant side window, he then crawled through it. He reached back into the smoke to twist the car's ignition key in the self-destruct. It began to bleep. Coughing and breathing deeply in the relatively fresh air, he scrambled up the embankment over pieces of his car, back to the road. His injured hand was now bathed in a throbbing sting. Then a wave of scorching wind knocked him over, as the inverted car exploded behind him. Lying on his stomach, over the singing in his ears, he heard a motorcycle approaching.

He crawled on his elbows into the weeds at the side of the road, relieved to see the motorcycle was still some way off. In the opposite distance, Giertz could see the helicopter had already followed The Bad Actor's car further up the road. Knowing there would never be another chance, Giertz fumbled urgently with the gun. He focused the complex arrangement of trigonometric lines and digits of the telescopic sight, still not knowing what they all represented, onto the rider's head.

The rider was progressing cautiously, knowing he was now a 'survivor,' but seemingly reassured by the sight of the explosion, he began to speed up. Giertz had never tried sniping before, apart from in one of his holygames, *It feels cold-blooded and strange, despite knowing the situation demands it.* It was another reminder the rules were different today, and would never be the same again for Giertz, as his faith in Ceebix's 'game' dissipated still further. Giertz squeezed the trigger anyway, telling his conscience, *This is poetic justice, if nothing else.*

Not specifically designed for sniping, the gun still heaved vengefully in Giertz's hands, just as the rider saw him. Luckily there was no wind to deflect the too-light, but high-velocity micro-round. Even so, the bullet sailed past the rider's helmet. The motorcycle wobbled slightly, then began to accelerate. Giertz became aware he'd missed, but forgave himself, *Sniping was never a skill I paid any attention to in training, not thinking I would ever use it.* He knew the rider would be arming his motorcycle's missiles now.

Giertz tried to calm down and re-focus on what his reflexes were telling him, but the second shot missed as well. With the third shot though, Giertz aimed well ahead of the rider, and this time his head gave an involuntary snapping movement, tilting at an odd angle. He pitched forward over the controls, and the bike followed him. His body then acted as a cushion for the weighty machine as it hit the ground. It slid along on its side for a few more yards, throwing up sparks.

Giertz jumped up and ran unsteadily to where the rider sprawled, blood rushing onto the road from a massive wound in his neck. In spite of this, he was still able to scream a mixture of pain and delirious obscenities, and something about his mother. Giertz had been dreading this kind of confrontation for a long time, *It isn't like killing in the heat of a situation.* He reached down to undo the clasp on the motorcyclist's helmet, but he grabbed weakly at Giertz's arm. Giertz tried to ignore the gesture and not to look, or listen, as he wrenched the helmet off. To save ammunition, he broke the rider's skull with a blow from the gun's ergonomic butt. There was quiet.

Giertz felt sick and almost was, as he pulled on the rider's helmet. It wasn't just the disgust, but a feeling of the day's general strangeness overwhelming him. Nevertheless, he sprinted up the road to where the motorcycle lay, still making the rumbling sound of a stunned animal. He dragged it upright. He noticed the helicopter in the periphery of his vision, hoping the pilot hadn't witnessed the incident.

Giertz mounted the bike and pushed the control for its cyclone injector up to its maximum. *It will burn out the engine in a short time, but hopefully what I'm about to do will be over in a few minutes anyway. He was right.*

**Chapter 100 Attacking Run**

Giertz wasn't at all familiar with motorcycles. Apart from the one at Uncle Joe's party, he'd only ridden them in his holygames. The bike leapt forward, wrenching his arms and neck, but for a moment it sat almost stationary as the back wheel span freely, then ignited. So he eased off the throttle, and it finally flew forward on its rear wheel.

The sensation of speed, and the realization there was only his sense of balance between himself and the tarmac rushing beneath, was immediate and terrifying. He felt frozen by the air rushing through his flimsy Combat Youth jacket. He still put more pressure on the throttle though, as if the machine had become an expression of the feeling now burning in his stomach. He couldn't even feel his bandaged hand.

Strangely however, he found he was reluctantly viewing his predicament in a detached manner, *Really, this machine is going almost too fast for my body to react to it, even with my reflexes.* Then he saw the helicopter coming back, *I wonder what the pilot now knows? Can he see someone in a Combat Youth uniform is riding a Consumeordie Youth motorcycle?*

The pilot obviously did suspect something, as the machine passed so close to Giertz the beat of its rotors almost sucked him off his mount. Giertz saw it was trying to contact him on the motorcycle's radio, but as the receiving light blinked at him he knew, *There's no use in answering as I don't know their call signs.* Then he watched the helicopter in his rear-view mirrors, sweeping around for an attacking run.

The motorcycle came to an 'S' bend, designed to slow down the suicidal traffic in the almost perfectly flat terrain. *Obviously something pre-dating the World Transport Corporation,* Giertz observed. The front tire gave a small shriek of warning, but this made him more optimistic, *The road is curving to the left and right for the foreseeable distance!* He began to zigzag on the already zigzagging road as much as he could, trying to make it even more difficult for the pilot to aim. Giertz listened for the first shot as he tried to understand the controls for the motorcycle's heat-seeking missiles. In fact, they were fairly familiar, *Just like in one of my holygames! It's easy!* They were also already armed, *So for all my doubts; I shot the rider just in time.*

Trying to throw off the pilot's timing, Giertz braked unexpectedly, then accelerated rapidly once more. Giertz was congratulating himself on the way his reflexes were preserving him, when suddenly a trench seemed to dig itself diagonally along the road, almost in front of the bike's front wheel. It was so close, a ricochet tore away part of the motorcycle's cowling. Giertz now stared at the surging road over a jagged plastic edge, turbulence tugging at his helmet.

Still slightly surprised, Giertz reassured himself, *The pilot still seems cautious, keeping his attack short and not coming in too close. He probably knows I've got the missiles ready by now.* The helicopter flew parallel to Giertz and at a distance, waiting for the ideal moment. Giertz also knew the motorcycle's rockets were small and not very accurate, meant mainly for dealing with cars and other motorcycles, not aircraft.

Then, Giertz unexpectedly saw ahead of him the speck of The Bad Actor's battered, ugly limousine turning onto another, larger road packed with traffic. *Now I understand why the helicopter pilot is so worried. That's who he's trying to protect! The Bad Actor must have been warned by now as well. Therefore the helicopter will have to make its attempt on me before the main mega-highway, where it will be more difficult.* As he expected, the helicopter finally came in at a narrow angle from behind, and Giertz got ready to fire the missiles.

A panel opened in the cowling on either side of the machine, exposing four plastic tubes. He moved his damaged hand towards the firing switch, but then almost too late understood the pilot's strategy, *I can't use my defenses! A direct hit by my missiles at this range would destroy both of us, but for the same reason, the pilot can't use his either. If he fires again, I will have nothing to lose.*

Briefly, he wondered why the pilot was so desperate to protect The Bad Actor, *I guess they'll probably blame the pilot if anything happens to a Bad Actor, and then the pilot will face some hideous retribution.* This may have been why the pilot did something unexpectedly stupid as the road ran out.

**Chapter 101 Agonizing Second**

The helicopter pilot panicked and broke away, trying to end the stalemate, and to get a clear aim at the randomly weaving bike. Giertz almost sprained his thumb on the firing stud, but for an agonizing second - nothing happened. Then the machine shook as all four rockets launched simultaneously. For a moment he was riding in a cloud of acrid smoke, and he coughed.

The pilot, now conscious of his fatal mistake, was already turning the helicopter as the tails of smoke curled upwards directly into its hot exhaust. Giertz opened the throttle completely and passed the helicopter, just as it turned into a plummeting ball of fire. He didn't have time to gloat though, *I have to try to formulate a plan for what I will do when I encounter The Bad Actor!* Giertz thought frantically, but couldn't arrive at one. Therefore he took stock, *The motorcycle has no missiles left, and my gun and the hand grenade will probably be of little use, especially because the helicopter pilot has probably forewarned The Bad Actor.* Giertz decided to wait and see.

When he came onto the mega-highway, the traffic was even heavier than he'd expected. In an effort to catch The Bad Actor, Giertz rode between the lines of vehicles. The combined slipstreams subjected him to steady buffeting which threatened to throw him off. As was usual these days, cars were randomly pulling out in front of him without a signal, and he dropped back into his lane only just in time. In his desperation, at one point he grazed the back of a car with the motorcycle. *Even if I can see three seconds ahead, it's not going to make a lot of difference in this situation.* Bare hands shaking and, in spite of the cold, sweating on the rubber handlebar grips, he fought hard to control his nervousness.

When he finally saw the back of The Bad Actor's car again however, Giertz was so feverish with revenge and terror he almost lost his balance. What surprised him was The Bad Actor waving to him out of the open side window. Giertz didn't understand this at first, but then reasoned hopefully, *It's possible he may have switched his radio off, probably trying to relax after the conflict, or maybe it was damaged? Therefore he might not have been warned!* He also noticed some silver scarring and bullet holes in the car's paint. Giertz smiled to himself at Kadski's 'legacy.' Then he guessed, *From where The Bad Actor is, he can't see my uniform either. The pessimistic thought followed though, Or this could be a trap?*

Knowing he'd little to lose now anyway, Giertz tried urgently gesturing back with his injured hand. He could see The Bad Actor speaking into his microphone once more, and the voice came booming out of the loudspeaker again, 'What's the problem?' The voice didn't sound so self-assured since cameras weren't around. Giertz gestured wildly again as if he had important news, then reached for the last hand grenade and bit out the pin. He muttered an incoherent prayer to omnipotent Xerak for this one not to be a dud.

As he approached the enormous, damaged car, it was plain The Bad Actor was already thinking twice, *After all, disgruntled Consumers are always making attempts on his life.* Therefore The Bad Actor's hand sprang back inside, and just as Giertz came along side it, the window that had opened so readily began to go up again. So he reached over the motorcycle's controls and jammed the grenade into the remaining gap, but strangely it appeared to only hang in space. Then he saw the edge of the thick, bullet-resistant glass had only wedged it against the frame.

**Chapter 102 Swerving Violently**

There was a strange, timeless moment as Giertz and The Bad Actor stared at the grenade between them wondering what to do, as the fuse burned out. They even looked at each other, and Giertz saw The Bad Actor's face up close for the first time since their duel. Giertz wondered if this was the same Bad Actor who'd defeated him at Uncle Joe's party, *Does he recognize his former opponent?*

Giertz perceived a perspiring nervousness now overlaid the Bad Actor's general tiredness. His steel-gray hair was disorganized. The slightly disheveled appearance, which he usually de-groomed so carefully, now just looked a mess. *The recent events have obviously been more of a strain on him than his public persona would admit. No wonder he switched his radio off, he needs to relax. Strange, you're trapped in what you do, probably as much as we all are, and maybe you don't even enjoy it much anymore?*

Giertz hypothesized that being 'The Bad Actor' was just some kind of purgatory a top executive had to go through to achieve his particular career-goal. This one probably saw himself as meant for 'finer' things, but was only stuck on this sordid level. Giertz couldn't feel any sympathy though, even if he'd tried to, which he hadn't.

They still stared at the bomb for a moment longer, but Giertz was the first to act. He gave it a sharp blow with his elbow. It dropped in through the window, which obediently finished closing. Giertz tried to accelerate away on the bike's rear wheel, to the sound of the car swerving violently from side to side as The Bad Actor groped on the floor for the grenade. Then there was a thunder-sound, and Giertz felt the air all around him turn hot and vibrate.

Going too fast, the shock from the explosion made the bike unstable. Giertz tried to slow it down, but somehow he didn't feel strong enough to control it. He jammed on the brakes, and the front discs glowed red.

Exactly what happened next, Giertz wasn't sure. When the motorcycle went over, the fuel tank ruptured, spilling over the red-hot engine and the bike exploded. It catapulted Giertz through the air, turning him into a blazing human meteor. His body flew over the crash barrier and into the weeds and thorns of a post-industrial deadscape of rusted trash.

He sprawled, twisted at an odd angle, and there was silence for a while. Further back he was only vaguely aware of the cars and trucks of The Consumers going too fast for their brakes, slamming into the burning wreck of the car, spreading it further across all the lanes. Other cars slammed into them in turn, creating a chain-reaction automotive Hades.

Giertz was beyond contemplating the consequences of his actions though, reminding himself, *Everything is simply the will of Xerak,* and an incredibly sweet unconsciousness threatened to smother him. Perhaps it even did for a few seconds. Then some instinct for self-preservation took over as Giertz heard the sound of another helicopter coming.

The arm with a damaged finger was now dislocated and broken in two places, and all the skin had come off his thigh and hip on the same side. *Otherwise, I'm not badly injured,* he thought, trying to ignore the smell of his burning clothes, and first and second-degree-burned skin, but eventually Giertz's legs and good arm also stopped working, even attempting to stand up was impossible.

Therefore Giertz crawled under the bushes, through oily muck and slime. Clutching at his mangled arm, he slid down the embankment into the open landfill on the other side. Through the pain, he was still overwhelmed by the general shock of the changing rules, *My second act of revenge against The Bad Actors has not compensated for anything! The sure knowledge there's a remaining Bad Actor to take his place only makes it worse.*

Crumpled painfully on the ground, actually rusted, disused railway tracks, Giertz finally stopped caring about where he was, or anything else. He lay for some time conscious, but in a mental void. He noticed the helicopter now hovering above him, but didn't bother to ascertain which side it was on.

When he saw Kadski standing over him, Giertz decided, *Surely this must be too good to be true!* He even wondered for a moment if this was yet another hallucination, but he also questioned why Kadski didn't seem happier with their mutual survival.

Giertz surfaced again momentarily on the floor of the helicopter, with Kadski sitting nearby, Giertz's stomach bouncing around with the helicopters defensive, return flight-path. He stared at Kadski analytically, trying to gauge whether he was a hallucination, but Kadski just appeared to be uncomfortable about the day's whole scenario.

'You did relatively well,' was all Kadski said, as usual, but the compliment came across as contrived somehow. Now there was no mistaking either the expression forcing itself onto his face. It was the same expression Giertz had seen on Kadski when Giertz had killed The Bad Actor previously, but this time Kadski had more trouble hiding it.

*It definitely is jealousy!* Giertz recognized, shocked.

As Giertz slipped back into darkness, he found it strangely unpleasant to realize Kadski could be jealous of him. The idea had never fully registered with Giertz, and it was a final irony on this day when the initially smooth path of his Combat Youth career had twisted in a way that creased it forever.

## Chapter 103 Randomly Attacking

That evening Giertz awoke from the anesthetic in the Rapid Healing Clinic as the buxom, blonde nurse in a low-cut, white uniform, peeled the antibiotic-bandages off his almost-healed arm and hip. She was saying something to him in a foreign language with the tone of voice she probably would have used for very young children. Then, as Giertz wobbled unsteadily out of bed, she started shouting at him with it. While the fog in his brain was still clearing, and the nanobots still fizzing in his bloodstream, he pulled on his uniform again and ran shakily down to his new car.

He wasn't interested in the state of his damaged body. Even the remaining pain in his partly-repaired arm seemed distant, but he knew, *There is something inside me more important that will never heal.*

Some other Combat Youths were stenciling his name on the car's door, and the paint wasn't yet dry. He smudged it as he climbed in and drove home, not paying attention to running in the fresh engine either.

He fell through the front door of his crumbling Victorian terraced house and stumbled over to the old holyscreen in the living room, which even still had a retro, art-deco, brown Bakelite surround. He switched to Real Life, despite having sworn he never would again, several times. Just as he'd feared, he was on there with Kadski, briefly glimpsed through the bullet-pocked windshield. Giertz could even read his own lips, recalling what he'd been saying, but it would mean nothing to the audience.

At the same time, Pandora was spinning, spinning, and spinning her glittering Wheel of Destiny, as the numbers rolled and the audience gasped. Giertz had never hated his love for her more than at that moment. Giertz also knew he could never forgive the audience for their laughter either, as Nailbrand disappeared forever, in agonizing slow motion.

Other heavily-edited scenes were also action replayed, to much gasping and applause. Of course, it now looked as if the Combat Youth had begun the fight, randomly attacking The Bad Actor while he was just out for a pleasant afternoon drive. Of course, the cars of the Non-men and the motorcycles where not even there at all, erased by some electronic process. Of course, The Bad Actor appeared to have fought all the Greedeluxe Youths off single-handedly. (There was even a stunt-man impersonating Kadski, with whom he had a fictional fist-fight to the death.) Of course, The Bad Actor extracted himself from the situation without even a scratch. So, of course, the audience fully believed it was all going out as 'news.' Giertz wasn't consoled by knowing they'd not been able to use much of the real footage from the actual event.

The strange thing, however, was Giertz realizing somehow 'Real Life' was ultimately right, *It really is all only a 'game'! In spite of the ideologies and rhetoric, in the end, it's just a case of winners and losers, and I'm simply not a winner.*

Giertz also now assumed though, *The Bad Actors are more expendable than they seem.* After Giertz destroyed the camera helicopter, they'd not been able to record his entire final, lethal episode with The Bad Actor, but Giertz knew by now they would never have broadcast it anyway, *It will all just be on some digital 'cutting-room floor' - somewhere. No amount of editing could have turned those last events around, after all.* He grinned.

The grin soon faded though, as he saw now, *It's all pointless. In the end, it proves nothing.* Somehow it was too much, seeing Ceebix's 'Game' for what it really was, only another game. Today just seemed the final dead end to this summer's journey of disillusionment, so Giertz knew he had to act. He had to do something. He had to do anything. Only this time, at least one possibility was obvious.

**Chapter 104 Sickening Nature**

Giertz stayed up in his parents' old, empty, house, knowing the ambush had highlighted thoughts he'd been having for a long time, so that he could no longer avoid them. In spite of his near-recovery from his physical injuries, he was still feeling ill, but not so much physically.

In vain he tried to confront the lessons that today, and the whole summer, had taught him, while still not sure what they were, *I still don't see any point in joining the Combat Youth, or even know if my motives are pure. The youth will never be united. There's no way I can make them destroy reality.* The latter didn't even seem relevant anymore. Paradoxically, each event over the past few months seemed to have just taken him further away from his final goal.

He still wondered also about his 'basic training,' considering his actions ever since, and the number of times he'd gone into his ODS. Some part of him that was still vaguely human asked, *What did they do to me? What did they turn me into, and what for, in the end?*

He tried thinking more deeply, *Despite the sickening nature of everything I've witnessed since my first Situation, there was always an overall motivation which has kept me going until now. I've forced myself to think at least 'something' would be achieved by the Combat Youth, in the end, but now I know, whatever it was, it won't be.* It was an idea Giertz just couldn't face.

Right from his sword fight with The Bad Actor, Giertz thought of everything he'd done as just a string of serious mistakes leading him into this crisis, *Now I have to lead myself out of it.* He couldn't see any direction, at all though. Therefore he recognized the only option open to him now.

He knew he had to die; the only question was how. He'd already considered joining the Suicide Squad. A handful of Combat Youths had already done so, but they hadn't been given any orders yet. They looked disappointed. Giertz couldn't see it making any difference to him anyway, *It would only be a continuation of my original mistake.*

Generally, instead of any feeling of camaraderie, joining the Combat Youth had only made Giertz realize he'd always felt incredibly isolated, even when he was with people he knew. Well before he'd heard the theories about his disease from Dr. Kortex, Giertz had already believed his personality operated in a different dimension to everyone else's: a strange, sterile, geometrically simple world inside himself, where there was only himself. He could perceive the other people outside himself as no more than insubstantial ghosts, *It's as if there's a solid, invisible force field of isolation surrounding me, trapping me, and there's no possible escape from it.*

During conversations, it was more as if other people were making indistinct murmuring sounds at him, which he would make an effort to interpret, from time to time. In his heart, he had to admit, *Being a Combat Youth is not helping any of my problems at all. It's probably even making them worse.* He also wondered if he'd been deluding himself about any three-way bond with his girlfriend and Kadski. Deep inside Giertz knew, *I'm not one of those two, either.*

Over-all, he wondered what he was really afraid of. What it was always twisting around inside him like some parasite, straining the knots of his insides, threatening to plague him with ulcers, and worse.

Meanwhile, dominating the day's whole ordeal was the death of Nailbrand. Another section of Giertz's mind wondered, *Why should his death have affected me more than all the other deaths I witnessed in the past few weeks?* Giertz still only knew, *I will never have that conversation!* It was more as if he had a question only Nailbrand could have answered. So Giertz began to try to prepare himself for the end.

**Chapter 105 Safety Catch**

Desperately making one last attempt to look for an answer, he wandered through the dead house and stopped briefly in the kitchen. He stared at the covers of his useless books again. He saw the small hard-cover book he'd thrown away on the first morning, poking out of the rubbish pile, and thought about the dead words he'd written in it, but anything appeared to be worth a try now. He picked it up again and read his untidy handwriting from several months ago, 'There is something wrong with my mind.

I HAVE TO ACT.'

He now felt it was advice he'd written to his present self.

As he contemplated it, he noticed he was unconsciously toying with the handle of his switchblade machete, *In many ways I've a lot more respect for this as a weapon than my gun.* Often when he used it, he almost felt it develop a mind of its own. *There's something so primal about it, about using a sword, which is what it basically is. It's as if it contains an inherent sense of purpose. Perhaps that's because swords evolved with humanity, and are probably almost as old as we are.*

From experience, Giertz knew the spring in the mechanism had enough strength to drive the blade through a human body. He released it now, and the blade snapped out, ready for work, with a metallic click that he felt through his whole arm. Something else this particular weapon had, as an improvement on the blades which had previously carved history, was a small rocket motor in the base of the handle. In an emergency, this had the power to shoot the blade out of the handle for some distance.

Giertz now also noticed he'd put the blade in his mouth without even thinking. He aimed the razor at some point well beyond his brain. He'd never needed to activate the charge in it so far, but he calculated that when he did, *The power of the blast alone will be enough to take my head off, even without the blade.* He felt his index finger caressing the safety catch.

**Chapter 106 Without Warning**

In his general despair, Giertz had thought about suicide a lot before, but he'd only ever tried it as an end in itself in a couple of half-hearted attempts when he'd still been living with his parents. Barely an adolescent, his general feeling at the time had been, *Death has to be better than life, because surely nothing could be worse than this?*

Then today, laughing slightly, he wondered, *Why have I never done this before?* Instead of thinking about why he should press the button on his machete handle, he was now considering why he shouldn't.

He was also surprised at how what he was contemplating felt so good, *It's almost like making lust!* In a crude way, it gave him an unaccustomed feeling of power over his own life, and destiny. He also felt nervous though, as if his body suspected something was wrong again, the way it often did when he drove his car.

He thought vaguely about what kind of mess the rocket-machete would make of his head, and about who would find his mutilated corpse, if anyone. He theorized about what effect his death would have on his girlfriend and Kadski, and the Combat Youth in general. He had to admit, It will probably be negligible. *They're used to people disappearing without warning, so it would be nothing new to them.*

He began to wonder instead what the actual moment of death would feel like, if he would feel anything at all. Then he tried to imagine what the absolute nothing after death would be like. *Falling down the bottomless black pit forever, with no light anywhere, and no escape.* While with his entire heart he believed there was nothing at all after life, just as Xerak promised, he still found it impossible to face that completely. These final thoughts were also making the present experience less enjoyable.

The handle of the machete was now shaking so much in his hand the blade had drawn blood from the roof of his mouth. *I understand now there are two definite sides to me. One wants me to die, and one wants me to live, and now they're struggling with each other for my fate.* He began to feel frustrated, not so much because he wasn't dead yet, but because he felt unable to act decisively.

He wanted to take the machete out of his mouth because it made breathing difficult. Saliva with a trace of blood was running down the handle, over his quivering hands, but his arms were more like the hydraulic appendages of a robot, out of his control.

*There's a ten, (or is it five?) second delay on the charge;* he reminded himself. He thought again about the words in his notebook, *Yes, I was right! I have to act!*

The next thing he became aware of was that he'd flipped the safety catch off and activated the charge. The machete handle made a soft bleeping noise, counting the seconds. A small red diode flashed between his fingers at the same time. He saw sweat fall from his large nose and run down the handle. Meanwhile, just as it had so many times recently, he watched his whole life jump in front of his field of vision.

**Chapter 107 Totally Hideous**

As the seconds bleeped away, Giertz's memory unraveled. There were moments he'd appreciated with Nailbrand, Kadski, and even his girlfriend. There were the 'better times,' when his younger brother had been alive, and they'd been allowed to play in the backyard of the house.

He tried to help the process, straining his memory now, going as far back down its tunnel as he dared, but the further he ventured, the darker it became. In the end, he couldn't see anything at all. The earliest thing he could locate was some totally hideous, unspecified event. He guessed it might have been his birth, *But then again, it might not be.*

Sitting here in the living room, he realized he hated this house. Once it had seemed like the whole world to him, but now his memories were ingrained into everything in it, and they were all bad. As he looked around, he forced himself to remember what he was usually trying to forget, and all the dusty furniture and other domestic clutter appeared to come to life, threatening him with the past.

A faded wedding photograph in a cracked frame on the mantelpiece confirmed his memory of his parents being younger, perhaps even the same age as he was now. His father was a taller, slimmer and more optimistic young man, with a head full of hair. He could also remember his mother being almost attractive, in a bovine sort of way, but in spite of the photographic evidence, it didn't seem possible now. Giertz knew his memory told him lies.

His clearest memory was of when he'd accidentally explored into the house's small basement one day and caught his father staring into a square, black, wooden box, about the same size as his head. There was a door open on the front of it from which a greenish glow illuminated his face. Giertz's father was wearing welding goggles, with perfectly circular lenses, to protect his eyes. He appeared to almost be in some kind of hypnotic trance as he murmured softly into the glow. Giertz could just hear him say, 'Yes, I shall obey...'

Giertz had quietly closed the basement door, but had never stopped wondering, *Who gives him his orders?*

Giertz's clearest memory of his mother was when he'd accidentally confronted her one day, completely naked, dancing on the landing of the stairs. Her pale, pendulous breasts and buttocks had been swinging violently to Frank Sinatra's rendering of 'Come Fly with Me.' She seemed to be aware of Giertz's presence, but carried on anyway, staring in front of herself in a kind of forced ecstasy. Giertz winced painfully now, remembering the cellulite landscape of her arms, hanging folds of white phlesh, a map of blue lines running under the surface, augmented by green varicose veins. After that first time, the dancing became almost a regular event.

Giertz recalled that her final words in any argument were always, 'What will the neighbors think?' *She was still saying that even when most of the neighbors had become mutants.*

He'd been conscious from an early age of being the pivot around which his parent's off-center relationship revolved. Giertz felt somehow responsible for their physical decline, and the way it mirrored the decline of their relationship, despite not seeing the logic in his guilt, *I was made to feel totally out of place in their story, as if I was a lightning bolt from a cloudless sky.*

As Giertz got older, after being taught to read and write by his holygames, while he sat with his books the parents would indulge in spiteful arguments about his past, present, and future. *Even though they've done nothing besides the absolute basics of introducing me to survival, they always treated the responsibility as if it was too much.* The gist of these arguments was their tossing the accountability for Giertz's 'problem' to each other, as if it was a ticking bomb.

He knew anything physical between his parents was entirely out of the question, *The closest thing to it was just a sort of guilty sideways glance at each other. Even that made them both uncomfortable, but nothing more. It's likely they tried it just once, or even twice, but something cataclysmic, probably my arrival, or my brother's, or both, made them give up forever.*

Giertz's knowing they still slept in the same bed together just made it all seem colder somehow, *It's as if what kept them together was some steely, dogged, sense of purpose, but exactly what they were trying to achieve is impossible for me to fathom.*

He looked around the room at the fake-gold plate, flaking off the genuine plastic ornaments, Yes there definitely is something wrong. He hypothesized that, *If a family is meant to be built on some kind of emotional foundation, this one is built on nothing - an emotional void. All the violence is just the turbulence which inevitably surrounds a vacuum.*

In later years the 'family' had used to sit around the old holyvision watching an early incarnation of Pandora. This show was the only entertainment Giertz was ever grudgingly allowed, before they gave him the holygame station, trying to tempt him away from exploring outside the house. Otherwise, his father just watched hours upon hours of middle-aged, balding men droning on and on and on about industrial output. Occasionally Giertz's father would raise a buttock from his armchair, to relieve a sulfuric wind.

The only time Giertz had ever felt 'close' to the 'family' at all was when one day his father had sat back on the remote control by accident, and for a change, there was a Greedeluxe sponsored educational program. It was a science documentary about the lifestyle of the amoebae.

Beautiful, floating, microscopic blobs of jelly had danced in front of them. The amoebae lived in a world of infinite shades of blue. For a moment the 'family' was hypnotized. Amoebas were dancing in the sea; amoebas were bumping into other amoebas, amoebas were dividing effortlessly into new amoebas. As if in a trance, Giertz's father had said, 'I wish I was one of them...' The other two had just automatically nodded.

**Chapter 108 Total Control**

One of the noteable things about Giertz's upbringing was that during most of his early childhood his mother had never allowed him outside the house. As a result, he'd developed into a withdrawn and physically weak child. His parents had even boarded the windows up to prevent what little view he had contradicting anything they told him about 'reality,' but occasionally he'd been able to sneak exciting glimpses of chimney-stacks, the backs of other houses, and even the enigmatic sky through chinks in their carpentry. Consequently, he'd spent most of his childhood sitting on his bed thinking, trying unsuccessfully to form a picture of the world outside the house, and his relationship to the two god-like figures who dominated the universe within it.

Why his parents had done this was a mystery to Giertz. He could only assume that, for some reason, they'd wanted total control of his mind, from birth. Giertz smiled now at the irony, *Even I don't have total control of my mind!*

Eventually, when he'd escaped for the first time, he found what his parents had told him contradicted what he was seeing with his own eyes. At first this wasn't enough to understand they were entirely lying, but when the revelation did come it was the biggest shock Giertz had ever had, up to that time. Initially he'd not even been hugely interested anyway, since his mother had told him if he ever found the courage to venture outside, 'The Sleethe' would capture him and subject him to weird, abstract punishments.

In the end though, despite the legend of 'The Sleethe' turning out to be at least partly true, Giertz found this mutant monster to be only a minor horror compared to some of the others he would meet on a regular basis in 'reality.' He would still willingly have chosen to confront any of them however, over living with his parents in *that* house.

**Chapter 109 Remaining Seconds**

Back in the present, with the machete in his mouth as the seconds melted, Giertz looked around the kitchen again. He noticed another of the objects he hadn't seen at all for years was a wooden cupboard hanging high up on the wall. It looked far too small to be of any practical value, but he knew now the memories it contained were so awful, he'd almost successfully hidden them from himself. He only vaguely remembered that they had something to do with the first time he'd tried to escape.

The child Giertz had thought at first, from their casual attitude, his parents were going to overlook his first escape attempt, but they'd nodded to each other. (This in itself was strange because it was one of the few times he'd seen them agree on anything. It even made Giertz wonder, *Is the constant, ongoing argument really just some kind of ritual they enact?* His mother had then climbed onto a chair to reach the cupboard and took something out of it.

She brought down an object like a small totem pole, about nine inches high. It was made of some waxy-looking substance Giertz couldn't define, a sort of dull greenish yellow in color. She placed it on the empty table in front of him. Looking more closely at it, Giertz could see it was topped by a swollen bald head, larger than the shaft. On the head was a spoilt, greedy, little face. It was smiling.

Giertz thought it was the most revolting thing he'd ever seen. It still made him shiver to think of it. He'd looked pensively at his mother and saw she was smiling expectantly at him. Then she'd put her hand on the back of his head to apply a gentle, yet firm pressure.

When Giertz resisted, the pressure increased, until she'd one hand clamped around the back of his neck and another around the effigy, forcing the two together. Giertz cried and wailed and fought, doing anything to avoid the confrontation, but in the end, she crushed his face against it. He went through the motions of pursing his lips, wet with tears and mucous, enough to satisfy her. After this, it was some time before he dared to venture outside the house again.

Curiosity overcame even this fear though, and when he did eventually escape for good, he found reality generally disappointing. The world inside his head was far more appealing.

## Chapter 110 Disordered Mind

The strangest thing to Giertz was that in spite of all he'd gone through, even now he was still terrified of his parents. For a long time, Giertz had mistakenly believed the key to his disordered mind was hidden somewhere in his parents' 'relationship,' or lack of it. So he would analyze it incessantly, dredging his every mental resource, but it never did any good. In fact, Giertz was still not sure who terrified him the most, his mother or his father.

Giertz thought now, intensely, about his father, who he believed was an impotent man, in every sense, *Which is why he works extremely hard to maintain a facade, however flimsy, of alert, virile energy.* 'I am the wrath of God!' His father had once declared as if it was an explanation, when Giertz looked unhappy after a particularly vicious beating.

It wasn't the physical injuries that had pained Giertz though, even when his father had tied Giertz's wrists to one chair to beat him with another. Giertz could probably have put up with worse if the bruises and fractures were given in some spirit of 'parenthood,' but he knew they were not.

While beating Giertz, his father would affectedly spit across the room, or gulp down whole cans of Consumeordie 'By-Product Beer'. (This was the actual trade name.) Belching, he would also rebuke Giertz for not being a 'man' because he refused to drink alcohol at all. (Giertz never drank.) Sometimes his father would eat his lunch and attack Giertz at the same time, bits of food flying out of his father's mouth, along with the curses and condemnations.

Giertz half-heartedly tried to analyze it now, *One of the most frightening things about my father wasn't that he was, at least initially, bigger than I was, or more violent. It's my vision of all the chemical and spiritual poisons accumulating inside him, and reacting in some terrible cocktail, to give him that unnatural, unpredictable, sickly energy. He never appeared to be able to burn it off sufficiently either. Most of the time he just sat in his armchair and dammed it all up.* Shuddering, Giertz recalled seeing the involuntary tremors of hate passing over his father's face in waves, as the colors from the HV screen danced around it.

Now and again the boiler-like countenance would swell and get even redder. Then the safety-valve mouth would open, to hiss an obscene condemnation of any defenseless minority Dr. Zed had been howling about on the broadcast, as if Giertz's father had thought of it himself. These pronouncements could often end in a wracking, coughing fit, *As if the unhealthy aura of my father's own loathing was wearing him down.*

His father would also arbitrarily drawl declarations to Giertz, related or unrelated, to what was taking place on the holyvision screen, such as, 'Industrial output must rise!' Or, 'We must entirely eradicate disorder!' And, 'Inferior species must be exterminated.' Giertz would always stop what he was doing and listen with absolute respect to these decrees, no matter how clichéd and inane.

One thing Giertz would give himself credit for was his ability to maintain a proper air of respect for his father, while not respecting him at all. Giertz would stand up when he entered the room, shake hands with him and call him `Sir,' despite having fundamentally less than no regard for him, but it never made any difference to anything.

Sometimes his father would rush in from the street, as if in retreat. He would dance stumpily around the room, arbitrarily breaking things, his livery muscles seemingly inspired with a weird, manic electricity as he yelped insults at the world, behind its back. *They were all essentially limp gestures though, as if he was inside an invisible straight jacket,* but all this would end abruptly when Giertz's mother would literally call her husband to, 'HEEL!'

**Chapter 111 Fundamentally Ugly**
While his father worked on Giertz's body, his mother worked on Giertz's mind. He wondered desperately about

this a lot because, strangely, it seemed to be some pact his parents had made with each other in advance of his birth. In fact, sometimes Giertz got an unsettling feeling it was all just some kind of 'show' for his benefit. To him his parents were just two actors, only playing out some weird Vaudeville routine day after day, to get some reaction from him, *It's as if they are experimenting on me! Towards what end though?* Giertz had even hoped to find that reaction in himself, so they would finally stop. When it eventually would cease however, and Giertz would get his answer, he would never see himself in the same way.

His mother had never hit Giertz once in his life, or in fact hardly touched him at all. His father's problems with her also appeared to be integrated with Giertz's own. His father argued with his mother all the time, but he lived in total fear of her, as if she knew some fundamentally ugly secret about him. She would consistently chide Giertz's father about things most people would probably have killed not to hear, but he just seemed grateful she kept quiet about the worst one of all. Giertz was thankful also, as he genuinely didn't want to know what it was, feeling he knew too much already.

His mother would often, deliberately, make a display of Giertz's father to him. For example, she kept a multi-tailed whip by her armchair. On impulse she would burst into the room, dressed in her husband's clothes, and start beating him with it. At the same time, she would pelt him with her own garments off the drying rack in front of the electric `coal-effect' fire. She wouldn't stop until her husband sat fully embarrassed, tearful and bleeding, dressed as Giertz's mother. Then she would smile down at Giertz, like a satisfied teacher.

Consequently, Giertz was also equally scared of his mother, but for different reasons. He wasn't entirely certain of what these reasons were, but he had terrible sensations of guilt in his mother's presence, without knowing why. He knew she didn't have 'something on him,' the way she did his father. Even so, she clearly hated him. On random occasions she would say nonchalantly, 'I hate you, Jimmy.' Therefore he almost envied his father's bruises and scars, *At least he's focused on something tangible.* Giertz's problem was more abstract.

Giertz's mother had always dominated the entire social order within the house. Even Giertz's toothless grandmother hadn't escaped, as her daughter fed her a diet of laxative porridge, and then derided her ferociously for her incontinence. Giertz had fully expected his grandmother to expire from sheer loss of dignity, *If she hadn't been a vegetable, she would have been reduced to one anyway.*

His mother would also regularly call Giertz a 'liability,' and many other such labels. He was reminded continually of how giving birth to him had been one of the vilest experiences she ever had, and how she wished she'd never bothered, assuring him, 'I was *pure* before I had you!'

'I never asked you to! You cretinous liability!' Giertz would rejoin. Somehow he always found it difficult to manufacture the same degree of respect for his mother that he did for his father.

**Chapter 112 Final Fractions**

Whenever this particular argument started he would always follow up with, 'You only married him because you were having me!' She would choose not to hear this though, wrapping her arms around the plastic curlers crowning her head, and would trump Giertz's accusation, in her own eyes, with, 'And you were the reason your little brother died. You caused so much damage coming out I couldn't have him properly. Otherwise he would

have been better than you! He couldn't have been worse!'
Giertz would only guffaw heartily at this,

'What! That gimp? You always were defective!' Giertz
could still remember his brother however. *He might even
have been my twin!* Giertz didn't know.

A strange, white, featureless little thing who never
cried, he just made abnormal whining noises and refused
to grow. He'd heard his parents discussing the diagnosis,
in quiet, guilty tones, 'Chronic failure to thrive.' Giertz
had guilt-soaked memories of even torturing him on one
or two occasions. At the time Giertz had viewed these
actions as a kind of twisted benevolence, based on his
parent's example of 'love,' trying to inspire his brother
into life, or get any reaction at all. Giertz soon became
bored though, because his brother didn't even react much
to anything. His had died after only a few years, *As if life
couldn't interest him enough.*

Giertz had to admit however there was something
about his brother he missed, even now. He still had
dreams about the times when, for an extra-special treat,
they'd been allowed to play together in the unkempt
backyard, surrounded by the towering brick walls. This
was a concession his parents had made after Giertz's fifth
escape attempt, knowing he was now strong enough to
prize the boards off the windows, even if it broke his
fingernails.

He could still remember the sun coming through the
one scraggy bush, posing as a tree. It had played patterns
across his brother's small, white, apathetic face. The rusty-
barbed-wire fringed yard had appeared enormous to
Giertz then, more like some mystical Eden. This was
mainly because he'd nothing to compare it to, but even
now, the dreams he had about it were so intensely
beautiful he awoke with tears in his eyes.

Giertz could remember enough to know he wasn't responsible for his brother's death, and could now discount most of the things he'd done to him as naive experimentation - almost. Somewhere inside however, Giertz still felt a seed of guilt towards his brother. No matter what he did, he couldn't reason himself out of it, and he knew his mother knew it too.

Today, after remembering so far back, he felt he could just as easily project his mind into the future. *The future I will never have now,* he reflected, without remorse. *It holds something ugly as well, something even uglier than death.* He also wondered, *Exactly how different is my perception of time to other people's?* He tried to count the final fractions of a second as the timer on the machete bleeped them off. He also tried to remember how many it would take for it to explode, but found both impossible.

Strangely though, as if it had been planned, just as the last second was about to bleep from the machete, he heard the front door open. He guessed it could only be a mutant that had somehow managed to pick the cheap lock. Death was one thing, but the idea of some hideous mutation eating his mortal remains, and doing Xerak knew what else to them, was just too much. Then Giertz found he'd taken his finger off the button, and clicked the safety-catch back on. The bleeping stopped.

He reached tiredly for his gun, but a shrill greeting echoed through the dirty house. It was a far too non-human sound even for a mutant, making Giertz's teeth feel unpleasant in their gums. Something deeper also made him wish it had been a mutant, even one of the worst ones, instead of what it was.

# PART 3

## Chapter 113 Systematic Conditioning

Giertz recognized his mother's voice calling, 'Jimmeeeeeeeeeeeeeeeeeeeeeeeeeeeeeeeeeeeeeeeeeeeeeeeeeee!'

If Giertz's parents had come on any other day, they probably wouldn't have found him in the house, or the mood he was in. Therefore the resulting cataclysm might never have happened, but his parents seemed to have an uncanny instinct for where he would be, and what he would be doing. Later though Giertz would reflect that, *Whatever the day, the whole disaster would probably have happened sooner or later anyway*.

Giertz tried to take an objective view of his parents. His mother blundered into the living room, *Smiling like someone sweeping dust under a carpet*. His father dawdled in listlessly behind her, *As if attached to her by an invisible piece of elastic*. They'd also both aged a lot since Giertz had last seen them, which hadn't been so long ago.

Again, Giertz was overwhelmed, more powerfully than ever, by a serious doubt that these people really were his parents. After years of their systematic conditioning, he felt no emotional bond of any kind with them at all. The question was always there however, *Then who created me? Or what? So why these impostors?*

Giertz knew by now the house was about to somehow morph into a court of 'law,' *A trial with two prosecutors, and I have to provide my own defense*. They entered just as Giertz was pulling the blade out of his mouth, with a trace of blood on the end of it. The embarrassment he felt about this only added to his unsavory frame of mind, while the parents were already looking around furtively, as if sniffing for further evidence. *Of what?* Giertz was well aware that the rapid-healing splint on his arm, and his other dressings, didn't help his case.

As was now usual, neither side bothered with any greetings. Knowing he was in the dock, as always, made him incapable of manufacturing any respect for them whatsoever. Giertz jumped straight out of the chair clutching his head, while his mother provided the charges, 'We saw you on holyvision today, and what you and your gang did to That Nice Man.' Giertz knew they meant The Bad Actor. People who liked him referred to him as 'That Nice Man,' or something equivalent, instead of his more common, but less complimentary label. *So that's why my parents are here...*

'And did you see him kill me? So why am I not dead?' As usual, though, they merely ignored this piece of solid evidence. Giertz knew this was a useless line of defense with them anyway, *Like just about everyone, they believe what's filtered through the holyvision more than what they see first-hand, with their own eyes.*

As usual, his father weighed in with Exhibit 'A,' in an accusatory tone, 'You're trying to kill yourself again!' Just what this proved he didn't say, only smiling broadly at Giertz. *It's the smile of someone who's finally found what they've always been looking for.* Giertz responded by providing his central piece of evidence, but he didn't know what it proved either,

'Well now I'm a Greedeluxe Combat Youth, and that's what we do!' In fact, he didn't understand why he was answering his parents at all, *It's more a kind of ritual we enact any time we meet.* His mother's only reaction was to give no reaction, and his father gave a small shrug as if it was just more of what they'd come to expect from their son.

Giertz's mother turned to him, and this time she wasn't hysterical or screaming, but this just served to put Giertz on his guard even more. In a carefully rehearsed speech, with the air of a surgeon explaining a simple procedure, she conjectured quietly and directly, 'You're *diseased* Jimmy. You're a diseased limb on our family tree, and like any diseased limb you must be either healed, or cut off.' *It sounds like a conclusion they've reached after long hours of debate.*

Yet Giertz knew the logic of this was flawed on two levels, *First of all, we have no family tree, apart from my grandmother, who is practically a vegetable, and a dying one at that, if she isn't already dead. Secondly, my parents can't 'cut me off' either, because they don't support me. I receive my portion of tokens in an account from The World Bank every week, the same as every other Consumer.*

Since his parents had 'won' the episode of Real Life, and moved to their 'bijou' 'micro-apartment in the clouds,' Giertz knew he could keep the house for as long as he wanted. *No one in their right mind would ever buy it, and with the pervading unhappy miasma, even a mutant would carefully consider living here.* In spite of all three of them knowing his parents' argument was making no sense, he wondered though, cautiously, *So what do they intend to do?* Knowing their conversation never did make sense anyway, didn't relax Giertz at all.

**Chapter 114 Screaming Unintelligibly**

At the same time though, the frightening thing to Giertz was his not knowing why his parents' attitude should concern him in the slightest. Giertz was short by any standards, and his parents barely came up to his shoulder, but somehow he still felt intimidated.

'You're the *disease*,' said Giertz, calmly, but trembling slightly. 'Whatever is wrong with me I caught from you *congenitally*. Your chromosomes are *diseased* because your fundamental existence is *corrupted*. You can't bear looking at me because it's like looking into a mirror, showing you both what you really are.' This idea scared Giertz also, more than he was letting on. He was always terrified of seeing his father staring back at him from the looking-glass one day. Giertz also seriously wondered, *Exactly what did my parents' conditioning put into my mind, and how do I deal with knowing I can't change it?*

His parents were more surprised by the calmness of his answer, the form of his reply, rather than the content, which they'd never really listened to anyway. Also, for once he wasn't screaming unintelligibly, or trying to pretend they didn't exist. So at least this time they went through the motions of listening, but more out of curiosity than anything.

'So you've come here to amputate me?' Giertz asked, folding his arms and staring at them. His mother smiled benevolently,

'No, we're going try to *heal* you.' *So that's the sentence,* Giertz saw. *The process is the punishment.*

'Well I'm joining the Sacred Vow of Judazz Suicide Squad, and I'm going to...'

'OH NO!' Exclaimed his mother. Her intricately permed, purple-tinted gray hair, powdered with sparkle-dust, almost appeared to stand on end, like a wire brush, as if jolted with several hundred volts. This was what Giertz understood least of all, *It's obvious my mother loathes everything about me, but as usual, at any hint of me being removed from her life, she reacts this way. Perhaps they don't like the idea of my death because then they'd have no one left to torture anymore.* He couldn't even be sure of that though.

After the initial shock, his parents reacted to his announcement, as always, by arguing with each other as if he wasn't there. Each had an air of superiority, but instead of Giertz covering his ears and retreating into his imagination as usual, this time he joined in, 'The will of Xerak flows through me!' He recited directly at their faces, and then began quoting Zytopharbb on the Idea, 'Their world shall end,

They shall be destroyed,

266

Their great engine shall rot,
It is foretold!
Metal shall melt,
Stone shall crumble,
Their wombs shall bear monsters,
It is foretold!'

Nevertheless, the domestic hysteria continued as usual, but then something different happened. Giertz's father appealed to him, 'Your mother's right! Your mother's right!' He gesticulated with an air of finality, but looked at the floor. It was a superficial, patronizing gesture, but for some reason Giertz's mother's hysteria subsided. This was probably because of her astonishment at her husband finally agreeing with her about anything. 'Your mother's right,' his father grunted again, but with even less conviction.

Giertz's congenital slouch straightened slightly though. He sneered, and his father looked confused. They all knew it was just another of the meaningless paternal clichés his father was always reciting. He looked everywhere now but at Giertz's gaze.

By now, however, Giertz felt so emotional about The Idea, tears accumulated in his eyes,
'A young, insane warrior,
Shall smite the swollen-headed monster,
In his tower,
It is foretold!
There shall be death,
And death within death,
There shall be no forgiveness.
It is foretold!' He realized for the first time in his life he'd shouted his father down, instead of the opposite happening. Giertz repeated more quietly, mostly to himself, but with a feeling of achievement, 'It is foretold!'

He grasped desperately at the moment of surprised calm it created. 'You've got it wrong,' he affirmed.

They were definitely listening to him now, but at the same time, he had a giddy feeling this words were going nowhere. He pointed his bandaged and splinted finger at them, 'I was sent here to heal you liabilities! I'm...' Before he'd finished though, he stifled the impulse to tell them specifically what the answer to their problem was, because for once he felt he might have his parents' full attention. *Perhaps by not losing my temper, I can cling to it for longer, and get answers to some of the things I never understood?* He tried a tentative question, deliberately laughing slightly to mask the gnawing curiosity, 'By the way, how do you think you're going to *heal* me?'

His parents said nothing but just nodded to each other. It reminded him painfully again of how their marriage seemed more like some bizarre, scripted and rehearsed play, enacted for his benefit, *They behave like two executioners, happy with their work, and it's so, so strange to see them agreeing on something.* The scene also had an eerie sense of familiarity for him. Giertz started to tremble, visibly, mostly with a primal fear, but also felt his ODS welling.


**Chapter 115 Domestic Effigy**

Giertz's aging mother just managed to climb onto a creaking kitchen chair, to reach the small wooden cupboard still hanging on the wall. Giertz studied the bunches of bulging purple, blue, green, and yellow varicose veins hanging from the back of her legs, under the seams of her phlesh-colored nylon stockings. She opened the cupboard, and for the second time took out the most hideous object Giertz had ever seen.

Giertz had been able to face The Terror in his soul at The Situations, even using it to his advantage. He'd survived whatever he'd confronted at the Xeracist Tabernacle. In fact, he felt he had a new relationship with fear as a Combat Youth, but somehow, this particular event paralyzed him. He was seven years old again, *It makes no sense whatsoever! Surely it couldn't even appeal to my parents' weird sense of justice to play this scene again, as a punishment?* It only reinforced his feeling they were really agents for some influential outside force, which was making his life hideously unpredictable. Quietly, he began to cry.

By now he almost didn't care anymore, *Nothing ever made sense.* He'd given up trying to analyze his family, but what he did understand about them was becoming unbearable, more like a nightmarish sense of unreality. In some ways, it was even worse than his hallucinations, and he didn't even know if this was one. Now, too late, he saw at last, *There is no pattern.*

His mother placed the domestic effigy on the table again. His father pushed a chair behind Giertz, and unwillingly obeying his conditioning he sat, as if he had no choice. They both looked down at him, smiling expectantly. Giertz twisted his face away, but his mother put one hand on the back of his head, and one around the idol - applying a gentle, yet firm pressure.

Giertz saw the smile on its swollen, obscene, little head coming closer, and then he clearly recognized it again. *It's the same smile I've seen on the posters advertising The Festival of Greed, and on Ceebix's face, and just about every other face I've seen recently.* For a moment, in a way, Giertz finally began to see the temptations of what his parents were offering. Afterward however, Giertz would try not to remember the tidal wave of events that came next.

Still trying to reason, Giertz continued resisting. He turned in vain to his father, who just studied him through his spectacles with perfectly circular lenses. So Giertz continued to cry hopelessly, shouting, 'Dad!' He thought desperately, attempting to find something to focus on in his confusion. He felt he had to do something. He had to do anything. Then as if something had just exploded inside his damaged mind, Giertz thought of The Idea.

Immediately his course of action became obvious. This time he didn't just kiss the idol, but nodding slightly, placed both hands around the shaft and put his lips around the head. He saw his parents smiling with pleasure to each other at this sight, his mother's eyebrows flaring slightly.

Then, even when it cracked one of his teeth, Giertz bit its head off.

He spat it out, right in his mother's face. Something else broke too at that moment. Instantly he felt the air pressure in the room had been reduced to zero, and the blood in his arteries was turning to gas. Despite seeing three seconds ahead in time, he was altogether unprepared for what he did next.

**Chapter 116 Emotionally Numb**

Giertz's father flinched as the idol's head ricocheted from his wife's face and into his spectacles, breaking one of the lenses. His mother just gaped at the sight of the decapitated effigy, and her insane son. So Giertz picked up the headless shaft and rammed it into her open mouth with both hands. Like a failed sword swallower, she staggered backward with the green totem projecting out of her face. She was so surprised that all her careful cultivation of Giertz's psyche had come to this, her arms flailing, she couldn't even pull the obstruction out of her windpipe. *It's all so inevitable, Giertz reflected, poetically rushing towards its terrible justice, with no one at the wheel - or brakes. Their little prodigy has now become their little nemesis.* He saw his hand fly out and grab his father's throat.

'I AM XERAK'S ANSWER TO YOUR PROBLEM!' Giertz bellowed, as the house suddenly became a microcosm of hell. His mother watched disbelievingly as Giertz went into his ODS, and what his bare hands were capable of doing to her husband. The cheap furniture went up in a fountain of splinters, and blood recomposed the flower-patterned wallpaper. When she saw it wasn't just another of Giertz's 'stunts,' she started trying to scream spasmodically, *Like someone giving birth,* Giertz noted, but even this wasn't enough to dislodge the totem.

When he'd finished with his father, Giertz turned and faced his mother. She stopped trying to scream and fell silent, not daring to even try to breathe. Giertz now recognized that as far back as he could remember he'd measured his appreciation for women's bodies on a scale ascending from his mother's, as he'd always found it so repulsive. Now though he discovered himself diving on top of her, tearing at her layers and layers of corsets, *More like some weird body armor.*

Giertz also had another secret theory, *My father was probably the first, and last, man to do this to her, and the experience was probably such that she would never let him do it again.* Giertz knew if anyone so much as brushed against her she would wince violently. By the time Giertz had finished, her face, still impaled by the idol, had turned a strange greeny-blue. He knew, *Even CPR wouldn't work now.* Not that he would have tried anyway.

A few minutes later, in the darkness, he dragged the two bodies into the backyard. He began digging a shallow pit by the insignificant bush, which had once appeared so significant. Giertz had expected to feel guilt of Oedipal proportions, but while he didn't want to blind himself, he was still just sane enough to realize that perhaps he should. As he dug, he turned up the soil-filled skull of his grandmother's dog, and found it more interesting than what he was burying.

Over-all he just felt emotionally numb and confused, but another part of him felt nothing at all, wondering again, *Who were these people really, and what should I feel about them?* Also, he found it strange that, *My 'basic training' appears to be almost a seamless continuation of my upbringing.* Then he noticed something very small that at first glance at could have been mistaken for a mole.

Tattooed on his mother's upper arm were two crossed lighting strokes on a white disk, in a red rectangle. Tearing his father's sleeve, Giertz found the same, small, Greedeluxe logo, *But they always supported Consumeordie!* Although Giertz finally had a clue, confirming there was more to his 'parents,' and their conditioning program, it only posed further questions to him - but when he eventually found the answers, he would rather not have known them.


**Chapter 117 No Warning**
As the end of the year came close, under the sweltering winter sun, The Festival of Greed had arrived at last. The media had consisted of virtually ninety percent hypnotic commercials for months, ramming The Festival into The Consumers senses from their holyscreens, by blasting their retinas with mesmerizing images. Any ethical stops there ever were in advertising had been ripped out of their sockets, as every trick of 'aggressive market penetration,' was being exploited to capture The Consumers' tiny attention spans. Families with bodies like Greek gods were shown lazily living 'The Good Life' in homes akin to palaces, as they gorged themselves in orgies of consumption every day, and ostensibly were cumulatively happier for it.

Of course, the major sacrifice on the altar of every family dinner table was a generous, steaming lump of raw meat, or 'Phlesh.' The larger, the better.

Sometimes the commercials were two hours long, more like movies, with the products so subtly introduced they were not consciously noticeable. The adverts had much bigger budgets than the HV programs, which only lasted two minutes now, and were peppered with repetitive commercials anyway. The Consumers were even openly called 'liabilities' for consuming Brand G over Brand C, and encouraged to chide each other. All the ratings revealed this year's Festival was to be a record one as well, with consumption breaking every record, as it did every year.

While he patrolled the dying city though, Giertz looked closely at the angry, dissatisfied, bitter faces of The Consumers as they drifted past again. Their alcohol and Preparation X315/J despondency was blurred and distorted by the bright green-tinted rain running down the windshield. *It's the same every year. Even when they get more products with every Festival of Greed, somehow they always feel more cheated.*

He'd heard somewhere The Festival had once had some religious significance, celebrating the birth of some prophet, or genius, but it was only a rumor.

Also, this festival had a particularly bitter under-taste due to further rumors, and rumors of rumors, of The Producers' not-so-secret mass-extermination plan for The Consumers. Like everyone, Giertz knew gossip about 'The Sanitization,' was being fanned into fact by documents 'leaked,' with increasing frequency, from 'various corporate sources.' *They are "leaking' them deliberately, the same way they prepare The Consumers for any unpleasant news, to acclimatize us to our forthcoming doom. In fact, he was surprised, Everyone seems to accept it so passively!*

*Like beasts shambling to the slaughterhouse, they are only curious as to when and by what means. It can't be long, so I have to find some way to end reality, and soon!*

He also believed it was partly because of this, and The Festival, that his relationship with his girlfriend changed so quickly, and drastically. It was also the reason why, consequently, his connections with the Combat Youth, and life-in-general, were never the same afterward. Why he felt he had to do something. He had to do anything. This time though, to some extent, he already had.

It was the last official day of The Festival of Greed when Kadski was taking longer than usual in the rapid Healing Clinic, so Giertz was patrolling with his girlfriend in the passenger seat, as she sometimes was. Then, with no warning, she started screaming with near-primal intensity.

**Chapter 118 Dead Silence**

Shocked out of his driving trance by the girl's shrieks, Giertz immediately started looking around for their attackers. The car was on a narrow road running somewhere on the city's outskirts, amongst the dead factories with broken windows. It was several seconds before he realized there were no attackers, and what was actually happening occurred to him. He stopped the car. 'What's the matter?' He sighed, even though it was the first time she'd done anything like this. She sat saying nothing for some time, her silence just made louder by the soft throbbing of the engine's tick-over. Then he saw tears in the corners of her eyes. Giertz experimented with a more gentle approach, 'Tell me what's wrong?' She still said nothing however, pouting at the dashboard, one tear running down her face.

He wouldn't admit he was disconcerted, but was forced to concede, *This is very unusual behavior for her, like a lot of things recently.* For Giertz, the atmosphere of The Festival was highlighting a strange interior feeling he could somehow not discuss with anyone. It was the legacy of his murdering his own 'parents,' and the way it had interrupted his urge towards suicide, yet only temporarily. It seemed to be reflected now in his girlfriend's facial expression, and his knowing she was hiding something else behind it. It was more of the same feeling he'd had on seeing her strange, destructive, utter contempt for her fellow Consumers possess her in her first situation, and now it concerned him a lot.

He turned the car and drove it slowly off the road, deep amongst the 'trees' of a 'forest.' She noticed a small stream running nearby, and was already pushing the door up when he switched the engine off. Her bullet-retardant rubber mini-dress and thigh-length, Synth-O-Leather boots creaked loudly against the Synth-O-Leather seat, as she leaned out and vomited. She went unsteadily to the stream and was about to wash her face in it, but Giertz quickly pointed out to her it was sterile, with no life in it or near it at all, so was probably heavily polluted. He offered her the car's water ration instead, which she used without thanks, and then just sat hugging her knees.

Giertz sat on the car door sill looking around. He never knew what to do when confronted by nature, almost feeling as if he was on an alien planet. On the very few occasions when he'd been near it, he only felt confused, but even he perceived there was something wrong with this particular piece of 'nature' today.

He couldn't make out exactly what it was at first, *This scenery is almost sickly, the greens and other colors are much too bright; the leaves look almost dyed, more like something out of a fairytale - someone's idea of how nature ought to be.* When he experimentally touched a leaf he felt mildly shocked for a moment, *This is all made of plastic! It's no more real than the synthetic plants in an office foyer, which require no attention because they've never been alive. The soil underneath here must be completely dead!*

Now he understood someone had carefully landscaped these hills, he also noticed the sounds of birds singing and insects buzzing just kept repeating. *It's only a recording, on a loop!* There was no scent of pollen or chlorophyll either, only the kind of overall mild perfume which hung around packaging materials. In fact, he tried to think of the last time he'd heard any real birds sing, and found he couldn't. The closest to it recently had been the sound of the local mutants screeching in the night.

A small mechanical grasshopper clicked by. It wasn't even a good imitation, more like a toy, the rivets on its legs easily visible. Giertz guessed correctly it was probably a miniature surveillance drone. From further up the stream came the faint sound of the mechanical pump that was the stream's 'source.' *I'd always assumed the occasional patches of green, amongst the pervading brown, flashing past my car windows were 'nature,' but now I know there's more to it, or maybe less.* Over-all he felt a strange sense of disappointment, an emptiness he couldn't define.

In the middle distance was an enormous neon sign, explaining the land had been benevolently `reclaimed' by Greedeluxe Corp. after their 'agricultural operations.' Giertz tried to resign himself to the scene of synthetic pastoral bliss; *I suppose Greedeluxe can't do everything right. The soil under this plastic grass must just be dead, barren...* Generally though he still felt cheated, somehow, and his non-communicative girlfriend, crouching by the sterile stream, somehow compounded the feeling.

**Chapter 119 Forced Innocence**
They both returned to the car, his girlfriend almost back to normal, but as she sat in the passenger seat she still said

nothing.  'Please,' he said finally, realizing he was now verging on pleading, 'What's the matter?'  Hesitantly she responded,
'It's this Jimmy.'
'This what?' He asked, still looking for something physically real to her, but invisible to him.
'This relationship.'

From feeling cheated, Giertz felt the inevitable, ugly truth beginning to envelop him. Someone else now believed what he'd always suspected, and he could no longer tell himself it was just his imagination. Even so, he tried to cling to his illusions, pretending not to know what she meant, still hoping she might mean something else. 'What relationship?' He inquired, with forced innocence - and then the dam burst.

She was as hysterical as he'd ever seen her. She shook her head, screwing up her eyes, crying, her makeup a melting mask, 'I feel you and Kadski have trapped me in this awful thing between the two of you, whatever-it-is. All the fighting and Situations!' She was almost shouting, 'It just goes on and on, doesn't it! What's it all for? I - I *believed* in you.' He just sat however, still looking blank, so she explained, 'It's always the same. I just swapped one "rut" for another. You're just an animal! And phony! A phony animal! When you came back, I was ready to give you another chance, but it's a waste of time...' He said again,
'The will of Xerak himself flows through me! I won't stop until Consumeordie Corp.'s profit margin....' He could see she wasn't listening. Again he tried quoting The Idea at her, 'A young, insane warrior shall smite the swollen-headed monster...' However, at the same time he knew, *Even this just sounds like another standardized answer to the standardized questions surrounding the Combat Youth.*

'Of course you will!' She replied, with the kind of corrosive venom she secreted these days.

'What do you know?' Demanded Giertz dismissively, but with an unpleasant inkling he'd begun to sound like his parents. He also suspected, *She really does know something.* She started again spitefully,

'I know a bit more than you do! I...' Then instantly she caught herself, and he saw, plainer than ever, She definitely is hiding something! It began to torment him. Therefore in a mocking, taunting, childish whine, which he knew was guaranteed to irritate her beyond endurance, he demanded,

'What do you know?' Again there was just silence, but this time of a different kind, *It's not that she's unable to speak, it's that she's trying not to.* 'Of course you do...' He added patronizingly. He was reaching for the ignition when she turned on him like a cornered animal, with a look he could never have imagined, to say something that would change their situation forever.

**Chapter 120 Virgin Priestess**

'I'm Pandora.' She said.

Giertz laughed out loud. It was too silly, *If she was claiming to be The Sacred Virgin Priestess of the Xeracist Tabernacle, it couldn't be more ridiculous!* His laughter grew forced though, as he saw there was no evidence to the contrary. Experimentally, he tried to imagine her with a wig, certain makeup, and a white dress... Now the secret was out, her body crackled with a new confidence. She swept a string of mousy hair across her eyes, almost obscuring them, staring down into his face as if from a great height. 'Good evening, fellow citizens!' She crooned in a deep, almost-whisper, with just the right degree of contempt.

Giertz had never left a car so fast. Drawing his gun as a reflex, his eyes automatically scanned the surroundings for helicopters, Non-men, Bad Actors, and nineteen fifty-nine Cadillacs, but he saw nothing. Even so, the event he'd day-dreamed of all his life was terrifying. 'Go on, shoot me then!' She said in her normal voice once more. It was almost her usual manner also, except there was a mocking edge to it now, as if she almost pitied him.

Giertz found he was aiming the gun directly at her. 'Don't worry, *they're* not here!' She taunted him further. 'This isn't "Real Life"!' Embarrassed, he lowered the gun and slumped uneasily back into the car. She started laughing with a tinge of sadism, saying, 'Oh by Xerak you should see yourself!' For a time he just couldn't think of anything to say, or think, apart from, *Those dance routines of hers, she wasn't copying Pandora, she was rehearsing them for her!* He decided though the best strategy was to start with general questions, gradually narrowing down to the specifics.

So he began with the most obvious one, but he had to ask it without looking at her, 'How? I mean, how did you get the job?'
'I just applied. "Girl under twenty wanted to work in holyvision, in glamorous occupation, etc. etc." The advert sounded too good to be true, so they didn't get many applicants. They told me after the audition they'd worded it specifically to appeal to somebody with a particular neurosis, but they still couldn't believe their luck when they turned me up.' Then her tone changed, to become more like pleading, 'I'm two separate people in the same body Jimmy. I can't...'
Despite still being stunned, he cut her short. He wasn't interested in her psychiatric problem, but later on, too late, he would be. His mind began working once more, as he sensed something more important to him, *Perhaps this*

*is it? The will of omnipotent Xerak has guided me to this point at last!* Suddenly his dead parents and failed suicide attempt appeared to make some sort of sense, *This revelation could be my key to destroying reality!* So he started to probe relentlessly, 'What's the job like?' He snapped. With a barely perceptible sigh of disappointment, she described,

'Oh it's only four or five hours a week recording my bit, but it's still hard work, the dance routines and so on. It's all rehearsed, of course. There are a lot of make-up tests. I almost enjoyed it at first, but I hate it now. I hate the whole 'Real Life' lie, no matter how hard I've tried to convince myself. They won't let me out of my contract yet, but they say when it's finally up they'll replace me with a computer-generated image.' She threw her arms out in the small cockpit, 'Then I'll *truly* be immortal. The Wheel of Destiny is all preplanned, as you guessed. They don't pay me much, actually. I suppose they know I need them more than they need me, but I do get a lot of free products.' She noticed he was looking at her chest. 'Oh, the ones I wear on the show aren't real, by the way.' Giertz felt strangely disappointed, as if she'd struck some fragile, major illusion with a big hammer. 'I don't mind the work itself. It's just the people, we're all living a lie...'

Then he asked the major question, 'Do you really make lust with The Bad Actor?' Giertz was unable to mask the concern in his tone, but she laughed at his naiveté,

'He's seen me without my makeup.' He was surprised to hear her sounding disappointed, but he would soon learn just how disappointed she was, and how dangerous it could be.


**Chapter 121 Suicide Squad**
Giertz began to see she'd bared her soul to him, and in spite of everything else he genuinely felt, *I must owe her*

*something in return.* Also, seeing her in this state did something to him that he'd never felt before. He was about to tell her *his* truth, that he'd joined the suicide squad, but he stopped himself. He still had a deep sense though, that he was somehow making another mistake, when he declared instead, 'Listen, I still don't believe you're Pandora.' Her hand came up involuntarily and grabbed his skinny arm.

'You must!' She insisted, defenseless terror now substituting the laughter in her face. 'I don't know what's real anymore! I...' Tears were accumulating in her eyes once more, but he still demanded,

'I want proof!' As he'd suspected, *If no one believes her story, she really will be trapped in her dual identity, not knowing at all who she really is, or even if 'she' really exists. So surely she'll have to tell me what I want to know?*

She became abashed however, which surprised him because knowing her as he did, he'd expected her to spring at the opportunity. Also, now he knew she was Pandora, he was only just beginning to understand what it meant to her, *In spite of her complaints, there's something addicting her to that job that she would be very reluctant to let go of, but at the same time she's also very frightened by it.* She said slowly, as if dreading his reply, 'What proof do you want?' Mercilessly he answered,

'I want the security code to Consumeordie Corp. Headquarters.'

She knew straight away this could mean only one thing. Becoming an impaled insect for a moment, she writhed silently in her seat, then responded quietly, 'You're going to kill him aren't you?' Her tone seemingly begged him that it shouldn't be so. At the same time, he detected the same, frustratingly dualistic undertone in her voice, somewhere, betraying hope that he would. Giertz laughed sarcastically,

'Well, what do you think? I'm a Greedeluxe Corp. Combat Youth! I can't throw away a chance to assassinate Dr. Zed! I'll show you how phony I am.'

Secretly, he also knew, *I'd have been happy just to eliminate The News Dummy, but if I kill Dr. Zed, then Consumeordie Corp. ceases to exist, and it really will be the death of civilization. Greedeluxe will have no competition, so everything will fall apart! After all, The Globecon can't exist when supply dominates demand, can it? It will be the final push over the edge that this 'reality' needs!* Mainly, he was just pleased she feared there was a possibility he could succeed.

Exasperated, and with a hint of anger, as he now recognized what she meant by, 'two separate people in the same body,' Giertz declared, 'Look! You've got to make your mind up! You're leading a double life! You know what that makes you? If either side finds out, do you think Greedeluxe will believe me? Do you think Consumeordie care about you at all? What's going to happen when your contract is up? Where are all the previous Pandoras? I don't see any of your predecessors around. If you really want out of your contract, I can be the one to release you.' Finally, she broke,

'There isn't a security code. There's a bio-print machine at the entrance. The Non-men are there as well. Even a perfect clone of me wouldn't get in. I've got Grade B clearance. I'm your only key.'

'What's "Grade B"?'

'It's the same as The Bad Actor's. He can take in anyone he likes, so why shouldn't I?'

She sat radiating resentment however, as if Giertz was a successful torturer. He still didn't understand exactly what he'd just done to her, but he wasn't curious enough to ask why. Without any further prompting though she told him the geo-coordinates. He was surprised it wasn't the place he'd thought, and she gave him another surprise, 'That building in The Security Zone they always show on the holyvision is a dummy. It's empty. The workers sitting at the desks are mannequins. They built it as a decoy for people - like you. The real one is right here, in Consumer Zone D.'

He reached tiredly for the ignition, The last few days have all been too much. Before he twisted it, she grasped his upper-arm once more. 'Do you believe me now?' She implored him with the same sense of urgency.
'When I see it.' He sang, softly.


**Chapter 122 Concrete Answers**
'Jimmy?' She said tentatively. Something about the way she said his name made him stop as he was about to twist the retro key. 'Jimmy let's just go somewhere else?'
'Where?' He asked.
'I don't know,' she replied confusedly, as if contemplating the idea in depth for the first time. 'Somewhere! I mean, away from here?'
'Where?' Giertz repeated, this time with frustration, as if he would appreciate some concrete answers.
'I don't know!' She was almost crying again. 'Anywhere. I don't care! We don't need all this Jimmy...'
'All this what?'
'...Dr. Zed, the Combat Youth, The Situations, all of it. The two of us don't need it Jimmy!' The similarity between this conversation and the strange one he'd had with Kadski in the cafeteria recently struck Giertz for a moment - but only a moment.

Then her emotions began to spill in a torrent of words, 'There's no point in killing Dr. Zed. He's a thing, Jimmy. Somebody made him. He never had a mother. He just runs on batteries. I'm not kidding. That's why he can do the things he does without feeling anything!' Giertz had guessed this already, but he was too preoccupied even to disguise the fact his mind was elsewhere. 'He's not made of phlesh Jimmy; it's something else.' This fact caught Giertz's attention because he'd also gained this impression from what contact he'd had with Dr. Zed at Uncle Joe's party, but Giertz didn't want to ask how she'd gained her more intimate knowledge. Unable to stop now, she continued, 'Even if you killed him, they would only replace him with something else.' Giertz wondered who 'they' were, but he wouldn't have to for long.

'All this fighting all the time Jimmy, it's not going to help anything. If you and I weren't here, it wouldn't make any difference. It's bad here, but it's always been bad and always will be, but there are loads of places...' She tried again, harder this time, to think of some, but just concluded, 'There's got to be somewhere?' She was having difficulty holding back the tears now, but his mind was far away. Then just for a moment it came back,
'When I have killed him,' he prophesied, as if in a sort of semi-trance, 'then we will go somewhere, and be alone together.'

As Giertz started the car, she seemed almost satisfied with this, but he was beginning to glow inside. The feeling he'd had recently, of everything he'd done so far being a series of mistakes, appeared to be almost neutralized, *Xerak has led me to this chance not only to destroy reality, but to convert my previous errors!* Giertz never even considered he could be making yet another serious mistake, and perhaps the most serious one of all.

He only began to feel a cold, questioning feeling however, when in the context of his horrific 'memories' of the Xeracist Tabernacle, he said to himself, 'The will of Xerak flows through me!'

## Chapter 123 Normal Weapons

Pandora did the final driving, while in the passenger seat Giertz shaved his head with Kadski's electric razor from the glove compartment, checking the effect carefully in the vanity mirror. Giertz had kept his hair short for some time now, much shorter than even Kadski's, so the operation didn't take long. Around his naked cranium Giertz wound a sweat-band of pure, white cloth, symbolizing The Sacred Oath of Judazz Suicide Squad. It had been tossed to him by Ceebix as a reward for volunteering, and was now emblazoned with hieroglyphs written in Giertz's blood, quoting the Sacred Oath of Judazz to, 'Exterminate all uncircumcised fornicators.' (Even though Giertz wasn't circumcised, and fornicated at every opportunity, he felt no sense of hypocrisy about this oath at all.)

Pandora hid the car close to the generic-looking area of uniform office blocks she knew so well, as Giertz sent a coded message on the radio to the other patrolling Combat Youth, telling them where he was, and what was happening. Enthusiastically they agreed to converge on the spot, and inform the Combat Youth who were on stand-by, and all the other allied gangs. Last of all they would inform Ceebix, but it was a responsibility no one wanted, as he'd become so unpredictable recently. It was clear by now he never liked the idea of his operatives behaving fully autonomously, as he'd dramatized to Giertz. He didn't care by now though, just beginning to realize what he'd set in motion, *Nothing will have been known like this before. The word will spread faster than flames on a pool of Synth-O-Gas. It will be the biggest single Situation ever!*

He and Pandora both checked that their guns, and the spare gun, were all fully loaded. Giertz added extra belts of grenades and ammunition to his usual weapons. He also wore a new device issued to them recently. It was a compact reel of a specially reinforced nylon, attached to a bolt-firing mechanism, with a tiny, yet powerful winch. As Giertz strapped it to his right arm he knew, *This will enable me to climb almost any vertical surface!* In passing, he read the warning sign on the side,

'DANGER! ONLY USE FOUR TIMES!'

He didn't think much about it however - at that stage.

As they advanced towards the building, Giertz thought he'd never seen such a boring rectangular, generic, brutalist slab, *It's so much like any other office block, it looks more like all of them than they do!* Now he understood what Pandora had told him earlier, *They designed it to look that way as a kind of camouflage, 'hiding in plain sight,' the complete opposite of the spectacular, post-neo-obscurist folly everyone thinks is Consumeordie Corp.'s headquarters. Clever!* There was something unsettling about it though, and the whole area, which at first he couldn't quantify. Then gradually he understood what it was, *No mathematical graffiti! Anywhere! Strange?*

Giertz also became aware Pandora was saying even less than usual, and abruptly he felt a twinge of something he assumed must be conscience, realizing, *I've never considered her feelings on this imminent assassination attempt.* In fact, thinking back, he couldn't remember a time when he'd really considered her feelings about anything. Guiltily, what was left of the human being in him touched her arm gently, saying, 'How do you feel about this?' She shrank away however, as if his fingers were red hot, shaking her head to avoid the too-little-too-late question. He learned then, *I suppose compassion is a skill - which I've never cultivated.* Consequently, he felt an unfamiliar sense of regret, which would continue to grow.

As they came closer to the building, Giertz somehow sensed Dr. Zed was up there. Giertz accurately visualized him staring down his nose through the bulletproof shutters of his office with a well-aged drink in his hand, the late afternoon sun reflecting off his tinted spectacles. In the same way Giertz felt that Dr. Zed knew he was coming, Giertz could already feel the tendrils of Dr. Zed's awareness probing for his mind.

Following Pandora's reassurances, Giertz didn't attempt to conceal his weapons. The reception area was empty, no one was at the desk. He commented optimistically, 'The building seems unguarded!' They passed through the first set of laminated, bombproof-glass main doors, as thick as Giertz's arm, with no trouble. As they did, he noticed the walls of the building were also thicker than he was tall.

'Good morning Ms. Pandora,' said a friendly riveted steel box, with a circular pattern of holes drilled into it, bolted to the wall.

This washed away Giertz's the last dregs of disbelief, *So it's true!* He was surprised it left him feeling disappointed though, the fear of what he was about to face almost overwhelming his need to destroy it - but not quite.

'The gentleman with me is my new bodyguard, that is why he's armed. His body-print is not on record, but he's covered by my security classification,' she said to the box, adding in a whisper to Giertz, 'I've done this before. There's no problem.' He wondered silently, *Who with?*

There were a few soft mechanical clicks as the box sorted the information. Finally, the speaker repeated in the same friendly tone, 'Good morning Ms. Pandora.'
'Stupid machine.' She whispered, but there was a thud and a sucking sound from the heavy glass doors in front and behind.

They pushed at the doors frantically, but they remained solid. Pandora turned white. Reflexively she prepared to shoot the glass, but Giertz flicked the safety catch on her gun three seconds earlier. 'A ricochet in here would shred us both!' Even before he'd finished though, Giertz felt his last words were coming from a distance. Then he noticed a faint hissing sound from the box. As everything went black, he distinctly heard the speaker on it say, in precisely the same tone, with absolutely no sarcasm, 'Good morning Ms. Pandora.'

**Chapter 124 Boiling Claustrophobia**

When Giertz awoke, an executive was holding each of his arms. They were marching him along a corridor painted with cheap white emulsion, under even cheaper strip-lights, around sharp bends. He became aware of being swaddled in shiny chains, and that while the businessmen were not heavily built, behind them marched two Non-men. Abruptly they turned through an office door which looked like any other.

Giertz was dumped, more as a bundle of chains than a human being, on the shallow-pile carpet of a surprisingly small, cheaply furnished office, the flaking imitation wood furniture looking as if it might even be second hand. As he landed with a dull, jingling thud, everyone looked up except for Dr. Zed, who sat behind the one small desk in the office, thin veneer peeling off the chipboard. He was concentrating on what Giertz at first thought was just an executive toy, *It probably demonstrates some Newtonian principle of physics or other.* He would soon find though he was very wrong.

Also, behind the desk was a large, washy, post-neo-obscurist painting. Giertz knew it had to be an original, worth billions, *But probably produced by one of Leonard Kornn's apprentices.* To Giertz it appeared to be totally out of place in the Spartan room, the oily colors only underlining the general drab bareness of the other décor,

It's most likely only there for investment value. However, he was wrong about that also.

The office felt even smaller with all Dr. Zed's disciples cramped in there, sitting on chairs with the stuffing poking out of them, Giertz saw Pandora sitting in one of the threadbare chairs, next to The Bad Actor, who smiled smugly down at Giertz. She kept looking across at Giertz with an increasingly pessimistic expression on her face. Both she and Giertz tried to conceal how they were ringing their hands in consternation. They felt the heat on their backs from the eyes of Dr. Zed's young, sun-bronzed disciples, their facial muscles knotted into cocksure expressions. Giertz noticed though, *Plainly they are all politely bucking for promotion over The Bad Actor's head.*

With so many people in the small space it was overheated and lacking oxygen. At first, Giertz thought it was almost funny, *Anyone would expect a hypermultinational corporation to have something at least bigger!* Then Giertz realized, *There are probably bigger, showier offices on other floors, but they are only for impressing the easily impressed. It's in pressure-cookers like this one that the real business is conducted, in boiling claustrophobia!*

Despite all this, something distracted his attention. It wasn't the kind of item one would usually see, but Giertz's odd position on the floor put it at his eye level. On one wall was a small group photograph in tasteful black and white. It showed three young men, taken long ago. Two were smiling, but the tall one in the center wasn't. He wore dark glasses and had a strangely shaped head. It was obvious he was a youthful Dr. Zed, and Giertz was surprised another of them looked familiar also, but at first he couldn't identify who it was.

Despite the evidence deposited before him, Dr. Zed appeared to have completely ignored one of his most important disciples, Pandora, turning traitor. Giertz was puzzled, *It all appears to be beneath his attention, he's more interested in that toy!* Giertz also saw, *In a way, this incident has accidentally served Dr. Zed's purposes: I'm just providing another demonstration of the 'Real Life' he's continually grinding into his followers, and the world in general.*

Curious now, Giertz observed the 'toy' more carefully and saw that, far from a Newtonian principle, it was a lattice of planes of various colors, shapes, and sizes, all inter-linked and flexible. In some magical way, they were able to shift around each other and change shape constantly. Dr. Zed was manipulating it dexterously, like a master of some complicated gambling game in a far-eastern marketplace. Instantly Giertz froze. *It's the exact model of my disease I saw in The Happylands asylum!*


**Chapter 125 Skull-Face**

There were other things on the desk also, an object like a small totem pole, about nine inches high. Made of some greenish-yellow, waxy-looking substance, it was topped by a swollen, bald head, larger than the shaft, with a spoilt, greedy, smiling face. There was a crack running under the neck, amateurishly repaired with cheap glue. Already frozen with shock, this was nearly too much for Giertz.

Then he saw Pandora's diary, and also the cheap blank notebook he'd written in, and a small silver key. Giertz felt violated, realizing it was as if Dr. Zed was trying to piece together some forensic puzzle, *He possesses all the evidence, but he still doesn't understand how it all fits together. How much does he know about me overall though, and how does he know it?!*

Giertz knew he would never have an opportunity to study Dr. Zed so closely again, and so he struggled to regain his composure. Giertz saw, *Dr. Zed has near-absolute self-control over his every action and thought, he seems to do everything deliberately. Even his blinking is conscious and measured. It's as if he has no unconscious!* Somehow it was intimidating just to be in this behavior's presence. Giertz felt a sense of wonder, *In spite of Dr. Zed's defect, or perhaps because of it, he pieced together an organization like Consumeordie Corp.*

So Giertz began to question, *Who, or what, could have created something like him?* He looked again, closely, at the black-and-white photograph of the three men. Suddenly the one who looked familiar lost his anonymity. Giertz had yet another shock as he knew he was seeing Dr. Asclepius, before the years of late nights in the laboratory had given him the gaunt features that earned him the affectionate nickname, 'Professor Skull-Face.' *So who's the third one?* This now became Giertz's overriding question, which he was about to have answered also.


**Chapter 126 The Beast**

The tiny office was even smaller than it looked, because one wall was a bulletproof window, giving the illusion of space. After a few minutes, Dr. Zed abruptly lost his fascination with the model, and with a drink in his hand, walked over to the window, to view the panorama of the dying city. His strange face was washed orange by the evening sun, burning between the bulletproof shutters. He murmured something, and they hissed completely open. He murmured something else, and the window itself opened. The breeze licked at the few remaining white hairs on his vast scalp.

Everyone went quiet, and Giertz knew Dr. Zed was setting the stage for another of his impromptu speeches, that he liked to give at random. He began using his voice like a blunt instrument, 'Consumer Man chooses to say "it is too late for the truth." Indeed, our civilization is fat, bloated, wasted. The world my lamented partner and I created now devours itself,' he looked directly down at Giertz, 'rotten with a cancer. Our ideals lie bleeding in the gutter.'

Then Dr. Zed quavered reverently, 'The tome my lamented partner and I wrote no longer applies.' Everyone in the office knew the name, but not the face, of who the 'lamented partner' was, including Giertz, *Byron Reed - the co-author of their blueprint for a Consumer utopia called 'Empire and Genius.'* Giertz reminded himself, *He'd held an equal shareholding in Consumeordie, but disappeared mysteriously on a skiing holiday at Dr. Zed's summer villa.* For some reason, the face of Byron Reed had always been kept secret. No one knew if the name was genuine, or even if there really was a partner. Giertz looked again at the photograph. The third member of the party was a shy, intelligent young entrepreneur, but despite forcing a smile, he didn't look happy, in fact almost ill. It was then Giertz knew the elusive face he was looking at, *So that's Byron Reed!*

Dr. Zed concluded, 'Our ideals have merely been divided up and cast to the masses, but still, as always, I submit to the demands of my Consumers.' Then, theatrically, he gave a command, as if it were some climactic announcement, 'Drag in The Beast!' At first, Giertz thought this was a purely metaphorical statement, until he noticed everyone looking towards the door, and immediately The Beast was dragged in, by a harassed-looking executive, turned zookeeper.


**Chapter 127 Strangely Human**
'The Beast' wasn't quite what Giertz had expected. It was an animal he'd never seen before, like some cross between an orangutan and small bear. It had long, yellow hair all over its body, and strangely human eyes, all of which made it extraordinarily ugly. It too had a larger than

human size head. A chain tethered the animal, the thickness of which appeared to be well out of proportion to its strength.

It was a popular rumor that Dr. Zed's pastime was genetic research. In his speeches, he was always repeating his belief that civilization was 'improving' all the time, and that it would eventually reach perfection, but only if Consumeordie Corp. gained full control, of course. Holding back the process were the human beings themselves, which now needed the improvement, rather than their surrounding society. The coming 'New Consumer Eden' required a 'New Adam.' Giertz concluded, *The foot has to fit the shoe, I suppose.* Giertz remembered, *It's also an embarrassment to Dr. Zed that, due to his peculiar genetics, attempts at reproducing himself, even by cloning, are hopeless. So he has no heir to the Consumeordie throne.* Therefore Giertz had no doubt, *The prototype 'New Adam' will also be the new CEO of Consumeordie Corp.*

Looking at The Beast now, Giertz felt a twinge of sadness, and sympathy, *It was probably one of Dr. Zed's failures in his genetic experiments to create the perfect Consumer, but he unexpectedly found a use for it.* It was hard for Giertz to believe however, *Maybe he even feels some affection for it as a pet?* Giertz would be very surprised though, to find out what the real relationship was.

Giertz was puzzled however, to notice how, despite The Bad Actor's fanatical dedication to Dr. Zed, he didn't seem to like The Bad Actor much. Giertz concluded, *Dr. Zed probably sees The Bad Actor as a failed experiment, because it's plain to everyone that, even with all his skills, he's not going to make an adequate replacement for Dr. Zed, and I've already killed him twice.* The Bad Actor seemed only too aware of it, shuffling and scratching his nose, as Dr. Zed ignored him. Giertz guessed, *Therefore a large part of Consumeordie's research and development budget must be going into Dr. Zed's human vivisection project.* He also now saw it was carried out on a hit-and-miss basis, *Dr. Zed probably has a whole menagerie of such failures, even more pathetic than The Beast, hidden in a basement somewhere. I suppose I should feel privileged to witness the results, and even more so to see a mutation Dr. Zed found useful.* Somehow though, Giertz couldn't make his feelings match the thought.

The Beast was shaking visibly at the sight of the office full of people, rolling its eyes in seeming terror. At Dr. Zed's signal it was let off the chain and allowed to scamper around on all fours, squealing, and defecating on some of the executives' tailored suits, as if these were people it hated. Dr. Zed turned and watched this with a silent, detached contemplation, a quirky trace of emotion on his face. Despite its status as Dr. Zed's pet, Giertz now heavily empathized with the creature, *In all its scramblings, The Beast seems to be looking for something. Perhaps it's hoping for affection, or even just an emotional response out of someone?*

A gleeful Giertz also observed that most of The Producers present just saw the creature as a disgusting, smelly annoyance, *They would dearly love to see it dragged out again, and shot preferably, but they are forced to accept it as an eccentric whim of Dr. Zed's, which they must tolerate.* Some even made an effort to interpret this 'Real Life' gesture of Dr. Zed's, trying to learn something from it. One even attempted to smile through the filth it had left on his face.

Briefly The Beast settled on Dr. Zed's shoulder, as if he was the only person it could trust to any extent, and Dr. Zed managed the closest he could to a smile. For a moment, looking at the silhouette of the weird creature next to the economy-size head, with the backdrop of the twisted landscape outside the window, Giertz had the first, strange inkling, *Perhaps things are not at all they seem?* And he was absolutely right.

He would never be prepared though, for just how right he was.

**Chapter 128 Therapeutic Value**

After The Beast had been dragged out again, a new atmosphere of calm appeared to emanate from Dr. Zed. It was as if seeing the animal, that he obviously liked more than his executives, embarrass them so thoroughly had some therapeutic value for him, while they were only more agitated.

After a moment though, the deep guttural drone continued, exactly from where it had left off, as if nothing had happened, 'The Consumers believe I show them Real Life, but they have never, and will never, see Real Life! I don my cap and bells for another day. I show them murder, mutilation, obscenity, on their holyvisions as they just nod and put another piece of `Dairylux' Chocolate between their `Plastident' dentures and say, "Ah! Yes, that certainly is Real Life!" I even receive love letters from aging spinsters saying, "Thank you Dr. Zed for showing Real Life to us!" Yet I have looked into the face of life itself,' his voice rose to a shout, 'and I say it is more vile than that of death!' Giertz felt a strange quiver of recognition with this statement, which caused him to recall his experience in Xerak's Tabernacle, *Oh by Xerak, Dr. Zed is talking about The Idea!*

'In my nightmares I see the faces of my Consumers, Dr. Zed continued, 'walls of them, reaching out to me for... for...' At this point he grasped his strangely shaped temples, closing his eyes and staggering slightly, his voice dropping almost to a whisper, '...but all I can do is give them goods and services...' Then he regained some of his bearing and declared, 'That is why they must be given Phlesh!'

By now however, Giertz had heard enough. 'I suppose,' he interjected, 'that you intend to win me to your point of view, so that you can display me like any other of your puppet-actors!' He sneered as he nodded towards The Bad Actor. Perspiring unhealthily, the eyes behind Dr. Zed's tinted spectacles becoming even more distorted than usual, he turned on Giertz,

'No!' He replied. 'You see that gallows out there?' He indicated to his entourage a structure of rusty iron girders on a roof nearby, clearly visible from the window. Giertz saw it was no ordinary gallows either. There was no trap door, but a system of pulleys by means of which a strong executioner would winch the unfortunate victim to be eventually strangled by his own body weight. The 'rope' was a steel cable. Giertz could see it was kept well oiled, and now understood the fate of the executives who failed Dr. Zed, as he continued, 'I'm going to have him hung, drawn, quartered, eighthed, and anything else I can think of on that! His remaining offal shall be thrown to the wild beasts of the circus in prime time! His poems will be torn up and burned before his eyes!' This last line staggered Giertz, even though he hadn't written any poetry yet, and he wondered again frantically, *How could he know about my secret ambition?* Meanwhile, Dr. Zed turned to Pandora, adding, 'And she will officiate, contract or no contract!'

Dr. Zed hadn't mentioned Pandora joining the Greedeluxe Youth in her spare time. Therefore Giertz had mistakenly thought of this as an indication of forgiveness on Dr. Zed's part, but now Giertz understood this omission was only yet another demonstration of his total uncaring for her, and anything she felt or did, as long as it didn't interfere with her contract. *Or his precious 'Real Life'!*

**Chapter 129 Hell's Dogs**

Laughing on only one side of his face, Dr. Zed turned his bespectacled stare on Giertz once more and said, 'I see you affect the shaven head of an assassin. You Hell's Dogs, you think you are so in touch with reality down there, don't you.' Giertz smiled inwardly. *He thinks I'm one of The Hell's Dogs gang, because they are the ones who get the most publicity. He doesn't even know they're a Consumeordie gang, on his side. Then again, why should he care either way?* Then Dr. Zed looked away and said with emotion, 'But you are not, and of this, you must be made aware!' Giertz noticed Dr. Zed almost appeared to be pleading for everyone in the office to understand something, gesticulating as he repeated, 'You must be made aware! You must be made aware!' He turned back to Giertz, and now he saw tears running down Dr. Zed's chiseled cheeks, many different expressions on the countenance all at once, but not quite mixing, like oil and water. It was a horrific, pastiche of a face. Dr. Zed showed all his entire bottom row of teeth as he repeated, 'You must be made aware!'

Then, like a juggernaut train switched onto a new track, he started on a fresh subject. A single, clear, optimistic expression flooded the huge face, and the tears stopped flowing instantly. The remaining wetness now looked totally out of place. As Giertz had anticipated, the speech eventually came around to Dr. Zed's favorite topic, Consumeordie's marketing strategy on fresh meat, or `phlesh' as he referred to it, 'My totality encompasses all extremes, and more!' Dr. Zed resounded, 'From the savage in its jungle to The Noble in his mansion. The desire for phlesh! Phlesh itself! The ultimate product! Still pulsing and bleeding, fresh from the slaughter!' Clutching a handful of the air before him, he came closer to Giertz, demanding, 'Have you ever thought about Phlesh? What

Phlesh *feels* like? What Phlesh *actually* is?' Dr. Zed worked his fingers on the emptiness to emphasize the point, 'You eat it, reproduce with it, and exist within it! Perfect Phlesh should be firm, like the fat covering a monopoly!'

At this point, Pandora unexpectedly jumped to her feet and began expressing herself confidently enough, at first. She gestured towards Giertz. 'They don't need you! The Consumers don't need you! They're sick of seeing your ugly face everywhere telling them what to do and what to think! You take away their dignity and pay them in...' She gesticulated as if physically groping for elusive words in the ether, '...filth! Rubbish!' Meanwhile, Dr. Zed just carried on preaching, in the same monotone, 'The market price is given and adjusts to it as a reason other than the shape of reality...' She pointed at Giertz again, 'Why can't you just leave The Consumers alone? You only manipulate them to fulfill your profits...' She gave up though, shrugging, almost in tears once more, and sat down again on her hands.

The harsh neon strip-lights dancing on his glasses, Dr. Zed gestured broadly at Giertz, as if desperately trying to make him understand, 'Now my Consumers are devourers of unclean phlesh, worshipers of hollow idols. Yet I shall still give them what is total! What is absolute! What is pure! I shall give them goods and services! I shall give them Real Life! I shall give them Phlesh!'


**Chapter 130 Weird Reverence**

Despite Giertz's loathing, as Dr. Zed's speech continued Giertz couldn't help feeling a paradoxical admiration, *Dr. Zed is really going! He's probably making his greatest speech ever! The ideas soar well beyond any of the stale concepts he's come out with before.* Almost all the other faces in the office were also looking up at Dr. Zed with a weird reverence. Some had tears of inspiration on them. One or two were begging him to stop, because the economic theories were too much for their limited minds to handle. 'To anti-manage in monopoly is what it's all about!' He continued mercilessly. 'The real threat to the economy is between A and B. So we associate A and B with a different dimension. Our mutual task is to deal with this possibility, to compensate the losers (the previous winners). Then mankind falls short of his optimum allocation of resources! A priceless move from B to A for the winners...'

The sweat was running off Dr. Zed's enormous forehead in rivulets, while the lines on it heaved and contracted as if it had a separate life of its own. Huge veins stood out, pulsing on his temples, as his entire body seemed to be pumping the ideas themselves into his brain. He strained to force the concepts out of himself, as if the gargantuan train was now ascending a steepening gradient. 'This is the age of sales, net assets, etc., so if it is not reason ruling management, there will be a greater potential!' Some of the disciples in the office began whooping and cheering as he paused for breath between statements, encouraging him not to hesitate in placing the insane building blocks on top of one another, while Giertz noted, *It's almost as if they've had laid bets on his performance!*

Dr. Zed was now unstoppable, proselytizing, 'Consider three standard models supported by slaughter-competition! When an animal is presented to firms, i.e., by a very low degree, such as will produce a carcass at least relative to the total market, the important determinant of the way firms are phleshed throughout developing levels of outputs, prices and profits are all moderately well phleshed. The forequarters models of price theory...'

While everyone was mesmerized though, Giertz's mind was working. He noticed one of the executive's eyes were not only glazed over with the same ecstasy as all the others, because he also had the honor of holding all Giertz's and Pandora's guns, grenades, and ammunition. He displayed them as pathetic relics of some failed rebellion. A slight, balding, bespectacled man, he stood by the doorway, with the two Non-men just behind him. They appeared to be indifferent to everything in the office, and the world in general. Giertz looked at the key to his chains. It also dangled temptingly from the executive's hand. Then Giertz looked at Pandora. He found she'd already seen it, but staring directly into her eyes; he saw only a confused coldness there.

By now Dr. Zed's whole head had turned red, and then to a frightening shade of dark purple, as he continued to thunder, 'The relative reality is not to keep it free! Indeed, a change of non-price competition, social political and economic standard models of price theory, are perfect in every dimension! A force other than theory suggests prices will exceed if it is not reason that rules....' Giertz was awestruck, *It looks as if his brain is about to explode from the sheer tension of being the single component holding all the complicated, irreconcilable logic of Consumeordie Corp. together!*

Dr. Zed then raised his eyes to the ceiling, craning his neck at an unnatural angle, as if the words were written up there. As he mentally staggered towards the grail of the final concept, some of the executives were clearly experiencing orgasm. The wine glass in Dr. Zed's hand exploded into a cloud of fragments, but he still only stared upward as the 'blood' dripped from his hand to the carpet, and he croaked out the last few words. 'Therefore I say, the Consumer... must devour... his own...' He grunted with effort and then choked out the final word, '...PHLESH!'

*So that's it!* Giertz was shocked. *That's his extermination plan for The Consumers! For me! The Sanitization. It makes perfect sense, no weapons, no nothing. He's just going to have The Consumers consume each other! Themselves! Perhaps he's even convinced himself that's what they ultimately demand from him, in the end. Getting them to eat raw animal phlesh is just a necessary stage, then it's only a short step to having them consume human phlesh, one another's, their own...*

With this thought, Giertz instantly felt he'd gained an entirely new perspective on what had happened to him in the past year, and everything else in general. He too began to wonder what, 'All the fighting...' as Pandora had put it, what the corporate youth gangs, and The Situations, were actually for. *Perhaps the corporations just want the youth to destroy itself?* Now also, Giertz felt he almost understood Dr. Zed's point of view, *I suppose, to him, it all represents progress, civilization, his 'reality,' reaching its 'final fruition.'* More than ever now, Giertz felt his mission was just, and his motives perhaps pure after all. It reaffirmed his belief that, *Somehow, I have to make a quick, clean end to this civilization, before it's too late for it.* Yet Giertz's thinking was interrupted by a sudden, added threat.

## Chapter 131 Fervent Faces

As if the run-away-train of Dr. Zed's thoughts had mounted the hill-crest, and was now charging down the other side, he bellowed, 'PHLESH! PHLESH! FOR MY CONSUMERS! PHLESH! PHLESH! PHLESH!' While saying this, he picked up a heavy, steel, post-neo-obscurist lamp from the desk. One of the more weak-hearted young executives present, probably horrified by witnessing similar scenes in this office before, had a sudden attack of idealism. At the same time, Giertz noticed old bloodstains here and there, which had never quite washed out of the shallow-pile carpet.

The Idealist leapt to restrain Dr. Zed's arm, but only found himself hurtling between the bulletproof shutters of the office window, out into space, still clutching the lamp as if it were some consolation prize for his idealism. As his screams of terror faded with descending altitude, Giertz was amazed, *So Dr. Zed not only possesses super-human intelligence, but strength as well!*

Dr. Zed's large hand now picked up a cheap, tubular-steel chair. All Giertz could think was, Oh, he's going to kill me! Giertz didn't know how long he'd been unconscious, but guessed pessimistically it must have been long enough for the Greedeluxe Combat Youth to react to his call, *They probably had second thoughts about it. Maybe they assumed it was another trap, or just some aspect of my unpredictable behavior.* He hadn't wanted them merely coming to the rescue either; he'd wanted at least to throw them Dr. Zed's misshapen head as they mounted the first steps to the building.

As Giertz considered this, Dr. Zed began to pound him into the blood-stained carpet with the chair, in time to the final word, now a war-chant for The Producers in the office, 'PHLESH! PHLESH! PHLESH!' They heartily stamped their genuine leather shoes in time to it, and Dr. Zed would probably have continued until there hadn't been enough of Giertz left to hang, but then somewhere an alarm sounded.

The squawking klaxon obviously had some specific meaning for everyone in the office, including Pandora. It instantly changed all the fervent faces present to disbelieving terror, and perhaps even those of the Non-men. The unnatural color quickly drained from Dr. Zed's visage also, and his arm froze in mid-stroke. Then there was a deep rumble from the foundations of the building, and the walls of the office visibly shook.

Giertz knew immediately it was the Greedeluxe Corp. Combat Youth placing heavy thermal-demolition charges on the armored front doors. He felt ecstatic, despite the pain, *They will be firing grappling hooks onto the floors above, and planting charges on them also! Then Consumeordie headquarters will be wide open to any visitors, for once!*

Ironically the heap of multiple, steel links had protected Giertz to some extent, like chain-mail armor. Now a fist projected out of it, catching Dr. Zed under his jaw. His ungainly body did a disjointed backward somersault over the desk. He fell in an undignified pile of reports, cables, and broken executive toys. 'You eat it!' Giertz shouted, but was drowned out by the unmistakable sound of a Situation brewing in the background, and an anonymous, disbelieving, fearful voice screamed out of the intercom, 'It's come at last! A plague of them! They cannot be contained on the lower levels! Initiate all contingency plans! Destroy the access codes...!' Before it was abruptly cut short with a yelp of pain.

**Chapter 132 Collective Realization**
What happened next seemed to take place almost faster than anyone in the tiny office could think, because they were all still getting over the idea that someone had actually hit Dr. Zed back, including Dr. Zed himself. Therefore there was no sound but the blaring klaxon for a few seconds. Then Pandora stood up again, her rubber dress creaking against the cheap vinyl upholstery.

Everyone thought she was just going to speak once more. Therefore they didn't take much notice, but she stepped towards the executive holding the weapons. There was a sudden collective realization of what she was about to do, but everyone just looked on helplessly. The insignificant man started fumbling to get an arm free, but her steel toe-capped, thigh-length, Synth-O-Leather boot swung up  in one of her whirling kicks, and crushed his groin.

He dropped everything and fell back, paralyzed with pain. She knelt and picked up the key and one of the guns. She threw the key to Giertz, and then shot the two Nonmen as they stupidly stepped forward with their arms outstretched. They vaporized, leaving a strange odor like acrid incense. Their clothes collapsed in two smoking piles on the floor. Another executive moved towards her, but she shot him through the eye. He was already dead before he crumpled onto the faded carpet, his head staining it crimson. She shot the man she'd kicked, who was kneeling, wheezing on the carpet behind her, and he keeled over to lay still. As she did this, another made a dive for her legs, but she turned in time and whirl-kicked him hard in the head, and he collapsed also. Then she stood surveying the office, her mind seemingly blank, wondering what to do next.

Giertz's multiple bonds were only held together by a single lock, which he'd undone easily enough, but it took some time for him to untangle himself from the yards of chain. As he struggled feverishly, he saw Dr. Zed crouching behind the desk. 'Shoot him!' Giertz shouted to her. She looked at the desk and uncertainly pointed the gun at the crest of the bulbous skull, just visible over it. She could have killed him on her whim at that point, but did nothing. Then they heard a movement at the other end of the office.

They turned just in time to see The Bad Actor opening a fire exit at the far corner. She switched the gun across the room, but he was already slamming the door in the faces of his colleagues, who were desperately trying to follow him. They were sprayed with chips of wood, glass, and ricocheting bullets as she rapid-fired at where he'd been standing. As Giertz finally sprang out of the chains, he noticed a movement by Dr. Zed's desk.

Taking advantage of the distraction, Dr. Zed dived head-first through the painting behind his chair, disappearing through the wall. There was a corresponding noise of running in the corridor outside. Giertz cursed everything, running over the smoldering ashes of the Non-men to the office door. He reached out for Pandora to throw him his weapons, but she didn't respond. In the corridor he saw Dr. Zed's back accelerating away from him with enormous strides, as Pandora stood numbly, just looking at Giertz.

Suddenly she raised the gun at Giertz, deciding whether or not to shoot him as well. It was this that finally made him comprehend what her job with Consumeordie, and being Pandora, meant to her, *The psychological addiction I'm asking her to sacrifice, how could I have been so naive, expecting her to believe in my dream and not theirs?* Now he also saw what she meant by, 'I'm two separate people in the same body,' and wished he'd listened more carefully.

He decided the best tactic was to feign ignorance, pretending he didn't understand, urgently extending an arm to her. She appeared to realize then that killing Giertz wouldn't mean much to him, because life didn't mean much to him. He might even thank her. Then an evil, vengeful, little smile crept over her face. Giertz was disturbed, because by now he'd seen it before on so many faces. After thinking for a moment, she just threw the belts of weapons to him. He looked at her for a moment longer, knowing it was probably the last time, and then leapt out into the corridor. Pandora then turned on her former colleagues, her gun hosing them randomly with micro-bullets, her aim distorted by tears.

**Chapter 133 Bullet-Dodging**
Dr. Zed was almost at the end of the long corridor when Giertz landed in it, firing from the hip. Even the highly

cushioned recoil of the gun shook his whole body as it ejaculated each of the ultra-high-velocity projectiles. 'You're the liability! Liability! LIABILITY!' He shouted in time to the shots. He saw them hit Dr. Zed exactly between his shoulder blades, but he just continued around the corner at the end of the passage, the points of impact hanging in the air after he'd gone.

Giertz rushed with all the speed he had down the corridor, but crashed into something invisible that threw him on his back. Picking himself up, he saw the bullets had bounced off a sheet of some transparent material, which had slid across after Dr. Zed passed. It was no thicker than Giertz's thumbnail, but he only hurt his hand as he punched it with all his strength. He decided to console himself by following a corridor leading off to his left, *At least it's going in the same direction Dr. Zed has taken.*

He was soon reassured also, by knowing he was running down a corridor parallel to the one Dr. Zed was negotiating. From time to time Giertz saw him at the end of a connecting passage, and would fire directly at his big head, but again the impacts only hung in mid-air again. *It's apparent Dr. Zed had this escape route planned well in advance. He must have been anticipating this assassination attempt for some time.*

Giertz found he was now running through deserted offices. Filing cabinets had been left open and monitors unattended. Cups of coffee steamed on blotting pads, Like the Marie Celeste. The staff had wasted no time, but Giertz wondered where they'd gone.

Then gradually the scenery began to change. He was running between laboratories full of glass tubes and oscilloscopes. He saw biological specimen jars full of organs floating in preserving fluids, some of which Giertz recognized as human. He saw other body parts, but couldn't be sure what animal they'd come from, or even if they were from any known animals.

Then looking ahead again, Giertz saw he was running towards The Bad Actor. He wore a long, black coat down to his ankles, with a red carnation in the lapel. His hands were sheathed in a pair of thin, black leather gloves, making them look small and insect-like. He had a big cigar clamped between his teeth, and a large, retro Thompson sub-machine gun with a drum magazine, but it was modified with a modern infrared sight and suppressor.

He fired at Giertz in an expansive burst. He twisted himself in the bullet-avoidance techniques taught to him by Ceebix in the 'live-fire exercises.' Giertz rolled out of the way as he'd been trained to, but only just in time. He ducked and jumped, firing back at the same time, as computer panels and filing cabinets rattled with hits and ricochets all around him.

Somehow though, the situation lacked any real surprise for Giertz, *It's just like one of my holygames. It's easy.* In fact he was overwhelmed by the similarity, and Giertz couldn't help wondering at the comprehensive emphasis Ceebix had put on this side of basic training, *I could almost believe I was coached specifically for this very event!* This idea gave Giertz a strange feeling of suspicion, that he couldn't account for.

After checking the next corridor was clear, Giertz began racing against Dr. Zed once more. He now knew though, in the same way he was hunting Dr. Zed, *The Bad Actor is now hunting me, and it's clear he's only playing with me. It's probably just beneath his sense of style to kill me too quickly.*

Occasionally a Non-man would spring from nowhere, and Giertz would shoot it down, like no more than one of the cardboard targets in the shooting gallery. He never quite got used to the strange smell when a Non-man vaporized, but they presented relatively easy targets. The irrational fear they instilled in Giertz however, made it difficult to limit himself to one bullet for each of them.

Giertz also noticed the specimen jars now began to contain entire unborn creatures. Most of them were visibly human, but with others he couldn't be sure. Some of them were so ugly he almost stopped, but he didn't want to take a second look. Then he came to the cages containing living specimens. Naked, with matted hair on beds of dirty, stinking straw, they had surgical scars all over their heads and torsos. Most looked relatively normal, but their behavior was exaggerated after some bizarre pattern. They either threw themselves at the bars, clawing to get at Giertz, or groveled in terror of his footsteps. Then he saw others that hardly looked human at all. *So this is where Dr. Zed keeps his other genetic-experimental-failures. Now I know where most of the human flies and crabs originate from! There must have been some mass escape years ago.*

Giertz wondered if Pandora knew about this, and concluded, *She must do!*


**Chapter 134 Warped Imagination**

The further Giertz penetrated the building, the more he began to see, Its new architectural exterior is only a facade of offices, grafted onto a very aged structure. As he twisted through the clean, white corridors, they were gradually turning into narrow brick caverns. Soon the walls were running with damp, thick with centuries of mold. *It's like an interior from some eighteenth-century nightmare, but whose?*

The pain of physical exertion started to grow in Giertz's chest, and then he heard a voice he didn't want to recognize. He saw cheap metal megaphones screwed to the ceilings, from which echoed The Bad Actor's cheap metallic laughter. 'No, you don't get out that way, "Dr." Giertz,' the speaker bellowed. 'And another thing, Greedeluxe shares plummeted another two points as I speak! Ha Ha!' A string of bullets chewed into the wall by Giertz's head. *He always knows exactly where I am!* He just glimpsed The Bad Actor's Cheshire-cat smile disappearing around a corner in a cloud of gun smoke.

Then the Bad Actor's voice crackled quotes from Dr. Zed, 'Democracy comes not from over-Consumers! Xerak is criminally insane!' To help counteract them, Giertz began to recite lines from 'The Thoughts of Zytopharbb' to himself,
'Their world shall end,
They shall be destroyed,
Their great engine shall rot,
It is foretold!' Somehow though it didn't help much, and he still didn't want to remember what he'd confronted in The Tabernacle.

At first Giertz believed he could recognize the sources of the stolen genes for the mutants in the cages around him, but the deeper he went into the building, the more difficult it became, *Some must even be part vegetable! Ultimately they seem to be synthesized entirely from some twisted imagination!* He passed more cages in which there were things he thought even he couldn't have hallucinated, and there were always still worse. Some appeared to be well aware of their condition and, and with what language they had, begged him for death.

Reviled, Giertz wanted to oblige, but noticed his ammunition was already running short. He also became still more concerned when he saw some broken cages, the bars bent and snapped from the inside.

**Chapter 135 Brain Abnormalities**
Giertz ran past a sign proclaiming:

Now in a series of enormous, dank chambers with high, vaulted ceilings, he observed rows of large, green, glass spheres. They contained strange, naked bodies, suspended upside-down in the fetal position. Giertz noticed with surprise, *Many of them look like Dr. Zed's disciples, They must be volunteering their DNA! As crazy as it seems, the gamble must be worth it for them. I suppose if they hit lucky and their body becomes the prototype New Adam, they will also be the new CEO of Consumeordie. What a way to get promoted though!*

There wasn't much light about, so he couldn't see very well, despite the dusty columns of sunlight slanting through huge arched windows along one wall. They illuminated gray piles of misshapen skulls and various abstracted bone formations. Other still-living life forms, with apparent brain abnormalities, scrambled amongst them, searching for sustenance. Their eyes lit up with a hateful hunger at the sight of Giertz's skinny frame.

The place was full of broken, obsolete, scientific apparatus, covered in inches of dust and cobwebs. *It smells like nowhere on earth! Obviously, this is a cathedral to Dr. Zed's search to create the New Adam in his own image, but here the gargoyles are alive!* The closest thing to holy music however, was the inhuman bellows of rage and confusion echoing around it.

He could only just see indistinct things scrambling away into dark corners as he approached, for which he was thankful, because he didn't want to look at them. *Here the evolutionary process goes off at a peculiar tangent. The escaped specimens breed, the fitter subsisting on the less adapted. What's it all evolving towards though? What might it have evolved already?* This last thought put Giertz even more on his guard. He could face the idea of being killed and eaten by them - just. What he couldn't deal with was that, *Like the human flies, they might contaminate me with their distorted chromosomes, and I will end up a part of the bizarre survival-struggle in here for the rest of my existence!* Then something he couldn't quite see grunted to his right.

He fired reflexively in its direction. There was a primeval-sounding exclamation of pain, and the something shuffled away urgently. Then he found himself confronted by something worse.

**Chapter 136 Strangely Shaped**

The something worse was filthy and dressed in ribbons of what had once been a business suit. *It's even still wearing a tie!* From its non-human physical appearance, Giertz would have expected it merely to grunt. Then he noticed it was trying to speak to him, but he couldn't understand what it was saying as its mouth, or mouths, were so malformed. It looked as if it was asking him a question, but he took no chances and shot it twice. Then he discovered he had an audience.

He could just see multiples of strangely shaped eyes watching him from a large shadow. He tossed a hand grenade at them. The explosion rocked the floor, sending up billows of dust and animal screams. He raced to the far end of the chamber shooting everything that moved. He fired in self-defense, then in terror. In the end, he just kept firing, no longer caring about the ammunition he used.

Giertz looked back and realized, in spite of this, through the dust he could just make out the silent, deformed crowd. *An army of misshapen phlesh!* They shambled purposefully towards him, chasing him towards a large, circular pit at the far end of the chamber, between himself and the exit. From the pit Giertz could hear loud, even breathing from a pair of lungs unlike those of any natural animal. It occurred to him, *There must be some form of hierarchy operating amongst these mutants, and what I'm approaching must be at the top.* He threw another hand grenade at them.

There was a white flash of heat which jolted Giertz backward and illuminated their distorted faces for a moment. When he sat up his ears were singing a strange, discordant note, and everything sounded muffled. He was only vaguely aware it had been another grenade with a dodgy fuse, this time going off too early. He saw it hadn't thinned their ranks either, or deterred them. *After all, the worst I can only do is kill them, and they'd probably welcome it.* For the third time since his first Situation, Giertz felt not just The Terror, but something worse. *The Bad Actor has guided me into a trap!* Giertz felt he was no longer playing with death, but he was death's toy.

He almost no longer cared about killing Dr. Zed. Now Giertz just wanted to get out of this menagerie at any cost. *Then again though, do I have a choice of destiny? I've used most of my ammunition shooting my way in. There isn't enough to shoot my way out again.* He understood there was no turning back, he could only go onwards, but once more he was forced to reconsider what he'd volunteered for, wondering what further horrors awaited him, *In the end it's purely the will of Xerak carrying me towards the confrontation I once craved so badly, whether I want it now, or not.*

**Chapter 137 Twisted Curiosity**

Giertz adjusted the pulley device on his arm. He'd only used it in the simulators, but understood the general principle. He aimed it at the ceiling just beyond the pit and fired hopefully. His arm jerked with the recoil as a bolt, trailing the thin nylon line, snaked upwards out of sight. He recalled the warning to use it only four times.

*That's one,* he noted. He heard the distant clink of metal on stone as it struck home. Tugging on it he heard it twang like a guitar string.

He also heard movement in the pit, and so he pulled the pin out of a grenade. While swinging over the pit, he dropped the grenade in. As he'd half expected, some hideous appendage groped hungrily out of the reeking darkness towards him. He just had time to notice it was covered in hairy suckers, each like a small human mouth.

Drawing his legs up to avoid it, he fell on the other side of the pit, scrabbling to organize his gun, but then the grenade went off. A fountain of smoke and slime was ejected out of the hole, and he recoiled from a few, disgusting drops of it splashing onto his leg. An echoing scream from the bottom of the pit accompanied the explosion, and Giertz was disconcerted by just how human those lungs now sounded.

In their eagerness to reach Giertz, some mutants couldn't stop themselves falling into the pit, but there was nothing between him and the door now. He lay panting, remotely detaching the bolt so it automatically rewound onto his arm. For a while, he'd given the mutants a common cause, but as soon as they knew he was beyond their grasp, they just turned on one another again. Giertz was tired, but he still got up and went to the doorway, mainly to avoid witnessing the carnivorous spectacle.

He ran more tiredly down a narrow passage lined with large, rust-covered industrial pipes. There was also a strange kind of mold. Looking more carefully at it he realized with additional revulsion there were life forms clinging to it. Barely recognizable as human, their metabolisms had merged with the mold, somehow managing to subsist on it, *Reduced to being parasites upon a parasite. This tunnel contains an entire ecosystem!*

He could also see though the mold was dying, and so were they. They reached out to him with their strangely evolved hands, as if they wanted to suck the life directly out of him. Some managed to catch him, but didn't have the strength to hold on. Giertz carefully ran the gauntlet between the walls and ceiling of groping arms.

The corridor was long, but seemed even longer. Further down it, he noticed the walls themselves were pulsing and breathing. Here and there an eye in it opened and tracked him. The horrors became even worse the further he went. In the end, he didn't dare look. All he could try to do was stop this from reaching his memory, and wonder where it would end, just hoping it would be soon. *There seems to be some definite sense of purpose to it all, but it's on some unfathomable scale of a twisted curiosity. So this is Dr. Zed's future Utopia!* Therefore, despite his mounting fatigue, he unreservedly knew what he must do, reminding himself, *I am the agent of Xerak's purpose: to destroy this unholy reality. It truly is his will itself flowing through me!*

Ironically though, Giertz also had a strange feeling, now overwhelming him, that somehow he was the one who was personally responsible for all this. *When I shoot at the mutants, it's like firing into a distorting mirror of myself. Therefore is this just another hallucination? I'm prepared to believe now, perhaps everything is a hallucination, even my whole life. Perhaps I, Dr. Jimmy Giertz, am just a figment of someone else's imagination?*

Shrugging away such thoughts however, on reaching the iron door at the end of the corridor at last, he found he was shaking at the idea of seeing what was on the other side. Reassuring himself it couldn't be much worse than what he'd just been through, he threw the remaining hand grenades, except for one, down the corridor, set to explode under anything following him. He dropped the near-empty spare gun also. He was glad to be rid of the weight, and it motivated him enough to open the door.

He slammed it behind him and dived, clutching his ears. The blast heaved the door off its hinges. As the dust settled, he didn't want to get up or look at his surroundings. Coated in dust, curled in the fetal position on the floor, still protecting his ears, he waited for something to happen - and it soon did.

**Chapter 138 Dimly Lit**

The Bad Actor's voice echoed around him once more from one of the tinny megaphones, 'Well Dr. Giertz, what did you make of that experience?' He spoke in the matter-of-fact tone one would use to a child. Giertz tried to think of something to say, but no words came. 'So let's see how you tackle this one!' Giertz tried to ignore the voice as he tentatively lifted his eyelids and looked around.

He seemed to be in an unremarkable corridor, with no mutants or anything else in evidence. He couldn't see anything strange at all, except for the very dimly lit, bare concrete walls, and ceiling. He noticed a bend at the end of it. He stood up and began running towards it. On reaching it, he found he was just traveling down another corridor, towards another bend, and another. After turning more corners, The Bad Actor's manic laughter crackled out of the speakers once more. It didn't take Giertz long to find, *I'm in a maze, and consequently a trap!*

He stopped and leaned against a wall, his scrawny chest heaving. Then a burst of Thompson sub-machine-gun fire cut through the opposite wall. It hammered across the one Giertz was leaning on. To narrowly avoid being hit, he ducked below his own chest height as Ceebix had trained him to. Giertz found the walls were of some thin concrete sheeting. Another burst sliced through the wall vertically, and he rolled out of the way. 'Now you're beginning to understand...' Said the disembodied voice, but Giertz didn't understand at all. *How can he be so detached sounding, so calm about his actions?*

Turning the sensitivity on his infrared gun-sight up as far as it would go, Giertz fired back into the thin wall in the direction the shots had come from. He thought he saw an indistinct green blob on the tiny display that could indicate The Bad Actor. He fired at it again, but a moment later another burst cut through the wall near Giertz's head. He understood now, *The Bad Actor, with his infrared sight, is tracking me through this maze in the same way I'm tracking him.* Giertz fired back again, but was still not quite sure where to aim.

This went on for a few minutes as he ran through the maze, firing after the vague, man-shaped image on his gun-sight, with the walls spitting back bullets. Giertz gymnastically avoided them, but was growing cumulatively tired. Then he saw light issuing from around a corner. Following it, he saw it was coming from a doorway. Instinct told him he'd reached the center of the maze. 'Oh I wouldn't go in there if I were you...' said the voice, mockingly. Defiantly, Giertz jumped through the doorway. The voice laughed again, but now with satisfaction.

**Chapter 139 Mind Grinder**

Giertz landed in an empty, cube-shaped room. He ran his hands over the scrubbed concrete walls and floor. Looking up at the center, he saw a single electric light bulb. The only other feature was another megaphone screwed to the wall. He was halfway across the room, going towards the doorway on the other side, when he instantly clutched at his temples.

He then experienced something that was difficult to quantify. As if someone was removing the yolk from an egg with a straw, he experienced his whole mind being sucked out of his brain. It was agonizing. He screamed, but the scream seemed to be coming from somewhere far away. He collapsed in the center of the floor. He saw the concrete surfaces had turned to mirrors, and the doorways had disappeared. The walls, floor, and ceiling were now tunnels, full of nothing but himself, going off into infinity - everywhere he looked.

The emptiness terrified him, *There's absolutely nothing here to reassure me I exist!* He'd never felt so incredibly alone - as if he didn't even have himself for company. Light-years away, he heard the loudspeaker crackling again, 'Congratulations Dr. Giertz! You have just entered "The Mind Grinder"! I'm sure you have observed fruit placed in a blender? Well, that's what has just happened to your entire psyche! Ha ha ha!'

Giertz noticed a thought floating through his head, *He's right!* However, it felt more as if his mind had shattered into crystal fragments. The room was somehow sucking them down the mirror-tunnels, into infinity. He was sitting in the center of the floor as they slowly span away from him. He believed he could quite clearly see the various components of his personality, now no longer a part of him.

In a way, he felt warm and relatively comfortable with the situation, but then he saw one fragment still within reach. He snatched at and caught it, holding it up in front of his face. Looking into its semi-opaque surface, fascinated, he could hardly remember what it was. He could just faintly hear the sacred message somewhere from the past, buried in his subconscious: the voice from The Tabernacle in the Desert of Death. It was The Idea.

Now he understood, it had told him everything he needed to know, and like a reversed film of something exploding, the facets of Giertz's strange mind all came fluttering back. They formed a single, solid crystal once more. Soon he could just make out the concrete walls of the room again. Meanwhile, the speaker on the wall was still laughing.

Giertz was only vaguely aware of his gun lying beside him, but he still picked it up and shot the megaphone. It clattered off the wall in a shower of sparks, smoking, bent, and full of holes. What was left of the mirrors now shattered, and cracked images of himself flew everywhere. The doorway returned, but the relief was short-lived, as he felt someone, or something, grab him from behind.

**Chapter 140 Vegetable State**

Giertz couldn't see the featureless face, but somehow sensing the empty countenance behind him, he could tell it was a Non-man holding him. Before Giertz could do anything, it had clamped its strong, cold hands around his elbows. *It must have been sent to collect me when The Mind Grinder reduced me to a vegetable state.* Giertz's innate fear of Non-men had made him slow to act. It stood him up and marched him out of the room, then stood still, as if waiting for orders. At first Giertz struggled to get free, trying to aim the gun to shoot the Non-man's feet, not sure he wouldn't hit his own, but then something occurred to him.

He could move his hands just enough to look down into the infrared sight, but not aim the gun accurately. As he'd expected, he could see an almost perfect infrared view of The Bad Actor. *He must be very close, just behind that wall!* He'd noticed this Bad Actor always appeared to aim for about chest height. As he saw the image of The Bad Actor raise his gun, Giertz made a desperate lunge forward, doubling up from his waist. The wall in front of him exploded once more, but he felt the clammy, lifeless hands of the Non-man wince and then release him. Giertz heard it collapse behind him, its non-life over in a puff of vapor. Giertz immediately went down on one knee, firing back into the wall.

He reached into his jacket and pulled out the last grenade. He looked at it wondering about the fuse for a moment, before throwing it at the wall, while ducking around the nearest corner. Then he saw just how thin the concrete was when it blew out, not only one wall, but holes in two others, as well as the ceiling, letting in more light. He instantly jumped through the dusty gaps, and discovered himself in a brightly lit corridor, back in the more modern part of the building. Then he heard a faint rustling on his right. Turning, he found he was face to face with The Bad Actor once more.

Giertz was surprised to see that, yet again, The Bad Actor looked just as scared as himself. He was sweating a lot, not looking a fraction as confident as he'd sounded on the PA system. *The last few minutes must have been just as strenuous for him as they were for me!* Giertz also mused on how similar this one's panicked facial expression was to the other Bad Actor on the highway a few weeks before, and to the one Giertz had rammed at The Situation before that. For a moment that seemed like hours, they did nothing, just standing fifteen paces apart, staring at each other.

Their guns hanging at their sides, they both waited to see what would happen. This time they had the same idea, but Giertz was the first to act. He raised his gun and fired, not even conscious he was seeing three seconds ahead. At first he thought it he'd achieved nothing. The Bad Actor was still standing, but Giertz noticed his arm was hanging at an impossible angle. Then it dropped off, still holding the gun. He silently collapsed soon after, still with the same under-confident expression on his face, and then with none at all.

**Chapter 141 New Facade**

Giertz looked around, wondering which direction to take. The Mind-Grinder experience had affected him in the opposite way to the one intended, and given him a brief rest, so now he felt his sense of purpose as never before,. The unmistakable message he'd received in The Tabernacle from Xerak himself, had escaped from Giertz's subconscious into his conscious, and was now screaming inside his head again.

He saw two elevators at the other end of the corridor. *This building has a new facade, but all the appliances in it are old.* These two had an antiquated arrangement of a kind of clock above their doors, each with a rotating hand indicating which floors they were on. He saw one was gradually traveling upward, around the Roman numerals, and it occurred to Giertz, *This has to be Dr. Zed's escape route, and no doubt there will be a VTOL private jet waiting for him on the roof.*

Giertz ran to them and checked his gun as he waited. With a loud chime, his arrived. They were both old and slow, and Giertz saw he was only five floors under Dr. Zed, so Giertz had an idea. He fired several shots into the control panel for the first lift, and wisps of bitter-smelling smoke escaped from it. He heard machinery somewhere above crunching unhappily, grinding against itself. Looking up he saw that, better than he'd hoped, the floor indicator had frozen between the top two floors, just before he entered the second elevator.

As it neared the top of its destination, his elevator didn't sound happy either. Frustrated with its slowness, he jumped out and ran up another two flights of the fire escape. Then he saw where the emergency exit door should have been on the penultimate floor; there was another modification to the old building. He was facing just a plain wall, with no continuation of the staircase.

To his left though, he saw a partially open door to another small office, and something inside it caught his attention. Ready to fire, he barged through the door, but the room was empty. However, in the center was a single, cheap table, with one, very old, portable control-terminal on it. *It's just like the one Uncle Joe kept by his bed, and Ceebix's for that matter.* Filling one wall next to it was a bank of holy-monitors.

Their purpose was obvious enough. *These control all the security for this building. They must survey everything from this room! Like the office downstairs, it's deceptive about its significance.* On the screens he could already recognize several of the areas he'd just run through. On the lower floors he saw the faces of people he knew - killing and being killed. He also saw, *The fight is even more furious than I'd expected!*

Now he knew where all the staff had gone. Arming themselves with their expensive guns and grenade launchers, they hung their impractical, tailored business suits with belts of ammunition. They'd tried to barricade themselves into the lower corridors, but it was useless. Disaffected youths were flooding in through the huge blast holes in the corridors' flimsy walls. The executives shot most of them the moment they entered, but the hordes kept coming, clambering over the mounds of bleeding dead, and horribly moaning wounded.

Dr. Zed's private bodyguards didn't last long, despite being picked men from the corporation's forces. Their chrome-plated helmets and black uniforms, with silver skull and crossbones insignias, appeared only to enrage the rabid mob even more. The small force's years of training and loyalty were no match for the Combat

Youths' numbers and fanatical zeal. Giertz watched the army die to a man, still struggling with their heavy, complicated weapons. *Their minds just seem fettered by tactics!*

Even Giertz winced as he saw the gold-braided general being torn apart by their bare hands. The overwhelming look of surprise didn't seem to leave his face, even as his head departed his body. Giertz found himself recalling Ceebix's smile, and Giertz visualized it a little broader now, and with a hint of sarcasm, *I have just witnessed the perfect demonstration of Ceebix's theories.* Then he realized something else, *I am his idea bomb!*

With the last line of defense gone, the executives in the screens seemed to know they were going to die. Speaking for the masses, despite no one hearing him, Giertz said quietly to them, 'Here are the people who've had enough "Real Life," enough Bad Actors and Pandoras, enough production and consumption, enough supply and demand, enough debates, enough promises, enough words, enough Phlesh! Here are the people won't eat any more of it, who say, "You eat it!" This is not revolution in politics, or theology, or ideology, or any 'ology. This is revolution in blood! This is revolution in the phlesh!'

**Chapter 142 Panic Stricken**
Turning to inspect the terminal carefully, Giertz noted a heavy combination lock on its armored case, with a notice etched into it,

'WARNING: WILL EXPLODE IF WRONG
COMBINATION USED!'

When he looked at the terminal itself though, he had the peculiar sensation of remembering something he'd never directly experienced. He noticed a small information window in one corner of the holy-display:


'CONSUMEORDIE Corp. FILE ACCESS CODE DESTRUCTION UTILITY. WARNING: CANNOT UNDO!'


His artificial Ph. D, Snodgrass's experience, told Giertz straight away, *This must be the terminal which monitors all the operations of Consumeordie,* but Giertz could have guessed what he was looking at anyway. *It seems someone was disturbed while in the process of sealing Consumeordie Corp.'s entire filing system, just as the voice on the speaker in Dr. Zed's office announced.* The central computer was urgently requesting a continuation of its orders. *Who was doing the destroying of the access codes though, and where have they gone?*

From the silence around him, Giertz guessed he was probably alone on this floor of the building. He concluded, *What the operator has seen on the monitors must have panicked him into joining the general exodus.* Playing with the terminal's control, Giertz immediately knew he now had access to every piece of information for Consumeordie Corporation's operation. *Amazing how I arrived just in time! If the operator had already erased the file codes, it would have taken more than a genius to access this.* Consequently Giertz found, *I have the ability, right now, to entirely destroy everything that is Consumeordie Corporation, forever. I can erase their core system and seal it, permanently! It all has to be the will of Xerak!* For a second he was giddy with power, but the floor shaking under his feet with the rumble of demolition charges, closer now, quickly returned him to reality.

As he scanned the masses of data, relating it to Snodgrass's learning, Giertz gloated over what an ungainly, obsolete dinosaur Consumeordie was, *For all his massive intelligence, Dr. Zed has overlooked fundamental weaknesses in the corporation's structure over the years. The whole company is like this building! They built its modern facade over an antiquated framework. Dr. Zed and Byron Reed never planned Consumeordie with any capacity for evolution, just to get bigger very quickly.* Giertz now knew the unspeakable truth, *Despite its size, Consumeordie hasn't fundamentally changed from the basic, cut-price chain store it started as!*

He smiled to himself as his fingers danced across the control, rapidly making small adjustments. *It's as simple as the gearbox in my car. Add one extra tooth to a single gear, and within a few minutes the timing will have been upset. The precision machinery will grind itself to dust. All the sub-corporations under Consumeordie Corp. will start supplying The Consumers with the wrong things at the wrong time. It's just like one of my holygames. It's easy, but almost too easy?*

Giertz rapidly analyzed the top-heavy Goliath, but then began to recognize another pattern. At first, he was surprised and confused by what he saw. Then abruptly, a moment of unbearable enlightenment filtered through Snodgrass's knowledge, and Giertz understood everything. Staring at the figures on the display, he knew they answered nearly all his questions. *Now I know how Dr. Zed knew so much about me!* The realization was sickening, and at the same time Giertz felt foolish for not recognizing it, when it had been so obvious. Breathing heavily he sagged against the table, suddenly feeling very tired. It couldn't have felt much worse if someone had hit his heart with a hammer.

After a moment of indecision however, he started again. The work didn't take him more than a few minutes. For his finale, he adjusted the codes so no-one could access them without making the problems worse. He saw, *I could even order tactical nuclear strikes against every major Consumeordie distribution center in the world, if I felt like it!* He knew now though, It's all pointless. He didn't feel the glow of satisfaction he'd expected. Instead, he only felt the crushing privilege of one who knew too much.

He looked more carefully now at the monitors on the wall, and noticed, *Almost every allied Greedeluxe Youth group has converged on this spectacle.* Even some of the Consumeordie gangs had quickly changed sides, and the remaining Greedeluxe Combat Youths were the spearhead. Giertz impassively observed the now terrified Consumeordie executives, fumblingly with their expensive, over-sophisticated, unfamiliar weapons. They were vainly trying to hold their flimsy barricades of overturned desks, photocopiers, and water coolers against the hordes of Greedeluxe Combat Youths, with sweatbands emblazoned by hieroglyphs written in their blood, tied around their shaven heads. Holding heavy demolition charges, they ran with suicide screams against tidal waves of bullets. Giertz witnessed acts of self-sacrifice and brutality he wouldn't have imagined physically possible. *It seems they all hate 'reality' just as much as I do.*

Giertz studied the identical look in all the executives' eyes, as they finally woke up to what 'survival of the fittest' really meant. *No amount of team-building, paintball outings could have prepared them for this.* The foundations of the edifice were shaking regularly now, and still the gangs kept coming, sweeping out of the alleys, out of the gutters, out of the sewers, in their hundreds, thousands. Even people who weren't in the gangs, just ordinary Consumers, were swept up in the fight. The entire population of the city now appeared to be converging on 'The Ultimate 'Situation.' In the light of Giertz's new knowledge however, none of it filled him with any inspiration, only despair. 'It's all totally useless,' he murmured out loud, to no one. He only wished he had the heart to call them over the PA system to tell them so. Somehow though he knew, *They'd rather die with their illusion, than live out the rest of their lives with the truth, as I will now.*

He was just searching for it in his heart to tell them anyway however - when he heard a noise behind him.

**Chapter 143 Upper Thighs**

Giertz's sense of defeat was so total it had even blunted his reflexes. Turning, he saw The Bad Actor standing in the doorway. Giertz struggled to come to terms with knowing, *So the rumor was wrong, there must be four Bad Actors and not three!* This one was wearing a light-gray suit with a blood-red carnation as usual, but now held a small, silenced machine pistol. Just like the others also, this Bad Actor's cool was completely gone. He looked panic-stricken and older than he was, and then Giertz felt the bullets stabbing through him like white-hot irons.

At first, Giertz was only aware of the weight of pain, crushing him. He'd known his turn would come sooner or later, reminding himself, *I've long lost count of the number of people I've killed after all, and I know I've been more than lucky, on many occasions, even with my reflexes. So it was only a matter of time.* He still felt a sense of injustice though, *Why did it have to come now, when I'm so close?* Giertz knew however; there was no mystery about the sudden appearance of The Bad Actor. *His voice must have been coming from this room as he was sealing the file codes. He saw me kill his replica on the CCTV, so he went and tried to find me for vengeance - and now he has found me.*

As it gradually came to Giertz he hadn't been killed outright though, he tried to develop some objectivity about his predicament. He became aware of the pulsing agony being isolated in his legs. He dared to open his eyes and found himself lying next to the table. Looking down he saw he'd been shot in the upper thighs. *It's pretty obvious where The Bad Actor was aiming.* Luckily Giertz's reflexes had still managed to make him jump high enough to make all the difference.

He looked up at The Bad Actor in the doorway. He was smiling to himself now as he took his time reloading the gun. Giertz looked across at his own gun, which had been expertly shot out of his hand. It lay in pieces against the wall, and Giertz had to admit, *That was a good piece of shooting by The Bad Actor.* He tried to reach down for his machete. He realized there wasn't much he could do with it though, *The delay on the rocket motor precludes its use.* Giertz began to panic, thrashing about aimlessly on the floor. The Bad Actor's Cheshire-cat smile grew wider.

**Chapter 144 Desperate Move**

Then, remembering something, Giertz made a last, desperate move. He aimed the bolt on his arm at The Bad Actor, releasing the safety catch. The Bad Actor saw what Giertz was doing and fumbled to finish loading the gun as Giertz pressed the firing button. The nylon line whipped across the office and struck The Bad Actor directly in the chest. *That's two,* Giertz recorded, as The Bad Actor reeled against the doorpost, dropping the gun. It clattered to the floor with the magazine just halfway in.

He clutched both hands to his chest as he collapsed forward. He lay on the floor rasping for breath for a few moments, and then pulled himself up onto the bank of security console monitors, with his last strength. He began feverishly pushing buttons, his gray hair hanging over his face.

Giertz lost interest in The Bad Actor's plight though, and turned to his own. One leg had only taken a single bullet in the muscle, and he quickly forgot about it, but the other was a different matter. It had taken two bullets, and from the gnawing, toothache nature of the agony, he knew one of the shots must have clipped the tibia, if not gone through it altogether. It wasn't bleeding profusely, *So at least by some miracle the artery must be intact.* He tore part of his already blood-stained jeans off to bandage the wounds. Bearing on the table, he managed to stand up, but found the leg was virtually useless.

He struggled over to The Bad Actor, whose lungs were wheezing and bubbling as if with terminal bronchitis, but he was still smiling, showing his bloodstained teeth. As he pressed a final button on the console, another loud alarm started ringing somewhere, on top of the first one. Giertz had taken The Bad Actor's actions for some paranoid delirium of the dying, but now Giertz became concerned. He saw, *There is probably some method in it.*

He picked up The Bad Actor's machine pistol and finished pushing the magazine in, as The Bad Actor only laughed. Almost delirious with pain and revenge, half choking, he said, 'You have killed my replicas Dr. Giertz, and you have killed me, but I have set this building to self-destruct. It will take you and all your expendable-liability 'comrades' with it. You will never assassinate the leader of this corporation, and you will never touch Consumeordie's core investment, which is still averaging a dividend of...' Giertz didn't listen to the rest of the speech, which quickly tailed off into the usual blend of statistics, accusations, and obscenities, becoming incoherent and senseless. Finally, it degenerated into his coughing a great stream of bloody saliva onto Giertz's uniform. So Giertz shot him.

The Bad Actor's chest made strange cracking sounds through the expensive, tailored shirt, as Giertz prized the bloody bolt out of it, winding it back into the reel on his arm. Next, he tried to find the code for disarming the building's self-destruct system, but knew there wasn't time. He did discover the control for the public address system however, and screamed warnings into the microphone on the desk. He saw on the screens the youths were beginning to take some notice, but it was clear most of them believed it was a trap, or bluff, and they were too engrossed in the slaughter anyway. Finally, Giertz emptied The Bad Actor's gun into the self-destruct panel, but it achieved nothing. Exhaustion, pain, and futility made Giertz fall to the floor.

He assessed his new quandary while checking The Bad Actor's pockets but discovered, *He must have used the last of his bullets reloading the pistol. Even if I did find Dr. Zed now, there wouldn't be a lot I could do anyway.* Then Giertz remembered, *I do have another option.*


**Chapter 145 Claw-Like**
Giertz pulled the brass locket given to him by Professor Asclepius from around his neck, split it with his thumbnail and it hinged open. Inside was a hypodermic vial. He took it out carefully, and then contemplated, *Asclepius made it quite clear to me what this will do, and I've felt complacent carrying it, until now.* The idea of actually using it terrified Giertz however, along with all his other terror.

It wasn't just having no guarantee the effects would be only temporary, although he still trusted Asclepius - at this point. It was more that it went against what little Giertz still believed in, especially now. He noticed his jacket was ripped, already exposing his upper arm, and so he just said, 'Oh, in the name of Xerak!' Jabbing the vial in, he reminded himself, *There's nothing else I can do.*

The agony in his legs seemed less important now, when he felt as if his blood had caught fire. He cavorted around on the floor as his body was at once dosed with concentrated sedatives, stimulants, and nutrients, to prepare it for the massive molecular changes. He was numb by the time the thick hairs sprang out of his arms, and his eyes began to divide themselves into multiple, small lenses, and the antennae sprouted from his forehead.

As this was happening, he was still conscious enough to realize, *Asclepius has virtually perfected the process of induced, rapid mutation, well beyond anything Dr. Zed's clumsy experiments have achieved!* The whole process took no more than three minutes.

When Giertz stood up, he even felt a certain degree of pride in his new, yellow-and-black exoskeleton. The world looked different through his compound lenses, but he was surprised he could still reason. He inspected his new arm and claw-like fingers. *Asclepius's formulation has blended the best characteristics of both the human and the insect.* Giertz's leg was still damaged, but as he'd hoped, the mutant exoskeleton had made it usable again.

Something else told him though, *This has got to be impossible! Surely even Asclepius couldn't achieve this? Induced mutation takes at least days, sometimes months, and the subjects don't always survive the metamorphosis. I must be hallucinating.* It felt real enough though. *What does it matter either way? Even if this is another hallucination, it just feels so right!* Then something drew his attention to the security panel again. Light was showing through the bullet holes he'd put in it.

Giertz wrenched at it, and it hinged out, revealing another flight of stairs. *A secret escape route!*


**Chapter 146 Unreal Ecstasy**
Giertz hesitated for a moment at the sight of the stairway. Knowing the truth, what had seemed so clear a few

minutes ago now appeared to be more confusing, but nothing had reversed his feelings regarding Dr. Zed. Also, when he thought about it, *The lie I've just uncovered on that terminal only makes me hate Dr. Zed even more - if that's possible. One way or another, I suppose this is still my best chance to destroy reality, or at least put a significant dent in it.*

Despite still limping slightly, Giertz bounded up the stairs, getting used to his acquired agility, bursting with a peculiar, new, optimistic energy. He'd already forgotten Pandora, the Combat Youth and everyone else, as if they all belonged to someone else's life, long ago. The only thing he could think about now was killing Dr. Zed. So as Giertz leaped onto the top floor, he felt a kind of unreal ecstasy at the sight of Dr. Zed trying to struggle from between the doors of the old elevator.

It was half-submerged between two floors, but on seeing Giertz he snarled, and made a final, mighty effort to free himself - which succeeded. Giertz wondered, *What is Dr. Zed thinking at this point? How do I, Jimmy Giertz, look to you? Mutated like this, dirty, coated in sweat, dust, and blood. Here's some 'Real Life' for you – your nemesis!*

Giertz had to remind himself though, *Dr. Zed spared my life after the duel, but that that was probably more a conciliatory gesture towards Uncle Joe.* Even so Giertz felt a sense of poetic justice as he unclipped the spare machete from his belt and threw it onto the floor in front of Dr. Zed.

Giertz said through his mandibles, 'Here's the sporting chance for you I never had! This time it will be a fair fight!' Although it didn't come out clearly. Now Giertz felt the contest was on his terms at last, but as Dr. Zed picked up the machete and came at him, Giertz saw that Dr. Zed didn't see it that way at all.

**Chapter 147 Considerable Agility**

Dr. Zed slashed at Giertz's injured leg, but Giertz rolled out of the way, and it glanced off one of his bullet-resistant, titanium shin-pads. Giertz went for his knees, but despite his age, Dr. Zed jumped with considerable agility. He swung at Giertz's head, and Giertz felt splinters of concrete stinging his mutated face when he ducked in time, as the machete bit into the wall. This maneuver left Dr. Zed himself exposed, and Giertz swung at the ribs under his arm, but only nicked the skin beneath his armpit. Dr. Zed stared at Giertz through his glasses for a moment, as if reassessing the threat Giertz posed to him. Then he threw a second, even more violent blow at Giertz's head. This time Giertz put his machete up to deflect it, but the top end of the brittle weapon broke off, and cut Giertz's mutated forehead.

He fought Giertz down the corridor, towards the roof door, and then Giertz fought him back up again. All Giertz could hear over the alarms were grunts and snarls, mixed with the ringing of two pieces of high-carbon steel. To Giertz, Dr. Zed was just an overwhelming silhouette, and he wondered again what he now looked like to Dr. Zed. *Probably just some distorted little wasp, he decided, who is giving him more than the usual bother.*

They both slashed on, soon covered in sweat, cuts, their own and each other's blood. Giertz had to notice though, *Dr. Zed's 'blood' has an unusual coloring, more orange than red!* This reminded Giertz of what Pandora had said about his phlesh not being 'real.' Then through the blur of emotion, two things began to nag at Giertz's remaining reasoning. The first was, *This machete fight has gone on longer than any other I've known. Perhaps he had lessons from The Bad Actor, or vice versa?*

*It's also strange in how many ways Dr. Zed and I are perfectly matched, my youth versus Dr. Zed's experience, my mutant body versus his mutant body. His hate for me versus my hate for him...* The other was that Giertz could now see, despite having gone into his ODS, it hadn't made any real difference. Dr. Zed was still able to match him blow for blow, and reluctantly Giertz had to admit, *This fight is going Dr. Zed's way!* As well as that, a new pain began to grow in Giertz's body.

It told him the temporary mutation was already wearing off, *My cells are starting to revert to their normal state.* Giertz wasn't that bothered by this. He knew he would be dead within the next few minutes anyway, when the building exploded. He had no escape. *If I can just prevent Dr. Zed from leaving the building, so we both go with it?* Was Giertz's only strategy.

Perhaps as a result of all this though, Giertz began to hallucinate mildly. He visualized his and Dr. Zed's machetes had turned into flaming swords, great tentacles of fire leaping from them as they clashed. The opponents' bodies and purposes had grown to gigantic proportions, so whole galaxies crumbled with every blow. Giertz felt the presence of the entire cosmos stretching around them, watching for the outcome, but then Dr. Zed did something Giertz didn't believe possible.

Somehow Dr. Zed was able to expertly slip inside Giertz's hallucination, as if Dr. Zed even knew exactly what Giertz was imagining. Dr. Zed's already horrible face began to melt and crumble before him. New and more terrible faces surfaced out of the morass, each more unbearable than the last. Giertz was shocked, *It's just like the particularly bad hallucination I had while driving that time!*

His last dregs of hope finally gone, he now knew how exhausted he truly was. Seeing he'd lost the fight, he collapsed, clattering to the floor. He half-heartedly swung up his titanium arm-protector, to deflect the last blow Dr. Zed threw at him, but Dr. Zed didn't wait to finish the job.

He just turned and ran up the corridor towards the roof door. Through his compound-lensed eyes, Giertz watched him go. He'd never felt such a pure sense of defeat since his sword fight with The Bad Actor, but even so, something still made Giertz act.

Giertz picked up Dr. Zed's machete from where he'd dropped it, and flicked the safety catch off the firing button on its rocket motor. Giertz leaned his whole weight against it, as it began to bleep away the seconds. He watched Dr. Zed run further away with his long strides. Giertz was just thinking the weapon might not fire at all, when his entire body was wrenched, as a jet of acrid smoke belched up the corridor.

**Chapter 148 Damaged Toy**

Just before he was about to round the corner, Dr. Zed exploded in a mass of servos, electrical components, synthetic organs and artificial phlesh. Shocked again, Giertz thought, *So that's the explanation! Pandora's perception was right. He was just a machine!* Giertz was too exhausted however; even to feel pleased with himself. What he did notice through his multi-lensed vision was something moving further up the corridor. From behind a recess in the concrete wall, he observed an eye studying him. Then Giertz recognized it, *The Beast!* It looked terrified as always.

Cautiously it emerged and examined the scattered, smoking hydraulics and artificial limbs, poking at them sadly. In spite of its privileged position, Giertz felt even more sorry for The Beast. Giertz also felt a paradoxical glimmer of guilt at having destroyed its master, but then The Beast did something strange.

From somewhere about itself, it produced a small control unit. It started rapidly punching commands into the intricate instrument, speaking into the mouthpiece in a high-pitched, child-like, but assertive voice. Some of the limbs twitched in response to the commands. Fingers flexed. The Beast's words emerged from the remaining part of the head, still wearing the cracked spectacles. 'One two, one two, testing...' Yet the monotonous drone now sounded weak. Giertz felt overcome with a particularly unpleasant form of helplessness, as his earlier inkling in the office, that things were not all they seemed - was confirmed, and he began to understand even more.

The Beast threw the control unit away, as a child would a damaged toy. It turned and shambled towards Giertz, stating, 'For a liability you see yourself as relatively smart, don't you Dr. Giertz? Your conspiracy against me with Professor Ceebix has gained a minor foothold on this day, but I *shall* rebuild my creation, and optimize my profit margins as never before. I will create a new puppet for myself...'

'You think Professor Asclepius will, you mean!' Giertz croaked awkwardly from between his, now shrinking, mandibles. The Beast stopped, visibly startled, and Giertz continued, 'Yes, I know who you are, Byron Reed! The phlesh-robot he created for you, Dr. Zed, was just a temporary measure, as he worked on repairing your mutation. It went badly wrong, didn't it, leaving you hopelessly deformed. He'd improved your brain, but when he found his creation conflicted with his personal interests, he abandoned you. That's why you've been doing your independent mutation research ever since, trying to reverse the process, and correct his bad workmanship.'

The Beast - Byron Reed, cocked its head to one side, forced to contemplate the painful facts, and the additional fact that now someone besides The Bad Actor and Asclepius knew them. 'You are mostly correct, Dr. Giertz,' it said reluctantly. 'I was a young, successful businessman, but like all such men, I still wanted more. Actually, after my brain mutation had been initiated, Asclepius already knew he'd irreversibly miscalculated. Therefore he created the Dr. Zed puppet for me, trying to compensate for the physical side-effects of my mutation, as they gradually got worse.' *Yes*, Giertz reflected in a gloomy moment of empathy, *There are always side-effects to induced mutations...* As it continued, 'It's true though, that it was still my mutant mind which created Consumeordie. Yes, when Professor Asclepius saw what he had done to me, and my anger over it, he lost the courage of his convictions, defecting instead to Professor Ceebix. Now Dr. Asclepius is trying to eliminate me by sending you, but it is my mutant mind that will recreate my share in this corporation. It will be stronger than ever before! Believe me, Dr. Giertz, I was known as "The Beast," well before Professor Asclepius experimented on me, and you are entirely correct, he still owes me favors...' What does he mean by Asclepius 'sending' me? Giertz half-wondered, but in the context of what Giertz had seen on the terminal, things were now beginning to slot into place.

Then Byron 'The Beast' Reed, saw that from nowhere, Giertz had somehow become galvanized with a mysterious new energy. He was already picking himself up, and his broken, but still very useable, machete. Terrified once more, Reed turned and scampered up the corridor, leaving a trail of excrement.

In spite of the pain and exhaustion now racking Giertz, something still drove him to run unsteadily after Reed. Perhaps it was knowing there was still some minimal chance, even when Giertz could hear the executive jet already warming up on the roof above. He staggered up the steps, but found the door locked from the outside.

**Chapter 149 Half Human**

There was just enough strength left in Giertz's mutation for a hand half human, half hairy and claw-like, to burst through the thin wood of the door, and tear the lock off the other side. He fell out into the air mixed with hot turbulence from the VTOL executive jet's thrusters. Covering his aching ears, he was in time to see it jerk upwards into the cloudy sky. For a moment it appeared like some weird, ungainly bird, but then its undercarriage folded, making it sleek and ready for flight.

At each corner of the square roof were deserted heavy machine-gun nests. Giertz ran over to one and sent a line of green tracer bullets snaking out after the jet, but his eyes were in the process of reverting to a human being's once more. More some incensed prehistoric horror, it had already rounded on him, and was firing its small heat-seeking rockets as Giertz rolled out of the sand-bags. The heavy gun exploded in molten pieces.

The large aluminum mouths of ventilation chimneys dotted the flat, concrete roof. Giertz crawled behind one, then from one to another, trying to reach the next machine gun, but the jet's Gatling cannon rapidly chewed up the three other nests. Giertz knew, *At least now the plane can't use its heat-seeking missiles on me, because they will be made inaccurate by the fires now burning in the nests.* It was small consolation however.

Instead, the jet began to perforate the thin aluminum chimneys. Giertz rolled from one to the other in the hope of confusing the pilot, the cannon hammering each one in turn, as Giertz thought, *It doesn't make sense. Why doesn't he run to escape the coming blast? After all, I'll soon be going up with the self-destruct anyway. Byron Reed must hate me so badly he really wants to see me die!*

All Giertz fervor had by now just degenerated into a fundamental need to survive, even if it was for just a few more seconds. For protection, he crawled on his stomach to the concrete enclosure that held the elevator motor, quite close to the edge of the parapet. Somehow, he squeezed into the narrow gap between the enclosure and the edge of the roof. He hoped he'd found a fairly safe place to endure the rest of his reversion from an insect to a human being once more. Then the pilot made a bad mistake.

The jet flew even closer to the roof and prowled just above it, as Giertz tried to hide. Finally, the pilot must have caught a glimpse of Giertz's half-mutated limbs poking out from behind the wall. First the large caliber shells slammed into the enclosure, and it collapsed on top of him. Then Giertz had the sickly feeling of dropping through the air, falling out over the parapet, into nothingness.

His reflexes however were unaffected by the ordeal, even while his body was suffering. Without thinking he fired the pulley device at the remains of the enclosure, as he saw it fading into the distance above him. *That's three.* It didn't make contact though, just bouncing off the remaining wall, and he realized as he fell, *The angle's too steep!* He'd already fallen several floors, with a sickening glimpse of the distant road below, when he tried for the last time. *That's four!*

As the bolt struck home into the parapet, he was more relieved than he could ever remember, but only for a moment. Even with its built-in shock absorber, the line instantly became taught, wrenching his arm almost out of his shoulder. He swung in an arc, slamming against the rough concrete. As he dangled for some time, he contemplated, *This almost seems like some punishment for surviving!*

He managed to operate the small power winch, and it dragged him up the abrasive wall, even gathering enough momentum to throw him back onto the roof. As he struggled to establish a foothold, the shrieking aircraft floated a short distance above him. He guessed the pilot was by now probably looking for definite proof of death. Then Giertz spotted an inspection cover on the rear of the jet's fuselage, and had an idea.

He knew he'd used up all the bolt's life, but he aimed the blunt point anyway, just above the cover, and fired. *That's five!* Somehow it penetrated the hull, and the winch dragged him across the roof and up into the sky with it. Suddenly he was close enough to undo the catches on the cover, tearing at them with his semi-mutated fingers. Probably realizing something was wrong, the pilot began to gain altitude.

As the wind started to tear at Giertz, the inspection panel fell open. Giertz didn't even look at what was inside, but plunged his broken machete into it with what strength he had left. He was showered with sparks and splashed with a burst of warm, rubbery-smelling hydraulic fluid. Instantly he felt something start to happen as the machine gave a slight jerk, then began to lose power - and height.

**Chapter 150 Few Seconds**
The aircraft turned, and its landing gear came down again. The pilot was trying to take it back to the nearest available surface, the roof it had just left, but whatever Giertz had done seemed to have affected its ability to land vertically. Therefore it only skimmed the landing pad, attempting to slow down.

Giertz rapidly lowered the winch and rolled as he was dragged across the concrete, crashing into one of the ruined aluminum chimneys. He struggled to cut the device from his forearm as he watched the aircraft travel over the roof, a thin trail of smoke running out of its tail. Instantly the last strap was torn from him as part of the landing gear broke off against the parapet on the far side.

The pilot turned to make another attempt, but the machine dropped out of sight below the level of the parapet. Then there was an explosion that compressed Giertz's chest, and he felt the whole construction rock a few degrees on its foundations, but before he had time to feel any satisfaction, a hairline crack ran across the roof by his legs. Then it began to grow wider. In a moment it was already a dusty chasm, revealing rusty steel reinforcing, and old, iron girders.

He felt the side of the roof he was sitting on slipping. He attempted to lunge back onto the other side, but didn't quite make it. He felt himself falling again and grabbed the most secure thing to hand. He discovered he was straddling an iron girder, projecting from the remains of the roof. He was clinging with his only good arm and leg, but even his insignificant weight was enough to make the rusty bolts on it sheer, and he swung out at an angle, over the abyss. He couldn't maintain a tight enough grip anyway, and saw the rest of the bolts at the other end were sheering, one by one, with dull ringing sounds. Then he heard the sound of an approaching helicopter.

He guessed it was more Non-men, or even another Bad Actor. *The building will go up in a few seconds anyway,* he thought, surprised it hadn't gone already. He found it strange that he wasn't too concerned about the idea of dying now, but was somehow nearly welcoming it. His sense of achievement at killing Dr. Zed, The Beast and the remaining Bad Actors was hollow when illuminated by what he'd discovered on the terminal. *Since I don't know for certain The Beast was even in that jet, there's also a seed of doubt I succeeded anyway.* Resigned, he felt the beat of the helicopter's rotors, and waited for the first bullets to strike him.

**Chapter 151 Flaming Masonry**

As Giertz waited for death, nothing happened, but he didn't feel any anticipation because his body was just too tired. In a way, he wished they would just get it over with. Then he saw a hand in front of his face. It was covered in a black leather glove, reaching for him.

At the other end of the arm was a smile, inside a yellow and black pilot's helmet. Giertz grabbed the hand and was pulled off the girder and onto the helicopter's Gatling cannon. He was still hanging out of the side, but with his healthy arm he grabbed the bottom of Kadski's pilot seat. The helicopter turned and flew rapidly away, with Kadski still holding onto him with one arm. Then Giertz felt the side of his face being seared.

The light helicopter bucked and jumped in the blast, and he felt its turbine laboring as Kadski tried to control it. Behind them, Consumeordie's headquarters finally disintegrated in a ball of white heat. Chunks of flaming masonry fountained through the air.

Giertz was still hanging out of the side, and rolled on the ground as Kadski landed them safely by Giertz's car. As the co-pilot took the helicopter up once more, Kadski jumped out to help Giertz, but he noticed Kadski's facial expression didn't match his chivalrous actions. He was still smiling, but there was also something else behind the smile which Giertz couldn't, or wouldn't, account for - at first. He felt doubly uncomfortable because Kadski's attitude reminded him of the first Producer he'd met at Uncle Joe's party, when Giertz had borrowed his coat. In the end, Giertz had to face it though; there was no mystery about it, *Kadski can no longer successfully hide his jealousy, and is now almost unashamed of it.*

Nearby, the surviving Combat Youths were already picking over the hot rubble, dragging out and killing any surviving Producers, displaying grotesque, dismembered trophies. The youths' weird screams of joy made a strange, fitting background to Kadski's words to Giertz, 'So you were the one to finally play "The Big Role"!'

Giertz had said nothing, but he knew, *Kadski must have witnessed what took place on the roof, he would have known the head of Consumeordie was probably in that jet.* Giertz noticed now Kadski still had several rapid-healing surgical dressings poking through his uniform, and he didn't look well. *Kadski must have discharged himself from the clinic early when he heard what was happening. He wouldn't want to be left out of The Ultimate Situation, but he still got here too late. He'll never forgive me!*

Giertz still couldn't believe he was getting this kind of behavior from Kadski, and wasn't sure how to handle it either. Giertz was almost too tired to stand up anyway, or even think, and his seared face stung while his damaged leg felt ready to collapse for good.

Then there was blood streaming from Kadski's mouth and nose.


**Chapter 152 Anonymous Head**

Kadski sagged against the side of the car, but the expression on his face didn't change. Giertz saw an anonymous head disappearing on a roof just above them. *A Consumeordie sniper has shot Kadski!* Giertz felt the same sense of unfairness he'd felt when he'd watched Nailbrand die.

Forgetting his exhaustion, as a reflex Giertz quickly opened the driver's door. He swung the passenger door up from the inside, and pulled Kadski in. Somehow Giertz found the energy to start the car and drive towards the rapid-healing clinic, his undamaged leg and arm only just working the controls as he reminded himself, *I can't call the helicopter back, because Ceebix has them operating on his own, secret frequency.* Meanwhile, all of Kadski's blood began to seep through his uniform and onto the floor of the car, filling the cockpit with its bitter odor.

The breeze from the open side window lifted Kadski's thin, tinted-blond hair about over his forehead, as the orange sodium streetlights flashed silently on his face, and the engine made subdued thunder. Kadski was conscious, but only sat in the seat trying to breathe. Then he said, 'Do you know what I think Jimmy?' It was a real question and not just a figure of speech. Giertz said nothing, but Kadski answered it for himself anyway, 'I think we lost, and he won. I mean Dr. Zed. He wanted to destroy us, and he succeeded. Look what we've become?'

Giertz felt uncomfortable about Kadski's statement as Giertz thought about the facial expressions he'd just seen on the surviving Combat Youths, *They all appeared to have the same weird, carnivorous smile as The Festival of Greed posters.* Giertz still resisted believing it however, at this stage. Instead, he tried to reassure himself, *At least we've probably struck a fatal blow to the reality I loathe so much. Surely The Globecon can't survive now?*

He was in for an unpleasant surprise though.


**Chapter 153 Assassination Attempt**

Giertz didn't want to hear or think about what Kadski was saying, as the disinterested, dull faces of The Consumers floated by again, garishly illuminated by the pastel-neon shop fronts. Sometimes the commercial streets around them were deserted, The Consumers maxed out after The Festival of Greed. Giertz started to feel as if he and the dying Kadski were the only two people in reality - and wished it were true. Giertz also began to slip mildly into the hallucination they were traveling down the corridor between dimensions once more.

The car was disintegrating around them again, followed by their bodies. Finally, just their two essences were flashing down the darkening tunnel, but when Giertz almost missed a turn, somehow he managed to shake himself out of it. Meanwhile he couldn't hear a lot of what Kadski was mumbling, as he became more delirious. Eventually, Giertz just heard him coughing softly now and again, and knew, *Kadski's just trying to formulate his own epitaph. It's as if he's aged sixty years in the last few seconds.*

Then Kadski said clearly, 'You really want me dead, don't you Giertz.' Kadski's use of Giertz's surname immediately made him aware of the gulf between them now. It wasn't a question this time, either. The most painful thing was how the bond between them was now finally neutralized, in the same way it had been with Pandora a few hours earlier, *As if it never existed.*

'Of course not,' Giertz denied, attempting to sound sincere because Kadski was dying. Giertz was driving as fast as he possibly could to the Rapid Healing Clinic, but ironically he was still surprised to hear the lie coming out of his mouth. Somehow also, even without seeing three seconds ahead, Giertz knew what Kadski was going to say next, 'You know, it was me she really wanted.'

Giertz knew Kadski had said this not to inspire jealousy, but only as a statement of the truth. Giertz rationalized, *Perhaps the three of us were fooling ourselves it could work? Right from the beginning, it was something we'd wanted to believe in, because there was nothing else. Maybe it could have worked in some perfect, abstract world, but it was so pure, so perfect, the slightest imbalance destroyed it.*

*Now I understand who Pandora took into Consumeordie headquarters before me. She must have had a similar confrontation with Kadski, but he somehow failed in his assassination attempt on Dr. Zed, and unlike me, Kadski managed to escape. Afterward, they must have tightened security, so what Kadski said about her preference for him must be true. Why else would she have chosen Kadski to confess to first?* Now it all made sense, Giertz saw both Pandora and Kadski in a different hue, not feeling the same way about them anymore, but Giertz was surprised it should matter to him. *It was only another illusion, after all.*

Kadski said nothing for some time, until Giertz heard him mumble defiantly with his final breath, 'I feel the strength!' This was what a Combat Youth always said just before he died. *Perfect!* Giertz still felt an ember of his old admiration. *So perfect! Right to the end!*

Finally, Giertz stopped the car and just sat with Kadski's cold, yellow, dead body, the cockpit reeking of blood, excrement and urine. *It was not a beautiful death, after all.* The Rapid healing clinic was still half a city away. *There's nothing I can do,* Giertz reminded himself. *I did what I could for him, in the same way he did for me, just out of our mutual sense of duty.* Somehow though, confusingly, it still didn't seem enough. *In another age he would have been a 'great warrior,' but now he's just a piece of phlesh.*

He made the holy sign of Xerak over the corpse, but at the same time thinking, *It won't bring him back, after all.*

# PART 4

## Chapter 154 Private Room

Giertz awoke in a clean, fresh hospital bed, sunlight filtering into his private room through a fine gap between yellow curtains, tastefully patterned with primroses. His first question was, *Is this another hallucination?* He decided it wasn't as he watched a confused bee buzzing around more plastic flowers on his table. Then he noticed the bee was also artificial, something wrong with its off-key buzz, the micro-spot-welds on its back just visible. *Another surveillance drone.* Nothing phony about the poison sting though, it had been assiduously provided.

Before he became fully conscious, he began to hallucinate again. He was aware of being in bed, but he also believed he was so far away he was outside the entire universe, alone and moving incredibly fast, faster than light. He felt as if his body's weight was more than infinite, and time had ground to an absolute halt. He moved his hand slightly, and it felt like moving the weight of several galaxies. He heard himself breathing as if his chest was some tremendous cavern, as big as space, inhaling and exhaling entire nebulas. Drops of sweat the size of stars were standing out on his forehead.

A little later a blonde nurse entered carrying a syringe on a stainless steel tray. She opened the curtains, and the light reflecting off her sterile white uniform temporarily blinded Giertz. Then he saw the 'sunlight' was artificial also. Outside the 'window' there was just a concrete wall, with a set of light bulbs. He guessed correctly, *I must be somewhere deep underground.*

Then she noticed he was awake. 'Good afternoon!' She greeted him pragmatically, in a foreign accent, but looking concerned. She spoke urgently into a small two-way radio above her ample left breast. In the now-brighter room, Giertz noticed the bed was surrounded by racks of complicated, computerized, monitoring equipment:

oscilloscopes and thousands of LED lights softly squawking and bleeping. It was all linked to sensors on his body by a colored spaghetti of cables, but he had no other sensations. His mind was as blank as the bed's clean sheets. *Where am I?* He began to wonder. *Who am I?*

He couldn't make out the words from the other end of the nurse's radio, but from the tone of voice, Giertz gathered his awakening must be important news. She dropped the syringe on the table and ran out of the room. While he still didn't recognize where he was, Giertz had a strange feeling of nostalgia. He couldn't account for why until Dr. Asclepius swept into the room, surrounded by his white-coated disciples. *So, I'm back in his institute again!*

**Chapter 155 Shaven Heads**

The disciples now all had shaved heads, just like the doctor, even copying his welding goggles with perfectly circular lenses, as was the fashion. Also, they wore armbands on their sleeves with the latest insignia of Greedeluxe Corporation: the two black lightening strokes were now crossed inside a white disk on a background of blood-crimson. Asclepius was much shorter than all of them, but the clean young men and women looked up to him with shining reverence. The gaunt features that had earned him the affectionate nickname 'Dr. Skull-face' were even gaunter these days. Giertz also wondered, *Why does the doctor insist on shaving his eyebrows, which can only make his face look even more skull-like?* To Giertz the sight of the doctor in his spotless lab coat, the light gleaming on his bald skull, black jodhpurs tucked into real leather jackboots as always, was by now familiar.

In fact, the combined feeling of nostalgia and deja-vu became almost too much for Giertz. He now seriously believed he might be hallucinating this encounter also.

After all, he could be even less sure of what was happening in reality these days. Meanwhile, Asclepius began to run down a list of what they'd repaired on Giertz's body this time, using the latest rapid-healing techniques pioneered by the institute. It was enough to jolt Giertz into remembering his fight with The Beast's jet on top of Consumeordie headquarters, but nothing else, at first.

Nevertheless, as Asclepius continued with the list for some time, 'Major cranial rupture, trauma to the spleen and left kidney, broken pelvis...' Giertz found something stranger, *A lot of the injuries Asclepius is describing I've never had before! They don't match with the ones I had after surviving The Ultimate Situation.* Then, indistinct memories of being in the car afterward, for the last time with Pandora, slowly began to creep back to him.

By now he was sitting up in the bed and feeling like a new, if bedsore, man. He also found his hair had grown down his back again, and his beard had returned. So looking like a schizoid Jesus once more, he stared blankly at Asclepius, who seemed less pleased about Giertz's recovery, than worried about what Giertz was going to say. With cautious optimism he asked Giertz an explorative question, 'So how do you feel?' Giertz only answered with a question, 'How long have I been unconscious?'

'Err, six months, twenty-two days, eleven hours, fourteen minutes.' Then Asclepius added somewhat sheepishly, 'We couldn't help the female subject, I'm afraid.'

With that statement it all came back to Giertz: the memories of their last vows, her nonchalant laugh as he'd fired the car's ignition, her screams and her grabbing the wheel too late as the concrete wall, with,

'XERAK IS OMNIPOTENT'

scrawled on it in fluorescent green, had come flashing towards them. Giertz commented neutrally to Asclepius, 'I told her we would go somewhere and be alone together. The pact was my way of trying to fulfill a promise, but I suppose it's ironic I wasn't able to keep my side of it.'

Asclepius was only passingly interested in this though. 'You were badly smashed up,' he said, 'but we have almost perfected our techniques now, thanks to our medical experiments on the Combat Youth. Yet you must understand, Dr. Giertz, in her case there are certain types of tissue damage even we still don't know enough about.' It was at this point Giertz noticed for the first time Asclepius had the words 'DEATH' and 'LIFE' tattooed on the back of either hand.

Asclepius gave him more specific details about the crash and his injuries, as Giertz watched the doctor's disciples weighing every word Asclepius uttered. Nobody mentioned that it had been a suicide attempt, while Giertz noted it appeared to be embarrassing to them somehow. *It probably doesn't look good for Asclepius if one of his guinea pigs self-destructs.* Giertz even wondered if Asclepius was trying to atone for the ethical dimension of the entire experiment. His cheerfully positive intonation even seemed to be an attempt at reintroducing Giertz to life, launching him back into it with a verbal slap-on-the-back.

To begin with, Giertz decided to play along, but he felt very strange, probably due to a metabolism which had been stagnant for months, and saturated with medicines. He replied now to the first question with all the optimism he could muster, 'I feel fine now Dr. Asclepius, thank you, and I'm in possession of enough of my faculties to know that's the truth!' Asclepius was slightly relieved, but not entirely convinced. He was about to leave for the next case as Giertz said, 'There's just one other thing...' Asclepius immediately understood what this meant, and hurriedly ushered his entourage on to start on the next case without him. Once the heavy steel door was closed and locked, he stood waiting nervously for what Giertz was about to say.

**Chapter 156 Further Questions**

Giertz asked gently, 'Why was no one told Consumeordie Corporation always had the major shareholding in Greedeluxe?' Asclepius said nothing, but Giertz knew he had his full attention. 'You see,' Giertz continued, 'after I performed the assassination on Dr. Zed, or should I say The Beast, I had some time to think. What I came across while destroying the Consumeordie filing system led me to several conclusions.' When Asclepius eventually did speak, he faltered perceptibly,

'And what are these "conclusions," Dr. Giertz?'

'Dr. Zed, as in Byron Reed, was one of The Council of Ninety, wasn't he?' Asclepius's face remained impassive as Giertz added, 'You are too, and so is Ceebix. He tried to disguise his voice at the Youth Rally, but I recognized it, he was the first speaker carried in on a litter.' Giertz watched Asclepius's reaction carefully, *It's obvious he knows what's coming.* Giertz knew he was never going to get the truth out of Asclepius, but at the same time was aware, *Asclepius's unique brand of personal ethics will never allow him to tell a lie either.* 'The World Government really lost World War Seven, didn't they,' Giertz went on accusingly. 'The Consumers were never told the truth, that there always was only *one* corporation, and therefore no real economic competition. If they'd known that Greedeluxe versus Consumeordie was a contrived myth, it would probably have started World War Eight.'

'In my case,' Giertz continued, but already with the feeling he was talking into a void, 'as with all your experiments, there are side effects, which you've been

trying to cure ever since I was "born." You created me in your laboratory, didn't you. You deliberately had me "conceived" with my mind in another dimension. Byron Reed, The Bad Actors, and his Non-men were the main obstacles to you and Ceebix dominating The Council of Ninety, which governs all the corporations. So Ceebix wanted a race of assassins with superior reactions, able to see three seconds ahead, a wild-card up his sleeve so he could intimidate The Council. I am just the prototype. As I was growing up you and he were always monitoring my scores on the holygames I played, wherever I was. They were specifically designed to train and play me off against the best in the world, to evaluate me. That was the paper Ceebix had on his desk the day of my interview.'
Asclepius, looking at the floor, just replied,
'All work done by this institute is classified,' not fully able to conceal the unease in his voice.

Then he looked directly at Giertz. 'In *some* respects, you were one of our most successful experiments. Therefore I suggest you see Professor Ceebix, he would still like to debrief you.' Giertz noted something strange about Asclepius's tone however. Then, as Giertz expected, Asclepius ducked out of the door diplomatically, to avoid further questions, adding quickly, 'Good-bye Dr. Giertz. We love you!' Giertz didn't need Asclepius to fill in the rest of the conversation anyway, and so he just recited Asclepius's half of it for himself.

He spoke out loud at the closed door, 'Since even before the last world war, the world's global economy, or "Globecon" has been just one integrated cartel, a single monopoly. Uncle Joe was only another, albeit major, shareholder in it, along with various other members of The Council of Ninety. These included Ceebix, Byron Reed, and myself, Dr. Asclepius. They feel however The Consumers should be kept unaware of this. Therefore the

Consumeordie versus Greedeluxe marketing campaign is a necessary on-going deception.' *It would also explain,* Giertz thought to himself, *why nothing ever changes. Why we're always stuck with nuclear fission and the internal combustion engine, despite there being more efficient technologies around, and why the corporation treats the Consumer like garbage. It's not only economic competition which has been eroded to nothing, either. That's just one reason why reality hasn't been getting any better.*

**Chapter 157 Fundamental Motivations**

Giertz continued his monologue without an audience, 'Professor Ceebix discovered during his asymmetrical warfare research that one man, with the right physiological and psychological background, could probably succeed in altering the balance of power on the council, where armies would fail. This weapon would give our faction of council members an enormous psychological advantage, so Ceebix termed it 'The Idea Bomb:' a profound new idea which would end the stalemate. It was my belief, despite certain irrational aspects of the personality, the fundamental motivations of the 'The Idea Bomb,' in this case the subject Giertz, were understood, and therefore his behavior would be predictable within given parameters. Professor Ceebix even betrayed the Combat Youth radio scrambler codes at one point, in order to provide the subject with the necessary motivation.

'However, initially, because of the side effects of Giertz's mutation, Professor Ceebix had serious doubts about our ability to control the weapon we had conceived, and now so do I, Dr. Asclepius. This is because of the subject Giertz's suicide attempt, and other increasingly unpredictable behavior, which leads us to conclude The Idea Bomb project is not as manageable as was hoped. In other words, we are no longer sure of what we have created, or what its possible long-term effects might be.' Giertz then added silently, *That was why Ceebix ordered me killed when he didn't know where I was heading that day. Perhaps he believed I was joining the other side, or just going outside his 'parameters,' but then he called the attack off because, in the end, I was still too valuable. It must have been a very sharp, razor-edge decision for him. This whole Idea Bomb project was his enormous gamble, and he probably never was entirely confident about it.*

Giertz couldn't be sure about everything, but he was also now certain his childhood suspicion had always been correct, that his 'parents' were just masquerading as his parents, *They were only psychologists, briefed to 'condition' me with sadism in a mind control experiment. They tried to mold me into Ceebix's idea of the perfect warrior, but programmed me with their own destruction - their little prodigy became more than they bargained for! Obviously, my father's orders came from Asclepius and Ceebix, when he was talking to the box with the green light in the basement. That was also why my parents had Greedeluxe tattoos on their arms, even though they claimed to support Consumeordie, and my 'brother' was just another failed prototype. In reality, I have no family, and never did have.*

Giertz also speculated half-heartedly, *Perhaps even Pandora was in on it on some level?* Even when Giertz tried hard, he couldn't remember first meeting her. *Maybe Ceebix somehow set me up with her?* In the end she'd just always been there, so now Giertz began to wonder if she was also just another hallucination. *In other ways, maybe she was all along? Kadski was definitely involved in Ceebix's plan for me, but probably didn't know the whole score. Even the entire Happylands episode was probably only another experiment, a trial run, to see if I, the 'Idea Bomb,' could perform as expected. That's why they made me relatively physically puny as well, so that it was only my reflexes they were testing.*

One additional thing was clear; he now understood what had been at stake in his fight with The Bad Actor at Uncle Joe's party, *Uncle Joe's controlling interest in Greedeluxe Corporation. He must have gambled his entire shareholding on me, knowing all about Ceebix's 'Idea Bomb' experiment, and wanting to see if it was true. I suppose Uncle Joe must have also known he was going to die shortly, so he probably thought the bet was worth it. He was always trying to prove some point or other to that party-crowd anyway, but he ended up proving the opposite - because of me. How did Ceebix and Asclepius engineer it for me to gate-crash the party though? It looked so much like an accident, but then that's probably what they needed me to think. The duel with The Bad Actor was just another test as well. Or perhaps I hallucinated the whole thing?* Giertz still didn't know anything for sure, but didn't care anymore either. *What does it all matter now anyway?*

Overall, he found himself recalling Ceebix's enigmatic smile again, which was no longer an enigma. Giertz understood it all now. *Yes, Giertz decided, Ceebix was right, The Game <u>was</u> enjoyable, but it wasn't easy, and winning it was the hardest thing of all.* Giertz also had a feeling he'd yet to find out just how hard winning it could be. This wasn't what preoccupied him though. *What am I now?* Was his main thought. *Just another mutant? Only a pawn in a board-room battle?* The irony of thinking he was destroying 'reality,' while he was actually reinforcing it, by sculpting it to someone else's vision - which he didn't like at all, was still just sinking into him. *I suppose I am just a product; I destroyed my surrogate 'parents' too late. They successfully conditioned this Idea Bomb, preparing me for 'basic training,' and I'm still ticking.*

Giertz was well aware there would always be something terrible inside him, which he had no control over. He also thought again about the terrifying, ugly message he'd received from Xerak himself in The Tabernacle. Giertz felt that now, too late, he was finally learning what The Idea really meant, but simultaneously knew, *It probably isn't all over yet, and I am still compelled to see my destiny through.*

**Chapter 158 Deep Bunker**

Later, some of Asclepius's disciples came back, and took Giertz in a wheelchair to prove to him just how dead Pandora was. What remained of her body was preserved, floating weightlessly in translucent, green liquid in a transparent capsule, *It's obvious she ironically took the worst of the impact after trying to swerve the car.* The disciples were still positive there was no hope of a cure because, according to them, the research had gone as far as it could. One teenage prodigy-scientist declared, proudly, 'Even the cures we used on you were just off-shoots from the main research!'

Then the question that haunted Giertz came up again, when his wheelchair was pushed quickly past a cavernous underground warehouse, Am I the only one? It was full of glass jars with developing embryos in them, and he thought again about the serial number beneath his armpit. Giertz saw that the numbers printed on each jar were in the same sequence as his. Instantly he was optimistic, *If my brother was another prototype, perhaps there are others like me, and I'm not so unique in this universe?*

A few days later, after Giertz's rapid rehabilitation program had rebuilt his wasted muscles to some extent, and he'd learned to walk and feed himself again, he checked out of the deeply buried bunker of the Asclepius Institute, as he had so many times before. After formally shaking hands yet again with the 'good' doctor, Giertz signed the patient's register for the fashionably dressed, pretty, sweetly-smiling receptionist. He then walked up the long flight of steps and through the familiar heavy, armored doors, disguised to look like any other abandoned, boarded-up shop front, but hoping this would be the last time.

Instantly he hunched up inside his Combat Youth jacket against the icy summer breeze, blowing through the decayed neighborhood. *My uniform's not designed to offer much protection in this frigid weather.* He also saw, while it had been cleaned and repaired, it still bore some of the damage and ingrained stains from his career, especially his last fight with Dr. Zed. Instead of warmth, it only offered a kind of nostalgia, like something belonging to somebody else, in a previous life. Generally though, whatever it was supposed to represent to him didn't feel familiar anymore.

As if to confirm this he was surprised to find some non-cancer-free cigarettes in the pocket. He didn't remember taking up smoking again. *I must have been in a pretty severe state towards the end, to have restarted this teenage habit.* He paused and lit one, savoring the warm, reassuring smoke polluting his lungs again, but as always he found it didn't help at all. He took the half-finished cigarette out of his mouth, and screwed up the whole pack, throwing both away.

Outside, blinking in the evening light, he was struck straight away by the sight of reality. *Somehow it's still here, even after all my best efforts.* Looking around at the crumbling buildings, the feeling he was now back in its hard, bright, cold, tangible grip gradually overwhelmed him. *Nothing has got better either, only worse, and perhaps even that's because of me? Maybe that was my real mission in the Combat Youth; was The Idea Bomb just intended to make reality worse, without totally ending it?* The evidence was all around him.

The rusting skeletons of cars now lined both sides of every road. Preparation X315/J addicts in the final stages of their habit lay about everywhere. Convulsing uncontrollably, they muttered nonsense to themselves. They all had the same, strange expression on their faces, their eyelids drawn back from bulging eyes, staring into infinity - and seeing something terrible there. Some of the more optimistic were ineffectually trying to stand up again, jerking about.

There were more, and to Giertz, worse mutants too. He had to step carefully to avoid large, gray human slugs, who slid along at one block an hour, on steaming, silvery slime-trails. Blind, their antenna carefully probed their limited path in the world before them.

Beyond them, in the hazy, far distance Giertz could still see the silhouettes of the giant towers of machinery that ran the city. Some still stood to attention as they circled the outskirts, illuminated by what looked like fairy lights, with the greeny-black smoke still belching from their chimneys, but several now leaned at odd angles, or undermined by rust had collapsed altogether. They left gaps in the otherwise regular line of darkened, ugly shadows. *Nobody knows what they do anymore anyway,* Giertz reminded himself, still seeing some hope that reality might finally end. *When they go wrong, even the skills to repair them have been lost. Then what will this civilization do?*

He tried to console himself, saccharine-coating what he was still seeing with the thought, *Perhaps in spite of my failure, the end for this reality can't be long now, surely?* At this point though, Giertz couldn't have comprehended just how successful a 'failure' could be.

## Chapter 159 Unpleasant Wind

The breeze in the dry, cold, dirty street was now turning into an unpleasant wind, blowing dust, litter, and Giertz's long hair about. On still not-quite steady legs, he walked listening to the metal studs in the soles of his boots clicking along the cracked paving slabs. Not exactly sure where he was going at first, he recalled Asclepius hinting that Ceebix may still have a use for him, which was enough to make Giertz's feet take a familiar direction. He was enormously curious however, *Why does he want to debrief me though?  What is there to say; now I've fulfilled my mission?*

As he walked, he tried to form some perspective on what had happened to him. *So that's that, and Asclepius was only telling a half-truth about Pandora. It's probably just not politic to revive her.* Giertz extrapolated on the thought, *Asclepius can probably do anything now, repair almost any injury, maybe even bring the dead back to life. By rights, I should be dead. So the Combat Youth can't even be killed now. Therefore he and Ceebix will just repair the Combat Youths they think are worth repairing, like me for example. They will become unstoppable. Their weapons technology will continue to advance, and they will dominate everything. They will carve tomorrow!*

Being truthful with himself however, Giertz had to admit the idea didn't make him happy, *Soon the secrets of rapid healing and age-lock won't be secrets anymore. More of the rival gangs will gain access to the processes, the same way they did induced mutation, and the fighting will go on forever, no longer for an ideal, but just for the sake of the fight itself. 'The means justifying the means' - therefore the meek shall not inherit the earth.* Unwillingly he came to realize he may now be looking at his worst-case scenario, *'Reality' will not only continue, but it will also carry on getting worse - and even uglier.*

As if to confirm the thought, Giertz now noticed for the first time this long, straight road was lined with old, red-brick Victorian factories, towering darkly either side. *Some probably even dating back to the first industrial revolution.* He reflected on how, when they were first built, they'd been 'manned' by children, *Because they were cheaper to replace when they were chewed up and spat out by the machinery.*

Inside these plants now, Giertz could hear the robot production lines tirelessly doing the final assembly, from components made by clone-slaves in The Free Trade Zone. After seeing what was on Consumeordie's terminal, Giertz had a new outlook on it all, *Just what are they producing? Weapons, probably, but then nobody specifically knows anymore just what all the factories are making, or even why, because supply now dictates demand.*

Giertz easily visualized the robotized industry constantly feeding the never-ending destruction of reality with the necessary goods, services, and weapons. *The terminally sick animal of civilization is somehow dragging itself along, while forever decomposing, without ever actually dying. Reality probably can go on and on, no matter how bad things get, after no matter how many revolutions. After all, it's been in a state of corporate monopoly perhaps even since World War Four, and technically that's impossible.*

Giertz suddenly no longer looked forward to his extended, Age-Locked future. *I'll be undead, in an 'undead' world: a zombie world.* He now felt colder than he already was. Thinking about it all had just led him back to the same pointless point again, *I thought if I destroyed Consumeordie Corp. I would at least strike 'reality' a death blow, but somehow I only helped to perpetuate the problem. Ironic, isn't it?* Or so he believed.

**Chapter 160 Willing Believers**

Looking up he saw the dusk sky was preparing for an emerald sunset. The few intermittent sodium streetlights that still worked were glowing pink and buzzing as they came on. They ineffectually illuminated sections of the old, cobbled road at random, only making the others seem darker. Then on the other side of the street he noticed a group of young, bored Producers in their tailored business suits.

For something to do, they'd gathered on a street corner to intimidate and sneer at any passing Consumers. Laughing and exchanging pejorative remarks to one another, they were tormenting an elderly Consumer woman as she walked by. Even at a distance Giertz could see, *It isn't all that much fun for you affluent, ennuied boys, is it.* Then the ringleader, in his real silk tie and high, starched collar, noticed Giertz. Their strategy began as usual with minor insults, but even before they started his hand automatically dropped to the new machete at his side (provided by Ceebix via the Institute) which was a gesture everyone understood these days.

Giertz knew, *Despite my relatively wasted muscles; with my reflexes I could still kill all of you if I wanted to!* However, while Giertz now hated Producers more than ever, he also realized something in him just couldn't believe in Ceebix's 'Game' anymore. In fact, it had got to the point of Giertz concluding, *I don't even know, or care, which side I'm on now.* As Giertz came closer, and noting he was a Combat Youth, the gang quickly assessed that Giertz might represent a real challenge anyway, so they only made a few disparaging remarks, before turning back to the task at hand.

After a few more paces Giertz encountered the swollen cadaver of a male Consumer, stretched across the sidewalk. *He must have been dead for days,* Giertz guessed, holding his nose, but almost retching as he stepped over it, reflecting, *No one bothers with funerals for Consumers anymore; the dead are dumped like any other trash. Giertz guessed, His cadaver will just stay here until the mutant rats or orange carnivorous spiders find a use for it.*

A little further on, one of the hypnotic billboards detected Giertz's presence and began flickering and cooing its Siren song urgently. Now Giertz understood how the corpse had come to be there, snared by the web of the commercial's infinite promise. Knowing how easy it was to be trapped in the dreams they offered, Giertz did feel a brief moment of pity for the unlucky Consumer. Not wanting to risk ending up like him though, Giertz tried hard not to look at the mesmerizing image, but somehow he couldn't avoid noticing the pulsing billboard's message. A woman's small, red-painted mouth was biting the end off an enormous, cylindrical, Dairylux chocolate bar, again and again. *Whoever conceived the 'concept' obviously wasn't aware of how sickening it looks, how it has the opposite effect on me to the one intended, only adding to the sum total of ugliness all around.* Meanwhile, the dead body on the ground reminded him, *Yet there are always enough willing believers for those kinds of promises, I suppose.*

Giertz had also passingly noticed the mouth was Pandora's, and he remembered what she'd said about herself being turned into a computer-generated image. *Perhaps they've finally done it?* Then however, he returned to his earlier, more disturbing thought, *Or perhaps she didn't die after all? Maybe I hallucinated her life and death altogether?* Then he caught himself hoping the latter was true. Knowing that mouth so well, he felt a small memory glow somewhere inside him, remembering the day it had told him everything, almost. *One way or another, she certainly did know more than I did: killing Dr. Zed probably hasn't made any difference, at all.*

This caused Giertz to remember the alternative future she'd offered him, which he hadn't even really considered, *Maybe there was actually somewhere, some real place she and I could have gone together, and a way it could have worked between us?* This in turn caused him to recall her vengeful smile at him in Dr. Zed's office, a smile Giertz had seen on so many faces, but didn't understand totally until recently. Therefore he had to admit, *Perhaps she was right, I did throw something away with her, a chance to really escape together, that I can never get back?* Painfully, faced with a vision of them both playing on a beach somewhere, he had to face it, *So maybe that was the biggest mistake I made, of all?*

**Chapter 161 Hideous Dream**
As he contemplated this, he felt something in the breeze flop against his shins. He looked down and saw two used condoms wrapped in one of the old-fashioned newscomix, which nobody read anymore, but which the media still reeled out anyway. Amongst the lithographed photographs of young people shamelessly exposing their retouched bodies, he saw the headline,

'Dr. ZED NAMES FOURTEEN ENEMIES OF PROGRESS!'

Beneath it was a picture of the bloated, paranoid cranium staring from behind dark glasses, as always. Giertz was puzzled, *It must be an old edition, or perhaps I didn't kill him? Maybe that was just a hallucination as well? Maybe I hallucinated all of it?*

Giertz quickly shook the mess away from his legs and walked on. *Everything, Pandora and Kadski, the fights with Dr. Zed and The Bad Actor, feels as if it was just some hideous dream anyway, now.* Hallucinatory or not, the returned memories felt like some terrible burden he'd been carrying for too long. While it had all happened over half a year ago, it still made Giertz feel enormously tired.

In fact he knew now, despite having slept for six months, completing the rapid rehabilitation program, and not having walked far, he just felt physically and mentally exhausted. *So that's it*, he thought, hopelessly. *That's all of it.* He sat down on a large, almost brand-new holyvision set that was lying at the roadside, thrown out for just not being this month's style. He put his elbows on his knees, and his head sank beneath his shoulders. He had that feeling again, which had accompanied his first major suicide attempt, except now it was even stronger, *It seems every major decision I've made since leaving the Happylands asylum has just been one in a string of serious mistakes.* Even Pandora's collaboration seemed to have only given him false hope. *All my exertions have only led me to this pointless point.*

Then he felt a hand on his arm.

**Chapter 162 Star Quality**

A filthy man of about Giertz's age had appeared from nowhere. He sported a beret, and spectacles with lenses like two small crystal balls, which made his eyes look infinitesimally small. He began talking to Giertz as if he'd known him all his life. Giertz's meditations had blunted his reflexes, but before the man touched his arm, he just had time to notice, *This man's hand is covered in a strange red mottling, probably symptomatic of some new mutation of Virus 265/76G-F!* Giertz tried to snatch his arm away, but was too late.

Oblivious to this, with no introduction the man mumbled a strange tale, through strings of discolored saliva dropping from his mouth, 'I discovered Pandora recognizing her star-quality immediately.' It all spilled out in the same monotonous, self-pitying whine. His breath smelt of some cheap solvent, and he never even paused to inhale. 'I got her an apartment and connections but then she forgot about me and left me to rot in the gutter once she made it...' *I wonder why*, Giertz thought.

At first, Giertz empathized, *It's plain the virus has got into the man's brain.* So Giertz tried to listen, politely feigning some interest, but soon failed to maintain it. Becoming bored he stood up to leave, but the man still didn't let go of his arm. Giertz finally managed to twist his arm free and knocked the man down, but he still grasped at Giertz's leg. He kicked him hard in the ribs, but the man just lay there continuing to talk as if Giertz hadn't done anything. As he walked away, Giertz could still hear him talking endlessly about Pandora. Then it occurred to Giertz, *That man sincerely believed what he was saying! So who would believe me, if I told them my story - if I told them the truth, when I can't even believe it myself?*

In this state of mind, he walked past a young woman breastfeeding her mutant baby in an abandoned shop doorway. For a moment Giertz was overwhelmed by a blissful feeling, seeing the happy maternal expression on her face as she gave it all she had to give. She didn't care at all about its deformed, semi-insect head, or the strange noise it kept making as if it had already realized something was wrong. *I suppose the mutants' chromosomes have got into the gene-pool now, and soon there will be more mutants than 'normal' humans.* He tried to care, but in spite of his revulsion for mutants, really couldn't now.

Further on he saw many blind people sitting in the same kind of doorways. Their concave, closed eyelids somehow didn't seem entirely hopeless. Some just sat patiently waiting for 'something,' or called politely for it. The street was lined with them, singing songs, shaking rhythms out of maracas. *A street of the blind, perhaps they are lucky they can't see what I do?*

Further still, sprawled in the gutter amongst more brand new holyvision sets, and other unwanted products, were the forgotten veterans of The World Wars with their twisted, mangled bodies and distorted, abstracted faces. They were part men, part rusted machines with their cheap, prosthetic limbs. He even saw one who was just a human head on a robot body. *Most of them also appear to have bizarre mental diseases, inflicted on them by psychological warfare - even worse cases than I saw in the Happylands Institute.* Somehow though they still managed to hum a patriotic anthem, their eyes misted with military nostalgia, but beyond them were alleys full of beggars, openly displaying their disfigurements.

As Giertz continued his journey, the city grew darker around him. *Like the synthetic 'nature' I discovered, this is the urban 'reality' I've been driving past in this city, fast enough to ignore it. My own neighborhood is bad, and not getting better, but this urban trashscape is somehow even more terrible, and still getting worse.* Looking at the hopeless figures in these streets he now felt overwhelmed, *The task of destroying reality is no longer just an academic prospect for me.* Yet it also led him to ponder, *I suppose everyone is just trapped in their reality, but they all seem to be able to accept it somehow. So why can't I? Why do I still want to destroy it so badly? Even more so now, except I've already had my shot, and failed.*

When he'd last walked out of the Asclepius institute, Giertz had only been half-interested in the Professor's veiled promise that Ceebix might still have a use for him, but now Giertz wondered, *Just why did they reanimate me? After all, I'd served my purpose, surely, and Ceebix certainly knows he can't predict my behavior within 'acceptable parameters,' so they must have had a good reason.* Therefore Giertz now dared to see a glimmer of hope, that he still had a chance to kill even this reality. *Perhaps The real Game isn't over for me, yet? Anyway, Ceebix and the Combat Youth still offer the only option I have right now.*

Almost involuntarily, Giertz started to hurry.

**Chapter 163 Hate-Filled**

After several even more abysmal streets, Giertz eventually retraced his way to the empty warehouses by the disused wharf. The ever-more rusty cranes were still hanging over the thick, soupy water, before the Greedeluxe Youth Headquarters office block. As he came closer, in spite of how dark it was now, Giertz noticed it had been bomb damaged, a whole corner broken off the top. He could even see the hate-filled, satanic graffiti on the walls in the empty rooms that had once belonged to the Motorcycle Youth. So many letters were now missing from the dead neon sign up the side of the building, it now just read, 'EE OU H,' like some exclamation of disgust.

When he finally reached the building he encountered a crudely constructed razor wire fence now surrounding the broken edifice. Impaled on the stakes supporting the silver coils were the fizzing, severed heads of Consumers, on some of which the faces were still recognizable, and nailed around it were inverted crucifixions. Giertz could still recognize some of the spread-eagled bodies as the leaders of various opposing, and some previously allied, gangs. Giertz noted also that some of them were Motorcycle Youths. *The split between the Combat and Motorcycle Youths must finally have happened, since the death of Nailbrand.*

Their cadavers hung in a variety of stages of decomposition, like talismans to ward off evil spirits. Even in the cold weather, Giertz had to hold his nose against the sickly, near-sweet stench, but for a moment he found himself nearly envying the tortured bodies. He almost wished he could share the peacefully grinning expressions on their upside-down faces, yet not entirely.

Coming closer, Giertz strained his neck looking up at the masses of glittering barbed wire now entwined around the building, like some strange metal ivy. *The work was carried out after an air attack, but the heavy-duty concrete stood up to it pretty well.* There was now a makeshift wooden catwalk also, connecting the building directly to the new helicopter pads on the flat roof of the warehouse opposite. Otherwise though, the area was entirely disorganized.

He read graffiti painted in Xeracist hieroglyphs as he walked around bomb craters full of stagnant water. There were the twisted remains of yellow and black fake Lamborghinis everywhere. *They seem to have been deliberately destroyed in some strange bumper-car orgy.* Charred bones of species that Giertz couldn't quite categorize were also lying about on the ground. Psycho Kiss was blaring permanently out of the PA system, so loud though he couldn't even make out a song at all from the distorting sub-woofers.

The first Combat Youths he saw had long, matted hair, and some hardly wore any uniform at all. Many wore raw, uncured dog, and other, animal skins. They no longer washed. The women had decorated the men by painting their faces, bodies, and guns with intricate patterns, over their corporate tattoos and brandings. Looking more closely, Giertz saw these were in fact brightly colored hieroglyphs from the thoughts of Zytopharbb. *There are hundreds of Combat Youths now. Obviously, they've taken over the whole Greedeluxe Youth; there are no other sub-divisions, so probably every member is a Combat Youth these days.*

**Chapter 164 Self-Consuming**

In the road in front of the cracked, armored-glass, entrance doors, a sizeable bonfire was smoldering. It was created from a couple of upturned fake Lamborghinis, and some cheap wooden office furniture. *It looks as if some manner of celebration is taking place?* Giertz watched the youths dance maniacally around it to crude drumming, improvised by simply beating aggressively on the concave roofs of the other smashed cars, augmenting the music pulsing from the speakers. Someone even managed to find a beaten-up electric guitar, trying to get a bit of old, retro rock 'n roll going. There was nevertheless something eerily familiar about the dancing.

Then Giertz recognized the steps, *They are almost the same as those of the priests in the Xeracist Tabernacle!* The dancing youths also waved spears, javelins, and even flint axes. One or two had improvised bows and arrows. Giertz found this retro weaponry strange, *Why use those when there are more sophisticated weapons freely available?* What were even stranger to him were the human scalps hanging from their belts. *It all seems in tune with the whole scene though, somehow.*

He noted, *There seems to be a general air of anticipation.* Eventually, a wave of light helicopters swept in, breaking up the night air. Their navigation lights illuminated the otherwise lightless sky as they landed on the warehouse roof, back from a patrol. *It must all be done with helicopters now. The fake Lamborghinis are obsolete, in the same way the tanks were before them.* He didn't like the idea, *But it was clear which way Ceebix's thinking was leaning, well before my coma.*

Another group of disheveled Combat Youths descended from the aircraft, brandishing aloft some things Giertz couldn't quite see from his position, but the others clearly knew what they were. A great cheer went up from the revelers, and they fired their guns into the air. They threw the things onto the fire in bursts of orange sparks, and an even bigger cheer went up. After a few minutes, they pulled them out again and began devouring the things, eating with their fingers. Curiously, Giertz looked again at some of the carbonized bones scattered on the ground and then felt a queasy sense of familiarity. It wasn't that he couldn't recognize them. It was that he didn't want to.

Instantly he recalled Dr. Zed's last prophecy, of how the Consumer would become self-consuming, and knew Kadski's final observation had been right, 'Look what we've become!' *These are human bones. The Greedeluxe Combat Youth are consuming human phlesh!* Giertz now felt as if the truth was torturing him. *After all the fighting and sacrifice and effort, not only is reality still here, and even worse, but the real victory has been Dr. Zed's! We became what we were trying to destroy.* Somehow Giertz now felt fragmented.

He watched the youths' feverish faces, washed in the weird, flickering orange light from the fire. *It would be wrong to call them 'savages,'* Giertz decided, *because even the simplest culture has some intricately reasoned pattern behind it, but here, all they have to celebrate is that there are no reasons, that there is no pattern - at all.*

Then slowly, seemingly one at a time, the faces all turned towards him.


**Chapter 165 Endless Tunnel**

They all appeared to recognize Giertz at once. *I don't see any faces I remember, but everyone appears to know who I am, and what I've done.* They stopped what they were doing, and the drumming petered out, along with the music from the PA system. They stared curiously at him, and he felt slightly embarrassed at first. *In my relatively clean jacket and jeans, I must look like some specter from the past, sent to haunt them.* One or two of the Combat Youths even looked a little guilty about what they were doing.

He'd never believed he was fully one of them, but now Giertz felt *really* out of place. As well as knowing who he was, it was clear they also hated him more than ever before, but he found it strange, seeing the same cast of jealousy as Kadski's on their sweating faces.

Then looking carefully, Giertz noticed something else on the ground. A potent breeze was depositing the same kind of coarse-grained sand he'd seen in The Red Desert of Death, everywhere. Immediately Giertz felt hope at last, *It's happening! It's finally reached this far!* He saw there was in fact so much dust; it was building up in small mounds against everything. He reached down and scooped up a handful. He held it out in front of himself towards the revelers, and let it run through his fingers, redistributed on the wind. The youths were just confused, but Giertz knew, *They'll understand, soon enough.*

The silence continued for a few more painful moments, but then another helicopter suddenly dropped out of the starless sky behind him. 'IDENTIFY YOURSELF!' An amplified voice boomed. Giertz turned to face it, momentarily dazzled by the helicopter's spotlight, but then saw its infrared Gatling cannon was locked directly onto his head. He stared up the endless tunnel of its barrel and wondered what he should say, *I haven't got anything on me I can identify myself with, after all.*

Strangely however, he found he didn't care much. He only had one thought, *Wouldn't it be ironic to be shot like this, after all, I've survived?* Then however, the voice echoed, 'AH! Dr. GIERTZ, GLAD TO SEE YOU'VE RECOVERED. WELCOME BACK!' There was an uncertain edge to it though. Abruptly the helicopter arced back into the sky, the voice trailing behind, 'PROFESSOR CEEBIX IS EXPECTING YOU IN HIS OFFICE.'

**Chapter 166 Exaggerated Friendliness**

Old bloodstains, graffiti and bullet pockmarks now covered the raw concrete corridors leading to Ceebix's office, but the room itself was the same as it had been during Giertz's interview, except it was now in almost total darkness. As Giertz entered, Ceebix was watching something on the holy-terminal on his desk. The light from it made his face seem to float in mid-air, as he spoke with exaggerated friendliness, 'Welcome back! Come in!'

Giertz entered slowly, as if in a trance. He was mesmerized by what was on the viewer: a thin young woman in a white evening dress. She could have been any age, any height, and almost any nationality as she swept onto the screen. *You can tell she enjoys what she's doing, in a detached sort of way, but in another way she could take it or leave it.* 'Good evening fellow citizens,' she purred, her face as cold and heartless as a hypermodel's, with a hint of contempt.

Giertz sat down in the same metal chair as before, but heavily this time. *New Pandoras usually differ noticeably from their predecessors, but this one is a perfect replica. Perhaps it's a digital image, as she predicted. Or maybe they even found someone else, exactly like her. Or perhaps it was all another hallucination...?* By now though Giertz positively wanted to believe there was someone still alive in that holyscreen. He wished he could in some way become a disembodied impulse in the circuitry with her.

In another sense he realized it wasn't her, Pandora, he missed at all. Now Giertz recognized a kind of agony developing inside himself, but it wasn't quite the same as what he'd felt for the loss of Nailbrand or even Kadski. What Giertz missed was a mousy-looking girl, with no bust or hips to speak of. *Perhaps not even that, just that*

Ceebix snapped the holyvision show off, the switch still covered in adhesive tape, jerking Giertz out of his melancholy. 'Rubbish!' Ceebix declared, 'I don't know why I watch it.' The office was now almost entirely dark, but somehow Giertz could still make out Ceebix's silhouette. He turned to face Giertz, but picked up a small object that had been lying on his desk. He began to toy with it, paying more attention to it than to Giertz.

Then abruptly Ceebix asked him a blunt question, the same one Asclepius had asked, 'Well, how do you feel?' Ceebix looked up from his contemplations, and he and Giertz stared uncomfortably at each other in silence, then he tried to speak honestly,
'I feel confused. I know a lot more things now, but somehow none of it makes any real sense.' He looked carefully at Ceebix, trying to gauge his reaction, but failed.

Giertz found himself distracted by the movement of Ceebix's hands, and he looked down to see what they were playing with. Straining his eyes in the darkness, Giertz saw another object, *Just like one of Dr. Kortex's multi-dimensional models of my insanity I saw him manipulating in the Happylands asylum!* Giertz shifted uncomfortably, but tried not to show it. Looking around the desk he could also see the phallic, domestic idol, Pandora's diary, and his almost empty 'poetry' book, but this time he wasn't so surprised, *It just confirms what I pretty much already know by now.*


**Chapter 167 Ritual Suicide**
Ceebix talked meaninglessly for a few minutes, filling Giertz in on what had happened during the time he'd been unconscious. Most of it was what he'd already guessed, 'After the death of Nailbrand, the tensions

between the Motorcycle and Combat Youth finally erupted into full-scale war.' Beneath Ceebix's recitation, Giertz read the subtext, *All the other Greedeluxe gangs joined in on one side or another, but the Combat Youth won, at a price, due to their skill in eliminating key figures.*

Also, underneath the sub-text, Giertz detected a tone of bitter anger: a boiling, vitriolic loathing for himself. *Ceebix still really doesn't like me, at all.* It made Giertz highly uneasy. He found himself listening to this more than what Ceebix was actually saying. Giertz began to have the feeling he was trying to diffuse an extremely sensitive bomb. He was too distracted even to notice the irony of Ceebix's attitude being the exact opposite of what he, Giertz, had hoped to extract from him, for so long.

Then one remark Ceebix made in passing drew Giertz's attention. 'Unfortunately, the Xeracist Fundamentalist Youth chose the wrong side...' In spite of Giertz's experiences and theological studies, this news from Ceebix made Giertz see he had been relatively indifferent until now, taking his belief in the existence of Xerak for granted. *In the end, I suppose I only believed in Xerak half-heartedly, because I was so focused on destroying reality, and Xeracism just gave me further vindication.* Now however, Giertz knew, *Ceebix has just demolished a major supporting pillar of my life!*

Giertz unwillingly remembered though the priests in the mountain, their ancient faith, and the terrible message he'd received there. This statement from Ceebix now caused Giertz to question, *So why did Xerak choose me to try to destroy reality? There was a reason to serve that purpose, above and beyond The Greedeluxe Combat Youth, but by joining them, whose and what purpose was I obeying, really?*

Therefore Giertz interrupted Ceebix, to ask why it had been necessary to slaughter all the zealots in the ranks of the Greedeluxe Youth, 'So excuse me, but I mean where does Xerak come into all this now? You told us we were fighting a *holy war*!' The corner of Ceebix's slit-like mouth drew back in an unhappy half-smile. He now knew somebody had uncovered his disguise at the Youth Rally, but he appeared to be more concerned about this than Giertz's question. Ceebix answered, but looking down at his hands, 'They had served their purpose. The Greedeluxe Combat Youth must now just believe in nothing but the conflict between the two corporations, as an end in itself.'

Ceebix saw Giertz was still confused however, and a hint of Ceebix's barely-suppressed anger vented out. 'Oh come on! We're both intelligent enough to understand Xerak is just an opiate for them...!' He waved his arm roughly in the direction of the Combat Youth, who were still loudly celebrating nothing by the wharf outside the building.  'Asclepius and Kortex,' Ceebix continued to grind out, 'discovered that lunatic - what was his name? That "Zytopharbb," in an asylum, and ascertained his delusions could be useful.'
'So it wasn't ritual suicide that killed him, was it,' Giertz accused. Ceebix waved his arm dismissively now,
'He'd served the purpose he was contracted to. His highest goal was always just to be a martyr anyway.' Giertz had noticed by now though, *Ceebix is saying this mainly to himself. So it wasn't even about religion,* Giertz reflected, sourly, as his final illusion evaporated. *Ceebix's agenda was never about helping me to destroy reality. So what was it about?*


**Chapter 168 Abandoned Marionette**
Then Ceebix somehow managed to regain his composure, returning to his central theme. 'Well, you've proved what you can do for us, so far, but when you deserted your patrol that time, I had my doubts, about you *and* Kadski.'

Giertz nodded slightly, to let Ceebix know he understood by 'us,' Ceebix meant himself and Asclepius. 'But *The Game* is helicopters now, Jimmy. Urban warfare has gone three-dimensional. The cars are obsolete; we trashed most of those months ago. Do you feel up to it? Your scores on the flight simulator were always the highest. That was why I called off the helicopter attack on you, so you've already had one second chance.'

Dazzled by his own generosity at offering Giertz a third chance, Ceebix showed a total lack of awareness of the tears in Giertz's eyes, 'I killed four Bad Actors and Dr. Zed, and Byron Reed!' Giertz said hoarsely, a catch in his throat. 'I did everything you created me for and programmed me to do...'

'But *why* did you need to do it *before* we *sold* the shares? I created The Sacred Oath of Judazz Suicide Squad *just* for you. For *you*, Giertz! All you had to do was join it and then just follow orders. It was all about the share price, *Jimmy*!' Ceebix finally exploded, his safety valve blown out altogether, his teeth gritted, bitterly hammering both his fists down onto the desk in time to what he was saying, making everything on it jump, repeating in case Giertz didn't get it, 'IT WAS ALL ABOUT THE SHARE PRICE! *JIMMY*!? Asclepius and I were set to make a killing in the market! A KILLING! Twenty-five years of my life! The Combat Youth, this whole project, *you*, were more than twenty-five years of my life! I was a teenage genius at the Consumeordie Institute of Asymmetric Warfare when Asclepius came to me with your DNA profile. Now, look at me...' Ceebix was reaching across the desk to Giertz, with an upturned palm, grasping at nothing. Giertz was stunned, not just by what Ceebix was saying, but his over-all male-menopausal demeanor. Giertz protested, astounded by the accusation,

'You programmed the Combat Youth, me through my "parents," to do so! To just destroy Consumeordie! So that's what I did.'

Even as he said it though, Giertz understood, *So this was Ceebix's greatest fear, his Idea Bomb, his monster, getting out of his control, growing beyond him, to develop a mind of its own. His experiment wasn't to have an autonomous private army which mostly thinks for itself, questions orders and makes its own up, but just believes it can. One way or another I upset his plans by functioning too well, going beyond his suicide mission. I destroyed what Ceebix wanted to possess, when it was really all just about stock-market manipulation. I suppose even an atom bomb is useless if the timer doesn't work. Maybe even Pandora wasn't supposed to confess to me until later...*

Giertz also recalled again Ceebix saying, 'You will enjoy The Game.' Therefore Giertz now realized just how addicted to 'The Game' he'd become. Visualizing the nightmare of returning to the aimless days of driving the endless, empty roads, just playing pointless holygames in the Synth-O-Gas stations again, he couldn't hold the feeling down inside himself any longer. In an almost-scream of withdrawal, he said, 'You're destroying me Ceebix! You've got to give me something to believe in! I can't function anymore without anything!' Giertz searched his memory for something and clutched at a sentence desperately, '"There's no good or evil, only survival!" You yourself told me that!' To his surprise Giertz saw he was holding out *his* own empty hand to him, mirroring Ceebix's gesture.

The corners of Ceebix's mouth now drew down, and it was only then Giertz fully comprehended the crushing weight of how much Ceebix hated him. He labeled Giertz with 'liability' and every other insult possible, and a few Ceebix invented for the occasion. He ended the list by striking Giertz's face with the back of his knuckles. It knocked Giertz out of his chair, and he sprawled onto the floor, where he found himself lacking the will to move, like an abandoned marionette.

Ceebix quickly pulled his wheelchair from behind the desk and over to where Giertz lay. In spite of Ceebix's disability, he began kicking Giertz violently in the ribs. He recognized with revulsion he would have done anything for Ceebix at that moment, even the most degrading of submissions, under the hail of blows and blasphemies. He even tried to, but it only intensified Ceebix's wrath.

From his wheelchair Ceebix somehow manhandled Giertz out into the corridor, slamming across the metal door of his office. Giertz lay slumped against the wall, a trickle of blood and thin mucous running down the concrete from his head. Passing Combat Youths stepped over him, a few looking down curiously, but no one did or said anything.

**Chapter 169 Spectral Entity**

After some time, not knowing what to do, Giertz got up and began wandering around the building. Even in its damaged state, it was still open twenty-four hours. He went to the self-torture chamber, part of which had been burned by the attack, but he couldn't summon up the enthusiasm to do anything. He visited the shooting gallery with the cardboard cut-outs of Dr. Zed's head, but felt the same way. The Rapid Healing Clinic annex, while still fully intact and functioning, couldn't help him with this problem. Then he began to notice the other Combat Youths were now watching him, carefully.

At first, he thought it might just be paranoia on his part, but began to see there was no mistake. They still wouldn't talk to him either. By now he had an overwhelming feeling of being like some ghostly entity, which no longer belonged in their world, *Really, they are fundamentally afraid of me; in the same way Ceebix is of his prodigy. Like Kadski, they also resent the fact I spoiled their game by playing it too well. Now they are just not sure what to do with me.* He knew they couldn't let him leave there either. *I'm too dangerous and unpredictable, after all.*

Then, out of nowhere, came the screeching of an alarm, and Combat Youth issue jackboots were running urgently on concrete. An explosion followed, and the whole world seemed to rock. Giertz felt momentarily seasick, then saw everyone was running to the building's armory. When he arrived, they were handing out rocket launchers and anti-tank guns. Giertz joined them, but as his turn in front of the serving hatch came, nothing happened. The young quartermaster doing the distributing wouldn't hand him anything, but just stared through him. A queue of silent, impatient faces began building up behind Giertz.

He felt he had to do something. He had to do anything.

Until now, Giertz had generally been thinking, *I know now my motives are pure, and always were, but it hasn't made any difference. So what have I got left?* He finally understood that while they'd owned him, *I've never fully gained my membership of the Combat Youth.* His sense of losing something he'd never quite possessed was now at its most acute. What Kadski had been trying to tell him the day Nailbrand had died, 'We don't need the Greedeluxe Youth, Combat Youth or any other youth...' echoed for Giertz now. *I don't need them because I never had them anyway, and never will. There's still one thing I have though, my reflexes!*

Finally, Giertz lost all patience and pulled his gun up. From the hip he shot the figure in the armory before he could react, and then turned on the group behind him. They'd hardly unholstered their weapons before they all collapsed, groaning hideously.

**Chapter 170 Structural Weaknesses**

Giertz jumped through the hatch into the armory and found a thermal demolition charge. He set the timer on it for forty-five seconds, then, even with his still partly atrophied muscles, managed to heave the enameled steel box off the shelf, running out into the corridor. He was familiar enough with the building to know its structural weaknesses. When he reached where he'd intended to lay the charge however, he found a machine gun nest where there hadn't been one before.

Three Combat Youths were firing wildly at a group of helicopters whirling around the building, which were spraying it with shells and rockets. The machines carried no particular markings. Giertz guessed they were some hasty amalgam of survivors from previously allied gangs, which had been decimated by the Combat Youth. Seeing Giertz with his bomb, one of the machine gunners tried to turn the ungainly weapon around on him.

Thinking three seconds ahead, Giertz just managed to heave the explosive into their midst, then shot all three of them. As they lay moaning, he jumped to shelter behind a thick supporting column, jamming his index fingers into his ears. There was an enormous roar, which seemed to vibrate his bones, as the charge took almost half the side off the building. In the resulting panic, Giertz fought his way down through the rushing bodies and fog of dust to the basement.

As he'd hoped, his old, dented, red, fake Lamborghini was still next to the others abandoned by the Greedeluxe Youth. Waiting to be trashed, it was covered by a blanket of eighteen months of dust, but the tires weren't quite flat. While fragments of concrete ceiling snowed down on him from the war above, he quickly inflated them from the nitrogen line, picking up a spare battery from the store cupboard, and filling up the tank. Where shall I go though? He wondered, as he routed through the trash in the glove box, looking for the key, and then he found the dirty, embroidered table napkin from Uncle Joe's party. Giertz had been using it for a cleaning rag, but the geo-coordinates and security code, given to him just before his fight with The Bad Actor, were still just visible on it. 'This has to be the will of Xerak!' He exclaimed to himself, but he still wasn't fully prepared for where it would send him.

As if to reinforce his belief however, when he fumbled deeply in his Combat Youth Jacket he found the key still there. Quickly bolting the battery in place, he recognized, *Somehow I feel closer to this machine than I ever have to any human being, or ever will!* Therefore he vowed to the machine with absolute conviction, *We shall always be together!*

The engine turned over unwillingly at first, but then barked into life once more. He drove over where Ceebix had used to speak from, and up the ramp marked 'SECTOR H' for the last time. As always, Giertz just missed the door of the warehouse; then he sprinted for the improvised, razor-wire barricade.

By this time, just as he'd planned, the helicopters were infesting the now torn open, far side of the building. His headlights glinted brightly on the steel wire as the car ripped through the flimsy barrier. As he drove away, he glimpsed the battle in his rearview screen from time to time. In the darkness it looked like some bizarre fireworks display, until it shrank to a mere flickering pinpoint of light. *That's their future, their reality,* Giertz thought, *not mine.* He still carried the questions with him however, *What have they done to me? What have they made me into?*

It would not be long before he would find out.

**Chapter 171 Tank Traps**

Giertz drove over the Channel Bridge again, which was somehow still open and just negotiable, thanks to his reflexes. On the road the other side he drove throughout the night again. As well as the full tank, the car had the reserve tank he'd welded in himself during his repairs. He didn't have to stop. With the cyclone injectors on maximum, it was enough to get him to the place in his mind. The instruments glowed reassuringly red before him, the car's front beams cutting through the blackness, to unveil - nothing.

Disbelievingly at first, Giertz began to see how relatively quiet the rest of the world was, in contrast to the bitter hysteria he'd just left behind. *It's as if all the disagreements have finally been resolved, by canceling each other out. When I drove through here before, there were at least a few buildings still standing, something to rebuild civilization on.* Now however, the moonlight revealed only demolition, and an accumulation of red sand. *Perhaps the collapse of the Consumeordie share price was the final blow for The Globecon after all?* Giertz considered gleefully. *So maybe my personal battle against The Beast wasn't wasted, in the end?*

In the relative peace of the humming cockpit, he was now able to think without distraction, *There was no mistaking the message I received in The Tabernacle, and I destroyed 'the swollen-headed monster.' I made a series of bad mistakes, but perhaps, ironically, they've led to the right conclusion? Where I came from must just be the last, dying embers of The Consumer Zone, but nobody there realizes it yet, not even Ceebix. Perhaps his Idea Bomb, me, was more effective than even he could predict? So maybe civilization, and therefore reality will soon be over after all!* Somehow though, Giertz felt even more frustrated at this thought, because, *Even if the end is close now, it still can't come fast enough for me.*

As a green dawn cracked over the horizon, at first he saw a few surviving Consumers, radiation and chemical burns on their faces, pushing rusty supermarket trolleys over the wilderness of rubble. *They are trying to scavenge their shattered lives from this decomposed infrastructure, in vain.* He observed. Soon though, after even just a little more distance, Giertz knew he was looking at a dead landscape.

As he expected, from the epicenter, a wind even angrier than it had been last time was blasting more desert sand across the jagged surface. It was gradually eroding the broken concrete, wearing the scenery down, and soothing it with a smooth blanket of red dunes - forever. He felt a strange sense of relief at the sight. *It won't be long. Yes, it won't be long!* Giertz assured himself, trying to be patient.

He went reasonably fast, but he wasn't attempting to achieve anything with his car anymore, being as easy on the abused engine as possible. He drove carefully, but his contemplations morphed into hallucinations again, even worse than the last time he'd driven here, bizarre conflagrations of images melding into the smashed landscape. No longer knowing where he was, he just had the same-old feeling of driving through his nightmares - but then the view started to become familiar.


**Chapter 172 Security Zone**

The geo-coordinates and security code given to him so long ago by the girl at Uncle Joe's party, began to flash as digits on the car's retro direction finder, as he reached the first razor-wire fence, and first set of auto-guns. Giertz identified himself to them and gave the security code. Then he drove the fifty or so paces between the system of minefields and trenches full of tank-traps, to the second gate, and repeated the information. *So this must be the mysterious Security Zone! They hid it in The Red Desert of Death. I suppose it makes sense, in a way...*

Eventually, he reached the outer wall. It was enormous, angled outwards, curving off slightly at both sides. At the third checkpoint, there were black-uniformed human security guards with complicated anti-tank guns. They peered at him suspiciously from under their high-peaked caps with a small, silver skull and cross-bones on the front. Giertz just repeated the security number given to him at Uncle Joe's party, and they waved him through without further questions. *Almost as if I'm expected!*

As he continued driving, now and again he would see new machinery of some kind. He passed a water purification plant, then a large solar power array. Then he saw something he'd never seen before. *A robot farm!* The glittering machines were busily harvesting the genetically modified crops, diligently tending and slaughtering the fat, docile animals. *The desalination plants must irrigate it all. Now I know where the food at Uncle Joe's feasts came from.* It was enormous too, the artificially created, green fields spanned to the horizon, comforting his eyes.

To Giertz, the inside of the Security Zone was more like a kind of Eden, a total contrast to the hostile desert, and world outside. He saw other machinery as well, but wasn't quite so sure what it was for. Then he saw buildings, a small, ideal town, shimmering in the distance, under a giant air-conditioned, transparent, geodesic dome. *It's all brand new!* What struck him above all was the order, *How carefully arranged everything is, compared to the mess I left behind!*

Then he noticed a house some way off to the side of the road. There was nothing spectacular about it. It was just an opulent, comfortable, post neo-modernist residence, hinting broadly at Frank Lloyd Wright's inspirations, blending with the flatness of the horizon. There was a party going on, with brightly dressed people surrounding it, reminiscent of the ones at Uncle Joe's estate.

Giertz parked his dusty, fake car next to the VTOL jets and burnished, genuine Lamborghinis, Ferraris, and Bugattis, and then stepped out into the heat. Through the screen of transplanted palm trees he approached the large front door, carved from a single oak panel. It was open and swung easily on its hinges. As Giertz entered the enormous living room, he felt a cold shiver though, not just from the air-conditioning. It was the same feeling someone would have on blundering into quicksand. He realized he was surrounded by Producers again.

He guessed, *Many of them must have been at Uncle Joe's party, as they clearly recognize me.* He also noticed from their reaction things were not the same anymore. He was no longer just a 'court jester.' *It's obvious most of them know what I've done to Consumeordie's share price,* he thought, smugly, but after the initial stir, they didn't take much notice. He was secretly disappointed they didn't seem more intimidated. They even appeared to be glad he was there, to relive the ever-suffocating boredom.

**Chapter 173 Forced Laughter**
Giertz also felt stunned as he recognized the house. The lights, music and forced laughter blasting from its windows had made it difficult at first. *It's the same one I saw in ruins, when I went to the Xeracist Tabernacle in the mountain some time ago!* At first he assumed, *They must have rebuilt this edifice, at some expense.* He marveled at the exactness of the restoration. *Even the dead trees around it are now completely green and healed!*

The furnishings were also to exactly the same specifications as the last time he'd been here. Giertz sat down on one of a casual arrangement of Bauhaus chairs around a large coffee table. The real leather on the chairs was supple and new. He ran his fingers over a corner of the table that was polished and unmarked, and there was no hole in the ceiling. The sand drift that had been in one corner of the room had been cleared. Giertz thumbed through the glossy magazines on the table, full of bright, colorful images of Consumer products. The fish tank was full, and well stocked with gently flapping, exotic angel species. Leonard Kornn's signed, original canvases, from his celebrated 'vert' period, graced the walls. Looking out of the enormous window, through to the very-far distance, at the blunt, blue point of the mountain where the priests lived, Giertz considered, *It's ironic these Producers couldn't know they've constructed their utopia right next to what's destroying their reality.*

Peering around the room though, Giertz could already see a few grains of the red sand starting to accumulate here and there. Now he knew what he'd really seen the 'last' time he was here. Also, as he moved about, he noticed, *There's something different in the general buzz at this party, compared to the excited optimism at Uncle Joe's functions.* Giertz couldn't avoid overhearing worried anecdotes about lost fortunes.

By combining a bit of what he already knew with Snodgrass's math, and some intuition, he was able to deduce, *So by going beyond the parameters of Ceebix's mission for me, and destroying Consumeordie's core software on their terminal, I did have a permanent effect after all! While they kept most of the details of the collapse from The Consumers, something went seriously wrong with The Globecon six months ago, and nobody on The Council of Ninety is sure how to put it right. Now I see why Ceebix hates me so much.* So Giertz finally knew for sure, as he looked around at the worried partygoers, *Yes, it won't be long.*

He politely refused a clone waiter in a white tuxedo who presented him with a syringe full of Preparation

X315/J on a silver tray. Instead, Giertz asked him for a glass of distilled water. In spite of all the driving, Giertz wasn't hungry. Then he looked up at the net curtains billowing slowly through the screen windows, to see a woman wafting through them, as if entering from a dream.

## Chapter 174 Meaningless Conversations

Immediately he recognized the girl who'd invited him here, all that time back. She was flitting about, having the same kind of small, meaningless conversations that she'd made with Giertz, but now with a variety of men. Sometimes she rubbed her body up against theirs, only half-accidentally, as if it was some experiment. It all struck Giertz though as, *She's rather too old now for this type of behavior.*

When his glass of water arrived, Giertz discovered from the waiter her name was Anthea. As Giertz watched her, he also discovered he totally hated her. He hated her because he was attracted to her. *More specifically he hated what attracted him to her. In the time since I last saw her, she has succeeded in transforming herself into an exact replica of Pandora, down to every gesture, but with just enough of her own personality showing through to keep her human. She must have had facial and body augmentation surgery to complete the job, and it must have been very expensive.* She was already surrounded by an optimistic pack of young men in loose white shirts and narrow, Italian-look trousers, as was the fashion, but she didn't seem to like any of them at all. It was obvious what they saw in her.

Then turning her head, her delicately coiffured-to-look-natural hair swinging somehow in slow motion, she saw Giertz. 'Jimmy!' She cried gleefully, despite having met him before for only those few seconds. He was surprised she remembered his name because he hadn't even known hers. She came up to him and gave him an almost desperate hug, calculated to make her all-male entourage bark with jealousy. 'You're Jimmy Giertz aren't you!? I remember you had a ripping fight with The Bad Actor!' She said it in the best, genuine, finishing school tones, which his dead girlfriend, in her life as Pandora, had only been able to imitate. Then Anthea cooled somewhat as she remembered Giertz had lost the fight. She added after a moment's more calculation, 'Well at least you took him on, I suppose.'

Nevertheless she enthused, 'Oh, I'm so glad you're here! Maybe we can start having some *real* fun again, at last.' On saying this, she looked slightly lost for a moment, as if something she was trying to hide had accidentally shown through.

**Chapter 175 Happy Shell**

She guided him out to the enormous, multi-tiered fountain. Large enough to swim in, it was filled with clean, blue, chlorinated water at just the right temperature, fed by an artificial waterfall. 'Isn't this place wonderful though?' She effused. 'And it's completely self-sufficient! We've even got our own oil well and refinery! It's all automated, and most of it is underground of course. There are massive stocks of everything we could need, food, Preparation X315/J, even spare parts for our cars, and jets. The library database has got every movie and holy-game ever made. Everything's solar powered, and the sun shines all day!' She emphasized the final sentence however with the air of someone completely lost, as if her bright, happy shell was extremely thin, 'I mean, what more could we want?'

She relentlessly confided further though, 'Only a few people are allowed in of course,' and Giertz was struck for a moment, *What she has just described has a strange similarity to the Happylands asylum.* He also noticed some of the same symptoms around, while she continued babbling, 'The Council of Ninety says it's going to exterminate all The Consumers soon. They haven't given away the exact details of the plan yet, but you'll be safe in here anyway. There's even an anti-missile system in case anything goes wrong with their plan. There isn't only one Security Zone as such. It's decentralized, so any counter attack by The Consumers couldn't destroy all of it. It will all be broadcast on holyvision, in a Real Life special. The Evil Poet says we'll be watching history! It's the next, biggest step in human evolution since the extinction of the Neanderthals. Just think! Humanity will finally getting rid of all those Non-Productives!' She sounded breathlessly excited about it all. *So she isn't as naive as she wants everyone to think,* Giertz realized, so shocked that he wasn't able to respond.

'I'm afraid you missed most of the fun today...' She indicated with a broad sweep the disoriented and depressed-looking guests, lying around. He also realized with relief, *She means I've avoided the inevitable, embarrassing warm-up orgy.* The inebriated hedonists were in and around the fountain, looking bored and slightly disgusted with each other's tanned, bloated bodies. The aloof, human-clone slaves in white Tuxedos stepped over them carrying syringes on hand-engraved silver trays. Everywhere were the torn remains of designer under-clothes. Some of the party-goers, already having had enough, were trying to crawl back to their private jets and real Bugattis, getting ready to detox on the way to the next party, in another Security Zone, but she reassured Giertz, 'This party doesn't finish for another three or four weeks, so you're welcome to stay as long as you like, as my guest. Indefinitely...' She looked at the other men standing behind her as she said this. 'Then it's on to the next one!'

She began to chat breathlessly about something else as well, but still reeling from her disclosure about The Sanitization, Giertz couldn't be bothered to listen. Then just as quickly she drifted away again, distracted by an unfamiliar handsome face, but she left Giertz feeling suddenly more alone.

The party was a masked ball. Most of the guests wore elaborate faces made of jewels and feathers, trying to look like mythological birds and dragons. Only Anthea didn't appear to wear one, but Giertz observed from experience, *Even without their disguises, everybody here is pretending to be something they're not, hiding what they really are. As usual, I am the closest thing to 'real life' in this place.*

As he circled the fountain with his glass of water, he gradually began to realize most of The Council of Ninety's members were here. He now knew, *This is how they conduct all the meetings, at never-ending parties like this, and the one Uncle Joe threw. Each council member has an identical secure terminal like the ones he and Ceebix had: their own, private Internet, with which they monitor their secrets. So when they get together, all the games played at these parties, and seemingly trivial chatter and jokes, are really a complex code, defining decisions of world importance - and I thought I was just doing party stunts!*

Of course, Giertz still didn't know the specific details of what all his stunts, done with Uncle Joe's encouragement, had meant. Giertz could now make educated guesses though, at the gestures his benefactor was trying to make to his guests, *By introducing some random element in the form of myself,* but Giertz no longer felt curious anyway. In fact, the whole concept of his relationship to Uncle Joe now reviled Giertz, *In retrospect; the idea of my avenging his death seems a very peculiar notion.*

As Asclepius and Ceebix were notable by their absence at this bash, Giertz surmised the agenda of this 'party,' *It's really to deal with the threat to the rest of The Council of Ninety those two represent, now the balance of power has been upset.*

## Chapter 176 Cosmetically Repaired

Giertz turned to the person next to him in the hope of gaining more information about what was really going on, and then found he was staring into the damaged face of Shrieking Joe Megastar. Giertz was awed, *SJM had once been more beautiful than some girls, but now the roughly stitched-up scar from his spectacular motorcycle accident runs almost helter-skelter around his countenance! And he's still refusing to have it cosmetically repaired.* There were also some of the burns on it which had still not completely healed, one or two turning septic, *From the time he deliberately set fire to himself on stage!*

He'd been sitting next to SJM for some time, but Giertz hadn't recognized him because he looked even older close to than he appeared to be on the holyvision. SJM was also even less recognizable because he wasn't wearing his usual skin-tight, black-leather leotard either, but a three-piece business suit. *Just like any other Producer,* Giertz reflected, slightly disappointed. *He looks bored and self-loathing, just like any other Producer as well.* Then Giertz understood the awful truth, *Shrieking Joe is one of The Council of Ninety! Perhaps he was all along?*

'I was your biggest fan,' said Giertz conversationally.
'I know.' SJM replied, with no emotion in his voice and without looking at him. Then a group of half-naked girls also recognized SJM, and screaming with joy dragged him fully clothed into the fountain. He didn't put up much resistance.

The Evil Poet was there of course, haughtily disregarding SJM's 'predicament.' From where Giertz was sitting, he could just make out what The Evil Poet was saying today, to his usual audience of Stoic, balding sages with their long, white beards, 'The balance of morality,' he droned, 'on this planet is entirely arbitrary, and held in man's hands alone. There is no abstract 'good' or 'evil' surrounding his actions like some ether. No outside cosmic force is evaluating man's activities, or influencing them in any way. Witness: greed and cruelty are rewarded every day, whereas acts of kindness and self-sacrifice meet with overwhelming punishments. Therefore, the concept of a `good' or `bad' action is relative merely to the set of circumstances in which one applies it, and the will of the majority, of course. Thus to try to perform a `good' action is merely to take a gamble. Quite a responsibility isn't it?' Giertz still felt the same perverse respect for the Evil Poet's point of view, but somehow found him harder to listen to these days.

**Chapter 177 Notorious Lesbian**
Then, Giertz heard something of a commotion coming his way, and to his surprise recognized somebody that everyone knew, but rarely saw. *This gathering must be important, because even Fat Boy is here! Real name Artous Phattbye,* Giertz reminded himself, *the well-known international socialite, elitist, and poseur. Today is one of the few occasions he now dares venture out of his private pleasure palace.* This figure was so obese he had to be moved everywhere in an enormous tank of warm water, like a mobile Jacuzzi, in order to support his weight on land. It was lowered hydraulically from his modified private VTOL jet, by a team of nervous technicians who carefully transferred it to the party.

Deep zipper-scars covered his bulbous, naked body from the various spare-part surgery operations he'd undergone. Organs 'harvested' from healthy young athletes had replaced his own, which usually failed from under, or over-use. Nutrition was being pumped into, and waste siphoned out of him, through large transparent tubes grafted onto his ballooning torso at strategic points. Fat Boy's Sumo bodyguards would manhandle almost any teenager he liked the look of, kicking and screaming, into the complicated life-support bath, as he always just laughed and laughed, sending massive, tsunami waves around it. 'Ha ha ha!' And he constantly repeated his motto, 'Pleasure! Give me pleasure! Ah ha ha ha!' *Even if he was not the fattest man in the world, he would certainly be the most over-indulged,* Giertz concluded. *It's fairly clear he likes the look of Anthea as well, but he wouldn't dare try anything as her father is one of The Council of Ninety.*

Gritig was there also, still wearing his harlequin suit, but it seemed a little faded. In fact, he was looking particularly confused and unhappy, unashamedly playing the sad clown, because he'd just learned his notorious lesbian, ninth wife was divorcing him. Much to everyone's disgust he kept remonstrating about it out loud, 'I bought her a hand-built private space-shuttle, so why would she go and do that?' The problem was everyone carried on laughing around him, as if it was just another of his routines, and Giertz noticed, *They even seem to think he's being really funny at last!* From beneath his fluorescent-orange hair, Gritig looked around the room at them all, a psychotic Rigoletto, his eyes quietly muttering, 'When the time comes, you liabilities will be the first...'


**Chapter 178 Broken Toy**

*I could exterminate them all right now, if I wanted to,* Giertz thought with satisfaction. He even carried his Combat Youth weapons quite openly in front of all their various bodyguards, and secretly knew his old, Browning machine gun was still in the car's trunk, with half a belt of ammunition. Strangely though, the revelers were still not particularly bothered by him, seeming to know he'd learned his lesson, and wasn't going to make the same mistake again. Unlike Ceebix and Asclepius, they found Giertz entirely predictable. *It's as if they see my wiping out Dr. Zed and Consumeordie's share price as just another of my party stunts, that went too far.*

Then Giertz deduced from the general gossip that a man sitting nearby was Anthea's father. Giertz also noticed next to him the small, tasteful arrangement of a coffee cup, a pair of glasses, a newspaper and a towel. The cup was full of real, fresh-ground coffee, and Giertz had never seen a real newspaper before, with real news in it. Most of the headlines were screaming excitedly about The Sanitization, but he didn't want to read them.

There was nothing spectacular about the elderly man. He was just a rich, silver-haired old entrepreneur, who had dealt his way onto The Council of Ninety. He sat all day in his original Eames lounger, contentedly sipping vermouth. His facial skin was so tanned; any expression stayed for some time. In fact, Giertz had never seen a man so at peace with life, *It's almost strange the way he just smiles to himself most of the time – so quietly.* Giertz studied the smile carefully however, and recognized it yet again.

He found one thing confusing however, *He's brimming with fatherly affection and pride, even while it's unavoidably apparent his daughter is the most nauseating form of nymphomaniac. It's also clear she hates him, and almost everything she does is to draw his attention to the fact.* The heavily-lined patriarch even looked on unaffected though, as Anthea participated in one of the orgies, cavorting doggedly with her pack of young men.

In fact, as she splashed and screamed with her entourage in the fountain, his every expression and gesture appeared to say proudly, 'Look, that's my daughter!' Consequently Giertz was overwhelmed by curiosity. Eventually, he went over to him and asked, 'How do you feel about your daughter's over-all public behavior?'

'They are all just modern young people,' he said laughing, indicating the fornicators. 'How could an old man like myself hope to influence them? Ha ha ha.'

Anthea was close enough however to overhear this remark. Lulled by the spirit of the occasion, Giertz had left his weapons belt on the food table near the fountain. She instantly stopped what she was doing and struggled out of the fountain, snatching the gun up. She stood in her saturated, white dress and aimed the weapon at her father with both hands, shouting aggressively, 'I heard that! I heard that!' What could be so offensive in the words escaped Giertz. *Perhaps she just failed to get enough of his attention? It must be some personal thing between father and daughter, like that strange, last confrontation I had with my 'parents'.* 'So die you liability! Die!' She screeched, but the gun was specially designed so the trigger would only be sensitive to Giertz's fingerprint. Therefore it just clicked uselessly. The old man only laughed again, lovingly.

'It doesn't work!' She said, like an extremely spoilt child with a broken toy. She struggled with the gun's cryptic controls, and even put the muzzle in her mouth, but it remained impotent. 'It doesn't work! It doesn't work!' Adding a string of obscenities she threw it clattering onto the ground, and stormed off, but after a moment the party continued, as if nothing had happened.


**Chapter 179 Glittering Orgy**

Giertz ignored the glittering orgy for the rest of the night, politely refusing every invitation to join it. Even the glass of water stayed full in his hand because he hardly sipped it. He wondered now why he'd come here, I suppose it's more a case of where I don't want to be. Yet he still wasn't sure. *Perhaps I thought I could still help kill reality from here? Or at least hurry its death along?* Considering the over-all picture however, he now knew, *Even if I wiped out the whole council, it wouldn't guarantee reality's destruction going any faster, and might even slow it down.*

More deeply though, being honest with himself, he wondered, *Why haven't I got anything in common with these people, any more than I had the Combat Youth, or any other group?* He analyzed further, frustratedly, *The rest of humanity all seem to believe there's something in reality worth hanging on for. It gives them some sense of purpose, bonding them all together, despite knowing they all really hate each other, but I can't believe in it, whatever it is. I never did, but why do I still wish I was one of them, one of the human race? It was a puzzle he couldn't solve.*

He speculated, *I could probably make the jump here every Consumer dreams of, to become a Producer of some kind. Maybe I could even get a foothold on The Council of Ninety, with what I now know? After all, the major qualification is one should pose a large enough threat to it to be absorbed.* Somehow though, he knew this wasn't the point. *If The Consumers ultimately failed to help me to destroy reality, The Producers certainly wouldn't want to help, at all.*

As the evening ground on, he also began to see people at the party he hadn't expected to see. Much to his surprise, both his 'parents' were there. *So maybe I didn't kill them after all,* he mused. He was astounded as well to see Nailbrand and the Abominable Bastido Brothers. Giertz wasn't certain, but he also thought he saw his skinny girlfriend and Kadski somewhere in the crowd. *So perhaps they didn't die either, and I did just hallucinate it all?* He even saw Lee Harvey Oswald, the man alleged to have assassinated President John F Kennedy, and had himself been assassinated.

Then another, less pleasant thought occurred to Giertz. *Maybe, if they are hallucinations, my suspicion has been right all along. None of it happened that way, or at all? Maybe I'm hallucinating right now, but if so, where am I really? Where is the reality in the end, that I still want to see destroyed?* Despite this though, he couldn't care whether he was seeing hallucinations or not. He sipped his water, theorizing perhaps the whole party was being thrown just for him. *Maybe they've all come to celebrate my great hallucination, like actors bowing out at the end of a performance?*

Eventually, he couldn't bear to be near the orgy anymore: a living mass of bodies which seemed to be gradually merging into a single, ugly organism. It gave him the same feeling of nausea he'd felt at The Situations, but this monster with many mouths, arms, and thighs, groaned and heaved, existing in some weird, abstract state of permanent lust. He wandered outside. As soon as he was out of sight, he dropped to his knees on the grass and stared up at the indifferent moon. Yes, he thought again, *winning The Game was the hardest thing of all.* Still, the only hope he could see was in the small drifts of red sand he saw building up all around. Then he realized there was someone else standing behind him.

'Are you all right Jimmy?' He heard Anthea's voice, now sounding as if she'd completely forgotten the incident with her father, even though her dress was still soaking, and so transparent. *Things like that must happen between them all the time,* Giertz concluded.

'Yes,' he lied.

'Then why are you crying?' She said with genuine curiosity, as if she'd never seen tears before.


**Chapter 180 Strange Awareness**

Now Anthea had mentioned it, Giertz felt his face was wet, but she didn't wait for him to answer, saying, 'Do you know what I'd like to do?' Giertz still didn't reply, because he wasn't interested. He stood up, moving reflexively towards the car park, but she answered her own question, 'I'd like someone to drive me up the coastal highway, to a place only I know.' She said this as if she was bestowing a great favor, but when Giertz didn't react, she added aggressively, 'Well, come on then!'

He filled the car at one of the free, real gasoline pumps, and turned it back onto a deserted road she indicated, amongst the palm trees. They drove along the scenic cliffs, which looked like something airbrushed for a postcard. The sun was setting behind some eroded, needle-like rocks projecting out of the sea in the distance. It threw emerald streaks across the sky.

Giertz began to have a strange awareness that, with the girl sitting beside him, *I've somehow stepped into the world always shown to me by the holyvision commercials.* He was now in the seemingly unattainable 'Real Life' occupied by Pandora and The Bad Actor, which Giertz had once craved so badly, but he had to admit, *Ironically, I've never been more unhappy.* In fact, he was a lot more than unhappy. Attaining this dream somehow only made him more aware of what, and who, he'd lost on the way to it.

Despite driving at what he thought of as his slower rate, Anthea kept laughing and squealing with glee, as if on a roller coaster, complimenting Giertz as the 'craziest' driver she'd ever been with. Then she insisted on comparing him in specific detail with a lot of other people who had driven her around. Giertz was surprised by the way she kept such an exact list in her head. Then she began to talk about her and Giertz's 'relationship,' and how she thought Giertz respected her, 'Because you are the only one who isn't just interested in my body.' Then she moved on to how they would 'go away' together, and how he would give her 'that perfect sensual experience' she'd always been searching for, and perhaps she would even preserve his chromosomes in their child. The whole idea was bizarre to Giertz. *Go away to where?* He wondered again, but this time said nothing.

Eventually, and perhaps inevitably, she returned excitedly to her, and every Producer's favorite topic - The Sanitization, 'I'll let you into a secret: The Evil Poet said he will let me be the one to push the button that launches the "Patriarch" missiles. You know, the neutron bombs? To start the ball rolling! They destroy people but not property, don't they!' She almost whispered, 'Just think, my name will go down in history, forever! A world with no more of those useless-eater Consumers! And it will all be thanks to me!' She appeared to expect applause from Giertz, but didn't understand the expression on his face. *Yes, The Producers are different from 'us,'* Giertz reflected, *and it's not just money.*

In fact, for the first time in his life, even after confronting The Bad Actors, The Beast, and all the other twisted individuals, Giertz had an unsettling sensation that, *I must be sitting next to pure evil, whatever the definition!* At the same time, he felt something familiar coming alive inside him. He tried to control it at first, but discovered it was doing the same with him, as he started to see, *She is reality.*

Then she began to realize she knew practically nothing about Giertz, so she started firing prying questions at him about his personal life, to which he gave either evasive answers, or completely exaggerated lies. So eventually she demanded, 'Stop here.' Almost lacking any personal will any longer, Giertz halted the car on the top of a cliff. They swung the doors up, and both got out. There was a warm breeze blowing in from the sea, carrying the sound of the waves below. Then she revealed her plan.

Perceptively she said, 'You really love this old car, don't you Jimmy. After all, it's all you've got in the world, isn't it? There's nothing else, is there.' She leaned on the red aluminum bodywork, running a hand sensuously over her rival's old, battered, mistreated flank. Giertz didn't reply, and she continued, 'But if you really love me, you'd be prepared to push it over this cliff.' Then she raised the sleeve of her dress. A small tattoo on her arm showed two crossed, black lightening strokes, inside a white disk, on a rectangle of scarlet. She smiled at him, with a kind of coy, forced innocence.

He knew he had to do something. He had to do anything.

Giertz stayed silent for a moment longer. Then he walked around the car and faced her. He looked into her eyes and saw with little surprise, *She too is wearing a mask, after all.* Except it so closely represented her own face, he hadn't noticed she had it on. *Does she know it herself?* He wondered. He reached down and gently lifted it off her head, but the countenance underneath was identical, except it was almost worn out from wearing too many masks. *There are no surprises here, or anywhere.* He dropped her mask on the ground.

Carefully he snatched one of her arms, and as she was small enough, managed to lift her onto his shoulders. At first she giggled and kicked playfully, thinking it was just another of the things men were always doing to amuse her. Then, as she began to realize it wasn't, she screamed and kicked hard to get free, but Giertz projected her over the cliff edge. Her screaming faded, getting lost in the breeze, until there was a distant crash as she hit the water below.

He tried hard, but soon admitted, *Strangely, I find it impossible to consider whether she may have survived an impact with the water from this height, or not.* He walked slowly back to the car, the studs on his boot crushing her fragile mask on the way. He knew the term 'ODS,' would have meant nothing to her. As with his 'parents,' he didn't feel any guilt at all, but somewhere, at a distance, suspected that, *Maybe I should?*

He drove further along the empty coastal highway, lined with gracefully swaying, replanted palm trees, down to a section running parallel to the beach. Finally, he stopped the car again and climbed out. He waded through the long grass waving gently on the dunes, onto the beach, feeling the red sand give beneath his boots' studded soles. He sat down in the myriad grains and closed his eyes, listening to the waves surging.

He sat and listened to the waves for some time, waiting until reality began melting and distorting before him again.

He felt he had to do something. He had to do anything.

**EPILOGUE The Seer**
The Seer blinked, opening his eyes...

**THE END**

IE Kolenda, Manila, 2012

**Also by I.E. Kolenda from UtopiOmatic2000:**

The Death Wish Man- An Outer Space Novel - ISBN: 978-0-9572080-6-3
Amazon Search: ASIN: B09LJS38H1


Wiche fought against the chrome levers, trying to bring the space vessel under control. Everything else not bolted down was thrown like a scattered pack of cards, and his body thrashed against his restraining belts. Then suddenly he saw on the screen, whatever I do, it won't make any difference - in the long run. Although visually the screen showed nothing but black space at their exit point, the other readouts going crazy told Wiche something else – altogether, we are plunging head-long into Sector-X, whether we want to go there, or not!

Wiche reassured himself, my destiny is in there, but he couldn't have imagined what form it would take.


I, Oswald – The Fictionalized Autobiography of JFK's Alleged Assassin – ISBN: 978-0-9572080-5-6
Amazon Search: ASIN: B08HVL91YR


'In the TSBD 6th Floor sniper's nest was myself, who was running around in a stupor as if hypnotized / Lawrence Factor, who probably did the shooting and was a very good shot (Mafia man Roderick MacKenzie knew this because he'd shot with him) / Ruth Ann Martinez who was known as a 'hit lady,' who was skilled enough to have taken the shot. She has been identified as the 'girl in the polka-dot dress' who ran out of the RFK assassination scene saying, 'We've just killed the senator!' (It was said that she killed men with a hatpin while making love. Apparently, she had come from a 'carnival' CIA traveling safe house known as ZR Flatstore.)'